The Almost Sisters

The Almost Sisters

Joshilyn Jackson

HARPER LUXE

An Imprint of HarperCollinsPublishers

HarperCollins
PUBLISHERS
—————— Since 1817 ——————

HarperCollins books may be purchased for educational, business, or sales promotional use. For information please e-mail the Special Markets Department at SPsales@harpercollins.com.

FIRST HARPERLUXE EDITION

ISBN: 978-0-06-267084-7

HarperLuxe™ is a trademark of HarperCollins Publishers.

Library of Congress Cataloging-in-Publication Data is available upon request.

17 18 19 20 21 ID/LSC 10 9 8 7 6 5 4 3 2 1

For Jacques de Spoelberch

The Almost Sisters

1

My son, Digby, began at exactly 3:02 in the morning on the first Friday in June. I don't mean his conception or his birth. I mean the moment he began for me, which happened between those two larger events. It was a start so small I almost didn't notice. I was very, very busy panicking about my job.

I'd finished penciling and inking a limited series for DC Comics, the last contract standing between me and the prequel to my own graphic novel, *Violence in Violet*. Every word and every line of *Violence in Violet* had been written and penciled and lettered and inked and colored by me. I was proud as hell of it, but I hadn't continued it as a series. I couldn't. *V in V* ended in a full apocalypse. Literally nothing could happen next in Violence's world, because there *was* no next. Everything was over, and it stayed over until Dark Horse Comics came to me with the offer for a prequel. They wanted Violence's origin story.

Every superbeing has one. Peter Parker gets bitten by a radioactive spider, Bruce Banner is caught in a blast of gamma radiation. Dark Horse wanted the story of how Violence came to be.

I said yes near instantly, excited at the prospect. It was a backdoor route into my own invented world, the chance to work with my own characters again. For the first time as a professional, I'd have full creative control over the script as well as the art. I was thrilled, even. Right up until I actually had to do it.

I loved Violence—as much as anyone can love a sharp-toothed, purple, vigilante cannibal—but I'd never explained what she was or where she came from, even to myself. She was simply a busty force with crazy eyes and silver thigh boots, acting out a bloody revenge fantasy that spoke to anyone who'd ever had their heart jerked out and stomped flat. Now I had to know how she began. I'd signed a paper promising I'd know, and comic-book artists don't miss deadlines.

I always got my best ideas at bedtime, drifting in and out of sleep, the membrane between my conscious mind and the black and salty marshes of my undermind grown thin and permeable. In my industry, pictures shaped story, and pictures were my jumping-off point. I closed my eyes and waited for colors that had no name to splash into shapes on my inner eyelids, forming images that would become the panels. But I couldn't fall into that deep green swampland of near sleep where all the best ideas were born. When I closed my eyes, all I saw was my deadline. It felt like it was coming way too fast. Coming *at* me, even, and with bad intentions.

I thumped my pillow and rolled onto my side, and there he was. He started. Digby.

I knew he existed before that middle-of-the-night in June, of course. Intellectually speaking. I'd had a small, almost casual suspicion back in March, when my period pulled a no-show. That was a couple weeks after I'd been a featured artist at a comic-book convention in Atlanta and that whole debacle had happened with a Batman. So, technically speaking, it was possible. Barely.

But I was thirty-eight years old, not some hyperfertile twenty-something who could catch pregnant like it was a cold. *Skips and late starts are my new normal,* I told myself when I hit ten days late. I had to stop by CVS for razors anyway. I threw a Coke and a pregnancy test into my basket. I drank the first on the way home, where I used the second.

I leaned against the sink, waiting out the timer. The

test itself was resting on the back of the toilet, in plain sight, on top of a tissue. I didn't peek, though. I kept my gaze trained on the pair of steampunk fishes I'd hung up on the wall over the tub. A local artist had made them out of "found objects," which was art-fart talk for trash. Chipped and rusty gears, nails, springs, and bits of broken tools had found a second life as fishes on my wall. I'd always liked them, but now it felt like they were staring back at me. They had very round eyes made from bits of vintage telescopes and fat rubber-tubing mouths that turned down.

"Oh, shut up," I told them. I'd never realized that fish were so judgmental.

Two minutes later I was looking at a pink plus sign.

I stood there squinting as if my eyes had gone wonky and were seeing wrong. I was in the outsize master bathroom that, along with the skylight studio upstairs, had made me fall in love with my funky Georgian house. Now the room seemed cavernous; if I yelled, it might echo. The test's pink packaging looked frivolous sitting on my sink, much too silly to be the bearer of real tidings.

I didn't want to go to my regular lady-parts doc, as if I had a UTI or needed to schedule a Pap smear. Instead I called my friend Margot Phan.

"Can you give me an emergency appointment?

Now?" I asked. She and her husband had been in my tight-knit clot of Tuesday gamers for twelve years now, but I'd never been to see her as a doctor. She was a pediatrician.

"My waiting room is stuffed with snot-filled toddlers. I'm on yellow alert here, Leia," she told me.

"I'm past yellow. This is a big, fat, blaring red," I told her. "You see teenage girls, right? You can check for if I'm pregnant?"

"Oh, shit!" said Margot. "Batman? Are you kidding me? Come right now."

Margot installed me in a tiny exam room with puffy cartoon forest animals all over the wallpaper. She did another pee test, which was positive, and then at my insistence took the world's most awkward look at my cervix.

"Leia, honey. You are knocked up," she told me.

"All the way up?" I asked, even though Margot was one of my closest friends. She wouldn't screw with me on something medical. But this still felt like some elaborate prank, as if she were about to pop up between my thighs while my feet were in the stirrups, holding a waffle iron and saying, *Look what I found!* "Maybe you should do a blood test?"

"That would be gratuitous. Much like this," Margot said, standing and heading for the door. I sat up, clutching the sheet around me. "Get dressed and then come to my office, okay? Let's talk. You're not in this alone."

I was so gobsmacked that for a second I thought she meant that I had *Batman* on my side. The real thing. Not a one-shot superhero in an Etsy cowl named Matt or Mark. Or Marcus. I couldn't quite remember.

I did remember that he was from someplace that ended in an *a*. Florida? India? Maybe Canada, like the beer we'd drunk in between tequila shots. He was taller than me, but who wasn't? He might have been genuinely funny; he'd certainly seemed funny at the time. He was black—I was pretty definite on that—and his smile, his jawline, had been absolutely beautiful. At some point he must have taken off his pointy-eared iconic mask, because I had a fuzzy memory of oversize brown eyes, slow-blinking and shy, with a thick fringe of lashes. They made his whole face sweeter than the cocky smile had led me to expect.

I also remembered that he loved *Violence in Violet*. He'd recognized me at the hotel bar and came over to describe all his favorite panels. He'd noticed the birds and little animals I'd hidden here and there in the artwork, disguised as shadows or curls of Violence's hair. He'd asked when the prequel would be published, saying he couldn't wait to get his hands on it. His admiration had been balm, and I had needed balm. Earlier that day I'd gotten so damn burned. Plus, tequila never was the handmaiden of good decisions. I'd asked him up to my room.

We'd started kissing in the elevator, where he'd grabbed fistfuls of my long hair to tip my face back in a way I liked so much. I remembered my hands working up under his chest piece, seeking warm and living skin. I remembered his naked body sprawled across my hotel carpet, me naked, too, hops and agave leaking out our very pores, rolling, me on top now with my head thrown back—had I put on his Batman cowl and cape?

Yes. Yes I had, I remembered with a whole-body shame flush. I'd worn them both, laughing like an Arkham-level maniac astride him.

In the morning I was dog-sick and alone. He'd left a note on the pillow—*You're amazing. Can't wait for the prequel*—and a phone number with an area code that for sure was not Virginia. It was probably fake, and anyway, I was flying home to Norfolk in a couple of hours. I couldn't call and try to un-one-night-stand him with some legit dating. I'd thrown the note away, and with it any chance I had of finding him. Batman wasn't going to be a factor.

I got dressed, but I didn't go to Margot's office. I sat staring at a wall covered with smiling rabbits and baby deer in cotton candy colors. The raccoons all looked so smug, like they were laughing at me.

And why not? Unplanned pregnancy is tragic when the mom is a kid herself, but at my age some elements of comedy crept in. Shouldn't I by now know better than to drag an anonymous Batman back to my room by his utility belt? Shouldn't I at the very least understand the proper workings of a condom? People might not say it to me, but they'd say it to each other. They would think it at me, really loud.

And my parents! I dropped my face into my hands, cringing at the thought of their reaction. They were suburban Methodists, both originally from very small towns, the poster couple for conventional. I could picture my mother tutting and hand-wringing, while my stepdad, Keith, stood awkwardly behind her, trying to give me money. Plus, telling Keith was tantamount to telling Rachel, and that would be the worst.

My stepsister had never had a fender bender, much less an accident involving reproduction. She had made herself a family in perfect order, as if it were as simple as a playground song: *First comes love, then comes marriage, then comes Rachel with a baby carriage.* I couldn't even get step one right.

The last thing I wanted was for Rachel to know that I had fetched up pregnant. She would be so irritatingly sorry for me. She would make excuses for me to our parents. *We can't blame Leia,* I could hear her saying. *She must be so lonely. Otherwise she'd never have engaged in such a desperate, tawdry incident with an unfindable Batman.* And the worst part was, she would genuinely be trying to help me. Rachel always helped me, sometimes so relentlessly that I wished I had a safe word.

There was a quick tap at the door, and Margot stuck her head back in.

"Do you have your pants on? You've been in here a while," she said.

Behind her, through the open doorway, I could hear children playing in the waiting room. Little piping voices. The bang of plastic toys and thumpy feet. I had barreled through that crowd of small, sniffling humans and their mothers on my way in. It was all mothers, though presumably each child had a father. Someplace. I had barely noticed the children, eager to get back here and let Margot correct the home kit's obvious mistake. But I heard them now.

Through the thin wall, in the room next door, a baby burst into a noisy squalling, rich with outrage. My head tilted toward the sound.

"What's wrong with the baby?" I asked.

Margot shrugged, tucking the ends of her jet-black

bob behind her ears. "Poor little 'roo, he's getting vaccinations."

She came all the way in to close the door, but I could still hear him. He sounded so affronted. Thirty seconds ago he'd been as innocent as the pink rabbits on the wallpaper. He hadn't even known that things could hurt. Someone should have warned him that the world had jabby things in it and that adults would stick them in his blameless thighs. On purpose.

But even as I thought it, he began to quiet. He must be in his mother's arms, being bobbled and soothed, already forgetting. A real, live human baby. I put one hand on my belly. It felt soft, a little rounder than I would have liked, no different from usual. Yet inside, secretly, it was not the same. In the mortifying shock of being pregnant, I hadn't thought about getting a baby. But that was pregnancy's endgame, after all.

"It's going to be okay, you know," Margot promised. She sat down beside me and put her arm over my shoulders.

"It's so weird to think that sex actually works," I said.

"Reproduction" was a high-school-textbook word. It was like photosynthesis or oxidation, just another process that I'd had to memorize to pass biology. Now here was biology, being true and relevant, working as intended in the darkness at the center of my body. If all went well, a whole and separate person would enter the world. A tiny person, made inside myself. My person. My son or daughter.

"You want to talk about your options?" Margot asked, but I was already shaking my head back and forth.

"I'm thirty-eight years old, Margot," I answered, slow and serious. "Aren't I running out of options?"

Margot was my friend. I could see her wanting to tell me that it wasn't true. But she was also a doctor, and I was dead single and a year and change away from forty. I'd walked away from every man I might have married. No, I'd run. The playground song in my head went, *First comes love, then comes hideous betrayal, then comes endless regret requiring expensive therapy.* It was a terrible song. It didn't even rhyme. But it was mine, and I hadn't made a family, even though I'd wanted one.

I still did. I wanted to fall in love, marry a dork like me, make more dorks. I wanted game nights, summer nerdcations to Ren fairs and Orlando, a better reason than my own sweet tooth for baking Yoda cupcakes. I had imagined what it would be like to leap in and make a life with someone. Make babies that were a blend of us. It must be a kind of magic, to create a kid with my husband's nose and my own deep-set eyes.

This kid, though? He might be born with Batman's nose, but how would I know? I couldn't remember Batman's nose. This kid would be biracial; he could get my deep-set eyes, but we still wouldn't look like family to my racist neighbor. Or to anybody's racist neighbor, actually, and the world was full of them. I'd be raising him all alone, too. I wasn't exactly living the dream here.

It didn't matter. No matter how embarrassing the origin story, no matter the potential hazards, a tiny piece of family had crash-landed in my uterus.

"I'm making a baby," I told Margot, and I sounded terrified.

Even so, underneath the shake in my voice, I heard joy. Margot must have heard it, too, because she grinned and hugged me tighter.

"Yeah, you are, Mama," she said, and wrote me a prescription for prenatals.

For the first few months, I kept it a secret between me and Margot and my ob-gyn. I bought a book called *Late Bloomers: The Pregnancy Handback for Women Over 35*, and it advised me not to tell, at least until I'd gotten through the first trimester. That made sense to me, and not only because telling everyone would be uncomfortable and I actively dreaded telling Rachel. I had another, deeper reason. At my age pregnancy was classified as high-risk. I had extra doctor appointments and tests, and in my heart I didn't trust that it would stick. This didn't feel like something I would get to have.

So I worked, I hung out with my friends, I put out cat food for the wary stray who lived in my backyard. I went to church and hosted Tuesday game nights. I took out the recycling. It all felt exactly the same as the thousands of times I'd done this stuff unpregnant. I missed having a glass of wine with dinner, but Night of the Bat aside, I wasn't a big drinker. I wasn't nauseous or any moodier than usual. I didn't find myself salting my ice cream or eating sidewalk chalk. Another few weeks and I had to move into my fat jeans, but that was no big deal—it happened every Christmas.

At my fourth appointment, my ob-gyn took some of my blood, and the fetal platelets told us my baby was genetically sound and definitely a boy. I was officially in my second trimester.

Now, *Late Bloomers* said, shit got real. Maybe not in those exact words, but the book and common sense agreed that it was time to make the guest room over into a nursery, buy some onesies and a Diaper Genie, and hey, maybe mention I was pregnant to my family and friends. I didn't. I was carrying a viable, whole, human boy, but he still seemed so intangible. He was like a drawing after I had the idea but before my pencil moved along the paper.

I didn't even tell my grandmother, my only living relative on my father's side. She was seven hundred miles away, down in Birchville, Alabama, busy making sure her pansy bed was immaculate and disapproving of young people and her own racist neighbor. She would have been the perfect test case, both because she'd never rat me out to Mom and Keith and Rachel and because she loved me so damn much.

I reminded her of my dad, who had been short and dark-haired and built on the thick side, just like me. And just like me he had been a haunter of used-book stores, an eater of Easy Cheese, a roller of many-sided dice. In my favorite picture, the one I kept in my purse, he was wearing Spock ears. The dork was strong in him. He had picked baby names when I was just a bump inside my mother, but he never got to see if I was a Leia or a Solo. He was killed by a drunk driver three weeks before I was born, Birchie's crowning sorrow in a hard life full of lesser ones.

She deserved to know she'd soon have a great-grandbaby, but even though I called her at least twice a week, I didn't bring it up. Childbirth—the kind with a child at the end of it—seemed improbable and distant. Telling Birchie especially felt like promising something I could not deliver. I didn't believe in it—in Digby— until that first Friday in June, 3:02 A.M., when I was riding out insomnia and failing to come up with even one idea for the prequel to *Violence in Violet*.

Maybe because I'd written *V in V* so long ago? I'd begun sketching Violence two decades earlier, when I was a senior in high school—practically a fetus myself. Those drawings got me into Savannah College of Art and Design, and the completed graphic novel had been my senior project for my B.F.A. in sequential art.

I'd taken the finished graphic novel to a small con in Memphis, where I showed it to a guy who hired artists for DC. He liked my shading, and he offered me a contract. I'd put *V in V* in a box and gone to work, parlaying that first job into a freelance career. I was good, and I got better, and I never missed a deadline. Over the years I'd worked for every major publisher in the business, penciling and inking characters from Ant-Man all the way to General Zod.

About six years ago, while updating my website, I'd scanned and uploaded the opening pages of *V in V*. It was mostly a whim—an easy way to pad my content.

The first month it got a couple hundred downloads. The next a couple thousand. By the summer's end, I had more than twenty thousand shares and linkbacks, and the traffic was crashing my server. My social media blew up with requests for the whole story.

I self-published it, making a print-on-demand paper edition and an e-book, and I sold more than a hundred thousand copies in the first year alone. *V in V* was still selling, and now, instead of sitting on panels, I was paid to be a featured speaker at comic-book and fantasy/sci-fi conventions all over the country. When I penciled for other series, my name on the cover boosted sales, and Dark Horse had made a truly motivating offer for this prequel. The only problem was, I had zero ideas.

I thumped my pillow, restless, trying to focus inward on my sharp-toothed antiheroine. How had Violence learned to fly, to bite, to wield her clever, crooked knives? When I started the graphic novel, twenty years ago, I'd concentrated on Violet, the heartbroken girl that Violence comes to protect. Violet was based on me in a lot of ways, so I knew her character down to the bone. Violence had been only a means to an end. To a lot of very bloody ends, actually, and I'd never thought past that. It was an absence in the book, and now I had to fill it. I sank deep into the dark inside my body, waiting to see a story begin, waiting for colors and shapes to come and show me. I was almost dozing, but not quite, and I turned onto my side.

When I came to rest, a smallness deep within me kept on turning. I felt it. It was a silent trill of something like a sound. It was the smallest key, spinning in a lock I'd never known was present at my center.

The movement was in me, but it wasn't me. It was another little something, a someone, willfully choosing to flex his flippery future arms, or whatever it was he had by then. It was a choice, but I hadn't made it. It was inside me, and mine, but I did not control it.

Right exactly then, my son started. He became real in ways he hadn't been five seconds before. Much realer than he had been almost four months back, when I was cleaning up my hotel room in Atlanta, finding only one used condom but remembering two sexes. A second condom had been on the bedside table, speaking to good intentions but still mint-in-package. Now I could feel him making small decisions inside me, and I already knew his name. It was a nerd reference so obscure that nobody but me would ever get it.

"Hello, Digby? Is that you?" I asked him, listening in that same odd, inward way for a sound that was not a sound.

It came again, as if in response. Alien and tiny, unfeelable under any other circumstances.

"Oh, my stars and garters, you're really there," I told him, though *Late Bloomers* said he was a few weeks away from hearing yet.

Quickening, my book had called it, and it was the perfect word, because when he quickened, my whole life sped up, too. I was pregnant, and this baby didn't even have a crib. Right now he had only me. I had to tell people. My Tuesday gamers ran a meal train every time someone had a baby or got sick. I'd made umpty casseroles and quarts of soup over the years; now I would need a turn.

Most important, I had to tell my family. Fast. My parents needed time to get over their initial shock before the baby came, so Mom could teach me to breast-feed and Keith could show me how to properly install the car seat that I didn't own yet.

Every Sunday afternoon Rachel hosted a family luncheon after church. I'd sat through more than a dozen since I'd gotten pregnant, eating shrimp scampi or beef medallions for two and keeping my mouth shut. This Sunday, I resolved, I would simply say it.

Something sure smells good, and hey, I'm spawning. Boom and done.

I'd pre-forgive Mom and Keith for any less-than-ideal initial reactions. They were going to be so embarrassed. I'd bright-side it for them, reassure them that I was healthy and happy and remind them that they were finally getting a second grandkid. In the end they weren't going to love Digby any less for being father-less or browner than they were. But the end seemed a long way off.

Rachel would back me up, but the minute we were alone, I'd get an earful from her, too. She'd be pissed at me for setting a bad example for her thirteen-year-old daughter. So would her husband, probably, but screw him. Of every jackass currently stomping around on this blue planet, Jake Jacoby was the last one who was allowed to have an opinion about me.

I'd eat whatever crap they needed to shovel at me, and then they'd rally around me. Around us. They had to, especially with Rachel there to make them. Rachel could rally so fast and so hard, and I had to be ready for that, too. Before Sunday I needed to go online and order everything I wanted for a bright blue Superman-themed nursery, before Rachel could swoop in with trendy neutrals and distressed wood and those horrify-ing Swedish animals from GOOP.

Sunday night I'd call my grandmother down in Alabama. If Birchie had been any other small-town ninety-year-old southern lady, the thought of telling her might make me cringe, but she was her singular self. Sure, Birchie lived stiffly, and by rules, but they were rules of her own making. That call seemed more like a reward I'd earn by weathering the storm of telling Rachel and my parents.

When I told Birchie about Digby, I knew that my prim grandmother would be . . . joyful. Joyful that she and I would not be the last of the Birch line after all. Joyful in the same soaring, secret way that I was—and right now? Feeling him move? I was practically giddy with it. I lay in the darkness, reveling in the flutter of this tiny, late, imperfectly got piece of what I'd always wanted.

Now I could hardly wait to call her. She had lived a version of this story: a single son, born when she was past thirty, that she had raised alone. Granted, she'd been a young widow. She'd had a proper husband there for the conception part. Even so, Birchie would understand better than anyone else how, in the wake of my son's beginning, I felt like my life was beginning, too.

I had no way to know that seven hundred miles south of me, the grandmother I longed to tell was coming to her end.

2

Birchville, Alabama, had its own origin story, so entwined with my grandmother's that there was no way to tell one without the other. The town itself was founded by Birchie's grandfather, Ethan, the eldest son of an old Charleston shipping family who had acted as blockade runners in the Civil War. They kept their money safely overseas, surviving the Late Unpleasantness with their fortune intact, if not their reputation. Their newly destitute social circle had small appreciation for southerners who had chosen prudence over patriotism.

By 1874 Ethan, who had been a child during the war, was chafing under the uncomfortable combination of wealth and the Old Guard's condemnation. He wanted a fresh start, and he was not the only young man in Charleston who felt that way. He left, taking several sons from the old families with him: a Darian, an Alston, and two of the impoverished Mack boys. The Macks had sunk all their money into Confederate government bonds; that family especially was so bitter that it penetrated the bloodline, genes-deep.

Ethan founded Birchville on the bones of a burned-out 'Bama town that had lost its charter in the war. He rebuilt the church first, then perched a big white Victorian house on the hill across the road. When both buildings were finished, he sent back to Charleston for his girl, to marry her in one and move her into the other. My great-grandfather, Ellis Birch, was born in that house, and my grandmother was born inside it, too.

At 9:00 A.M. on any given Sunday, Birchie would be sitting at her formal dining-room table in that very house, watching her town wake up through the big bay window. Behind her, on either side of the doorway to the kitchen, portraits of her grandfather and father flanked her, watching their town as well, stern and benevolent. Ethan looked proud, after the fashion of portraits in his day. Ellis looked even prouder, plus he had those creepy Uncle Sam eyes that seemed to rove around the room. I had never liked eating in the dining room under his painted gaze, but it was the Lord's day. Birchie would no more eat a Sunday meal in the

cozy breakfast nook than she would take up Prancer-
cise. I could imagine her there perfectly, spine ramrod
straight, ankles crossed, eating her egg and sipping
coffee with Wattie Price, her bosom friend.

I didn't have to imagine the wretched events that
awaited them across the street at Birchville First Baptist on this particular Sunday morning. I would see the
whole story unfolding in my head from a hundred different angles, because every church member who was
present—and a few who weren't—would later tell me
all the gory details.

As the church bells pealed ten-fifteen, Birchie and
Wattie linked arms to careful their way down the wide
steps of their front porch. Those two little old ladies,
round and soft and short and fragile, looked like a
matched set of salt and pepper shakers as they toddled
down the hill toward First Baptist, on schedule and as
timely as the tides.

Birchville's population was a little smaller and
skewed a little older than when I was growing up, but
there was still a family of Darians, plenty of Alstons,
and a slew of Macks who lived in the town. My grandmother was the only remaining Birch, though, and all
the old-name families were members at First Baptist.
As Birchie and Wattie made their stately way up the
left side aisle, folks cleared a path, offering smiles and

greetings. Birchie took it as her due, pausing only to exchange a speaking glance with Wattie as Martina Mack clomped up the other aisle in her enormous Sunday hat. It blocked the view, perched high and bright red over Martina's iron-gray witch scraggles, but Martina would neither remove it nor move back. She had to sit in the second row, right side, exactly opposite Birchie's pew.

Wattie's knees were bad, so Birchie helped her settle before sitting down herself, and quite a few folks in the congregation looked away. There were folks at the church who could not seem to remember that Miss Wattie did not work for Birchie. Wattie had never worked for us, in fact. That was Wattie's mother, Vina. She had been the Birches' housekeeper. When Birchie's own mother died in childbirth, Vina had rocked Birchie, and taught her songs, and tucked her in for naps in the kitchen playpen. She still had milk from her youngest boy, so Vina fed Birchie with her own body. A year or so later, Wattie came along to join my grandmother, and they had bonded deep as sisters. The two of them had put up jam together every August of their lives in that kitchen: as babies watching, as helpers too little to be truly helpful, as young girls, as married ladies, and eventually as jam masters who regularly took multiple ribbons at the county fair.

Around twelve years ago, I started worrying about Birchie living all alone in that big house full of staircases with her bad balance and worse eyesight. I'd wanted her to move to Virginia, into an assisted-living apartment near my house, but she would have none of it.

Meanwhile Wattie's husband had passed, and both her sons lived far, Stephen in Chicago, Sam in Houston. They were worried, too. Wattie's house was on an isolated road outside of town. She drove herself into Birchville almost every day with less and less regard for what lane the car was in. She and Birchie would sit out on the porch in fine weather or in front of the living room's wide windows when it rained. They would knit and talk and supervise town life. It was a relief for all of us when Wattie failed her driver's test and came to live with Birchie in the big Victorian. They could walk to the beauty parlor, the library, three restaurants, the yarn shop. The Piggly Wiggly didn't have a delivery service per se, but for Emily Birch Briggs? The groceries got delivered.

The longer they lived together, the more symbiotic they became. Church had been the last amalgamation. On paper Wattie was still a member at Redemption, the all-black Baptist church near her old house. Birchie kept her membership at First Baptist, too, but for years now they had gone to services together, half the time walking to First Baptist and half the time being driven to Redemption by one of the deacons. This was a First Baptist week, and they bent their heads over their shared church bulletin until the service started.

Birchie took tidy notes in the margins of her Order of Worship, upright and attentive, giving Miss Wattie small, decorous nods when the preacher got it right, frowning slightly when he got it wrong. There were very few nods.

Miss Wattie remained stoic. Her large, heavy-lidded eyes hardly seemed to blink, but a close observer would notice that her full lips clamped in tandem with every Birchie head shake. The Reverend Richard Smith was new to the church, and very young, and prone to passionate sputtering about the Beatitudes. He told everyone to call him Pastor Rick, and sometimes, when he mentioned hell, it almost sounded like he was putting air quotes around the word. Worse, there were no detectable air quotes when he mentioned dinosaurs. Neither Birchie nor Miss Wattie could approve of him.

The old pastor—a properly powder-dry fellow of their generation—had died. Instead of promoting Jim Campbell, the blandly handsome, middle-aged unter-pastor, the church had called this new boy. He'd been born respectably enough in Alabama, but he'd gone to Golden Gate Seminary out in California.

As far as I could tell, they'd returned him with his old-school Southern Baptist doctrinal stick-in-the-butt still firmly lodged, but he also owned a pair of man sandals and did not eat red meat. Worse, he'd alternately coaxed and needled every single First Baptist member onto Facebook. Even Birchie and Wattie had signed up, strictly as a kindness. He'd betrayed their goodwill gesture by making the church newsletter completely virtual. To save trees, he said, but it meant they'd actually had to learn to turn on the computer I had gotten them. To my grandmother all this meant he was now "from" California, which was practically Babylon—the setting of a thousand movies about fornication that she flat refused to see.

"And he sweats when he preaches," Birchie had told me on the phone. In her small, pursed mouth, "sweats" sounded like a curse word.

"I'm sure he can't help it," I'd told her.

"He most certainly could. The church has air conditioning."

Birchie should know, as she had single-handedly paid to install it in the 1970s, when she was going through the change of life.

"The pulpit is right under the vent, but he won't preach from it," Wattie chimed in. They were on speakerphone. They'd always liked to have a share in each other's conversations, but over the past couple of years they'd used the speakerphone more and more often. These days they took every call in tandem. It had happened so gradually I thought nothing of it. "He puts on that headset like a pop star, waving his arms around and jogging back and forth."

"It's true!" Birchie confirmed. "I feel like I'm watching that communist Fonda girl on one of her tacky aerobics tapes, what with all his gyrations splashed across those . . . screens."

"Everybody's using screens now, y'all," I told them. "And no one watches tapes. Or does aerobics, for that matter."

I heard a skeptical "Humph," but I didn't know if it was Birchie or Miss Wattie.

"They only put the lyrics on that screen," Wattie said. "How can people sing without the notes?"

Birchie said, "I swan, Lois Gainey has not been on key once since those screens went up. *He* says the hymnals were getting ratty, but I offered to replace them. Twice." I understood from her tone—anyone would have—that Miss Birchie's considerable resources had not been available to help with the installation of screens.

All this change notwithstanding, Birchie was happy in her pew. Today the church was holding its Summer

Kick-Off Fish Fry on the lawn. It was a tradition as long-standing and almost as venerated as Birchie herself.

As a kid I'd been to it every year; I'd spent every childhood summer down in Birchville. I wasn't a football fan or a fish-the-Coosa River sort, but I'd loved Birchville anyway. Birchie bought me chalk in every color; I'd draw comic strips a block long, every sidewalk square a panel. She'd made Batman and *Star Wars* patterns on graph paper to entice me to learn needlepoint, and I'd needed no reward but the pie to want Wattie to teach me how to make her perfect crust. She and Wattie together sewed me a new Wonder Woman costume every year. I was allowed to run all over town wearing it, acting out *Super Friends* with local kids until I heard Birchie ringing the porch bell that called me home for supper. In Norfolk I could only wear it in the house. *It embarrasses Rachel,* my mother told me, her pink cheeks testifying that Rachel was not alone.

For me summer began with the taste of catfish rolled in cornmeal and coarse salt, served up crisp and smoking hot on paper plates with sweet tea in Dixie Cups. Iceberg and cherry-tomato salad drenched in homemade ranch dressing. Cheese grits. Fried okra. Huge wedges of icebox pie for after. That meal was still the very taste of freedom to me.

This year it was drizzling outside, a thing Miss Birchie's prayers had not allowed to happen on Fish Fry Sunday for decades. Probably God weighing in on Pastor Rick. But there was no canceling or postponing the Fry. The youth-group boys simply crowded the tables into the fellowship hall. As Miss Birchie and Miss Wattie came in, arm in arm, Pastor Rick was there to greet them.

"Now, there's no need for you ladies to wait in line. Come have a seat. We'll bring you plates."

This was one thing he got right. No grandmother-aged lady or pregnant woman had ever had to stand in line at a church social. Pastor Rick walked Birchie and Miss Wattie over to his own table, already packed with deacons and Associate Pastor Campbell and his wife, Myrtle. Birchie took the seat across from Frank Darian, her lawyer, who lived and worked out of the big blue house two doors down from Birchie's. He was the only man at the table who wasn't part of church leadership, but his wife, Jeannie Anne, was the children's minister. It was a part-time job involving hand puppets, and therefore open to women.

Pastor Rick came back and set paper plates down in front of each of them, saying, "Here we go! Here we go!" His wife was right behind him with their drinks and napkins.

The plates were wrong, though. No catfish. No fried okra. No iceberg salad. Instead there was what looked to Miss Birchie like something ready to be mailed—a rectangle of parchment paper, tied up in a string.

"Well, now, what's this?" Miss Wattie asked.

"It's salmon. It's wrapped and steamed with fresh herbs and spring vegetables," Pastor Rick said.

A moment of silence. Wattie turned to whisper something, her lips almost touching Birchie's ear. A lot of Birchie's conversations happened with Miss Wattie whispering to her in full profile, Wattie's breath stirring the snowy fluff of tendrils that had escaped Birchie's bun. It was so common a sight these days that no one thought anything of it. Not right then.

"But this is the Fish Fry," Miss Birchie said, emphasis on "Fry."

"It's called salmon en papillote," Pastor Rick said.

"That sounds French," said Birchie darkly, but poor Rick missed the tone.

"Yes! Yes, it is French," he warbled happily. "And so much healthier."

Birchie looked like she might say more, but Wattie stayed close, her voice a breathy background noise, soothing Birchie down. After a moment Birchie's sparse lashes dropped, and she said, "Well, let's try it, then."

Miss Wattie turned to face her own packet. Her full

lips compressed into a wide, flat line. She'd calmed Birchie, but she made no move to try this wrongful food herself.

Birchie peeled back the wrapping to reveal a pile of bright green asparagus and a few cherry tomatoes, their skins wrinkled from the steam. Her mouth pursed and pruned into a dot, the exact opposite shape of Wattie's but expressing the same feeling.

Pastor Rick turned to Jeannie Anne Darian. "Did you find your last two volunteers for nursery duty at VBS?"

Jeannie Anne started to chirp an answer, but Birchie talked over her.

"Is there no cornbread?"

"Well, no . . . we thought . . . Carbs are . . ." Pastor Rick began unhappily, and Birchie overspoke him, too.

"And still and yet no biscuits?"

"There might be crackers in the pantry," he offered.

"This is nonsense," Miss Birchie said, and Miss Wattie leaned in again to whisper. Wattie had prevented more than one hyperpolite evisceration in her time. But no biscuits was too much, and Birchie turned to her and said, "No, Wattie, it won't do."

In the wake of this soft-spoken utterance, the table quieted. Pastor Rick was new, but even he understood the power of these words, spoken by the reigning

Birch in Birchville. He was almost cringing with pro-
pitiation.

"You should try a bite before you judge! It's so
healthful. And delicious. I know you'll like it if you try
a bite."

Birchie inclined her head away from Wattie's calm-
ing whispers. She pushed aside the vegetables with her
plastic fork, digging to find the salmon. It was shiny
with olive oil and tomato juice, dotted with bits of black
pepper and herbs.

"Oh, dear, no, I can't possibly eat that," she said,
her voice gone dangerously sweet. Sweet as icebox pie.
Sweet as sugar tea. Wattie leaned in closer, her whispers urgent now, but Birchie talked over her, blue
eyes bright in her powdered face. "It looks like Pastor
Campbell's penis, all pink and freckled."

The delivery was so prim and cheerful that it took
several seconds for the words she'd said to register.
Deacon Lester choked. He stifled himself, trying to
asphyxiate quietly in the dawning shocked silence.
Anna Gentry spilled her icy sweet tea down her blouse
and didn't so much as squeak. Jeannie Anne Darian
paused with her bite of fish halfway to her lips, her
eyes bugging in her pretty, pug-dog face.

It didn't seem possible that Emily Birch Briggs
would say the word "penis" or acknowledge the exis-

tence of such a thing. Had a six-foot penis gone running across the church lawn on legs, everyone would have expected Miss Birchie to go completely blind in a six-foot-penis-shaped blotch, right at the center of her field of vision. *Lovely sunset,* she might remark, peering through it to God's glorious vistas. But now she had acknowledged the existence of genitalia in the fellowship hall; worse, she'd said out loud that associate Pastor Campbell had a set. She'd described it in such great detail that it seemed likely she had met the member in question, which was purely, purely unthinkable. Sweat popped on Pastor Rick's forehead, and all the deacons were gaping. Pastor Campbell, hearing his essential self so maligned, opened and shut his mouth several times, with no words or even breath coming out.

Wattie, the only unshocked person in the room, stood up and said, "Birchie, we need to go home. Now."

Miss Birchie poked disdainfully at the fish with her plastic fork, saying, "Well, but it does, Wattie! Ask Jeannie Anne. She's seen that penis much, much closer. Hardly the assigned use for the choir-robe room, though I suppose that's not for me to say."

The air, already shocked and sparking, became fully live with electricity. The whole room went so quiet that folks nearby could hear Wattie fierce-whispering to Birchie, "Get up! Get up! We need to go!"

As if a current were running around the room, the congregation came to understand, one by one, what Birchie was matter-of-factly describing, and they stared at my grandmother in shocked horror. Birchie knew every sin in town, after all, but she heard gossip the way a queen heard supplicants. She never discussed what the town called "news" with anyone but Wattie, instead going directly and privately to First Baptist sinners like the apostle Paul, except with homemade soup. Her stern encouragements to put away wrath, tithe properly, or stop the coveting of other people's wives were done behind closed doors. Birchie was the scion of decency, and these words from her were as shocking as the idea of the adultery itself. All the horror was focused on my grandmother, right up until Jeannie Anne blushed.

Not a delicate blush either, the sort any lady might have touch her cheek when such vivid language landed at the lunch table. This was a crimson shame wash that started at the forehead and didn't end even at her throat. Her chest reddened in the V of her light knit top. Her skin became a scarlet backdrop for the glistening pink and pepper-freckled bite of fish still held at the portal of her glossy lips.

She saw it then, how she had that morsel an inch away from ingestion, and threw it violently away. The fork landed with a sad plastic clatter, followed by an unfortunate plopping as the fish hit the table. Whispers started at the closest tables to Birchie's center one, spreading outward like a rustling tide.

Frank Darian was the last to come to understanding. It wasn't until his wife shoved her chair back and stood up from the table that his expression changed from shocked to something awful. A disbelief. A pre-pain wondering.

"Jeannie Anne?" he said, and she walked away. "Jeannie Anne?"

She didn't turn or falter but kept twisting through the tables as whispers built and roiled around her.

Birchie watched her go, eyes overbright and an incongruous smile on her face, watching her verbal wrecking ball smash two key church marriages. Wattie stood helpless beside her, no longer whispering; her urgency was gone. She seemed oddly resigned, patting at the silver-white zigzags of her short hair as if putting them in order were her main concern.

"How could you?" Associate Pastor Campbell rasped at Birchie. He stood up, his chair scraping back, and slapped his hands down hard against the table. He leaned in toward her, threatening almost, and raged again, "How could you!"

"How could *you*?" his wife whispered, but he didn't seem to hear her.

"Birchie," Wattie said, calm and firm, "I need your help," but Birchie was scraping her own chair away, rising to her full five feet to glare right back at Campbell.

"Don't you raise your voice to me, you humping goat. I will turn you over my knee and paddle your saggy ass," Birchie said. The tone was right, frosty and imperious. But the words! These were not words that Emily Birch Briggs would ever, ever say, and they were followed by a high-pitched, crazy titter.

Pastor Campbell stepped back, away from the confusing sound, his face registering equal parts rage and disbelief. Then he seemed to notice his wife, crying in the chair next to him.

Wattie waited it out, standing beside Birchie until her awful cackle stopped. Then Wattie touched Birchie's arm, and Birchie turned to her as if she had just discovered her there.

"Did you see his saggy ass, Wattie? Did you see it?" Birchie said, and then mimed humping at the table.

Three hundred of the faithful sat frozen, watching Emily Birch Briggs having a mental breakdown, and only Wattie spoke.

"I surely did, but, Birchie, Mercy Lester is slicing up peppers by the hush-puppy batter," she said.

Birchie's avid face clouded into confusion, and she

stopped her obscene rocking. A few years back, Mercy Lester had put the Fry on the high road to apostasy when she'd tried to add cheese and jalapeños to the hush-puppy batter. Birchie had spotted her before they got mixed in. While Miss Wattie scooped the offending ingredients off the top, Birchie had put a forgiving arm around Mercy's shaking shoulders, like Jesus sheltering the woman caught in adultery. Instead of asking for a sinless someone to cast the first stone, Birchie had reminded the outraged congregation that Mercy had been raised a Presbyterian before marrying Davey Lester; could anyone expect her to know better?

To bring it up now was such a non sequitur that it looked as if Wattie were losing her mind right along with Birchie, but Birchie said, "Lord, that girl! Let's go and stop her," as though Mercy and Davey hadn't moved to Montgomery three years ago.

Her face stony and unreadable, Wattie began guiding her out.

"Well, now. Now. Well. Now." Pastor Rick floundered.

As the two of them made their slow way out of the hall, the congregation came one by one into this clarity: Miss Wattie's whispered soothings and asides had long hidden a crumbling at Birchie's center.

It was unthinkable. Miss Birchie, as they all called

her, smelled like rose petals and history. She was the last Birch living in Birchville, ninety years old but still with her perfectly erect spine, her interested eyes, her ancient collection of Very Nice Handbags. For many of them, Miss Birchie was the town. The idea of the town. She was the avatar of the town as it used to be in some Old South utopia that only existed if you were white and well-to-do and Baptist and didn't notice how folks who weren't all of those things had fared. Even before they made it out of the room, people were texting me. Once the door closed behind them, they started calling me as well.

I didn't answer. By then it was already past noon, and I was on my way to Rachel's house. My phone was turned off, and my mind was made up. I was ready to drop my Bat bomb, and I was braced for the kaboom.

3

I pulled up in front of Rachel's pristine Colonial in East Beach, with its black shutters and butt-ugly Tara columns. I was the first one here, but I parked on the street anyway. If I pulled in to the driveway, Mom and Keith might block me in; I'd be trapped, with no way out if the interrogation became unendurable. I'd baked a pecan pound cake, so that everybody would at least come to the conversation cheerful and full of sugar, but they would still want to know when and where and how I'd let this happen. Rachel especially could be so pushy.

I'd been penciling and inking far too long, leaving the scripts to other writers. I couldn't invent a good origin story for Digby any more than I could think of one for Violence. Digby himself, while very young, might be impressed to hear he'd sprung from a late-night encounter with a Batman. But what about Digby's older self? I didn't want to tell my parents or Rachel or my kid that I didn't know his father's name. Or job. Or medical history. Or even if he was a decent person, but that was the truth.

He had good taste in comics, I could say. *He was an excellent French kisser.*

As I trudged up the stairs onto Rachel's wraparound white porch, her husband, Jake, came barreling out the front door, blind, slamming it behind him. He almost ran me down. I tried to dodge and stumbled. He dropped the bag that he was carrying to catch me before I pitched back down the stairs with the cake carrier.

"Damn it, Lay!" he said, and then I flushed and he froze, his hands still on my arms. He hadn't called me Lay in years.

I had my balance, so I crabbed sidewise away from him, out of his grasp. I didn't like him touching me. Most of the time, I thought of him as Rachel's accessory, buckled on but irrelevant, like a wristwatch.

His hands hung in the air for a second, awkward and empty, before he dropped them to his sides.

"Damn it yourself, JJ," I said at last, giving him his old name back, too, as lightly as I could.

The letters made my mouth taste sour, and I had a hard time connecting them to the man in front of me. I thought of him as either Jake or Mr. Rachel. We hadn't been Lay and JJ to each other since we were kids. We'd spent our afternoons from third grade on in my family's basement rec room, reading new comic books as fast as they came in. We'd eat Fiddle Faddle and parse plot twists, trying to guess if our favorites would survive the cliffhanger endings. As we put each issue away into a plastic sleeve and filed it in order in the proper box, we'd discuss what superpower we would each want, debating hyperspeed or flight, teleportation or telekinesis.

I never said it out loud, but like most girls I wanted to be Super Pretty. Rachel had dibs on that power, though. Every boy I knew turned into a stammering wreck in her presence, even JJ. Maybe especially JJ, who blushed and puffed whenever she breezed through the rec room. JJ mostly wanted to be Super Not-a-Fat-Kid, though he never said that either. We knew these things about each other without saying.

Then when we were seniors, JJ's daddy had a massive stroke and died. In the wake of it, things went all kinds of wrong and weird between us, and he quit school to help his mom run Jacoby Motors, their used-car dealership. Our paths never crossed after that. We never spoke or even saw each other. Not once. His house was biking-distance close to mine, so it had to be on purpose.

Four years later he showed up at Mom and Keith's annual drop-in Christmas Eve party. I was on door duty, but I didn't recognize him. He was a tall, blond stranger, smiling and holding a bottle of Riesling.

"Merry Christmas!" he said.

He leaned in to kiss the air near my cheek, and, oddly enough, I recognized him then, by smell. He was three inches taller, with a gym body, subtle highlights, and maybe a nose job, too. For sure he'd done some kind of movie-actor nonsense to his teeth. Uniform and overwhite, they made his smile seem insincere. But under a dash of subtle aftershave, I caught the essential smell of my onetime best friend.

"JJ?" I said, boggling at him.

"I go by Jake now, Leia," he said, and then clapped me on the shoulder. Heartily. As if I were some bro of his in a beer ad. "Good to see you! We'll have to catch up."

He thrust the cold wine into my hands and breezed past, heading right for Rachel. He stayed with her all night, lounging against the wall, telling her all about how he'd saved the family business and now had a three-year plan to open up a Nissan dealership as well. He was Self-Made Ken, charming the pants off Holiday-Champagne-Buzz Barbie.

He'd called me Leia because you don't call the first girl you ever had sex with by her old pet name. Not when that name was "Lay." Not if you've always been in love with her stepsister.

Now I stood in the wake of our old names, clutching my cake carrier to my chest and feeling an odd, bad tang in the air around me. He bent down to stuff spilled clothes back into the bag he'd dropped. It was one of Rachel's reusable Whole Foods bags.

"Are you on a Goodwill run?" I asked him. Stupid, but it was the only thing that came into my head.

"No. What are you doing here?" He shoved his flop of blown-out blond hair off his forehead as he straightened up.

"It's Sunday," I said. "Where else would I possibly be?"

He raised his eyebrows. "Rachel canceled lunch. She sent you an e-mail."

A khaki pants leg with a razor crease ironed into it was hanging out of the bag. I tucked it back in and saw a baby blue shirt with pinstripes and a button-down collar. This was practically Jake's uniform. Then I realized that the gray knit wad of cloth on top was a pair of boxer briefs, and I flushed and made myself look back at his face. Really look.

He had dark circles under his eyes, and his face was puffy. For a moment it was like I could see the round, sad face of my old friend JJ. A ghost face, transparent and faint, superimposed over my brother-in-law's chiseled features.

"What are you doing?" I asked him quietly, human to human.

His mouth turned down, fiercely unhappy, and he said, "Nothing. I have to go."

He pushed past me and took the stairs, race-walking toward his red Nissan Armada.

"Go where?" I called after him.

He didn't so much as glance over his shoulder. He threw the bag into the SUV and climbed in after it. I hovered on the porch, cake carrier in hand, my original mission shattered. Part of me wanted to slink home, but after Jake's bizarre behavior I had to check on Rachel and Lavender. I tried the door, and it wasn't locked.

I stepped into Rachel's vaulted foyer, and immediately I heard her running toward me from the kitchen, shrieking, "I said get out, you motherfffffuuuu—"

Rachel sputtered out mid-profanity when she came into the archway and saw that it was me. She skidded to a stop just inside the dining room. She was barefoot, which Rachel never was. With crazy, tangled hair, which Rachel never had. And two black eyes.

"Rachel!" I said, my heart rate jacking, horrified. I was still trying to process this sudden alternate dimension in which Rachel would shriek the F-word at her husband, and now I was in a completely impossible universe, one where JJ would *hit* my stepsister.

Rachel blinked and fluttered at me, and even though her eyes were swollen, I realized it was only mascara and liquid liner, wept off and rubbed into black raccoon rings. Then I could breathe again. Barely. Poor Digby got instadrunk on the panic chemicals that had been dumped into my bloodstream. He fizzed like a shot glass full of 7-Up at my core.

After a fraught pause, Rachel's hands went to her hair, trying to smooth it, her chest heaving. It was funny in an awful way, because her hair was the least of it. Everywhere my eyes went, things were wrong, so many things that I couldn't catalog them all. The huge mirror over the serving bar was shattered, shards of green glass and what looked like red wine splashed all over the mirrored slivers. One of the dining-room chairs lay on its side, the others catty-whompered. All eight were usually spaced with mathematical precision around the table.

Rachel gave up on her hair and stepped to me, taking the cake carrier in a parody of a gracious hostess. She turned and plopped it onto the table and took the lid off.

"Is this your grandmother's recipe?" she said.

When I nodded, she reached out with one bare hand to tear a huge hunk off. I watched in disbelief as this strange, black-eyed creature who had replaced my stepsister started eating it, methodically, like it was a punishment.

That's when I knew that Jake was cheating on her.

Unfathomable. Rachel was the prize, longed for, fought for, reached at last. Sixteen years of marriage, and as late as last week his eyes still tracked her, greedy, whenever she was in the room. He looked at Rachel as if at any second he would grab her willowy waist, swing her up, and set her on the mantelpiece—the finest piece of art placed at the room's focal center. But he was cheating. I would have bet a million dollars on it.

Perhaps only because he'd called me Lay. In that single syllable, history had reared an ugly head so ancient it felt like mythology. My understanding rose from that sweaty, urgent, single incident of clasping that had passed between us, back when we were kids.

The day after his dad died, JJ came weeping down to find me in the basement. I took him in my arms, and he burrowed and clung, his hot face pressed into my neck, his tears scalding. He was a sad, soft animal, urgently snuffling and rooting at me, racked with shocked grief. I pulled him even closer, holding him so tight it was like I was trying to tuck all that desperation up inside my skin and soothe it. No matter how tight I squeezed my arms and legs around him, his unwieldy body squished out around my clamping, his sorrow much too large to be contained. Then we were kissing. It was sad and wet and frantic, his face slick with tears and snot, but I didn't mind. I felt a huge, ballooning love.

We shoved bits of clothes up and aside, pressing close and closer until I was taking him in. It hurt, a little, but I felt calm and welcoming and something else. The only word for it was "powerful." Powerful but not superior, not above him. It wasn't like that.

It was like I'd stepped off a cliff and found myself standing on air in an effortless, surprising hover. I'd always had this secret power, and I used it without thinking, without knowing that I always could have. Used it for good, I'd thought, to help my wounded friend.

It wasn't romantic. I'd never girl-crushed on him in some silly, ain't-he-dreamy way. I only loved him, whole. He was my best friend. He knew all my secrets, and he'd told me all but one of his. I'd cried facedown in his lap after my cat died. He was the last person I talked to every night, on the phone, and he was the first person I wanted to see every morning; we picked up our endless and ongoing conversation on the bus, between classes, at lunch, and after school at my house, with no need for segues or greetings. Now here he was in my basement, ruined in my arms, and it was good to wrap protectively around him as he rooted and pushed and sobbed his guts out.

Then he gasped and stiffened, and I felt it all come out of him. All that writhing misery, I pulled it right out of his body into mine. His rigidness relaxed into peace, and I felt a swell of pride that I could do this for him.

We lay in each other's arms for a dozen heartbeats, perfectly still, and still perfectly together. In that silence I felt something starting, and it was the story of me and JJ.

I teetered on an internal edge, feeling us tip toward the beginning of a whole, real life. *First comes love,* I thought, and even though I was only seventeen, I knew all the things that would be next. I could imagine me and JJ at college, at our jobs, at our wedding, all the way up to a baby we would make exactly like this. Somebody with his nose and my deep-set eyes. There was one next after another for us, so obvious and easy, and with no need to hurry. It was ahead of us, and we were paused, complete, our bodies linked, on the brink of our beginning.

Then he was scrambling away from me and trying to get all his clothes straight, his cheeks staining even redder when he saw the smear of blood on my inner thigh. He mumbled something about needing to get home. He wouldn't look at my face.

I was still mostly wearing my nerd-girl standard-issue uniform—a thrift-store dress with combat boots—but I felt so naked then. I had to sit up and put my left leg back into my panties, fasten my top buttons, tie my left boot, smooth my hem. When I looked up, he had gone. The next day he wasn't at school. He never came back to school, and he didn't return any of my calls. I went to his house, four times, but he wouldn't come downstairs to see me. He didn't speak to me again until the Christmas he came after Rachel.

I didn't get pregnant, that time. Which put me at a lifetime score of one for two on random, unprotected sexual encounters. I never told anyone about me and JJ. Not Rachel, not Mom and Keith, not the small tribe of nerd girls at my lunch table. It hurt too much to say; I'd been demoted from best friend down to a Kleenex.

It ruined something inside me. That was the year I started drawing Violence anyway. I'd been doing a funny strip starring a character named Violet who looked like me and who frolicked about accidentally thwarting crime. After JJ, prototypes of Violence starting hiding in the margins. Watching my toon. Watching over her. Violet changed, too, evolving into a version of me who did have Super Pretty as a power, and anyone who screwed with her met Violence. Violence ate men like they were snack cakes and was never, never sorry. That was Violence's true origin story. She came to be when I got my heart ripped out and ruined in under seven minutes, but that was not a tale that I could sell to Dark Horse.

Later, when JJ reappeared and Rachel got so serious about him, I made myself believe that he was a new guy—some stranger I'd just met. Especially after they got married and then Lavender came. I separated Jake from JJ, my ex-bestie who'd once wept and writhed and used me, spending his sorrows in my body while keeping his heart for Rachel, for later. It was this secret piece of ugly history that made me sure he was capable of thoroughly shitty sexual behavior now.

"This cake is amazing," Rachel said with her mouth full. She stuffed more in.

"Where's Lavender?" I asked.

Rachel shot me an irked look, her mouth now too full to answer. She stood in profile to me, chewing, breathing heavily in and out through her nose. After she swallowed, she dropped the rest of the chunk of cake onto the floor and dusted her hands together, adding crumbs to the carnage.

"She walked down the street to play at Olivia's house. Surely you don't think I'd let my child witness this."

She said it flat, rhetorical, but after the last five minutes I wasn't sure of anything. I'd never seen her this way—never. I hadn't been allowed to. Not even when I might have helped. As a kid she did her grieving in the laundry closet with no witness except Thimble, her stuffed bunny. Back then, at least, I knew when she was ruined. I would sit outside the closet in silent solidarity and be extra nice to her when she emerged. As an adult I couldn't even do that much. I didn't have the intel. I'd never seen her weep her mascara off, not once.

"What did he do?" I asked, meaning, how had Rachel caught him? And was it a true affair? A one-night thing? A hooker?

It didn't actually matter. I was on her side, period, because Rachel was a "step" in name only. We were both barely three when Mom and Keith got married. I had no concrete memories of a life before her. She was family, while Jake was like her garden shed, fabricated elsewhere and then added on. And the boy he used to be? JJ? He was a bullet I'd dodged years ago.

Rachel straightened up. She had five inches on me, even in bare feet. I watched her trying to gather the shreds of her cool blond dignity. She couldn't, quite. The raccoon eyes spoiled a lot of it, and the way her hands were shaking spoiled the rest.

"What are you even doing here, Leia? Didn't you get my e-mail?" The tremble in her voice wrecked her go-to tone of fond exasperation. She was trying to pretend her dining room wasn't full of broken glass and upended furniture. Like the problem here was my inability to check my messages.

"Let me see," I said, and it was a relief to look away from this nakedly wretched Rachel, scrabbling in my purse to turn on my phone. "Is this really what you want to talk about?"

"I don't want to talk at all," Rachel barked, suddenly so vehement that I looked back at her in spite of myself. Her hands fisted in her wonky hair.

The phone buzzed and pinged in my hands. A text was landing. And another. And another. My *Underdog* theme-song ringtone started, cheery in the fraught silence. The screen said Polly Fincher, a First Baptist member down in Birchville. I sent the call to voice mail, and I started to ask Rachel if I could at least help her straighten up the room before Lavender got home. I barely got two words out before the pings of more texts landing sounded. Then my phone started ringing again.

"What's going on?" Rachel asked.

I opened up Messenger and saw a host of familiar names. Lois Gainey, Chester Beckworth, Alston Rhodes, Pastor Rick, and more, all Birchville people. My heart stuttered, and I started flipping through them. They all said variations of the same thing:

> *What's the matter with Miss Birchie?*
> *Oh, honey, we are all sick worried!*
> *What does her doctor say?*
> *How long has she been this bad off?*

And from Martina Mack, that vicious crone: *Your granny surely showed out ugly in church this morning. . . .*

I looked up at Rachel, stricken.

"What?" she said. "Leia, what?"

"Birchie," I said. "Something's wrong with Birchie."

Bad wrong, too, because the phone started ringing again. Pastor Rick, but I didn't want to talk to him. I needed to talk to Wattie. I swiped him to voice mail, and still more messages were landing.

Childhood summers aside, I had never lived in Birchville. Since I'd graduated high school, I had never spent more than a week at a time there. But I was a Birch. The last Birch, so far as they knew, and this is what round two of all the texts was saying:

Come home.
Come home.
You must come home.

I reached for Rachel, blindly moving toward her, and instantly her failed rally made good. It was as if she teleported slightly above and to the left of her own human turmoil, ready to help me, to fix and manage my mess. This was her essential self, her place, always, as the rest of us mere mortals plodded through our tacky mud. It was sad, and it could be enraging, but it was also very, very useful when the world went south.

"Did she fall?" Rachel asked, putting a comforting arm around me as we peered into the phone. A fall had been my worry for a dozen years now. Those damn staircases all over that house!

"I don't know, I don't know," I said. I opened my e-mail, and the first versions of the day's events were already landing. Rachel and I read in tandem. I was too horrified to be relieved that Birchie hadn't broken a hip; this was somehow worse. She had survived so much, been so essentially and willfully herself. She was bull-minded, chock-full of strong opinions that often belied her genteel-bastion-of-the-Old-South looks. But now the texts were saying that with Wattie's help she had apparently snuck her way down deep into senile dementia or Alzheimer's. "I have to get there, I have to go!"

My hands were now the shaking ones, and I couldn't get the phone to do right. Birchie had refused to leave her town, much less her house, and before Wattie had moved in, she'd driven off a string of in-home nurses. She'd thrown her Life Alert away, saying that only dogs wore collars, and she rarely remembered to charge the cell phone I had bought her. Her sole support system was Wattie, who was almost as old as she was.

"Breathe, sweetie. We can't even be sure what we're up against until you go and see. I can book your travel while you're packing," Rachel said.

I loved her for that inclusive pronoun. *What* we're *up against*—the casual, unconscious declaration that she owned a share in my troubles.

"But you have things going on here, too, with J— Jake," I said. I wanted a share in hers as well. "I don't want to—"

"Shhh, we'll fix me later," Rachel lied.

I let her. My dear old Birchie, far away and failing, trumped whatever Jake was doing with his penis.

I kept flipping through the e-mails, and the more versions I read, the more I found that I was also furious. Those two devious old ladies had put one over on the whole town for God only knew how long, smiling and tatting antimacassars and showing up for church bake sales. They didn't want their lives to change, so they had deliberately hidden truths—oh, I was so angry! Going back to read the latest texts only made me angrier.

So many of our family friends assumed I knew. They were asking what her doctors said, how long it had been going on, and what I planned to do. Only Martina Mack assumed I'd been in the dark. Her latest Facebook message called me "irresponsible and either blind or very stupid" for abandoning a "poor old crazy lady" to "the slapdash care of an ancient, colored maid." I wasn't sure which of the three descriptions made me maddest, and then I was sure.

The first one. The one aimed at me. Because it was the only charge that was remotely accurate. I *was* irresponsible. I *had* been both blind and stupid.

This wasn't on the town, or even on my duplicitous old darlings. I should have noticed. I should have seen. I was Birchie's closest. Birchie's only. I was the one who shouldn't have been fooled. Who knew what damage had happened on my watch?

"I should have moved her here, by me, where I could help her," I said, and instantly regretted it when Rachel's eyes met mine.

She had a thousand I-told-you-so's she could rightfully say in response to this; she had long thought my grandmother had no business living in a town she called "a pimple-size backwater with nothing but a Walgreens doc-in-the-box and an equine vet." I could see her trying to choose the words that would best express how very right she'd been all along, as always, and in that pause we heard it. A soft snuffling sound, coming from somewhere above us.

We looked up, and there was Lavender. She sat hunched into a teeny folded packet on the balcony above the vaulted foyer. She stared through the white bars of the railing, her hands fisted around two of them like a girl in a delicately spindled lady jail. When Lavender turned thirteen, Rachel had taken her to the Clinique counter to learn makeup and skin care; now her eyes were ringed just like her mother's, with soft brown starter mascara.

The superior, wise thing Rachel had been about to say to me died in her mouth. She exhaled its ghost in a small, sharp gasp.

"Olivia wasn't home," Lavender said.

"Oh, no," Rachel said quietly, bereft.

I learned then that I already had mother hands. They moved of their own volition to my belly, two steps ahead of thinking, shielding Digby from any bad thing that might hurt him one day, later, when he was out of me and being his own self. Rachel's hands moved at the same time, rising toward Lavender. I could see in her reaching hands the need to hold her baby, hide her eyes, form cups over her open ears.

Too late. Whatever awfulness had happened between JJ and Rachel, my niece had been a witness. Unshielded. Lavender was witness to it all.

4

It begins with Violence.

No cause, no reason, no explanation. She just is: The Bad I Am.

Back in college I drew the first page as a single panel: Violence leaping over a grayscale city roofline in her sex-monster superhero outfit, a gaudy splash of color in the darkness. Her purple-black leotard was French-cut, with a deep, deep V-neck outlined in silver to suggest the letter. It was like Superman's S, but with boobs spilling out of it. Long, wicked knives were strapped to her naked thighs, above her boot tops. Her crazy purple hair blew behind her, becoming jagged strands of black lightning where it overlapped the big, round moon. Her grin showed teeth that were oh-so-faintly pointy.

I saw my style emerging in that opener. It was in the way the light bounced, the frenzied female body over a static background, the use of a limited color palette to pull the gaze right where I wanted it.

Once I'd left the airport and gotten out of Birmingham, I spun that image of Violence in my head. I could do this drive to Birchville on autopilot, because I'd been down this route at least twice a year since I was six months old and Mom moved me to Virginia. Birchie had paid for the move, and for Mom to go to Old Dominion University. It was the last thing Birchie wanted—to move the only grandchild she would ever have farther away—but Mom wasn't from Birchville. She'd grown up in nearby Jackson's Gap. She'd met my dad at a Dairy Queen right after high school, in the first summer of their lives when labels like "cheerleader" and "nerd" had lost their power. They fell in love and married fast and young, the way small-town people often did. After he died, Mom wanted a fresh start; Birchie made it happen, so Mom and I gave her all my childhood summers and my Thanksgivings in perpetuity.

I usually liked this drive. It was a low-traffic four-lane that shot through Nowhere, Alabama, on the way to my specific piece of it. I could drive it in a state of mind that was a little like twilight sleep, where the pictures formed and shifted.

I wanted to think about anything but Birchie's health. I was so angry with myself, so worried, and I wouldn't know how bad it truly was until I got there. I kept my mind's eye fixed on that first image of Violence, trying to see how she had come to be so I could write this prequel. The one I hadn't started yet.

I was used to working creatively to deadline, but in collaboration, as part of a team. Plus, my teams had access to deep histories and intricate worlds that had been invented by other teams of people, years ago.

V in V was different. It was the first and last thing I'd done that was wholly mine.

I had to remember how to work alone. While gestating a still-secret human. Also alone. While finding out what had gone so bad wrong with my Birchie and deciding what to do about it. While supporting Rachel long-distance as her marriage imploded, which was like attempting to cuddle a cat who didn't want to be picked up, and now the cat was three states away.

I had to try, though. I was the only person on the planet who even knew that Rachel was in trouble. Except, of course, for Lavender. Who was barely speaking to me. My niece was a hunchy thread of palpitating blond misery beside me, her face pointed decidedly away, out the window. I'd gotten nothing but sour nods and shrugs and one-word answers ever since I'd picked

up her and her ridiculous Louis Vuitton three-piece
luggage set at Rachel's early this morning.

She was so tiny that I wondered if she should be
in the front seat. She hadn't asked, though. She'd just
gotten in, and Rachel had said nothing. Lavender was
heading into eighth grade, and Rachel must have finally lost the "You have to be a hundred pounds" argument. Lavender had been born so premature that she
might never be a hundred pounds. Lord, if we got into
a wreck, the air bag might well kill her. Her head was
the size of a little cantaloupe, and her hands looked like
doll hands, folded under the brand-new breasts that
were pushing at her T-shirt.

"I'm glad you're with me," I told her, and it was
only mostly a lie. Usually I liked traveling with Lavender, who was into manga and Magic: The Gathering
and could use words like "Whedonverse" correctly
in a sentence. I made up for it by saying an immediate truth. "And sometimes it's good to get away from
home."

"Maya got a trip to Paris," Lavender said.

It was the longest sentence she'd said all day.

"You'd rather be in Paris? Me, too, babe."

It sounded lovely, actually, skipping off to eat me-
ringues and macarons and wander the Louvre with my
usually delightful niece. In We-Go-Straight-to-Paris

World, Birchie was healthy and hail, walking with Miss Wattie to the fruit stand to pinch-test the tomatoes.

"Well, I don't want to be in Alabama," Lavender said. "Maya's gramma took her for two weeks, and when she got home, everything was done already."

"What was done?" I asked, and even as the stupid question fell out of my stupid mouth, I regretted it.

"The stuff for the divorce," Lavender told the huge bank of kudzu we were passing on the right. "Maya got off the plane, and only her mom was there to pick her up. Her dad was waiting to meet them at the Scoopery. They bought her a Death by Chocolate sundae, even though her mom was always like, 'Sugar is the devil.' Her dad had moved to an apartment already. Her mom had packed half of her stuff to go in her new bedroom there. It was like, 'Here, this happened. Live with it, and have this ice cream because we think you're either five or stupid.' Now she has about a million pimples, because her dad lets her eat whatever she wants on his weekends to piss her mom off. Her mom's never home, because she's dating every creep there is on JDate, which, gross, and her dad's girlfriend moved in, and she's like twenty-six, so it's even grosser. Maya already tried pot, and she dyed her hair green, and she hates everyone. We're not even friends anymore, because she hangs with the burners."

The saddest part was how flat she said it. Like this was regular, and now it was her turn. Up until now she'd been so protected; she hadn't known that no one grew up without collecting dings and broken edges. I hated standing witness to this first hard blow, hated hearing the shiver and crack of her faith.

"Lavender, that's not going to happen to you," I said. I couldn't stop her hurting, but I wouldn't let it ruin her. Not if I could help it.

"I'm not going to smoke pot and get pimples?" Lavender said. "Or Mom and Dad aren't getting a divorce?"

She knew the answer to the second question better than I did. She didn't wait to hear my answer anyway. She turned her face to the window and popped her ear-buds in, jacking up the music on her phone so loud that I could hear the tinny whisper of some pop boy wailing in falsetto about love.

I took a cleansing breath and refocused on Violence, suspended in midleap over the cityscape. She's looking down, grinning her savage grin. There was only one word on that whole first page, written inside a small white square to show that it was Violence's thought, not dialogue.

Hello.

She's seen Violet, trit-trotting through the narrow,

trash-strewn alleyway below. In the second panel—
and in every panel where Violet is seen through Violence's eyes—her footsteps leave a trail of flowers and
vines and butterflies and yearning baby rabbits. It was
a little embarrassing to remember exactly how über-
pretty and pure I'd made my avatar. Violence, who has
landed on a rooftop now, looks right at her and thinks,
You are a living sunbeam in this black and filthy place.

On the next page, shapes rise out of the shadows
and coalesce into a gang that follows Violet. Well, I was
young, and hurting enough to turn one sad, selfish JJ
into a pack of evil boys, bent on mayhem. Violence,
watching them stalk the living embodiment of my
own innocence down an alley, thinks, *Like any light in
darkness, you attract.*

She follows the gang, slithering along the roofline.

The shadow boys call out to Violet. She speeds up,
looking for a way back to a busy street, a lighted store.
But she has taken a wrong turn. The alley dead-ends,
and the boys encircle her, blocking much of her yellow
light. She holds her purse out in front of her. As if they
want something so simple, so easily abandoned as a
purse. Her eyes are full of tears that have not spilled
yet. Nothing has been spilled yet.

From her perch Violence watches, and through her
eyes the boys are hunchbacked and long-snouted, more

hyena than human. She starts creeping down the wall behind them.

Your light has called these feral children. And something worse . . .

One boy bats the purse to the ground, and another knocks Violet's hat off. A third grabs at her shoulder, snapping the strap of her sundress with a ping.

Your light has called me.

Violet falls to her knees. As she covers her eyes with her hands, Violence comes to ground behind them. The snicking of her long knives being drawn gets their attention. Then it is all carnage, because this is what Violence brings. She tears and bites and slices, making bad boys into broken heaps and pieces.

Live, scrap of sunshine. Live to warm me.

As Violence swarms back up the alley wall, she takes one last look over her shoulder. Violet kneels in a fresh-made abattoir with her hands covering her eyes, seen but not seeing. The baby rabbits hide in her skirts. Her sundress is a red-and-yellow Rorschach test. A frightened songbird on her shoulder holds the broken strap to keep her covered.

By the time Violet takes her hands away, Violence is gone. But not entirely. Her colors, her shadow and its shapes haunt the margins of the frame until the next time Violet meanders into jeopardy.

I flipped back to the beginning in my mind's eye. There Violence says that Violet's light called her. What if she was lying? Or what if she was simply wrong? Did Violence know her own origin story? That was an interesting question, and I felt a little spark. The spark of *story* starting. What if—

"Is that a food baby, or are you pregnant?" Lavender asked, pulling me out of my dirty alley, landing my butt hard back in the rental car.

I was so startled that I turned toward her, jerking the wheel sideways. Our tires hit the rough tread on the shoulder of the highway, and I realized I'd been steering with one hand. The other, in its brand-new mother-hand way, had moved of its own volition to the bottom curve of my belly. It defined Digby, small-ballooning in his own decided little pooch in front of me.

I had to face front and grab the wheel with both hands to drag the car onto its proper course, but not before I saw that Lavender looked as startled as I felt.

"Oh my God, are you?" Lavender said, almost a squawk. She pulled her earbuds out. "I was totally kidding."

My face felt so hot. I wanted, very badly, to say, *Ha-ha, you're right, I'm fondling my abdomen purely for spicy-sandwich-related reasons!* But I was already sixteen weeks gone. In another month or so, Digby would tell the truth for me. Plus, I had a long-standing policy of not BS'ing Lavender. It was one of the reasons that we were so close.

"Are you really pregnant?" she asked again, insistent.

"A little bit," I said.

I risked a sidelong peep at her, and to my surprise, her hands were balled into fists in her lap and tears of fury had welled up in her eyes.

"No one tells me anything," she said. "You all just do what you want. You grown-ups. You do whatever you want all secret. I never know important stuff, unless I happen to find out by accident."

"Oh, honey," I said, instantly softened, because this was not about me, much less Digby. Not at all. "I don't know what's going on with your mom and dad, but I do know they both love you." She snorted at that, and I asked her, "Do you want to talk about it?" Lord, how I did.

I wanted to know what Lavender knew. Sunday afternoon Rachel had gone upstairs and taken Lavender into her room. She'd come down half an hour later, but I was on the phone with Birchie.

By then I'd heard and read enough eyewitness Fish Fry accounts to convince me that I had to get down to Birchville, ASAP. I'd called Birchie directly to tell her

I was coming. While Rachel sat in the wreckage of her dining room, calmly booting up her laptop, I blatted into Birchie's soft "mm-hm"s and Wattie's palpable silence, "I should be there Tuesday, at the latest."

I was hating the speakerphone. I felt my words thinning and flattening as they fell out on the other end, as if they were landing in an echoing black canyon instead of a genteel living room with damask curtains and twin Victorian love seats.

"No need for such a fuss," Birchie said.

"We're fine here, Leia," Wattie added, which was such a blatant whopper that it stole my breath for a second.

"I'm glad to hear that you're fine, Wattie," I said, my voice gone sharp. Birchie never would have been able to hide her failing mind for so long without Wattie's help. And now they both sounded truculent, unsorry and dismissive, like they'd simply been naughty babies hiding chocolate. "Are you both just fine?"

Birchie answered, her tone mild. Almost chatty. "Well, Wattie's knees have been a bother for her, I can tell you that."

I hardly knew how to respond. Maybe she was so deep into the badlands of the brain that she'd already forgotten what had happened. Maybe she was being Southern Lady Genteel about the brand-new Late Unpleasantness she had started down at First Baptist. I needed to see her to know.

As soon as the connection closed, I called my parents. Rachel looked up from pricing flights and rental cars for me when she heard me say, "Hey, Mom," pausing to listen to my half of the conversation.

"It's a lot for you to do alone," Mom said, when I'd gotten her up to speed. "Do you think I should go with you?"

"No," I said, near instantly.

My mother had a strong sense of doing what was right—and what was expected—but her presence would only make things harder. She and Birchie hadn't been close since Mom remarried. Birchie hadn't objected to the union; my father had been gone more than three years then. The rift came because Mom wanted to change my name and let Keith adopt me. Mom thought I would feel like the odd girl out, growing up Leia Birch Briggs when she became Clara Simpson. Birchie fought her bitterly, and it caused a lifelong coolness between them. After that, when Mom brought me down for my summers, she didn't stay the way she had when I was a baby.

Now that I was grown, I was glad Birchie had won. I would have been odd girl out by any name, a super-nerd who stood five foot nothing and had the Briggses' pale skin and the Birches' dark hair and light blue eyes. My tall, wispy mother looked like the mom who would come in the box set with Keith and Rachel. They were all long-boned and honey-colored and slim, and none of them had ever seen a single episode of *Xena*.

"I got this, Mom," I told her. My grandmother's illness was Birch business, and my mother didn't have a place in it. "And anyway, Rachel is helping me book—"

My stepsister was instantly on her feet, waving her hands back and forth to get my attention, shaking her head no.

I stopped talking, puzzled, and Mom said, "Rachel? I thought she had a stomach bug?" I remembered that Rachel had canceled lunch.

"Yeah, but I called her anyway. You know Rachel. She's probably finding flights from the bathroom floor."

Rachel gave me a thumbs-up and sat back down in front of the laptop. I got off the phone, thinking how weird it was to be on this side of Rachel's wall. Neither of us was ready to spring our life-changing family news on our shared parents, but I knew about Jake, and Rachel did not know about Digby. It was an odd reversal. As I came up behind her, thinking I should encourage her to get some support from Keith and Mom, I saw she'd put a second one-way ticket in her Delta shopping cart. It was made out for Lavender Marie Jacoby.

"Absolutely not," I said, but Rachel talked over me.

"Leia, you'll have your hands full there. You'll need a helper," she said, as if she were doing me a favor. "It will even be fun for Lavender, that big old attic full of furniture and letters and oh, the clothes! I used to be so jealous, seeing your summer pictures playing dress-up with real flapper gowns, bustles, poodle skirts, and that wedding dress. . . ."

"Yeah, when I was nine," I said. By the time I was Lavender's age, the attic seemed like a great place to get heatstroke and spider bites. I missed JJ's Super Nintendo so much that Birchie drove into Montgomery and bought me one to ensure I stayed through July. Rachel spent her own teen summers with Keith's parents down in Myrtle Beach, getting blonder and browner in her bikini, decorously French-kissing every cute boy in South Carolina. "No thirteen-year-old girl dreams of a vacation down in Birchville, Alabama. And I need to focus on Birchie."

"Yes, exactly," Rachel agreed. "But you also have to decide what to store and what gets packed for Goodwill. You're awful at that sort of thing."

"I don't know if I'm going to close down—" I began, but Rachel interrupted me.

"Yes you do." As she spoke, she kept right on typing Lavender's birth date and home address into Delta, as if it were already decided. "I'm sorry, but you do. You have to move Birchie here, to assisted living. You've already put it off longer than you should have. She needs more care than she can get in Eastern Jesus, Alabama."

"Maybe so, but Birchie will have her own opinions," I said, an understatement so enormous I was surprised it didn't get stuck and smother me on the way out of my mouth.

"You have to be firm. At a certain point, you have to take charge of things. With your grandmother that point came years ago." Now she was choosing two side-by-side seats on the plane diagram. First class, which was ridiculous. A thousand extra bucks for a hot towel, some leg room, and free cocktails that Digby wouldn't let me drink. "Lavender can help you. She's naturally an organizer."

It was true that Rachel's genetic legacy was visible in Lavender's alphabetized-by-author bookshelves and color-coded sweater drawers. But Rachel had never seen the Birch ancestral home in person. There were a hundred and fifty years of history in that house, most of it in the form of junk that had been stuffed and stacked and piled up in the attic. It would take four strong men a week to make a dent in it. Lavender would no more be useful than would Sergeant Stripes, the feral cat who lived in my backyard. I started to say so, but Rachel talked over me.

"That frees me up to find some places for Birchie to tour here. The nicest facilities all have monstrous waiting lists, I hope you know, but I can get her in almost anywhere she likes. People all over this town owe me favors." I think she still saw a big fat no on my face, because she stopped typing, looked up at me, and added, "Please, Leia. I need some room to think right now. Please?"

That stopped my refusal cold. Rachel was asking me for help. Unprecedented, though she'd been shoveling her own unstoppable help at me for thirty-five years now. Even back in freaking preschool, she "helped" me color. One of my first memories was Rachel lisping, *Pee-poo aren't green. Pee-poo are like dis,* while peeling an Electric Lime Crayola from my fist and replacing it with Flesh.

As an adult, she'd helped me choose everything from cars to Christmas trees to lip gloss. She'd bullied me into surviving after JJ screwed me over, even though she didn't know what was wrong with me. JJ was so socially beneath her that she'd barely noticed his presence, much less his absence. All she knew was that I'd stopped eating and washing my hair. Even my Wonder

Woman comics piled up unread. She'd stepped in, telling me that if I didn't get out of bed, I would molder. She force-marched me to Soup-N-Salad with her friends and dragged me to watch her current boyfriend do his sportsball things. When I sat blank-eyed through these events, she changed tactics, suffering through *Men in Black* and *The Fifth Element* and even a teeny local *Star Trek* con, anything she thought might spark my interest. She'd done my color chart, too, claiming that going off to college required a makeover, then took Keith's Visa and bought me a slew of spring-colored scarves to rectify my stark winter wardrobe.

"Just get some pink or this turquoise up around your face," she'd told me, and the enraging thing was, with Spring colors by my face, damn it all if I did not look fresher and bright-eyed. Less broken anyway. Twenty years later I was still winding a funky scarf in the correct colors around my neck, elevating my uniform—black top, boot-cut jeans, and Chucks—into an actual outfit. Her genuinely good intentions coupled with her self-assured rightness made the helping both exasperating and impossible to turn down.

What had I done to help her back? Nothing. She never let anybody help her. Even on those rare occasions when Rachel allowed a virus to get through her cloud of vitamins, she kept her freezer stocked with frozen quarts of homemade chicken soup she made out of organic bone broth and whatever root vegetables had the most antioxidants.

"Well, there's no harm in finding places for Birchie to tour, but only if they have two-bedroom units. Wattie and Birchie will likely want to stay together. I have to give them the option," I told her, digging out my AmEx. Rachel was on the payment page already. "And fly us coach. Those seats are big enough to hold two Lavenders."

She hesitated, eyeing my Digby-inspired larger ass. She noticed whenever I put on a few pounds and would gift me with fruit baskets and yoga-class cards until my jeans got roomy again. She reached for her purse, and I knew this move as well. She was about to get out her own credit card and pay to put me where she wanted me.

"Do you want me to take Lav or not?" I asked.

"Fine. I'll put you back in steerage," she said, and she even used my card.

Now here we were, Lavender and me, both under different kinds of Rachel-fueled duress. Me with only a best guess idea of what had happened between her parents.

"I don't want to talk about it," Lavender said. "No one ever talks to me about anything, so why should I talk to you? You're as bad as them, running around all secret pregnant, and I'm this dumb kid who gets to find out last. Or never."

Her hands were shaking, she was that angry, that helpless in the face of whatever was happening to her family.

"Lav," I said softly, "you're not the last to know, okay? You're first. Unless you count doctors, I haven't told a living soul I'm pregnant."

That gave her pause, and she asked, "Gramma and Grampa don't know?" I shook my head. "Mom doesn't know?"

"Nope. And I would like to be the one to tell her. Them. Everyone—in my own time, if you don't mind," I said, and looked over to meet her eyes, so she would know how serious I was. She nodded, solemn, and I looked back to the road.

After a minute Lavender asked, "What about, like, the dad? The dad of the baby? Does he know?" She was calmer, and that was good, but oh, what a complicated question.

Instead of answering directly, I told her, "The father is not going to be involved."

"But does he know?" Lavender asked, as persistent as her mother.

I shook my head, wishing I could be thirteen and stick my lip out and say, *I don't want to talk about it.* I didn't want to explain drunk and sketchy sexual decisions to a middle-schooler who had yet to kiss a boy. I could feel Rachel as a sudden, looming presence in the car, wanting me to tread very, very carefully here. Lavender looked up to me. It didn't help that she was full of brand-new estrogen and had just watched her own father storm out the front door with a Whole Foods bag full of socks and underpants. Hormones and daddy issues, the classic recipe for pushing girls way too early into boy arms. "What does your mother tell you about sex?" I asked.

"Oh my God, like, nothing," Lavender said, flushing. "I mean, she gave me a book about it. And she told me not to have it."

"That's excellent advice," I said. "Reproduction works, Lav. It only takes once, and it can happen even if you think you're being careful."

"So you went on, like, one date?" Lavender asked.

"No," I said. "It wasn't that kind of thing."

"What kind of thing was it?"

A no-date thing, actually, and I could not remember his real name. I had a flash of Batman, that cocky grin under the cowl, his surprisingly well-muscled arms and shoulders—I'd assumed that definition had been drawn onto the costume—and now I thought, *A really, really hot thing.* The thought came so fast I was already saying it. At the last second, I replaced the word "hot" in the out-loud version.

"A really, really stupid thing."

I didn't even cross my fingers on the steering wheel. I wasn't lying. It had been stupid. But also, I couldn't help remembering, plenty hot.

"I want to know what happened," Lavender insisted.

Nothing about this story was particularly thirteen-year-old-appropriate, but sometimes the world wasn't. Thirteen-year-olds still had to live in it and not be lied to. Even so, the spirit of Rachel was practically a force now; there was honest, and then there was too honest. If I would not lie, Rachel expected me to at least be a good object lesson.

"I was at FanCon in Atlanta, and I had an awful day. So I went down to the bar, which was a bad idea. This guy came up and asked if he could buy me a drink."

"What was his name?" Lavender asked.

"Doesn't matter," I said.

"What did he look like?" Lavender asked. Which was entirely not the point.

"I don't know. He was dressed as Batman," I said. "So I—"

"Batman?" Lavender interrupted, and then she snorted. Almost a laugh. "You love Batman! Was he a cute Batman?"

"I don't know. It doesn't matter," I repeated, but a sidelong glance at her told me that it did, to her. Well, at least it was a question I could mostly answer. "Um, he was around my age. African American. Deep voice—"

"He was black? You're having a black baby?" Lavender interrupted again.

"Well, it's half my baby, Lavender. He'll be biracial, so I don't know what he'll look like or how he'll think of himself."

She was staring at me, big-eyed and silent.

"What?"

"God, Aunt Leia. You are just . . . so cool."

Rachel was going to murder me.

"No, I'm not cool," I said. "I'm reckless, and I let feeling crappy lead me into bad decisions. For the record, it didn't make me feel better." Not strictly true, but in the morning I'd been half dead of hangover, so it was true enough. "He could have been a rapist, or a psycho stalker, and I brought him right up to my room. He could have had a disease. I had to get tested for a bunch of crap, which was scary and embarrassing, and I still have to take another HIV test in a couple months, just to be safe. I was completely out of control, and now this baby—who I'm glad about, don't get me wrong. I am going to love this kid. But, Lav, my kid is going to grow up with no father."

That one hit her close. Maybe too close. She looked away, swallowing.

"That's going to suck. Not having a dad," she said, and I wasn't sure if she meant for the baby or for her. Maybe both.

I backpedaled, picking a different moral. "When you drink too much, you make choices that you might not make if you were sober."

She rolled her eyes, accepting the subject change. "They told us at school."

"Well, I'm telling you again," I said. "It's easy to drink too much, especially if you're not used to it."

Lavender nodded, very solemn. "So you're saying I should start drinking as soon as possible and get used to it."

She said it so earnestly it took me half a beat to realize she was trolling me. I smiled, relieved to see the sassy kid I knew was still there, under the unhappiness.

"Exactly. Birchville is in a dry county, or else I'd stop and get you a sippy cup of bourbon." I turned us onto Main Street. "Look, we're almost there."

Lavender made a face, like she was smelling something less than savory. "This is Birchville?"

Up ahead we could see Walgreens and Subway across from Tiger Gas, a nod to Auburn. Alabama fans gassed up at the Shell.

"The edge of it," I said. "You'll see downtown after this intersection."

She sat up straighter, looking around as we passed Piggly Wiggly, sharing its parking lot with Movie Town.

"What is that place?"

"You rent DVDs there. They also have tanning beds in the back," I said. In some ways driving into Birchville was like driving thirty years into the past, the streets lined with colors and concepts right out of 1987.

"That's freaky," she said. "A lady on the corner is waving at us."

Dot Foster, a sweet older woman who headed the Prayers and Squares ministry at First Baptist, had spotted the rental car. I waved back, and she hurried off toward Lois Gainey's house. Within minutes the entire town would know I had arrived, toting an unknown adolescent. If no one remembered that I had a niece, they would deploy a scout to drop by to find out Lavender's people and provenance. In other ways driving into Birchville was a lot like driving a *hundred* and thirty years into the past, all the way back to 1887.

I stopped at one of the three traffic lights, studying Lav as she studied my town.

She was past Super Pretty—she was beautiful, and true beauty always came with a healthy shock of odd. Part of it was that she was so little. In the NICU she'd looked like a wrinkly purple apple with a few sticks attached, everything below the neck wasted to bird bones to protect her brain. Her body had never yet caught up. She was my height but built to scale, so that in pictures where she stood alone, she looked lanky and tall. Her face was wider than it was long, with huge eyes sunk deep and razor-sculpted cheekbones. Her nose was a small, sharp jab over a wide mouth. Now her body had changed, too, and tiny as she was, she didn't look at all childish. I hoped she wouldn't realize how spectacular she was until she was twenty-five and safely past letting it ruin her.

We were at the square now, the spire of First Baptist visible from any point around it. Here, on the far side, a park with benches and a fountain shared space with the library. The sides were row shops that ran around the corners: the Knittery, Sally's Hair Emporium, Read-Overs New and Used Books, Cupcake Heaven, Pinky Fingers Nail Salon. First Baptist itself took up most of the fourth side, and the center was all church grounds and the tiny, ancient cemetery. Most of the houses on the outer ring were Victorians that had been converted into offices and stores. A few were still residences, owned by the remnants and relations of the oldest families.

"That's Birchie's house," I said as we turned the last

corner, but Lavender's eyes had caught on the pale blue Victorian two doors closer. Both of Frank Darian's teenage boys were sitting glumly on the porch steps.

Frank or Jeannie Anne must have pulled them home early from camp. Was there some parental compulsion to move children across state lines when a marriage was in trouble? Or perhaps they had demanded to come home. Most of First Baptist's youth group had been at the Fish Fry, so no doubt Hugh and Jeffrey Darian had gotten their own slew of overdetailed texts and e-mails.

I wondered who was in the house with them. Traditionally, when marriages blew up in southern small towns, the home defaulted to the wife. But, also traditionally, the husbands did the cheating, plus Frank's law office was on the first floor. I was willing to bet Jeannie Anne had been the one to vacate.

"Cute," Lavender said, still looking at the boys. They both looked back.

The out-loud boy noticing was new. Maybe it came in a package with the curvy hips she'd recently acquired.

"Birchie owns that white Victorian with the wraparound porch. See the turret?" I pointed. "On the second floor, that round room has a daybed and curved bookshelves. I called it the Princess Room when I was little. You can sleep there if you want."

She glanced at it, and said, "Cool," but then she looked back over her shoulder at the boys. I felt a twinge of sorrow. The Princess Room would have excited last summer's Lavender, a secure and curveless twelve-year-old whose parents loved each other. This summer's girl was thirteen—hormone-soaked and heartbroken.

We pulled in to the drive. Miss Wattie waited in the cushy porch swing, her feet pushing the boards, slowly rocking. Her hair was too short to sway with her. She stood up and came into the sun. Her little curls looked like molten silver as she made her way down the stairs. Birchie was below her in the yard, wearing her big gardening hat. She knelt by of one of the beds, planting something, turning dirt with a small trowel. She straightened when Wattie lifted one hand and then rose carefully to her feet, but she didn't wave. She stared at the rental car, still holding the trowel, her other hand full of seeds, her face blank.

"I'll unload the bags and then come up and meet them," Lavender said. "Go say hello."

"You sure?" I said, and she made muscle-man arms. I was surprised to see the stringy definition in her biceps.

"I'm pretty mighty," she told me, making me smile back. I handed her the keys.

As I came to the foot of the porch stairs, Birchie startled, and her blank eyes finally fixed on me. She blinked rapidly, puzzled, and my heart sank. I'd come to see how bad it was, and already—it was bad. She didn't know me.

"Birchie?" I said.

She blinked twice more, confused, and said, "Oh, no, I don't think I got the turkey. Wattie, did we get the turkey?"

I had to work hard not to cry. It was a good ninety degrees, and Birchie was right beside a host of splashy summer zinnias, but recognizing me had dropkicked her into Thanksgiving.

"The Pig delivered everything we need," Wattie told her, coming to hug me.

Birchie bent to drop her trowel into the tool bucket. She threw the seeds behind her, and they landed on the black patch of tilled soil. They were small, round speckles of an orange not found in nature. It looked like Birchie had been planting little candies, maybe Tic Tacs. I kissed Wattie's cheek, then went to hug and kiss my grandmother, shutting my stinging eyes, holding her a little too tightly. I wasn't sure how to begin.

"Goodness," Birchie said, breathless. "You'll squeeze the life right out of me. I'm glad to see you, too."

When I finally stepped back, Wattie leaned in

toward Birchie, saying something about dinner almost too softly for me to catch, right into her ear. Birchie acted as if Wattie weren't speaking, reporting the information as if it were her own knowledge.

"We're having Cornish game hen."

"Sounds wonderful," I said. My voice sounded so thick.

My Birchie was planting candy, and she hadn't known me. I still wasn't sure that she'd realized it was June. I felt a small bubble of anger rising, that things had gone this far without my knowing.

Digby spun like a teeny whirligig inside me then, as if reminding me how easy it was to not tell. Even the things that really mattered. Even to the ones who loved you most. But still. But still. I couldn't help but say it.

"You should have talked to me." I aimed the words at Wattie, but she only looked to Birchie. So to Birchie I said, "I don't even know what's— Is it Alzheimer's? And what are y—"

"I don't have Alzheimer's," Birchie interrupted, suddenly present and looking quite affronted. "I have . . ." She paused and leaned toward Wattie, who was already whispering. "The Lewy bodies!" Birchie said, triumphant. "I have the Lewy bodies growing in my brain, and it isn't Alzheimer's at all."

"Lewy bodies," I echoed.

Wattie said, "It's like Parkinson's, but Lewy bodies are actual growths, made out of proteins. They aren't malignant, but they cause all kinds of trouble. Also, she's had at least two mini-strokes that have not helped one bit." It was a bullet of neat information, delivered in a matter-of-fact tone.

"That's really succinct, Wattie, thank you," I said, my anger now sharp enough to cut the grief. Did she think three sentences was all it took? "I don't know what the hell any of that means."

Wattie's temper did not rise to mine. Just as calmly she said, "It means Birchie says soap words, on her bad days. She gets tired and confused and ornery real easy. Now she's started saying things out loud in public that might be better said more quietly, in private, and she sees animals that aren't there."

"Rabbits," Birchie chimed in. "These days the whole town is chock-full of them. All doing what rabbits do."

She waved an irritated hand at the bottom of the drive. I looked and saw no rabbits. Just Lavender. The rental car's hatchback was gaped open, but the luggage was still in it. She was down by the curb talking to both Darian boys. Fantastic.

"Dr. Pettery has her taking Exelon and Sinemet," Wattie went on. The formal medical words sounded odd coming from her familiar mouth, as awkward as

I always sounded when I tried to use my high-school French. "They help her not shake, and they help her not fall down. He told her to take baby aspirin to keep a bigger stroke from coming. There's another drug that could help with the memory and the rabbits—"

"Such humping!" Birchie interjected. Wattie kept talking.

"—but there's a good chance it would make the shaking much, much worse. So we just live with those dirty rabbits, don't we?"

"I know those rabbits aren't there," Birchie confided. "Real rabbits behave better."

I shook my head. "You should have told me she was sick."

"Oh, honey," Wattie said, pitying and reproachful.

Birchie's bright eyes were on me now, alive and clever and thoroughly her own. Her dry hands patted at me, like I was a sad dog or a baby.

"Oh, honey," she said, her tone echoing Wattie's. "I'm not *sick*. I'm only dying."

Then she took my hand and led me up the stairs into the house.

5

"You know what you have to do," said Rachel in her kind-but-firm voice.

I'd had to call anyway to tell her we'd arrived safe. While I had her, I asked her to type "Lewy bodies" into Google. I'd already done it, sitting down at the desk the second I was alone in my room and booting up the old laptop I'd brought for Lavender, but it had been a mistake. The facts were laid out in such plain black font, stark against the website's white background. Scary phrases seemed to bold themselves and fill my field of vision. *Cognitive decline. Hallucinating animals or people. Anxiety. Dementia.* When I'd gotten to *Advances inexorably to death,* I'd snapped the laptop closed with more force than was good for it. Then I'd dialed my stepsister.

"I haven't made any decisions," I told Rachel, but my voice sounded faint. Well, good. Lavender was rustling around in the tower room next door, and the sounds of her unpacking reminded me how thin the walls were. I didn't want Birchie or Wattie overhearing. "I haven't even talked to Birchie's doctors yet."

"I know this feels like you're moving fast, but sweetie, no," Rachel said. "Not to be judgey, but you've been worried about Birchie and Wattie's living situation for a good ten years now. You let it slide and slide, and now you need to declare a state of emergency. Lewy bodies are frosting on a whole bad cake. You need to be firm with them."

I moved the closed laptop out of the way and pulled my sketchbook toward me. It had a pencil stuck down in the spiral binding, and I wrestled it out. I usually found myself doodling when I was on the phone. Or under stress. The pad was open to a simple drawing of Violence, leaping. Her knives were out. I drew a boogery shape in front of her, long and lumpy, as I spoke.

"I know, but, Rachel, this is Birchie. She's so freakin' invincible."

It seemed wrong that the banal rules of aging and the body would apply to Birchie. Rules never had before; she was a legend, and she came from legends.

Her grandfather had founded the town, her father had steered it intact through the Great Depression, and Birchie herself had saved it again in 1957.

That summer Ellis Birch left abruptly for Charleston in a swirl of rumors that the family fortune was in jeopardy. An embezzler at the investment firm, some folks said, or trouble at the overseas bank where, rumor had it, Birches still kept their blockading money.

"Them Birches din't diversify," Jelly Mack had said, with such a combination of ill-concealed relish and total ignorance of the definition of "diversify" that the remark had become famous. The local old folks still said it back and forth, chuckling, though Jelly had been dead now twenty years.

At the time it had not been funny. Most jobs in Birchville proper were tied in some way to Birch money, and the family owned most of the square. The rents could be considered acts of charity; they kept our downtown thriving.

Ellis Birch died of a massive heart attack right after arriving in Charleston, which made the rumor mill go even crazier. The sky was falling, and for the first time folks started asking what would Emily Birch do? She was thirty, and stout, and still unmarried. She'd had suitors as a girl, but no one good enough in Ellis Birch's proud, paternal eyes. He had discouraged them, which was a euphemism. One of the Mack boys had been discouraged all the way to the state line.

Emily hadn't been seen as an old maid, though. Her money and her name kept her separate from the ranks of the Perennial Hopefuls who sat aging in a clot of sad pastel at church socials. But if the money were gone? If she were just an impoverished lady of a certain age with an ever-rounding figure and no family to speak of?

Neighbors flocked to the big white Victorian with misty eyes and casseroles, but they found my grandmother packing, sharp tongued and sharper eyed, decidedly uninterested in pity. She boarded a train for the coast that very day. Folks assumed she was going to bring her father's body home, place it reverently in the crypt behind First Baptist, and sink into a life of genteel poverty and mourning.

They had underestimated her. She stayed, burying her father in Charleston in order to finish the fiscal rescue mission he had started. She took his meetings with lawyers and investment bankers, and she didn't come home until both she and the bulk of the Birch money had weathered the crisis.

How could mortality touch her? She'd kept a whole town alive, seen nearly a hundred years of history, survived her own early widowhood and the loss of her only son. Old age should not be allowed to grind her down.

"Do you know what 'syncope' means?" Rachel asked.

"Is it part of this? Of these Lewy bodies growing in her brain?" I asked. I didn't know that word, so it hadn't leaped out at me from the website.

"Yes, and it means fainting. Sudden fainting. It's in a list of physical problems that she has or will have soon. Also shaking, dizziness, loss of balance."

I had noticed that last one myself. That last one was already here.

Under my hand the boogery shape in front of Violence had grown spindly arms with claw tips. I gave it the suggestion of a thick-necked head with taut, blind bulges where the eyes should be. Added high, slitted nostrils.

"I'm not saying you're wrong," I said. "I'm only saying it's complicated."

"No it isn't. You have to take charge for her now. It's time. Ask yourself, how many sets of stairs are in that house? Do you want her to spend the last year or two of her life in traction? In miserable pain from a broken hip? She can't stay there. It's simple if you ask yourself the right questions." I'd thought I wanted Rachel's certainty, but she was as hard and sharp as those black letters on the website. She advanced inexorably, too. My pencil scratched across the paper, shading. "Are you still there?" she asked.

"I'm here, but I don't think family things get simpler if you ask the right questions," I said. I made sure there was no snipe or snark in my voice as I added, "Could the right question simplify what's happening with Jake?"

Now it was Rachel's turn for silence. I started drawing a second eyeless boogery monster. *Violence Versus the Lewy Bodies.*

"Point taken," Rachel said at last, her voice tight. "Just promise me you'll keep your eyes open. Those little old ladies have been lying to you. They'll fool you if you let them. The way you're talking, I think you really, really want to get fooled."

"I promise, but how are things with you? Have you heard from Jake?"

"No," Rachel said, suddenly brisk. "I need to go start dinner."

Which was code for, *Mind your own damn business, Leia,* because she was just going to nuke a Lean Cuisine. Lav was with me, Jake was in the wind, and she never cooked for only herself.

I unpacked and took a shower, trying to wash the road and a little of my mingled grief and anger off me. Rachel had a point, but was it wrong to want a single, peaceful evening? The smell of roasting hens, peppery and succulent, wafted up the stairs as I got dressed, like a sensory argument for respite. Birchie would serve them with fat slices of the summer's first heirloom tomatoes from the back garden and her famous cornbread. To make it, she saved bacon drippings in a coffee can by the stove, and she'd put some of that grease into the cast-iron skillet and set it in the oven. She'd make batter while the rendered fat got so hot that it was close to smoking. The sizzle of the batter landing in that pan was the kitchen soundtrack of my youth.

I didn't know if the urge for peace came from sweetness or from being scared, though. Was it cowardice to enjoy one dinner in the company of my favorite niece, my only living Birch relative, and my much-loved Wattie? Surely it was my best self that was saying I could start spying and deciding tomorrow.

But the voice of Rachel in my head was asking, could Birchie still make her cornbread? There was no written recipe. Did she remember? Maybe she was standing in the kitchen as blank as a sheet of brand-new paper while Wattie made it as part of their ongoing little-old-lady conspiracy.

I was too disheartened for any more conversations, so I sent brief updating e-mails to Mom and Keith and my friend Margot, who was feeding my feral cat. At six I tapped on the adjoining door that linked my bedroom to Lav's room in the turret. She was sprawled on the daybed, deeply immersed in the mysteries of her cell phone. There was no dresser in the round room, but I saw Lavender's shorts and T-shirts stacked neatly, color-coded, in the shelving. Four pairs of shoes and her rain boots stood in a tidy row on the floor.

"Dinnertime," I said, and she got up and followed me out and down the stairs, texting and talking to me at the same time.

"How long do you think we're going to be here?"

She didn't sound as aggrieved as she had on the drive, probably because she'd hung around outside with the Darian boys until their cell phones had beeped to call them home. That was new and yet the same; Birchville was so small, so known and safe, that kids still roamed at will.

When I was Lav's age, most of my summer friends' mothers hollered their names in long pig calls to retrieve them. The well-off ones sent their housekeepers out to do it. Birchie rang a distinctive brass bell from the porch. It could be heard from anyplace on the square, and woe betide me if I did not come at once. Birchie rang it herself; she was above pig calls, and she hadn't kept a housekeeper since her father died. She was famous for it. She'd come home from Charleston in mourning clothes, but a week later she'd traded them for bridal white and married her greengrocer, Floyd Briggs. Then she'd offered Vina, Wattie's mother, a fat pension so she could retire. Vina had worked for the Birches from sunup to suppertime, six days a week, for most of her life. She'd more than earned it.

Birchie "did for herself" after that, even the year she was pregnant. Her father had been a proud man, more revered than beloved. He'd been "Mr. Birch"—never "Ellis"—to every single person in town. My grandmother wanted it known that the new reigning Birch was not too uppity to keep her own floors clean.

In recent years I'd insisted on hiring a rotating cast of local girls to help her with the heavy work and laundry, but she still cooked and kept her garden. Although now, having seen her planting Tic Tacs, I guessed Wattie was doing more and more of those things.

"We'll need to stay a week or two at least," I told Lavender. I wasn't sure of anything, including how bad off Birchie truly was. How long could they have been lying to me?

On the way through the parlor, my Rachel-sharpened gaze caught on the two upholstered chairs, sitting side by side facing out the big front window, so close their arms touched. It made me stop short, noticing the Victorian love seats, facing each other in front of the fireplace.

Lavender rammed into my back.

"What?" she said, but she didn't look up from her phone.

"Nothing," I said. The love seat on the left had matching tables at each end, one stacked with Birchie's bookmarked Phyllis Tickle book and several novels, the other holding Wattie's giant King James Bible and *The Immortal Life of Henrietta Lacks.* Nearby the tiny round coffee table on the wide end of the wraparound porch had its two chairs pulled around to one side, backs against the wall of the house, ostensibly so they could both have a clear view of the square.

All the furniture in the house had been reangled and rearranged so Birchie and Wattie could sit like honeymooners crowding in on one side of a restaurant booth. It hadn't always been that way. It had happened in gradual steps, though, so I hadn't noticed from visit to visit. These days, even when they were standing, Wattie's bad knees and Birchie's poor vision kept them arm in arm, giving Wattie near-constant access to the best of Birchie's two good ears. How deeply did the Lewy bodies have their hooked claws in Birchie's brain?

I took a long, slow breath, trying to lower my heart rate. My pregnancy handbook had a judgey tone and quite a lot to say about the effect of stress upon poor Digby. I doubted it would recommend barraging him with oscillating grief and anger hormones.

We went into the kitchen through the dining-room door. Birchie and Wattie were at the stove, loading up the plates. By the back door, a recessed nook held a narrow rectangular table. It was set for dinner, telling me the same story as all the other furniture: I always sat on the built-in bench seat under the window, while Birchie and Wattie sat side by side, looking out over their backyard garden. But not this time.

I deliberately pulled out Wattie's chair for Lavender, saying, "You hungry? You can sit right here."

So much for peace and sweetness. Rachel was right; I needed my eyes to be opened. I needed to see how much of Birchie was still present, without her co-conspirator's whispered assists.

Lavender plopped into the chair, eyes still on her screen. She reached blindly for the glass already set beside the plate and took a big slurp. Her eyes widened, and she finally looked up from her phone, startled and so horrified I thought she might spit it right back out.

As soon as she could swallow, she stage-whispered, "Oh my God, what is that?"

"Tea," I said. Rachel brewed tea strong and served it sugarless, spiced with so much cinnamon and lemon it was practically an astringent. Lav gave me a look of such pure disbelief that I amended it. "Sweet tea."

Birchie and Wattie came over, each carrying two

loaded plates. Birchie came right to her usual spot, setting the plates and sitting without seeming to notice Lavender, but Wattie stopped short as she clocked my teenager-assisted coup. She gave me a long, reproachful look as she set her plates. I dropped my gaze. Wattie's part in this cover-up was not purely altruistic. Her own sons had wanted her to move into assisted living when her driver's license got revoked. She'd moved in with Birchie instead, a compromise that could work only as long as both of them stayed healthy.

"Bow your heads," Wattie said, sliding in onto the bench beside me.

Lav reflexively stuffed her phone into her back pocket. Rachel didn't allow phones at the table. We joined hands as Wattie launched into the blessing.

Wattie's husband had been Redemption Baptist's preacher for decades, and Wattie was as devout as they came. She settled in to thank God in great detail for food and family, safe travels, and the beauty of the day. All her words were aimed directly heavenward, not at me, but at the same time she had my hand in a grip so tight it qualified as a pinching. She was ill with me for giving Lav her seat, all right, and that in and of itself said quite a bit about how much cover Birchie needed these days.

I sneaked a peek around the table, and Wattie was

the only person with her eyes closed. Birchie glared disapproval at Lavender's hand, as if it were the blood-soaked paw of some unclean animal. Lavender stared off sideways, oblivious, not listening. When she saw me watching, she snapped an appropriately holy look onto her face and shut her eyes.

"In the name of Jesus, I pray these things," Wattie said. Eventually.

We all echoed her "Amen."

All of us but Birchie, who was now staring openly at Lavender, trouble written in the powdered creases of her forehead.

"I'm really glad you set the table in here," I said to call her attention.

I wanted to get Birchie talking, but I also meant it. Usually a single extra person was enough for Birchie to declare that we had "company" and move us to the very formal dining room with its massive walnut furniture. There a huge china cabinet loomed against the longest wall, chock-full of silver pieces and Birchie's mother's wedding china. My dining room at home featured a gaming table and the built-in china hutch held my Wonder Woman action figures. Eighty-seven mint-in-package versions, dating back from 1966. I did not do formal very well.

Birchie peered at me across the table. "Beg pardon?"

I said, "I meant I enjoy eating here, in the kitchen nook, like folks."

Birchie looked to Wattie's place, blinking with myopic suspicion when she found Lavender again instead.

"Pass the salt," Wattie said, and Birchie located her across the table. She smiled in obvious relief, handing the shaker across. Wattie held Birchie's gaze, cuing her. "This is a fine place for supper. As Leia's niece, Lavender counts as family."

"Yes. Lavender counts as family," Birchie parroted. I didn't like the way her words matched Wattie's so completely.

I said, "It's much cozier here anyway."

Birchie turned her bird-eyed gaze on me. "Well, I like a dining room at times. A meal with company should feel like something of an occasion. Still and yet, I do think it aids my digestion when my father isn't watching every bite I chew. He doesn't like for me to be so stout."

She said it as if her actual long-dead father were waiting in the dining room to disapprove of the butter on her cornbread. I hoped she was making a little joke, referencing his oil portrait, hanging on the wall behind the table's head.

I told her, "If you want me to, I can take your father's picture down. There's a ton of other paintings in the attic. I could dig out that pair of ship paintings you always liked. They're about the same size."

"You think it would be that easy to take my father out of this house?" Birchie said, amused. "It can't be done! You could burn that portrait, but he would still be present. My father was born in this house, and his picture has been hanging on that wall for decades. He never was an easy man to shift." And this was purely, purely Birchie. She was still in there, even if the lying had been going on for longer than I'd hoped. I buttered my cornbread, peeking sideways at Wattie. I found her staring openly at me, as if to say whatever the gramma version of "In your face" might be.

"So the portrait stays," I said, taking a bite. If Wattie had made this batch of cornbread, she'd done it perfectly. It had crisp edges and a tender middle, like a salty doughnut. It tasted like my childhood.

"I think the portrait must stay, yes," Birchie agreed, and then she added, "Even though Daddy could be a pluperfect asshole."

I choked on my bite, and Lavender released a snort of shocked laughter. I did not know which was weirder coming out of Birchie's mouth, the expletive or the criticism of her revered father.

"Birchie!" I said, when I could swallow. "My niece is here."

Lavender probably heard that word a minimum of nine times an hour at school, but never from the sweet, pink mouth of a little old Baptist lady.

"Oh, for goodness' sake, Leia," Birchie said lightly, casting her eyes heavenward. "Get off your horse. Everybody has an asshole."

Lavender was giggling openly now. I realized that, under the table, my treacherous hand had moved to cover Digby's nascent ears. That put me in danger of catching the giggles as well.

Birchie seemed to realize she'd said something wrong. She was looking at me, but her body canted ever so slightly toward Lavender, no doubt waiting for a whisper. Lav had both hands clapped over her mouth, trying to stifle herself. Birchie turned to look at the place where Wattie should be and was startled anew by my niece.

"Who is this?" she demanded. All at once she sounded querulous and very, very old. "Who is this girl? Why does she keep being here?"

"That's my niece, Birchie," I said gently, all laughter gone. "Remember?"

"Well, why is she staring at me like a gigged fish? Was the child not raised to have even one manner?" It was a very Birchie turn of phrase, said in her most imperious voice, which made it so much sadder somehow. She was there. But not all there.

I said, "Lavender was surprised to hear you say . . ." I found I could not repeat the word, not at this childhood table where once I said "poot" and then was stuck for an hourlong lecture about the relationship between my vocabulary choices and the moral decay of the nation. "She's my niece. Remember?"

"Of course I remember," Birchie said, still querulous, outraged. "Of course I do! But why is she here?"

"May I be excused?" Lavender asked, small-voiced.

"There is no excuse for you," Birchie trumpeted, turning on her.

Wattie said, "Enough!" in a tone that brooked no argument.

She rose ponderously to her feet, and at the movement Birchie looked and saw the shape of her friend. Her face wiped itself almost clean of expression, like an old-fashioned blackboard. Streaks of thought were still dusted across it, but they were unreadable.

"Change seats with me," Wattie ordered Lavender, swapping out their plates and cups with brisk, angry motions.

"Did I do something wrong?" Lav asked, and I felt sorry that I had put her in this odd line of fire.

"No, child, hush. *You* didn't do a thing wrong, except you've barely touched your hen, and you aren't as big as a half bug. It's only Birchie needs things to be a certain way these days, and changing them up, why, it's pure meanness to her. Pure and simple meanness." Just as when I had earned her disapproval as a girl, I felt myself shrink nine full sizes. Lavender and Wattie switched sides, Wattie still talking to me with hard-edged reproach. "Nights are difficult for her. Mornings are much better. Isn't that right?"

Birchie nodded, calmly reaching for another piece of cornbread. "I moved Garden Club to ten A.M., and Martina Mack acted like I'd said we were going to eat a baby. If I'd known she'd hate it that much, I'd have moved it years ago." Wattie handed her the butter, and Birchie took it, her body naturally canting toward her friend.

"I only wanted to—" I said, but Wattie spoke over me. "You eat up, too."

She cut her eyes at Lavender, and when they came back to rest on me, they were dark with angry promise. My niece's tiny person was the only flimsy barrier between me and something strong and filled with righteous fury. We all went back to eating, though I could hardly taste the food. Lavender stuffed five bites down, fast as she could. It was so deadly quiet I could hear the buzzy hum of texts and e-mails landing in her phone.

Into the fraught silence, Lavender said, "That was really delicious! Thank you." She'd been raised to say these words at any dinner, even if her hostess served up offal. "May I please be excused?"

I nodded. She gave my knee a quick squeeze under the table. She knew I was in for it. Then she squirted away, already reaching for the phone in her back pocket. I heard her clattering up the stairs, the slim wall of her protection gone.

"I'm sorry," I said to both of them. "That was low. The seat thing."

I wasn't sure if Birchie knew what I was apologizing for, but she inclined her head in gracious acceptance.

"Yes, it was," Wattie agreed. She leaned in toward me. "We can be plain with one another now."

That sparked me, and I got a little size back. "You should have been plain with me all along. Maybe I wouldn't have pulled that trick if you two hadn't done so much sneaking."

Wattie shrugged, an angry, sharp motion. "I love you, Leia, always have. But you aren't mine to fool."

That took me a second, but then Birchie said, "No. You are mine to fool, my sugar."

"So you're both saying Birchie made her own choices, like always. Okay. But how long ago was that?" Wattie's nostrils flared, a danger signal, but I kept on, asking the hard questions Rachel had pressured me to ask. "You're deciding things now, Wattie. One thing you decided was to keep me in the dark."

"Child," Wattie said, but with none of the patience she'd shown Lavender. "Birchie's right, you are perched so way up high on that horse you're liable to fall and break your tailbone. Birchie made these decisions while she could."

"She's keeping them for me," Birchie said. "I lose track sometimes. She'll tell you true."

"So hear me," Wattie said, so in tune their sentences almost overlapped. "She wants to stay here."

"It's not safe," I said, and Wattie and Birchie exchanged a speaking glance. Birchie actually laughed.

"And you think dying should be safe?" Wattie asked, equally amused.

"You know what I mean. Your sons have had this talk with you, Wattie, more than once. Same as I have with Birchie. You and she both need to be living someplace with no stairs, where there are doctors on call. You two should've at least had home help for years now, but you fought us on that, too, and we gave up. But now things have to change," I said, Rachel's points pouring out of my mouth like I was her hand puppet. "How long ago did Birchie get this diagnosis?"

"A few years back," Wattie said, evasive, but it was enough to make me feel gut-punched. Tears started up in my eyes, and, seeing that, Wattie's face crumpled a little, too, even as she sat up straighter, indignant. "I'm doing the best that I know how to do. And truth told? I wish it was me, because she would do the same as I'm doing. I'm losing my friend, and there's no one left to stand like this for me. My husband left for heaven way too soon before me. We raised our sons up to be fine people, but when she's gone, of course they're going to put me in a home someplace. For my own good, they'll say. For safety, they'll say. Just like you. We don't want that."

Birchie took Wattie's hand, saying, "Now, now."

Wattie looked to her, and the naked sorrow on her face undid me. This was hard, and horrible.

"It's not fair. I know there's nothing fair about it," I said, but I had seen enough to know that Rachel was right. As usual. I knew what I had to do, and I owed Wattie the truth of it, right then. She had given it to me, and so I gave it back. "I'm going to talk to her doctor, but I think you have a good idea of what he'll tell me. You and Birchie can't stay here. The closest hospital is thirty miles away." Wattie's heavy lids shuttered down over her eyes. For the first time, she couldn't meet my gaze; Dr. Pettery must have told her this already. "There's hard change coming, Wattie. And it is coming fast." I hated my own tone. I sounded like Rachel talking to Lavender, that time Lav announced that she was going to dye her hair hot pink. Wattie tried to exchange a look with Birchie, but Birchie wasn't looking back. As I had spoken, Birchie had checked out. She slumped in her seat, staring blankly past my head into the garden. I went on. "You need to talk to your sons, Wattie. I can talk to Sam and Stephen, too. If you and Birchie want to stay together, we can work that out. You get to have a say."

Wattie wasn't quite done yet.

"You want my say? You move down here. We can make the sewing room into a bedroom for her. So no stairs." *Except the seven on the front porch and the long, steep flight down from the back door,* I thought, but Wattie was still talking. "Move to Alabama." It was so matter-of-fact that I knew it was not a spur-of-the-moment idea. I had a spur-of-the-moment answer, though, and it was a resounding, *No. Hell no.* Wattie must have seen it on my face, because she got louder and more urgent. "Hear me out, now! You aren't married, and you don't even have a fella. Not for serious.

You can draw your pictures any old place. You only got yourself to think about, so why not think of Birchie?"

Her dismissal of my whole life hurt. She spoke as if work for me meant lolling in a cushy chair, scribbling and hooking back bonbons, not a real career with deadlines and travel. As if Mom and Keith and Lavender and Rachel didn't count as family and my Tuesday gamers and my church community were nothing. But even if I wanted to uproot myself, now there was Digby. I could feel him fluttering and flexing, a second heartbeat at my very center. I had to think of him first.

Pee-poo are like dis, Rachel had told me once, putting the peachy-pink Crayola that used to be called Flesh into my hand. As if all the flesh that mattered was that color. That crayon was called Peach now, but the ideas behind its old name were still alive and present. Present everywhere, all across the country, but more overt in Birchville.

I wouldn't raise Digby in the small-town South, even though there was a lot of good here. Kids still ran free in packs unafraid, unscheduled, still called home for supper by bells, only now the bells were kept inside their phones. We had good neighbors who made me caramel cakes when I visited and kept me in the Facebook group and on the phone tree even when I was seven hundred miles away. Birchie and my father and I had all been born here, and to me there was no prettier country than the deep greens and black-browns and sunny blues of rural Alabama.

But it was 1987 here in more ways than a movie-rental store. I didn't want my biracial son growing up in a town where Wattie was the only black face ever seen in the crowd down at First Baptist, especially since half the folks there pretended that she was the Help. Birchie had the only white face ever seen on the regular at Redemption. Here the white families with means sent their kids to a small, lily-colored private school one town over. The county's public schools were poorly rated, and the black kids and the white kids sat at different lunch tables.

I didn't want to bring my pregnancy up now, though. This conversation was hard enough to keep on track without the ultimate derailment my Digby news would bring. Plus, I wanted Birchie to hear it first, and as good news, not blurted in anger. I would not use Digby as my trump card in an ugly argument. Right now Birchie wasn't fully present, even though her eyes were fixed on me. Her body sat in her chair, listing more and more toward Wattie every minute.

"I'm sorry. Wattie, call your sons in the morning.

We need to plan a trip to Norfolk soon, so you can look at options. You two are going to have to move."

Wattie stared me down, silent, as sturdy and impassive as a wall. "We'll see," she said, and in the foyer the big grandfather clock began chiming seven. At the sound Birchie pushed back her chair and stood up as if on autopilot, her eyes fixed on the middle distance. Wattie stood, too. "I have to start doing her bedtime things now." I came around the table to kiss Birchie's powdery, soft cheek. She did not respond. I usually kissed Wattie, too, but she did not seem kissable just now. Her eyes on me were hard and dark as chips of onyx. Her pointed chin was tilted up at me.

"Let me help put her to bed," I said, propitiating.

She shook her head, no, and then, to my surprise, she kissed me. Her lips on my cheek were as cool as stones from the back garden.

"I do this every night, and she needs everything to stay just the same. You hear me? Leave things the way they are. You leave things lie," the stone lips said, and by the end it didn't sound like she was talking about putting Birchie to bed. It sounded like a warning.

6

A rustling thump from above woke me, way too early. I scrubbed at my eyes and checked the clock. Six-thirty in the morning, God help me. Just over my head, pattery footsteps ran across the ceiling, quick and light. So Lavender was actually rooting about in the attic. She'd spent the last couple of days roaming the town with the Darian boys or playing on my old laptop, but this morning was her last chance. It sounded to me like she was taking it.

I'd found the attic irresistible when I was a little kid. I'd spent the earlier, cooler hours of my long summer days trying on feathered hats and the old lace wedding dress or digging in the sewing table with its box of a thousand unsorted buttons. I'd jumbled things about as I played, dumping a shoulder-padded forties suit into a sea of whalebone corsets, mixing ledgers from the 1890s in with sweater vests and sci-fi paperbacks from my father's childhood. Knowing Lav, she was probably re-sorting everything by time period or color. At least she was exploring while she could. At 10:00 A.M., the estate-sale company I'd hired from Montgomery would be here to begin the assessment.

I groaned and pulled the pillow over my head. Sorting through the attic was a job for Hercules, and even he might have to call in the rest of the Avengers. Lav and I couldn't do it alone if we had three months and a backhoe. The main section took up most of a whole floor, tight aisles winding like a maze through mishmash piles of junk and heirloomworthy prizes. The narrow back room under the eaves was worse. In it, boxes and chests and wardrobes had been piled six deep with no aisles at all, packed literally to the roof with clothes and papers and furniture and books. I'd always been told to stay clear of that back area lest I pull out the wrong piece of keepsake Jenga and topple everything down and smash myself.

I'd disobeyed enough to know that there was a full set of Jane Austen in the crates right by the door. *Persuasion* held the powdery remains of pressed flowers, a remembrance of love gone wrong or right. Either way, they'd been dry bones when I found them and were probably dust now. I'd put *Persuasion* back; the flower's oils had wrecked the print, so on the pages where they had been laid to rest, the story was unreadable.

I'd hired the estate team to help sort trash from treasure and to let Birchie claim the things that mattered most to her personally while she still remembered. It was also a message, telegraphing change, like the assisted-living brochures I had printed out for them, like the speakerphone calls with Wattie's sons. Oh, but it was going to be an ugly day.

My little old ladies were not going gently into that good nursing home. Wattie fought me every living minute and Birchie on and off as she was able. Today would be the same, but squared. No, cubed. They had a lot of weapons in their crafty arsenal: innuendo, barbed asides, appeals to reason or pity or nostalgia. Birchie especially excelled at "soft reproach," looking wounded and yet so forgiving at the same time. When she was on point, that look landed on my chest and pushed in, a long skewer of sorry feeling that ran me all the way through.

It hadn't changed my mind, though. I'd had a lengthy talk with Dr. Pettery, and he backed my decisions. He'd been concerned for quite some time, but HIPAA and Miss Wattie had kept his hands pretty well tied.

Rachel had e-mailed me a list of Norfolk facilities with spotless reputations and memory-care units. I'd held off booking travel until Wattie and her sons decided if she'd be touring the facilities with us. Sam wanted her to move to Houston, near his family, but Stephen insisted it was Wattie's choice. I thought that in the end Miss Wattie would want to stay with Birchie, though so far she had only reiterated that neither of them was going anyplace, thanks muchly. The role reversal, setting rules for women who had half raised me, made me so sad and uncomfortable that I'd spent a lot of time hiding in my room, saying I was working. Which I was, as long as we could agree that "working" meant doodling endless Violences on scratch paper and not having any ideas for the prequel.

I curled up tighter underneath the covers. Closing down the house itself would be easy, when we came to that point. In the 1870s houses had been built to last, and, in this one, entropy had never been allowed to gain a toehold. It was so tidy I could pretty much throw out the milk and eggs, cover the furniture, and call it closed. Updated double storm windows gleamed clean behind crisp sheers. The furniture was old-fashioned but not actually old. Anything that began to sag or wither was banished—usually to the attic. And therein lay the problem. I was even now snuggled up under the stacked, unsorted weight of a hundred and forty-odd years' worth of Birch family history.

I was loathe to get up and begin this day, but Digby had no such hang-up. He was already being busy. I put my hand over the place on my belly where I felt his cheery fizz and jiggle. I pressed down, but at seventeen weeks, I could still only feel him moving from the inside.

I heard the familiar creak of the door between my room and Lavender's. This room had once been my father's—his glow-in-the-dark star decals were still all over the ceiling—and the tower room had been his playroom. I made my gummy eyes open and pointed them at the doorway. Lavender froze mid-tiptoe, my laptop in her hands.

"Good morning," I said, surprised to find her back downstairs and already playing on the computer.

"I didn't mean to wake you," she said. She came all the way in and put it on the desk.

"I was up," I said.

Her eyes cut away. She walked over to the fireplace and picked up the glass shepherdess who was perched, dustless and gleaming, on the mantel. My room, like every other one here, was like a cozy surgical theater—spick, span, and homey. Lavender, whose house was in a constant state of readiness for a Restoration Hardware photo shoot, had seemed right at home. But not just now. She studied the shepherdess with elaborate over-interest, as if Bo Peep were trending on Twitter.

Had she been e-mailing a Darian boy? Or maybe she'd been in Messenger with Rachel, telling her about Digby. Girls told their mothers things, even when they promised not to. I made a mental note to check the browser history later, because the kid was definitely up to something. God, please let her just be sneak-watching R-rated anime on my Netflix. I had too much on my plate already.

An enormous crash shook the ceiling; something heavy had fallen and hit the floor above us. Lavender jumped, and I was so startled I sat bolt upright as a landslide of smaller crashes tumbled in the wake of that first boom.

"What the . . . ? Wasn't that you up in the attic earlier?" I asked, kicking at the bedclothes wound around me.

"No," she said, and ran to see.

I got free of the duvet and hurried after her down the hallway toward the attic stairs in my yummy sushi pajamas. I had visions of Birchie, confused and broken, lying under a chest of drawers or a pile of heavy boxes.

Lavender threw open the door to the stairs as I

caught up, and the attic's heat rolled out and over me, thick and wet, salted with dust. I sprinted up the long, steep flight ahead of her now, calling, "Birchie? Birchie, is that you?"

"It's okay! We're okay!" a male voice said, and I halted halfway up. Frank Darian came to the railing and stood looking down at me, mopping his red face with a bandanna. The strings of his beginner's comb-over were scraggled, and he looked like he had aged a good ten years since I saw him last Thanksgiving. "Hey, Leia, sorry. A stack of book crates bit it, but we're all fine."

"You all? Who's with you?" I demanded. My heart still felt like it was Hulking out inside my chest, swelling and banging, trying to brute-force its way out of the prison of my rib cage. "Is Birchie up there?"

"Of course not," Frank said, and both his boys appeared beside him, their sweaty faces streaked with attic dust.

"Hey, Miss Leia," Jeffrey said, which made me feel about a thousand years old.

"Hey, Lavender," Hugh said, overly casual, cocking his hip like Elvis. He looked the way Frank had looked at fifteen, tall and lanky with a mop of sandy curls and a confident smile.

I became suddenly conscious that my niece was

wearing tiny cotton shorts and a camisole top. Thirteen woke up dewy and kitten-eyed and thoroughly adorable, and sashaying up the stairs had set her hips asway. I started back down, turning Lavender and herding her before me.

"Go get dressed," I whispered to her as we reached the hall. It was a palpable relief to step out into the air conditioning.

"I'm wearing shor—"

"More clothes," I hissed, and gave her a little push toward her room.

She rolled her eyes, calling "Be right back" to one boy or another. Maybe both of them. They were following their dad down the stairs, but they both paused to watch her twinkle along the hallway.

I shook my head and backed up, giving the Darians plenty of room at the bottom of the stairs. Thirty-eight and pregnant did not wake up so fresh and fair. I had bed head and no bra. My mouth was coated with morning goo and probably smelled like Swamp Thing.

"What were you guys doing?" I asked.

Hugh, down last, mercifully closed the door on the heat.

"We dug your trunk out and took it down, and then we were repacking that back room," Frank said, as if it were the most reasonable thing in the world for me to wake up to an attic full of Darians landsliding books around at the ass crack of dawn on a Friday morning.

"My trunk?" I asked. "What?"

"You wanted a sea trunk, out of the back room?" I shook my head no, and Frank said, "Well, Birchie called last night and said you did. Do you think she was . . ." He paused, searching for words. "Maybe she was confused. We all know that Birchie is . . ." He paused again, looking down at his feet. "Not herself." It was a kind finish, considering. I couldn't think of a worse way to learn of your wife's infidelity than having it publicly announced to your family, friends, and clients in the middle of a church social. I had a sudden urge to go find Jeannie Anne and smack her one. She'd been one of my summer friends, though by high school I was tired of her endless drama. She'd acted like she was on a mission to enact every plot from *All My Children* before graduation.

"I didn't have a choice. I had to do what my heart told me," she'd say, trading one boyfriend for another with a lot of overlap and sneaking. Twenty years of marriage and two kids later, it turned out she was still that girl. This time her heart had told her to get with Pastor Campbell in the choir room. By now she should've figured out that her heart was shitty, maybe told it to shut up.

Frank looked like hell. His eyes were puffed small with purple shadows underneath. The lines around his mouth and on his forehead looked like they had been scored double deep.

I felt swamped with empathy, though Frank might find that word presumptuous. Jeannie Anne had torched close to twenty years of shared life; on the scale of douchery, she deserved a higher score than JJ. But even so, Frank and I were two people standing in a hallway who knew what betrayal felt like.

"No, Birchie's not herself, Frank," I said, an indirect apology.

"She sounded good on the phone, though," he said, not meeting my eyes.

"What time did she call?" I asked, changing the subtext if not the subject, to give him some relief.

"Maybe eight?"

I frowned. Had Birchie snuck back out of bed to call him? "Was Wattie with her?"

"Yeah, on speakerphone. You know how they do. Maybe they mean whatever's in that trunk for a surprise?"

I didn't think so. Not a nice one anyway, considering our constant clash of wills the last few days. I had a vague but very bad suspicious feeling growing.

"'Scuse me, Miss Leia," Jeffrey said, and squirted

past me, Hugh in his wake. "Dad, can we go down? Smells like the rolls are ready."

Once he said it, I noticed it, too, the yeasty, sugared smell of Wattie's cinnamon rolls drifting up from the kitchen. She must have been up way before dawn; they had to rise twice and bake for forty minutes.

"Sure," Frank said. "But afterward you're going to help me restack those boxes."

They clattered down the hall, and Hugh paused at Lav's door. He gave it a casual knuckle rap. "Yo, Lefty, come have breakfast."

Lefty?

Lavender, now in a cotton T-shirt dress and tennis shoes, came out, and they galloped downstairs to eat a thousand calories in butter and sugary carbs that would slide right off their adolescent bodies.

"How are you holding up?" I asked Frank once we were alone.

He shook his head as if I'd asked a yes-or-no question, then gave me such a sad, cynical smile that my heart broke for him again. He was such a decent person, so good to my grandmother. In summer he sent his boys down to mow her lawn, and he acted as her man-in-the-house when the porch light went out or the doorbell stopped working. Now he was up in the thousand-degree attic heat before his workday started, moving boxes for two little old ladies who had blown up his marriage in front of his whole church.

"How are the boys doing?" I asked.

Frank didn't answer for a sec, his tired eyes searching my face, looking for some shade of schadenfreude or gossipy interest. I hoped he wouldn't imagine it there. I asked because he was our family friend, and because he was fresh broken in a way that I'd felt cracked my whole adult life.

Frank must have read me right, because his guard dropped. His shoulders slumped, and the dark pits of his eyes told me how hard he was working to keep himself together.

He said, "Hugh's shut down. I have no idea. Jeffrey, he's young. He can't hide how hard he's taking it. Watching him try, it breaks my heart."

"God, Frank. I'm so sorry," I said. I knew from Lavender that the boys were staying with him at the house. They'd been to see their mom a couple of times, walking over to their grandma's house where she was staying, a half mile off the square. "Have you talked to Jeannie Anne at all?"

"Yeah. I'm trying to be civil, even though she's seeing Campbell. They're in love, apparently. Martina Mack, God bless her black-hole heart, came by with a burned chicken casserole and that cheery news."

"Of course she did. She dropped by here with a melted carrot cake to tell me about her aunt's endless and agonizing death from Alzheimer's. I wouldn't let her in, but she shouldered into the doorway and gave me every awful detail. No one on any porch on the planet has ever so thoroughly relished a dead aunt." We shrugged simultaneously, with the weary acceptance of small-towners toward their homegrown horrors. I added, "If it helps, she also told me that the church fired Campbell." Adultery from the associate pastor was not a big congregational morale builder.

"Yeah. I couldn't set foot in that church otherwise. But in some ways it's bad. I'm scared she'll move away with him. I'm telling everyone who'll listen that I'm fine, it's fine. I keep reminding folks that she's hurting, too, and believe me, those words taste worse than Martina's casserole. But I have to. I don't want her driven out of town. I mean, I do. On a rail. Maybe coated in a little tar, some feathers." He smiled, wry and weary. "But if she goes, she'll try to take the boys, and the law leans toward the mother. I'm not letting that happen. I can't. I have to think about them now and not strangle her."

I swallowed, the lump in my throat grown even thicker. So this was what fatherhood looked like when it was done right from the beginning.

I wouldn't know. The Birch line had bad luck with fathers. Birchie was the last of us to have one all the way through adulthood.

I'd had Keith, and he'd been a great stepdad. He loved me, a lot, but I still called him Keith. Once, when Rachel and I were very little, still in preschool, Keith had been playing dollhouse with us in the den. I said, "No, rocka-chair goes here, Daddy." I didn't even notice I'd said it.

In the next breath, Rachel launched herself at me, punching and screaming. She bit my shoulder hard enough to make me bleed. Keith had to drag her off, still flailing. Mom came running as Rachel and I both burst into tears. She stopped in the doorway, fluttering and flapping, saying, "What happened, what happened?" I stopped crying first. Rachel sobbed and heaved in Mom's arms the whole time Keith was dressing the bite. Hard, racking sobs that ended only when Keith finished and went to hold her. I never called my stepdad anything but Keith again. Remembering, my hands moved to cover Digby, now the third fatherless Birch generation.

"You're doing the right thing," I told Frank.

"Yeah. And thanks for listening. I can't say this stuff to most people, you know? It will get around." Frank straightened, manually moving his shoulders back and down, as if they were relifting a burden. "I need to get home. Lois Gainey's coming by at nine to write her nephew out of her will again. That's why we came to get your trunk so early. Sorry we woke you."

I'd forgotten the trunk. "Where'd you put it?"

"In the den. Wattie wanted us to load it in your car, but I told her we'd do that on the way out," he said.

My suspicions were good and roused, and I turned to the stairs, saying, "Let's go see what the little-old-lady stealth brigade is up to." Considering they'd hidden Birchie's illness for so long, I could not imagine that I was going to like their new plan much.

Frank began to answer and then stopped. He tilted his head, listening. A car engine had started up outside. Close. So close it had to be coming from the driveway.

"What the hell," I said.

"Is that your car?" he asked, then shook his head no, as if answering his own question.

It had to be, though. The only car parked out there was my rental, but no one downstairs in this house had any business driving.

I was thirty-eight and pregnant, but I took the stairs in the old, fast, slide-and-leap I'd used as a kid, hands skidding down the banister. I sprinted through the den, where Lavender was sitting between the two boys on the sofa, my computer in her lap. They were all peering into the screen and eating cinnamon buns. They looked up at me with startled, sugary faces as I thundered through, Frank Darian right behind me. I flung open the front door, ran out onto the porch, and leaped down those stairs, too.

The rental car was already backing down the long crushed-seashell drive with Wattie behind the wheel. Birchie sat in the passenger seat. I could make out the hunched shape of a large chest looming in the back. Wattie must have had the boys move it while Frank and I were talking.

"Stop! Stop!" I yelled, running barefoot out onto the wet grass of the lawn.

Wattie hadn't had a driver's license for years now, and for damn good reasons. Where did she think they were going? Wattie's eyes met mine, and she stomped down hard on the gas. The car surged backward.

Frank zoomed past me on his longer legs, trying to get behind the car so they would have to stop.

"Frank, no!" I screamed, still chasing the car head-on. What if Wattie didn't see him? The Darian boys would spill out onto the porch just in time to watch their father be squashed.

The car was moving too fast, though. Frank wasn't going to make it. Wattie's eyes were still locked on mine, and she lost the angle as she came to the end of the drive.

The back left tire cut into the yard, and the car bounced and jerked. Wattie sawed the wheel the other way, gunning the engine, overcorrecting. The right tires veered into the yard, skidding on the grass, and finally she braked.

Too late. The trunk of the car smashed into the brick mailbox pillar with a horrific crunch.

"Oh my God!" Lavender yelled. She'd arrived with Jeffrey and Hugh at just the right moment to see the crash.

I was still running for the car. Frank got there first, to Wattie's side. He jerked at the door, but it was locked.

"Open the door!" he yelled through the glass.

Wattie wouldn't even look at him. She stared forward through the windshield, shaken and mutinous all at once.

I leaped awkwardly down the driveway to the passenger side, the crushed seashells biting into the bottoms of my feet. I peered in the window.

Birchie stared back at me with startled eyes, her fluffy bun in a muss.

"Unlock it!" I yelled.

She obediently clicked the button, and I hauled the door open before Wattie could relock it. She was actually trying, but Frank got her door open, too. I reached in, my hands feeling all over Birchie, running up and down her arms, her face and neck, her chest and ribs, looking for damage.

"Are you okay?" I said it way too loud, right into her face.

"Of course I am, honey. Such a fuss," she said, giving me irked eyebrows, pushing at my searching hands. "Leia, stop groping my bosom."

"Are you all right?" Frank was jacked up and yelling into Wattie's face, too.

"Let us go," Wattie said, low and intense. "We'll be right back in a minute."

"You crashed my rental car!" I was still yelling. I could not stop.

"Bah! Barely, and we have to go," Wattie said, angry and so very urgent. "The car will still drive. The air bags didn't even come out."

I was suddenly dizzy and sick, imagining if they had. Air bags going off like gunshots, striking at their frail old bodies, pulping them.

"Should I call 911?" I asked Birchie. "Does anything hurt?"

"Make her let us go," Wattie said, clutching Frank's arm, appealing to him.

In answer he reached across her and grabbed the keys, shutting the car's engine off.

"What's happening?" a voice called behind me.

I looked over my shoulder and saw the Barleys, Birchie's elderly left-side neighbors, tottering toward us from their house. It was too early for a lot of folks to be about, but I spotted Martina Mack bustling down the street toward us from the square as fast as she could, the very last bit of hell I needed right now.

Wattie slumped in the driver's seat, defeated.

"We're all fine, Lisbeth. You and Jack go on in the house," Birchie called to the Barleys. They didn't, but they stopped on the edge of their yard. Birchie clicked her seat belt open and swung her feet around.

"I don't think you should stand up," I said, but she flapped her hand at me and started climbing out anyway. I took her elbow and helped her. She walked me around the car, tutting at the crumple in the bumper.

"Is everyone okay?" Lavender called.

Wattie clambered out of the car, too, silent and stoic, her face unreadable.

"Get the trunk out of that backseat," I said to Frank, and that got her attention.

"You leave that be," Wattie said, but I spoke over her.

"Right now, Frank. I am not kidding."

"Frank, you need to mind me," Wattie said.

He paused, looking back and forth between us, and his gaze finally settled on Birchie. She was still blinking at the bumper. "Miss Birchie?" Frank said.

She peered at him. "Goodness. Did we crash the car?"

I put my arm around her and stood as tall as I could. It wasn't very tall, granted, plus I was wearing pink pajamas with cartoon California rolls and unagi sprinkled all over them, but I was still a Birch in Birchville. Maybe not *the* Birch, but my grandmother didn't seem up to the job this morning.

"Get the trunk, Frank."

Frank shook his head, almost an apology at Wattie, and then he did what I said. Hugh came down from the porch and helped him without being asked. Jeffrey and Lav trailed after, curious.

Wattie glared warning daggers at us all. Mostly me. We all stood in a cluster in the center of the lawn watching Frank and Hugh wrestle the trunk out of the backseat. Wattie stepped to Birchie and took her place beside her. They linked arms, clicking together as perfectly as Lego pieces. On Birchie's other side, I felt suddenly extraneous.

Frank and Hugh set the trunk on the grass. It was an old brown sea chest, the edges bound in rust-speckled metal.

"It's locked," Hugh said.

Sure enough, there was an old padlock with a keyhole, rusted but still in service, on the clasp.

Martina Mack had reached the lawn. "What's happening?" she demanded in her scratchy old-lady voice.

"Don't you dare trample my grass, Martina Mack!" Birchie ordered. "We have enough grass tramplers here already."

When the rest of us ignored her, she went to join the Barleys, whispering at the edge of the yard.

"What's in there?" Lavender asked Wattie. The boys flanked her, both their bodies angled toward her.

"Nothing," Wattie said.

"Bull," I said. Wattie had left the driver's-side door open. I went to the car, leaned in, and popped the trunk.

"The chest itself is pretty light," Hugh reported. "It's not books or anything."

"Were you running away?" I asked Birchie as I went around to the back of the car to dig out the tire iron. That was all I could imagine, that it was an escape trunk, packed full of orthopedic shoes and cotton drawers and nice housedresses, hidden in the attic in case I kept insisting Birchie had to come to Norfolk.

"Is that my hope chest?" Birchie asked, as if noticing the trunk for the first time. Mornings were usually her best time, but the crash had rattled her.

"It's like Pandora's box," I heard Lav say softly to Hugh and Jeffrey. "I don't think they should open it."

"It's not your hope chest," Wattie said to Birchie. She glanced at Lavender, then me. "There's no hope in it."

I turned away, lifted the tire iron.

"Don't you do it," Wattie warned me.

I smashed down on the old lock. The chest shivered, but it held.

"Want me to try?" said Jeffrey, with a teenage boy's enthusiasm for whacking things with sticks.

Birchie said, "It's my wedding dress. It's my married-lady linens."

I brought the tire iron down again, hard as I could. The lock held, but the clasp itself broke, falling down to seesaw on one of its hinges. The Barleys and Martina Mack crept a little closer, crossing the invisible border onto our property. The kids all three leaned in, and Lavender reached out to grab both boys by their arms. I dropped the tire iron. Put my hands on the rough wood of the lid.

There was a breathless pause as I swung it open.

I saw something pale, maybe white, wrapped loose in plastic sheeting gone so old it had yellowed. I peeled the top layer of sheeting back.

Lavender gasped, clutching the boys in closer. Frank said a very bad word under his breath. I could hear Wattie panting behind me.

"What is that?" Martina Mack said, bustling across the yard, aggrieved. "We can't see! You're block—" Her voice cut out abruptly as she came up behind me.

"Why, that's not my wedding dress," Birchie said. "You'll need to look again, Frank. My hope chest must be farther back."

I couldn't move, was barely breathing.

Birchie reached past me and gently, mercifully shut the trunk, covering the pile of bones and loose teeth littering the bottom. Covering the human skull resting beside its own detached jawbone, its crown decorated with a deep, unnatural cracking high up at the back. The trunk had the only lid left to close over the black pits of the eye sockets as they stared up from the depths, old and dark and empty of everything.

7

It begins with Violet.

She's not on the first page, but she's the light that calls my antiheroine. Makes her say hello.

So far I'd thought only about Violence, endlessly sketching her without finding her origin. The past few days, I'd even wished for a little more Violence in my makeup. Not the cannibaly parts, but as Wattie and Birchie fought me on a thousand tiny fronts, I'd longed for a scoop of her single-minded will. Violence was so certain.

I'd discounted Violet, even though when I started drawing her in middle school, she had my dark hair and strong jaw and deep-set eyes. She'd changed during my senior year of high school, post-JJ, when I invented Violence. I'd turned Violet Super Pretty, evolving her from Hilary Swank's less glamorous third cousin into a willowy blonde with big eyes and bigger boobs. She got so sweet that I hurt my own teeth drawing her, like an old-school superhero girlfriend. TSTL, in the vernacular: "too stupid to live." Violet skips with oblivious cheer down that first dark alley, and her near-constant state of jeopardy allows for a lot of sly feminist humor in the first half of the story. By the end it's not funny anymore, as she and the world become wreckage. Maybe I'd made her less like me so that it was easier to ruin her.

Violet begins to break in an abandoned warehouse where she and her boyfriend have been taken by a drug lord. It's a huge, dark space, filled with pallets of crates and stacked boxes, and thugs are stationed at the edges and entrances. The cartel guy wants to know what happened to his crew. The boys from the alley. As Violet cries and swears she doesn't know, the rabbits and sweet-faced mice and puffy birds begin to gather around her. Their pleading expressions match her own.

The animals are a tell; rabbits and robins are present only when Violet is seen through Violence's eyes. In the black-and-gray shadows near the frames, bits of her appear: a jag of hair, the edge of one boot, a sharp-nailed hand. Every distance shot shows one less thug guarding the perimeter, more viscous liquid pooled in corners and running down walls.

The cartel guy loses patience right after the last thug's feet disappear near the top of the frame. He steps close, and above him Violence's deep purple silhouette glows faint near the ceiling. She's clinging like a spider with the corpses of the henchmen draped and hanging in the pipes around her.

He pulls a pistol from his waistband and puts five bullets in the boyfriend.

"Last chance," he says to Violet, and brings his gun to bear.

That's when Violence drops between them, so lightly that the snick of her knives unsheathing is writ larger than her landing. There is a moment of surprise, some prefight banter, and then Violence is pretty much eating him.

The panels zoom in on Violet. Her face is in her hands, but she's peeking through her fingers. Her eyes are filled with tears, but her lips . . . she might be smiling. Her palms are pressed hard into her cheeks, though, so it might be the pressure of her hands pulling the corners of her mouth up.

It's hard to tell, until you notice the rabbits. While the mice and birds work tenderly, comforting Violet and drawing a corner of her skirt over the dead boy's face like a shroud, the rabbits are watching Violence. They stand up on their haunches, and their white pelts are splashed with gaudy blood. They witness this murderer get eaten up alive, and the rabbits kind of like it. They have begun to change.

Maybe that was why the graphic novel went viral in the first place; Violet's story happened to everyone. All of us, every innocent babe born on this planet, gets broken eventually. We could all reach back in time with certain fingers to touch those places: Someone you love died, you watched your mom or dad walk out the door, you had sex for the first time and learned exactly how expendable you were. Or you peeled back the lid on an old trunk.

I hadn't looked at Birchie since she'd closed it again for me. My eyes didn't want to turn that way. What would I see? Guilt? Defiance? Pure fury at my ham-fisted insistence? My grandmother, who made me ice-box pie and called me "sugar," had human bones hidden up in her attic. Who was this woman? I didn't want to look at Wattie either, not now that I'd let sunshine touch this thing that should have stayed in darkness. This thing that never, ever should have been.

But when I looked, I saw only my grandma and her bosom friend, small and frail and dear to me. Wattie was looking back, and the compassion in her large, round eyes almost undid me. Forgiveness, even, and under her gaze I knew I'd marched us all to this dark moment.

Once I'd hired the estate-sale folks to help sort out the attic, Wattie had to move that sea trunk. I'd given her no choice. And Wattie had tried to warn me. She'd told me on my first night back to leave things lie. She had begged me not to open the chest. I'd known her my whole life, but it had never once occurred to me to trust her. I hadn't thought, *If Wattie is stealing a car, then she must have good reason. Maybe I should let her take that trunk and go.*

Birchie herself looked stricken. Her lips moved, muttering or maybe praying. She stepped back from the closed trunk, and Wattie took her arm again, rejoining them at hip and elbow.

"Oh, sweet Lord! Who is that? Who did you kill?" Martina Mack screeched from the sidelines.

I lurched to my feet, saying, "Shut up, Martina."

It didn't matter whose bones they were or how they came to be there. Birchie and Wattie were standing right by human remains, but as I looked at them, I could not believe that they were murderers or evil things of any stripe. I didn't understand the bones, but I understood these women. I trusted them. I didn't need to know this origin story, or Birchie would have told it to me years ago.

I only wished I had let Wattie steal my car, let her drive that chest away and hide it elsewhere. Hide it better and forever. When I saw her backing down the drive, I should have grabbed two giant cinnamon rolls and gotten me and Digby drunk on sugar. I should've sat down with Lavender and said, *What's so dern interesting on my computer?* Thirteen's secrets would be innocent and fresh, sweeter than this box of bad history on the lawn.

"Is that . . . Was that a person?" Lisbeth Barley called. "Was that bones of a person?"

"I'm calling Cody," Martina Mack announced.

God help us. Birchville had five full-time policemen, and one of them was Martina's grandson. "Jackass" did not skip any generations, at least not in the Mack family. Cody was the last thing I needed in our yard right now.

"Miss Wattie, you and Miss Birchie go inside," Frank said quietly.

Birchie leaned in with worried eyebrows. "I need to put my trunk away," she said, one hand reaching for it. Wattie held her fast, kept her from touching it. "I need—"

I cut her off, saying, "Go on inside. It's okay."

I was scared of what she might say next. She'd just publicly claimed ownership of a box of human bones. I would not let the Lewy bodies convict her of God only knew what else on the lawn in front of the Barleys and Martina Mack.

Martina was already barking into her cell phone, "Naw, naw, Cody, I'm saying! You get your butt over to the Birch house, right away!"

"Come on, now," Wattie said. "Leia and Frank will handle this."

I nodded, reassuring, though I had no idea what "this" was. Once they were moving in the right direction, I turned back to Frank. "Should we take the trunk inside, too?"

"Don't you move that," Martina called. She was off the phone now and pointing at the sea chest with one quavering old finger. "That right there's a crime scene!"

Lavender and both boys watched, big-eyed and quiet. Hugh loomed over her, protective. Jeffrey had only a couple of inches on Lav, but he was doing his best to loom protectively over her other side. My bare feet were cold in the dew-wet grass. Down the road I could see the blue-clad teardrop shape of Cody Mack, already speed-walking up from the square. His officious gait set his Maglite swinging.

"It's not a crime scene, Martina," Frank said, mild and dismissive. "We don't know what it is yet."

"I own almost every season of *Law & Order* on DVD. I know a crime scene when I see one." She turned her beady glare on me. "Y'all uppity Birches! I shoulda known. I hope they bring cadaver dogs and dig up the whole yard." She gave the Barleys a knowing nod and added, "I bet you anything there's a whole slew of bones and folks and suchlike buried under there."

The Barleys actually looked alarmed.

"Don't be ridiculous," I snapped.

Martina looked down her nose at me, tilting her head back and flaring her nostrils so wide I could practically see all the way up into the dark cavity where her brains ought to have been. "My daughter took me to see *Arsenic and Old Lace* over at the Montgomery theater. I know what's what!"

She'd prepped her grandson about what was what as well, because as Cody bustled up, I saw he'd brought a roll of glaring yellow crime-scene tape with him. It was so old it was dusty.

"What in blue blazes is going on?" he snapped, glaring from Frank to me. "Gran says you've got a body in that chest?"

I started to answer, but Frank put one calm hand on my arm.

"We're not sure what we've got here, yet," Frank said.

"I'm going to need to open it," Cody said to Frank. "I need to see."

Frank waved his hand in a be-my-guest gesture. Cody pushed in close and dropped into a crouch.

I turned my face away and looked at the Barleys, huddled close and whispering to each other. I heard the chest's lid creak, heard Cody grunt. Down the road Della Brody was standing on her porch, peering over at us. Next door to her, the Maxwells had come outside, too, so First Baptist's super-efficient phone tree was already working. We'd have most of Birchville on our lawn within ten minutes. I kept my face pointed safely at the neighbors, watching them coalesce, until I heard the click and creak of the chest closing again.

Cody was asking Frank about the car with its smashed bumper and how the chest had come to be resting in the grass in the first place.

"It was in the back of the car."

"Where was it before that?" Cody asked. "Where did it come from?"

That was the real question, wasn't it?

"The attic," Frank answered, calm and brief, supplying truthful information, but only the exact things Cody asked for.

While they talked, I picked my way over to Lavender and the boys, the damp cuffs of my pajamas flapping at my bare ankles.

"You kids go make Birchie and Miss Wattie some hot sweet tea, please? Or cocoa. I think they're in shock."

"Can we have cocoa, too?" Lavender said, her kid-centric interest lured by chocolate and sugar. Jeffrey's smile sparked hopeful at the question, but Hugh's face remained grave, a mirror of his father's. He was only two and a half years older, but they were big years; I hoped that Lav had picked the safety of a crush on Jeffrey. Lavender wasn't ready for a high-school boy, minutes from driving, with a full complement of adolescent testosterone thundering through his body. But I looked at how close he stood beside her, so protective, and I knew he was there whether she was ready or not.

"Sure," I said. They started off.

"I'm going to need to question Miss Birchie," I heard Cody say behind me, and I whirled back.

Frank said, "I'm her lawyer. You can talk to me."

"That dog won't hunt," Cody said. "I been questioning you. You don't know jack-all."

"I'll have to do. I can't let you talk to my client. You were at the Fish Fry, so you know very well Miss Birchie is not competent."

"Bullpucky. Seems to me like Miss Birchie only

spoke some true words at the Fry. If what she'd said was craziness, your wife wouldn't be living at her mama's right now, would she?" Cody said, and Frank's lips went white.

Damn, but that was a low blow in a fresh wound. Why hadn't God made jackass genes recessive?

"Birchie has Lewy bodies." I stepped in, trying to sound calmer than I felt. "It's a form of dementia, and you can confirm the diagnosis with her doctor. You absolutely may not question her." I shot Martina Mack a look of pure venom. I'd seen *Law & Order*, too, if only once or twice. It wasn't really my kind of thing. "You talk to Frank and no one else, and you keep a civil tongue in your head while you're doing it." It was a line straight out of Birchie's lexicon.

Now one of our two police cars was driving slowly up from the square. It looked like the chief, Willard Dalton, was behind the wheel. He was a reasonable guy, older and calmer, worth about fifteen Codys. I willed him to drive faster.

Cody glared back and forth between us. "Get me Wattie, then. She hasn't gone demented, all sudden and convenient, has she?"

"*Miss* Wattie, you mean. Who raised you?" I was all Birchville in this moment, speaking for my grandmother and doing it well enough to shame him. He was in our own yard. Hell, he was in our own town. He should have called Wattie "Miss," given his age and hers, especially in front of his own grandma, and he knew it. "I see your boss coming, and he will talk to Frank, and me, and anybody else who might need talking to. You stand out here in the yard like the dog you are. Let human beings pick what happens next."

I turned smart on my heel and walked off toward the house.

"Wait here," Frank ordered Cody, and followed me up onto the porch. He leaned in, talking soft. "Don't you ask Birchie any questions. She might tell you."

"Tell me? Tell me what?" I said.

"Anything. You need to be careful what you know. Don't ask, and do not let her explain."

I was already shaking my head. "Frank, I have to—"

He interrupted me, quiet but urgent. "Hear me on this. These are old, old ladies, and Birchie is sick. I'm not going to let anybody question her. Not if I can help it. But for sure someone is going to question you. If you know the wrong thing, say the wrong thing, you could do a lot more harm than good. Let me protect y'all."

I held my hands up in surrender, though it would not be easy. As I went inside, I tried hard not to even think of questions to not ask, and failed. Who was in the trunk? It must be someone who belonged to Birchie in some way. It was her house, after all. Exactly how long had it been up there? I'd only had one look at the bones, but they were old. Old enough to unhinge entirely from one another. Also, the trunk had been buried deep in the back room. When I was a girl, that back room had already been too packed to allow me entrance. Had the trunk been present, moldering and foul, while I played dress-up? It could have been there longer than I'd been alive, the heaps of history growing up organically around it, burying it deeper every year.

I hoped it had been. I hoped it had been there for a century or more, a bad legacy passed down to Birchie from someone long dead. My storyteller's brain was hunting narrative. Ellis Birch was by all accounts an overprotective father, and also overproud. Perhaps these were the bones of Birchie's missing suitor, the one who was supposedly run off to the state line. Maybe they were older still, the remains of a Yankee soldier, killed during the throes of Reconstruction. They could have traveled in this trunk with Ethan Birch, the real reason he fled Charleston and founded Birchville. If this was only a box of bad history, then it would all be over soon. Remains that old required anthropologists, not cops.

All I had to do was wait. Let Frank get the story. He would tell me, and tell the police, too, in the best frame possible. The bones were something Birchie knew of, that was clear, but I could not believe for even a breath that they were a thing that Birchie *did*.

The kids were still in the kitchen. I could hear the clatter of dishes and the buzz of young voices. Birchie and Wattie were alone in the living room. They sat primly side by side on one of the Victorian love seats.

"Are you okay?" I asked Birchie, going right to her and kneeling.

"I suppose. Such a mess!" she said. "I'm so sorry. I never thought—"

"Hush, now." I kissed her. "Don't apologize. Don't talk about it at all. Frank says not to even talk to me, okay?"

She nodded, but I looked into her bright blue eyes until I was sure that she was there and hearing me. I turned to Wattie, taking her hand in mine. I could feel her own live bones, intricate and frail, and they seemed more fragile than her weathered skin.

"You and me, we have to get on the same page now," I told her.

"I've been on your page since the day that you were born, sugar," Wattie said, but then she added tartly, "Though all this week I wondered if you might be illiterate. Don't worry. I'm not going to let her say a word."

"Good," I said, though my heart sank. If Wattie didn't want her to talk, that meant Birchie had plenty more to say. I wasn't asking questions, and I was still learning too much.

Keeping Birchie quiet would take both of us. The Fish Fry proved that Birchie's illness had progressed past Wattie's powers to thoroughly contain it; Birchie might at any minute say the world's least convenient truths. Or worse, she might say self-incriminating nonsense. She did have Lewy bodies. She saw awful rabbits humping all over the town. What if the Lewy bodies made her remember things that never were?

I fixed Wattie with a stern gaze and said, "That trunk belongs to Birchie?"

"I thought we weren't going to talk about this," Wattie said.

"I'm making sure we're protecting the right person. Is it hers?"

Wattie's wide, full mouth compressed, and her sparse, white eyebrows knit, but after a moment she ducked her chin in a nod.

"Okay. Hear me now," I said, sounding just like Frank. "If the police ask, you say you only helped Birchie move the trunk because she asked you. I'm sure she was very agitated due to her illness. The illness that means she can't be held responsible for anything. So you probably agreed to help her move that trunk with no idea what was in there."

Wattie's nostrils flared. "My mother didn't raise me to be a liar."

"Well, you've gotten pretty good at it all on your own, then," I said sharply, but my heart sank. Of course Birchie had told Wattie what was in the trunk. She told Wattie everything. "Okay, that was cheap, but I had no idea Birchie was ill until last week, so maybe I was owed that shot." She looked away, but I saw that my words had landed with her. "For the record? My mother didn't raise me to be a liar either. Lucky for you, I don't always take her good advice."

"Hmf. The world would be a better place if we *all* listened to our mothers—and our grannies, too," Wattie said.

"Maybe. Did your mother teach you how to keep your mouth shut?"

"You're a caution, girl," Wattie said, smiling a little in spite of everything. "You spent half your childhood in that attic, and you never knew he was up there, did you? It's fair to say that I know how to keep things to myself."

I shook my head. "Hush, now. We let Frank talk, and we sit tight." But the information sank in anyway. *He.* The person in the attic was a *he.* A he was so much more human than an it, and worse, Wattie knew that the remains were male. Still, it didn't mean she had known the him personally, or that she had had anything to do with his death or his interment in a sea trunk. "Don't say another word. Frank believes it's better if I don't know who's in there."

"I told you already," Birchie piped up, agitated.

"Birchie, please, please, please stop talking," I said, reaching across Wattie to pat at her.

"I told you the first night you were here," Birchie insisted. "I told you at dinner."

It was morning, Birchie's best time, and she sounded so certain. Nevertheless, I was pretty sure we hadn't discussed who might or might not be dead up in her attic over the roasted game hens and fresh tomato salad.

"I can't remember how to make that cornbread," Wattie said, sudden and loud. Birchie started and looked at her, blinking. "I can't remember how much flour and how much cornmeal."

"Two to one," Birchie said. "Two to one, you know that. And three good-size fresh eggs."

Wattie shook her head. "You better start at the beginning."

Birchie seemed to sink back into herself. "I need to get your mother's bowl, because in that bowl we can eyeball how high to put the flour and such. I keep it second bottom cabinet, left of the stove. . . ." As Birchie walked us through the process of making her signature dish, I realized that Wattie had done this before. It was a coping mechanism for Lewy bodies, taking Birchie step by step through something that was second nature. Something she remembered in her hands and nose and mouth, not just her mind.

Lavender came in with a tray full of hot cocoa and a worried face.

"Where are Hugh and Jeffrey?" I asked.

"Eating fifty more cinnamon rolls. They are going to puke if they don't stop." She set the tray down. "Can we have the laptop back? We were doing something."

"Sure," I said.

It was still sitting on the coffee table. She picked it up and turned to go, saying, "And when you get a second, can you call my mom? I told her you were busy with the cops, but she's having kittens."

"You called Rachel?" I said. I didn't need Lavender's confirming nod. When things went to shit, girls called their mothers. My own mom smelled like chamomile and honey, and I half wanted to run home, crawl into her lap, and abdicate all pretense of adulthood. Instead, I had to call Rachel. She must be foaming. "Jesus, please us."

"Leia! Mind how you use the name of our Lord,"

said my grandmother. Who had kept a dead body in her attic for God only knew how long.

"How much grease goes in the skillet?" Wattie asked, insistent, pulling Birchie's attention.

"A goodly scoop. Use the spoon I keep right by the coffee can," Birchie said, back on track.

I touched Wattie's shoulder as a thank-you and then went upstairs. I had to explain to Rachel how it was I'd brought her only child to a house that had a body hidden in the eaves. An old, old body, I would need to emphasize. Just bones, really. When did a person stop being a body and become a piece of history? Perhaps when there was no one left alive who loved them. How long was that in a town that had a memory as long as Birchville's?

I didn't know.

I didn't want to know.

I closed my bedroom door behind me, braced myself, and dialed my stepsister.

8

Kittens was an understatement. Rachel was having Bengal tigers, and she fired a barrage of questions at me in a high, tight voice. I didn't have answers, but it hardly mattered. She interrupted every other second, railing and gobsmacked at the injustice; she'd evacked her kid from a marital war zone only to land her bang in the middle of a crime scene.

When I could get a word in edgewise, I asked, "Are you going to tell Jake?"

A small silence.

"Have you talked to Jake at all?"

"No. I guess I have to, if you're going to be finding corpses stashed right above his daughter's bedroom," Rachel snapped. As if I habitually dug up human remains all willy-nilly and now I needed Rachel to bring me in hand before I turned up Jimmy Hoffa in the zinnias. The fact that Rachel might call Lavender's dad was the only silver lining I could find here. I was not a Jake fan by any stretch of the imagination, but he was the only father Lavender had.

"So what now?" I asked.

"Lavender's coming home, is what now," Rachel said, in a tone that brooked no argument.

"Okay," I said. "You want me to call Delta?"

"I'll handle it," Rachel said, and finally let me off the phone.

I took a fast shower, and I was barely out when my phone started ringing again. It was Mom, calling compliments of Rachel, wanting to know what the hell was going on at Birchie's. Of course my parents needed to know what was going on, but I'd wanted to be the one to tell them. Gently. With a lot of context. I hadn't felt so tattled on since Rachel and I were six and she ratted me out for accidentally flushing Mom's emerald-chip earring down the toilet. And after I'd kept my mouth shut about Jake!

I stood dripping, wrapped in a towel, for a good ten minutes, assuring my mother that there was no reason for me to come right home with Lavender. I gave her my Yankee-soldier-bones theory and told her that any-way, with Birchie sick, I was pretty much the adult in charge here.

"Maybe so," Mom told me, fretful. "But you're still my baby. That never changes."

That made me put my free hand over my pregnant belly, wondering what the hell I had signed up for. As soon as I could get off the phone, I threw some blush and lip gloss at my face, hoping it would land in a way that made me look less fraught. I tried to get dressed, but my very fattest emergency jeans chose today to be insufficient to hold Digby. Perfect. I threw them in the corner.

As I turned away, I caught sight of myself in the mirror. Even at my fittest, I wasn't what you might call willowy. I was built thick, with stubby muscle legs and hardly any boobs to speak of. But these days my body was looking different. I'd gained a cup size, and my hips had rounded out along with my belly. I was heavier than I'd ever been, but I liked my body in the mirror. I looked lush and very, very female. Maybe even sexy. I stared at myself for a good ten seconds before I realized what I was doing.

"What is wrong with you?" I asked my reflection, then went to dig through my small store of packed clothes.

I knew the answer. My judgey preggo book said this was common in the second trimester. It was sex hormones, showing up all uninvited to the crazy hormone party already raging in my legitimately panicked brain. I put on a long Indian-print skirt, an outsize T-shirt that I sometimes slept in, and a lightweight baggy cardigan. When I checked the mirror again, I looked fat and maybe homeless, but not pregnant. Good enough.

By the time I got downstairs, the yard was innocent of bones, boxes, neighbors, and policemen. Frank was sitting in the breakfast nook, eating a cold cinnamon bun and waiting to give me an update.

"Did you talk to her?" I asked with no preamble.

He gave me a brief nod, but his face was grave. "I tried. Birchie was frazzled, and she didn't make a lot of sense. Wattie says she got up too early. Her routine is off. They're both lying down now. Be patient, okay?"

"Well, at least you kept that moron from filling up the yard with crime-scene tape," I said, grateful. The last time that yellow tape had so much as seen the light of day was when Movie Town put the tanning beds in the back room. Their little stash of rentable porn moved to a corner with an 18+ sign posted until a high-school boy got caught walking out with a copy of *Good Will Humping* stuffed down his pants. Cody—of course Cody—had then roped the corner off in glaring yellow, both to indicate a major crime and to try to keep teenagers out of the section. "Did Chief Dalton ask you a lot of questions?"

"Not much, once I agreed to let him take the bones off to be analyzed. He's being as careful as I am. This is Miss Birchie's house, after all. He knows where most of his salary comes from."

"That's excellent," I said, suddenly starving. I sat down across from him and chose a roll from the tray myself. I took a huge bite and asked around it, "Can't we tell them we came across the chest by accident? That we were pulling things of sentimental value down for Birchie and found it buried deep? Maybe Birchie saw the bones and panicked. Maybe she was even driving the chest down to the police station?" That was the polite title for an office about the size of a good walk-in closet tucked into the square by Brother's Café.

"You mean flat-out lie," Frank said, regarding me gravely.

"Yes. Hell yes," I said, vehement but still very, very quiet. The house was full of teenagers holed up someplace whispering about their own concerns and exhausted little old ladies having naps. My Birchie was ninety years old and grievously ill. Whatever she knew or witnessed or was party to, I forgave her. If she even needed forgiving, which I wholeheartedly doubted.

"Morality aside, that story won't wash," Frank said. "The trunk was locked shut when they tried to run off with it. Martina Mack saw you break that lock out in the yard, and she was trumpeting the fact so loudly I suspect they know it over in Georgia."

"So what do I tell people?" I asked.

The lawn and the street in front of the house were clear for now, but I knew Birchville. All over town, hot chicken casseroles and Bundt cakes were being assembled, and soon neighbors and members of First Baptist would be standing on the porch bearing food, hungry for information.

"Nothing," Frank said. "Less than nothing. Don't lie, for God's sake, just keep your mouth shut. Don't let your niece or Miss Birchie or Miss Wattie talk either. Tell everyone who shows up here that you aren't allowed because it's an ongoing investigation. I've already told Hugh and Jeffrey not to yak on pain of death or fifty hours of yard work, whichever they'd hate more. We'll let it play out. See what Chief Dalton does next."

"Do we need a criminal attorney?" I asked Frank. I thought we might, but Frank shook his head.

"Not yet, I don't think. I'll tell you if we get to that point."

I found this answer reassuring.

The doorbell rang, but I stayed in my seat. I was exhausted, and all this week I'd had a new kind of pregnant hungry that seemed to start in my very bones. I'd finished the roll, but I still felt like I had nothing in my stomach. Neighborly mac and cheese and avid curiosity were waiting for me on the porch, and I was almost willing to brave the latter to get to the former. Almost.

"Fucking fuck," I said, and buried my face in my hands.

Frank stood up. "I'll tell whoever it is that Birchie's asleep and to come back later. Can you find Hugh and Jeffrey and point them toward their gramma's house? They're late already, and I don't want to give Jeannie Anne an excuse to text me."

"Deal," I said, happy to exchange problems. "But if whoever that is has brought a casserole, please bring it in. I want to stress-eat about half of it."

Upstairs, I heard young voices, pitched low, coming from the tower room. The door was shut, and the tower room was technically Lav's bedroom. Not cool. Worse, I heard only two people talking. Lavender and one boy or another. They were being too quiet for effective eavesdropping, and I didn't want to be a sneak with my niece anyway, but I heard Lavender say the word "daddy" as I came to the door. So they were bonding over their newly smashed families, sitting in a closed room with a bed in it. Not cool at all. I knocked once and threw the door open immediately after, hoping I'd find Jeffrey.

It was Hugh, of course, who had broad shoulders and was almost capable of growing a mustache. Poor Jeffrey was still downy-cheeked and sliver thin. Hugh and Lav were pressed close, side by side on the neatly made daybed, heads bent over my laptop. They looked up as I came in, but they did not move away from each other.

"Where's your brother?" I asked Hugh, casual.

"I sent him to Gramma's. Mom texted. She's pretty freaked about . . . you know, the . . . um, you know," Hugh said.

So the news had already left the square and spread to the very edges of the town. Super.

"Yeah, well, maybe you should head on over, too," I said, stern enough to make Hugh rise.

"Yes, ma'am," Hugh said as Lavender set the laptop aside. "Bye, Lefty."

As soon as we were alone, I said, "Hey, *Lefty*, how's about you don't close the door when you have a fella in your bedroom."

"It's not like that. We weren't doing anything," Lavender said, and then she changed the subject. "Is Mom making me come home?"

"Of course she is," I said. No way Rachel was leaving her in a house where a body had been unearthed. Or untrunked, as it were.

"Aunt Leia, no! You were supposed to talk her out of it. It's stupid. It's not like we found a pile of freshly murdered teenage girls under the stoop. I'm not in danger."

I sat down in the overstuffed reading chair, pulled a throw pillow into my lap, and hugged it to my Digby tummy. "Sorry, Lav, but it's a done deal."

Lav said, "This is probably the single most interesting thing that ever happened to me, and I don't want to go before we even find out who got murdered."

"Don't say 'murdered,'" I warned her instantly. "No one said anything about a murder."

Lavender looked at me, fond and skeptical and patronizing all at once, the way I used to look at her when she was eight and still reverently setting out baby teeth for the fairy. I'd been almost sure that at that point she was in it for the money. But only almost.

"Come on, Aunt Leia. Hugh says unmurdered people get regular buried. Not stuffed up into attics," she said, and damn, but the kid had a point. Worse, if Hugh had already come to that conclusion, what was the rest of Birchville thinking? Most of the town loved Birchie, but not like I did, and I could only imagine the bile spewing out of Martina Mack's smug face. "Do I really have to go home?"

I said, "Your mom is probably buying you a ticket right this second. Tomorrow at the latest, maybe even tonight, we'll be headed for the airport. You better get packed, okay?"

"This completely sucks," Lavender said. She made no move to rise and get her suitcase out either. Instead she pulled her bottom lip into her mouth and chewed it. I clocked the look on her face. Guilt. She'd done something, and she wanted to confess.

Downstairs, the doorbell was chiming again. I needed to help Frank reassure the town, get some food into my pregnant body before I passed out, check on Birchie. I stayed where I was, though. Whatever this was, it was eating at her.

"Just tell me," I said, gently as I could. "What did you do?"

I hoped to God it wasn't Hugh-related. We'd only been here a few days, but they had been difficult, and I knew firsthand that the loss of a father could lead to fast, damaging sexual decisions. Her own MIA dad's bad choices had taught me this, when he and I were not much older than she was now.

Lavender flushed and said, "We didn't do much."

"You and Hugh?" I said.

She nodded.

"I think you should blurt it out," I said. "Fast, like taking off a Band-Aid. Yank!"

"I told Hugh about your baby," she said in a rush. "Don't worry, he won't tell anyone."

"Lavender!" I said.

This was so far from the confession I expected that it was in another universe. My personal universe, actually, one where she had zero business meddling. Worse, Lavender was already spilling to the neighbor boy, and she was headed home. My secret would not survive long in sharkier, more Rachel-filled waters. Rachel would go tattle on me more to Mom and Keith, and I would spontaneously combust from all the stress.

"Hugh's solid," Lavender said, so dismissively that telling Hugh couldn't be what she was feeling guilty about. "But we're both so sad, for the baby."

"Why on earth?" I said, but softly, because we were in it now. Telling Hugh my secret mattered to me, but this was the part that mattered to her.

She wouldn't look at me. She spoke so quietly that I barely heard her. "Because the baby won't have a dad. He won't have one at all, even to start."

"Oh, honey, that's the last thing you need to be worrying about," I said. Of course my kid's fatherless state was going to resonate with these kids. The last time Lav had seen her own father, he'd been charging out the door with a Whole Foods bag full of underpants and oxfords. Hugh's family was in equal disarray.

"Was the baby's dad . . . Did he seem like a mean person?" Lavender asked.

"I don't know. Do you think this might be more about your own dad and not the baby?" She shrugged, inscrutable. Thirteen was so much harder to read than simple, sugar-hearted twelve. "Have you talked to your dad at all? Maybe texted him?"

"Mom told me not to," Lavender said, waving the question away. "Aunt Leia, just answer me. What if I have to go to the airport in like five seconds? I need to know—when you met the baby's father, did he seem like he was nice?"

I took a deep breath and resigned myself to the conversation. Thirteen was urgent, and it came with tunnel vision. This mattered to Lavender so much that she was talking about Digby's dad instead of human bones or her own parents. I had to take it seriously, but I wasn't sure I had an honest answer. By the time I'd started drinking with the Batman, I'd been emotionally shipwrecked. I wasn't in any state to assess the character of my not-yet-existent-baby's father. I'd been bitch-slapped almost twenty years into my past.

A shame, because the day had started out so wonderfully. I'd packed a five-hundred-seat auditorium at FanCon. They'd had to turn people away because of fire codes. At the end, when Dark Horse announced that a *V in V* prequel was in the works, that whole host of glorious nerds had risen to their feet to give me a standing ovation, foot stomping and hollering.

After, as I walked around the show floor, people kept sidling up and shyly asking for my autograph. I saw at least twenty women and two men who had come dressed up as Violence. It was surreal, passing cosplay version after version of the killer I'd invented, each one with a pulse and purple hair. Short and tall, fat and thin, young and old, all toting pretend knives and rocking thigh boots. My favorite one had smeared deep rust red around her mouth, and when she grinned at me, I saw the same color in the creases of her pointy prosthetic teeth. I even saw a Violet in a sweetsy yellow sundress with a taxidermied songbird clipped to her shoulder.

This kind of thing only happened at cons. Nerd fame wasn't like real famous. I never got recognized at Harris Teeter, and non-nerds lost interest in my job the second they realized I wasn't in tight with Robert Downey Jr. or the Batfleck. My own family didn't subscribe to the series I penciled and inked; Mom liked cozy mysteries and books with *Chicken Soup* in the title. She found

Violence frankly disturbing, and Keith read only non-fiction. Rachel had never so much as cracked the cover of my graphic novel. She told her East Beach friends I was "a working artist," leaving out the embarrassing comic-books part. But at FanCon I was a rock star, and it felt pretty good.

The booths were starting to close, and I stepped out of the convention hall to get a Starbucks in my hotel lobby. That was when I saw him. Derek, my ex-boyfriend from my art-school days. He was by the exit, passing out pale pink cake pops from a bouquet. To his family. His wife and his children.

The wife looked like me, short and thick, pale skin, dark hair. Well, she looked like me if I were ten pounds heavier, I thought, and regretted it immediately. I didn't want to be that brand of bitchy. She was holding a little baby dressed up as Hulk, laughing, trying to eat her cake pop with the baby reaching for it. He ignored the one clutched in his own fat starfish hand. They had two tweeny-looking girls as well, one dressed as Scarlet Witch, one as some anime-style princess thing I didn't know. The girls were gabbling in tandem to Derek about some nerdgasm-worthy something they had seen at the con.

Fourteen years ago Derek had offered me this life, this exact one I was seeing.

Or he had tried to. I hadn't let him get the ring box out of his pocket. Hadn't let him ask the question.

He didn't know that earlier that week I'd gotten a long, ecstatic call from Rachel, asking me to be her maid of honor. Telling me about her ring. Jake, my former best friend, who had once called all games "sportsball," had used the Jumbotron at Pitt Field to ask her.

I'd looked at Derek, the ring box a tattling lump in the pocket of his ill-fitting suit coat. We were twenty-one years old, and he'd been flushed with the pride of legally ordering champagne that he could not afford.

Before he could get the box out, I had told him, "I think we should call it, yeah? Graduation's right around the corner, and I'm moving back to Norfolk. I mean, we always knew this thing had a timer on it, didn't we?"

I went to a friend's place while he got his stuff out of my apartment, leaving him to divide up our shared comic books. He snarfled all the Doom Patrol, which I took as proof that I'd been right to break it off. He knew exactly how much Robotman meant to me.

Now, looking at his life with a lobby and a crowd of milling nerds and the gulf of many years between us, I was sick. I was purely sick and reeling with an understanding that was way too late. He was a nice guy. He had loved me. I had maybe loved him, too, and I had walked. I had walked away from Derek, and later on from Jonathan, and from Kev, and finally, three years ago, from Jax. I'd had no good reason, just the broken and untrusting piece that JJ had created in my center.

I put my skinny vanilla latte in the trash and walked across the lobby and into the hotel bar. There I had myself some tequila. And some Batman.

The Batman had approached me, actually.

"Excuse the fan-boy freak-out, but you're Leia Birch. I love your stuff," the Batman said, a world of admiration in the words. "Can I buy you a drink?"

I liked his wide smile and the glint of his dark eyes inside the mask. I wanted to drink enough to stop thinking that I lived alone with eighty-seven mint-in-package Wonder Women and a cat named Sergeant Stripes. I wouldn't even let *him* in the house. I hadn't cared whether the Batman was nice or not. In the moment Batman was being nice to me. It was not enough, but it was something.

I had no idea how to explain this to Lavender, or even how much I should explain.

"I didn't ask him for any references," I said at last. "I'm not sure what you're looking for here, kid."

She shrugged. "I'm not looking for anything. Well, no, I am. We are. Hugh and I, we went looking for your Batman on the interwebs. But then I thought, what if he wasn't nice?"

"Lav!" I said, rocked to the core by so much naïveté. Put this kid in a yellow sundress and there was page two Violet—bunnies, birds, and all. "I told you, there isn't any way to find him. Please don't worry, okay? My kid is going to have lots of family. He'll have you, and Rachel, and . . ." I paused, not sure about Jake's standing. I skipped his name and went straight to, "Your awesome grandparents will be his, too."

But Lavender had checked out of the conversation. She pulled my computer back into her lap while I was talking, swiping her fingers around on the touch pad.

As soon as I shut up, she said, "I'm trying to tell you. Hugh went through your Facebook feed. We figured that the Batman must have liked your page."

I shook my head at her. "That's crazy."

My real Facebook page was under my legal name, Leia Birch Briggs, but professionally I had always used Leia Birch, as a tribute to Birchie. As myself I had maybe a hundred friends. My Pro Pages for Leia Birch and *Violence in Violet* were huge, though. Leia Birch had more than twenty thousand likes, and *V in V* had almost fifty thousand. There was no way Lav and her little boyfriend had looked through all those, assuming that the Batman even Facebooked.

"Hugh sorted them by sex," Lav said, still clicking at the keys. "Did you know that more than half your fans are women? Plus, you told me he was black, and there's so many white-boy nerds, you don't even know. Then we ditched anyone who looked old or like a kid or super gross. That got us down to nine. We started looking through old profile pics, and one of them cosplays. Guess what character he dresses like?"

She didn't say it. I didn't need her to.

As she spoke, she turned the laptop toward me. There he was. Digby's dad.

He wasn't quite as cute as I remembered him, but I'd had tequila goggles on that night. Still, he was grinning the cocky grin that had first gotten my attention, and it lit up the oversize eyes that made his sharp-jawed face sweeter than it had seemed inside the cowl. His forgotten nose turned out to be a good one, wide and straight and sized to fit his face.

"Holy shit. Batman," I said, like a potty-mouth version of Robin. I stood up, and the throw pillow I'd hugged to Digby fell onto the floor. My gaze flew from Batman's profile picture to Lav's face. "Please, please, tell me you didn't let him know about the baby?"

"No! God no," Lavender said, and I could breathe again. For almost a full half second. Right up until she added, "We only messaged him once. And then I realized that I should have asked you first if he was nice. Aunt Leia? Was he nice?"

"What did you say?" I asked her, my voice so raw and angry that she flinched. "What did your message say?"

"Just hello," she told me, defensive. "All we said was hello."

I took two steps closer. On the screen I could see that an icon at the bottom of my Facebook page was blinking.

The Batman had already messaged back.

9

I dreamed my abdomen was made out of curved glass, like half of a huge fishbowl jutting out in front of me. Rachel wanted to see the baby, so I lifted my shirt and we peered in. Digby looked like those cartoon sea monkeys from the old ads in the backs of my childhood comic books. He was cute and smiling, with three deely boppers on his head and flippery feet. He waved his tail fin at us in a friendly hello. I waved back, but Rachel said, "That's Aquaman's! How did you forget which Super Friend you fu—"

I woke up with a start. It was dark in the room, but a faint light at the window told me it was close to dawn. I sat up, scrubbing at my face, Rachel's oh-so-disapproving dream voice echoing stupidly around in my head—as if my stepsister had any clue who was in Super Friends!

I wrapped my arms around my real, much smaller, opaque belly. Digby was awake and whirring around, half mine, half mystery. I didn't need a psychologist to puzzle out the meaning of my dream. Had someone told me yesterday that anything could push the bones sideways in my subconscious? Well, I would have laughed. But Lavender had managed, and it had sparked the worst fight we'd ever had. I'd been appalled; she'd been truculent and unapologetic. I'd told her to pack her clothes and stay off my technology on pain of death, but her dabbling could not be undone.

Digby had been my secret. My accidental family. Mine. His father had been unfindable, an accepted absence. He was the end, Digby the beginning. There was no next for Batman. I'd told myself so, over and over, every time he'd crossed my mind. Now a pair of teenagers had found him almost instantly. It hadn't even been that hard.

If I'd wanted to find the Batman, then I would have. It was that simple. I hadn't tried, and that was pretty damning. I wondered if it was partly, even a little, because Batman was black. Had I bought into the stereotypes about black men and fatherhood and assumed he wouldn't mind not knowing? I didn't think so. God, I hoped not. But maybe, on a subconscious level, it was there. The thought made me extra guilty that I still hadn't read his message.

Lavender had contacted him through my public page, thank God, so he still knew me only as Leia Birch, artist, and he wasn't showing up in my Messenger or Facebook apps. They were only connected to my private account. My laptop was currently hidden down in Birchie's sewing room, but only to keep Lav off it. It wasn't like that was where they kept the Facebook. I could log in to my public page from my phone's browser or my Cintiq Companion, a monstrously expensive touch-screen tablet with a better processor than most computers. It ran all of my drawing software. I hadn't doodled myself into a real idea yet, so I hadn't unpacked it.

I needed to pick a machine and go read his response. He could not be unfound, after all. But when I thought about reopening that window, looking through it into his world, I couldn't picture it. He would have a whole, full, real life, and when I tried to imagine myself entering it, even virtually, my usually color-filled head filled up with blank, white space.

I got my sketch pad and took it over to the desk by the window, thinking I would draw some Violences. I knew from long experience that hand sketching was more than a good way to jump-start work. It was an inroad to my subconscious. My head didn't know how to deal with Batman, but my hands might. And if I accidentally drew my way into the *V in V* prequel I was supposed to be writing in the process? Even better.

I began with a dingy row of storefronts running up one side of the paper, but as they took shape, I realized they were more than a little run-down. They were ruined. I was drawing a postapocalyptic strip mall. This was the world as Violence had left it at the end of *V in V.* An odd choice, because that world had no next. I'd been hired to write the origin story, not draw the wreckage.

I darkened the sky above the roofline, hanging a few shredded jags of black cloud, and I put the edge of a crumbled concrete bench beside a small blighted tree on the corner. Now the buildings faced a park.

They looked a lot like the attached shops on the square right here in Birchville. I recognized the silhouette. I went back to add details until the faded lettering and broken goods scattered on the sidewalk had turned them into the ruins of the Knittery, Cupcake Heaven, and Pinky Fingers Nail Salon.

In the shading around the shattered windows and dark, listing doorways, I saw the amorphous shapes of the personified Lewy bodies I'd sketched earlier taking shape. I had four of them lurking in the shadows before

I realized that each of their misshapen faces and their eye lumps was aimed at a central empty space.

That's when I knew that I was drawing Violet. Violet had always been the object of every gaze.

Fine. The story truly began with her, and anyway, I was in no mood for Violence.

I wanted more natural light, so I pulled the drapes back open. It was still too early, but across the square the sky was turning all the colors of state-fair cotton candy. Shades that Violet liked, pale and baby sweet.

So Violet did have a part in Violence's origin; she was my way in. Maybe Violence couldn't begin without her, though I hadn't thought that Violet would appear in the prequel when I'd signed the contract.

But maybe she had to, I thought as I etched her willowy lines, imagining the butter and sunshine shades that made her hair and sundress. She knelt on a patch of scraggly grass, snuggling a postapocalyptic mutant kitten. Violet had begun as a version of me, and her innocence had called Violence. I couldn't imagine Violence without her. Had Violence protected innocence—or innocents—before Violet came along? I didn't think so. It felt . . . The word that came into my head was "unfaithful," though there was no indication anywhere that Violence and Violet were lovers. It felt unfaithful anyway, on a deeper level than a thwarted romance.

I was liking Violet's expression, joyful and oblivious as she clutched the nightmare animal cheek to cheek. She looked like she was saying, *Squee!* The cattish monster hung in her arms, its clawed limbs dangling, looking long-suffering and resigned. I liked it, too, but the more detail I added to the "kitten," the more he looked familiar.

He had long, sharp ears shaped like katana blades, and I'd frilled his neck and belly with barbs of black fur. He looked less postapocalyptic and more gothic. I set my pencil down, plagiarism bells going off in the back of my mind. He was derivative, but who was I stealing from?

Then I had it. He looked a lot like a vampiric Batman, the way Kelley Jones had drawn him in "Knightfall."

If I was looking for permission to put my Batman back in the closed-story file, instablocking him, my hands weren't giving it to me. They'd drawn him right into the picture. They had put him with Violet, too, and she seemed pretty pleased to have him. No one had ever accused me of being an optimist, but my hands were saying that Lav's coup could be a good thing. Were they right?

I stared down at the town square as if the answer might drive itself around the corner, but all that appeared was a white SUV. A Nissan Pathfinder. It was very new and high-end for a Birchville car, and so spanking clean in the sunrise light that it reminded me of Rachel's.

I stood up almost involuntarily, the chair scraping back.

Holy crap, it *was* Rachel's. As it came closer, I could see her blond head behind the wheel. It was like waking to find that the Statue of Liberty had yanked itself out of the Hudson while no one was looking, Weeping Angel style, and come speeding across the country toward me. I blinked and scrubbed my eyes, and when I opened them, the SUV had pulled into our driveway.

I reached for my robe and yanked it on, both to better hide my Digby bulge and because the town had seen quite enough of me standing in the yard in my yummy sushi pj's. I jammed my feet into my purple Chucks and hurried down the stairs with the laces untied and trailing. By the time I got out the door, Rachel was standing beside the open hatchback, dragging out a massive piece of luggage.

"Rachel, what on earth!" I said.

She let her very expensive suitcase tumble to the ground, bruising the leather.

"Thank God it's the right house," she said. Dark circles ringed her eyes, and her hair was scraped into

an untidy pony. She was wearing sweatpants, or whatever exalted name sweatpants that cost two hundred
dollars went by. They had crumbs stuck to them, and
she was breathing heavily, a fraught, pre-cry kind of
breathing. Her chest heaved as if this were a bring-your-
own-emergency party and she'd come fully equipped.
"Where's Lavender?"

"Sleeping. That's what normal, human people do at
this hour of the morning," I said, but very gently, because I'd never seen Rachel in such a state. I was already
coming down the porch stairs toward her, worried but
also the smallest bit fascinated. "Rachel, did you drive
all night?"

"Of course I did," Rachel said. Now she was haul-
ing an even larger piece of luggage out of the back. I
stepped over to help her. "I told you I was coming."

No, she had told me she would handle it. I'd assumed
she meant she'd make reservations and then send me
instructions, detailed and precise, in her usual level-
headed way. But I wasn't going to argue with her, not
when she was in such a ruined, un-Rachel-ed state.

"This is sure a lot of luggage," I said, overly hearty.
I ought to hug her, or pet her frazzled hair, something. In my darkest hours, Rachel enveloped me in
strong, medicinal hugs, firm and sure, like I was a tube
of sad toothpaste and she was trying to squeeze every bit

of sorrow out of me. Now I couldn't even put a friendly hand down on her shoulder; the very air around her seemed to vibrate with a touch-me-not unhappiness. "Are you sure we need to bring all of this inside?"

"I don't want it to get stolen," Rachel said, slamming the hatchback shut.

"It won't get stolen," I assured her. Rachel had never lived in a small town.

She grabbed the larger piece and began dragging it toward the house, saying, "You never know."

"I pretty much do know," I told her, but I pulled the handle out and started dragging the smaller bag. It was something I could do that felt like helping her. I followed her up the porch stairs. "We could leave it all in the car—unlocked, even—and it wouldn't get stolen. Or if it did, three witnesses would be calling the police and telling them exactly who was stealing it, by name, before the thief got halfway up the block."

"Tell that to the dead guy in your attic," she said.

Touché.

"You sure did pack a lot," I said in that same overly hearty voice, opening the front door.

"I thought Lavender and I might take a road trip. Maybe head down to Disney World. I told Mom and Dad that's where we were going. We. Like me and Jake were coming down here to get Lavender together. So maybe I should take her? I could stand to see the Happiest Place on Earth," she said.

"Oh. Disney sounds nice," I told her, even though it sounded crazy. I pictured Lavender, alternately texting and sulking her way through It's a Small World while this fraught version of Rachel wept and wiped her nose into her feral ponytail. Even so? It seemed less crazy than having an unraveling Rachel here, now spinning slowly in the middle of the foyer, looking up the stairs and down the hall and into the living room beyond. "Where is everyone?"

"In bed," I said. "Don't you think you should tell Mom and Keith what's going on?"

"God, no, not until I have some kind of plan," she said, and I was way too secret-pregnant to push her on it. She finished her turn, coming back around to face me, and now she looked almost forlorn. "Where is everything?"

"Rachel, I have no idea what you're talking about," I said.

"I thought . . ." She plopped down onto her suitcase like Anne of Green Gables abandoned at the train station. "I thought there would be people, and a chalk outline. And tape and dogs. Techs in jumpsuits. Where is everything?" It was rhetorical, and she didn't give me a pause in which to answer anyway. "What am I doing,

Leia? I'm so tired." Her eyes filled up with tears. "I drove all night to get here. And now look at this place. There's little birds singing outside. It's so clean. The whole town is so clean, and in here? I could serve food on that banister. It's like I came down here on an emergency rescue mission to pull my kid out of Mayberry."

"I tried to tell you on the phone," I said, glad that she was missing the undercurrent. I could feel how deeply the town was disturbed, whether she could or not. Even now, with the world asleep around us, there was an electric buzz of pent-up stress, like a cloud around First Baptist's steeple. Birchville had taken it in the teeth recently, what with public announcements of adulterous liaisons in the choir room, the subsequent firing of the associate pastor, the revelation of the One True Birch's illness, and now, worst of all, the bones. The bones trumpeted to us that our recent troubles were inevitable, and maybe even just; there had been something rotten at this town's sweet and sleepy heart for years and years.

"Look at that Tiffany lamp. What bad things could happen in a room with that lamp?" Rachel asked, sniffling. To her, an urban outsider, Birchville in a state of greatest frenzy looked as placid as an untroubled lake. "What am I doing here?"

"Running from Jake?"

At the mention of his name, she stood, instantly prickly, as remote and closed as a human Fortress of Solitude. But she'd driven overnight to plop herself uninvited down in the middle of my mess. It was as close to permission to jam my nose into hers as I was ever going to get.

"Rach, just tell me. Is Jake cheating on you?"

"Ugh, of course not!" she said, affronted.

"Okay," I said. I wasn't perfectly convinced. She hadn't really known Jake back when he was JJ. She'd thought of him as my creepy little friend, if she thought of him at all. She'd been shocked when Mom told her that the charmer who showed up at our Christmas party was the fat kid who used to practically live in the basement with me.

"Was he ever, like, your boyfriend?" she'd asked, overly casual, as we were helping Mom clean up post-party. Before I could answer, she was hurrying to add, "Because he asked me out, and of course I wouldn't date your ex."

"He was never my boyfriend," I said, because it was true, and also because I could see how badly she wanted me to say it. It came out terse, but Rachel didn't notice. Her shining smile in response made it clear that she wanted very much not to notice.

When she went to take the trash out, Mom said quietly, "Leia, if you're not okay with this, you should tell her."

"He never was my boyfriend," I repeated, although I had felt us start. I had held his body in my body, and I had seen a future.

"I could tell her," Mom said, but I could hear reluctance in the offer.

We both knew from long experience how much it hurt Rachel when Mom backed me in a way that seemed against her. I shook my head. It wasn't worth it. JJ wasn't worth it, and anyway, I thought, there was no way she'd get serious about him.

I never told Rachel about those seven sad, slick minutes in the basement, and I was pretty sure JJ hadn't either. Not that it mattered now. Surely sex had an expiration date; every human secret must eventually get too old to matter, disintegrating all the way past bones to nothing. But I thought a man who kept that kind of secret from his wife might well keep others.

"If he's not cheating . . . what? Is he drinking too much? Addicted to something? Porn or drugs or gambling?" Rachel glanced reflexively up the stairs, making sure no Lavenders were peering down through the banister. We were alone, but she still didn't answer.

"Is it something weirder? Is he obsessed with World of Warcraft or those videos of women in high-heeled shoes stepping on roaches?"

"Don't be gross," she said, and then she moved in close to me. She put her hand on my arm, and when I covered it with my hand, her fingers felt like icy sticks. I leaned in, and she bent closer to whisper, "He betrayed me." She barely got those three words out, as if each were a serrated knife she had to shove up her throat and out her mouth.

"How? How did he betray you?" I asked, getting frustrated. All that buildup, and for three words that told me nothing about Jake that I didn't already know. "Come on, Rachel, what? Did he build a doomsday device? Is he secretly a cannibal?"

She dropped her hand and wrapped her arms protectively around her middle. "I'm not comfortable talking about money."

That was not what I expected. It was better, actually. I hoped it was a money thing, because that seemed fixable in a way that cheating often wasn't.

"So he's in some kind of debt?"

She squeezed herself tighter. "Yeah. All kinds. The Nissan dealership is done. We're close to losing the house. Last night I told the real estate agent I've been talking to that we were ready put it on the market. I had to forge Jake's signature, and I left the papers in the mailbox for her on my way out of town. I should have done it earlier, but I didn't think I could stand the questions from my neighbors. She's probably at my house right now, hammering a sign into my lawn."

Now it made sense that she'd let Lav and me fly down coach. I'd even paid for both tickets, and Rachel—she who was always prearranging with waitresses to get the lunch tab and offering to replace my entire wardrobe with "some grown-up clothes"—had for once allowed it.

"I'm so sorry. What about his dad's old business?" I asked.

"I don't know. If the house sells quickly, and for a good price, he can maybe salvage it. Pieces of it. It's not my problem."

I boggled at her. "Not your . . . ? Rachel, if you and Jake got into—"

"*We* did not get into anything," Rachel interrupted, and there was so much frost in her tone that I felt it, a crystalline bite in my lungs as I sucked in breath. "Jake got us into trouble all by himself. He never gave me so much as an inkling. He let it get bad and bad and worse, and he hid it, and he borrowed to cover it. For God only knows how long, Lavender and I have been living in a house of cards, while Smiley Daddy took us to Greece. He bought me an eight-hundred-dollar pashmina, and he couldn't pay the mortgage."

"Okay, that's bad," I said.

It was a sin that Rachel especially would have a hard time forgiving. Jake had . . . well, he had Rachel-ed her. He had taken his stuffed bunny to the laundry closet and cried there, with Rachel locked out, not even knowing. It was stupid, too, because if he'd told her when the trouble started, Rachel could have fixed it. She could have fixed the living hell out of it, then started a budgeting blog and landed on *Good Morning America.*

It was a very Jake Jacoby thing to do, however. Not that I was taking his side. I would never take Jake's side, even if he tripped and staggered by accident into the right. But this time I could see it. I could even understand it. Jake had reinvented himself for Rachel. He'd defined himself as this self-made successbot who followed trends in man fashion and cared a great, hollering deal about March Madness. Back when he was JJ, he and I hadn't even known what March Madness was; I still wasn't entirely clear on it. Jake Jacoby was such a fundamentally dishonest construct, it was a miracle that lying about debt was all he'd done.

Still, it was all he had done, sounded like, and screwing up with money seemed forgivable. I recognized betrayal when it crossed my path, and fronting to stay successful in your wife's eyes did not rise to that level.

"That's very bad, but he's the only dad Lavender's ever going to be issued." Even as I said it, I realized what a hypocrite I was. Batman was the only father Digby would ever have, and a complete unknown. I wouldn't even look at him on Facebook, but here I was advocating father's rights for an absolute known jackass. This was not about me, however, so I soldiered on. "You could fix this."

She snorted. "My marriage, you mean? 'Can I fix it?' is not even the question. You're missing the point."

"Okay. What is the point?" I asked.

She flicked at the air with all ten fingers, as if the answer were hanging in the atmosphere around us, obvious.

"He never told me. He never planned to tell me. He was going to—" Her voice broke, and she clenched her eyes shut, as if Jake were standing right in front of us and she could no longer bear to look at him. "He was going to stick us with it, me and Lavender. Disappear and leave us in his mess."

"Oh," I said, a long-drawn-out syllable, full of a dawning understanding. It was what Rachel's mother had done when Rachel was three months old. It would hit her so hard and so directly that I wondered if her own history hadn't made her jump to that conclusion. I asked her, "Are you sure that's what he meant to do?"

"Of course I'm sure," she said, ice cold. "I was looking for an old recipe in MS Word, and I found a draft of a blubbering letter he was writing. It read like a suicide note. Leia, I thought it was a suicide note, but then I started digging in his browser history and e-mail, and he'd used our last dimes to buy a plane ticket to Oregon. Ticket. Singular. Just him. If I hadn't had a craving for Nana's lemon bars, he would have been gone."

Now, that was the JJ I knew. That was the JJ he'd always been. Of course he'd planned to poof, even knowing that it was something his wife could not forgive. When JJ did something so bad he couldn't stand himself, he disappeared, ditching anyone who'd been dumb enough to love him. It was time for JJ, version 3.0. I could imagine him in Portland, growing a giant beard and a craft-beer belly, maybe moving into one of those tiny houses. He could call himself Jac. Do whatever people did out there. No more Superman-loving dork and now no more sportsy yuppie. Maybe he'd even take up boccie ball. That unmitigated asshole.

Rachel said, "I confronted him that day, when you came over with the cake. I told him that he had to decide. He could stand and face his mess with us or run west like the lowest-crawling worm on the planet."

"Jesus, Rachel," I said. Birchie would have fussed at me for taking the Lord's name in vain, but this was, I think, an actual prayer. Lav had witnessed that fight. She knew that her dad had planned to ditch her. "What did he say?"

"He hasn't gotten back to me on that yet," Rachel said, both so glib and so bitter that it set my eyes to stinging. "I don't even know if he got on the plane. I told him not to speak to me or look at me or even think my name unless he was ready to man up."

So when shit got real, JJ had filled a Whole Foods bag with underpants and left. Nice. At least Rachel had called him on it. When Jake screwed me over, I'd given him the luxury of never having to explain himself. Of course, I'd had the luxury of not having his child.

"I know this hits you where you live, but Lav at least needs to hear from him. She—"

Rachel's eyes blazed. "I told him not to dare think her name either. Not if he's going to leave her."

If Jake weren't such a coward, he would have contacted his child anyway. I pushed through Rachel's touch-me-not force field, practically visible around her, and I laid one hand on her clammy arm.

"What can I do to help? Please let me help. I can get you caught up on the house payments so you have time to sell—"

She blinked, several times, rapidly, as if she had just noticed me in the room. Her lips curled up oh-so-slightly at the corners.

"That's sweet. I know you make a living with your art stuff, and that's great. So great, that you can do that. But it's freelance, and you're single. I wouldn't dream of taking your nest egg." She looked down at me like she was Supergirl and I was a toddler offering to help her lift a building.

I squelched down an orange surge of irritation, sharp as citrus zest. I drew for freaking Marvel, and for DC, and Dark Horse, for the love of God. Literally thousands of art nerds would trade a good chunk of immortal soul to have my career. Thanks to *V in V*, my own house was paid off. If I wanted to, I could get myself a Lexus and a purse dog and shoot my forehead full of Botox like her friends in East Beach. Instead I bought mint-in-package Wonder Women, and the contents of my dining room built-ins were worth fifty times more than her Spode china. She always acted like this, though. Like I sold lumpy handmade pot holders door-to-door, but not to worry! She'd be there to pay the electric bill when the whole thing went south.

I breathed through it. Rachel and I were two broken halves that had been glued into a family. The difference was, my dad had died; I'd never once thought he might come back if I were perfect. Rachel lived her whole life like she was mother bait, shining for a woman who never even sent a birthday card. Jake's decision to opt out had hit Rachel in her oldest open wound, and if patronizing me let her feel better, even for a second, she could have it.

"Okay, what then?" I asked. "What can I do?"

She looked around the room again, from the love seats to the lamps to the tidily filled bookshelves. "It's so nice here. Do you think that we could stay with you? For a little?"

I hesitated. Rachel was an alpha female, marching into a house that already held both Birchie and Miss Wattie. "Are you sure you would want to? After we found the . . . after what we found?"

"It isn't what I thought. Not at all," she said. She spread her hands. "I don't want to go back to Norfolk. I have no idea where Jake is, and I can't stand being home while Barb-the-perky-real-estate-agent drags families through my house. I can just imagine her leaning in, telling some yuppie bitch and her manscaped husband that they should make an offer, any offer, because we're desperate not to end up in foreclosure."

I needed Rachel here like I needed a good old-fashioned zombie apocalypse, but she was asking me for help. She never had before. A window had opened in the smooth wall she kept around herself, and I was being allowed to peek through it. Of course, inside that wall was a moat full of monsters and another, bigger wall and probably some dragons, but it was a start.

"Of course you can," I said. "If that's really what you want." She smiled, a true bright sunshine smile, even as I added, "You'll have to bunk with me, though. We are flat out of empty bedrooms."

"That's fine. That's great. It will be like when we were kids on family vacations," she said, as if this were a good thing.

Mom and Keith had planned one every spring break. They'd pile us into the van and drive across the country to aquariums or canyons or theme parks. None of us were really camping types, so we'd bunk at inexpensive family-style hotels that featured two queen beds per room and swimming pools and free continental breakfast. Rachel and I always shared the bed by the bathroom. Keith had to be by the door, as if he thought pirate brigands or hostile aliens might burst through and he'd need to protect his womenfolk.

"You hated sleeping with me when we were kids," I reminded her.

"Only because you always kicked me!" she said. "Anyway, I didn't have Ambien back then."

I tried to derail her truly bad idea one more time, but

without making that window seal itself shut. "Well, if I do bug you, you can always borrow my house in Norfolk. It's standing empty."

"Thank you, but Lavender's made some friends here. She's been texting me in an endless stream, begging to stay, and I would like her to have a little fun this summer. I can't really afford Disney right now," she said, and then some plastic came back into her smile. "Unless you would rather we didn't?"

"No, no," I said. "Stay. It will make Lav happy, you're right about that." And with Rachel here, boy shenanigans were both less likely and no longer my sole responsibility. "What can I do for you right now? Are you hungry? Want some hot tea?"

"A nap. If I could lie down for a minute . . ." She sounded so pitiful, and she had been driving all night.

I led her up the stairs to my room. I carried the smaller case, in deference to Digby, and it still felt like she'd thrown half her walk-in closet in there.

"Lav's right through here," I said, setting the suitcase down near the adjoining door.

She came to look, cracking the door and peering in. I saw a measure of peace settle on her face at the sight of her daughter, sleeping in a coil under a heap of covers. Lav's bright hair spilled across the pillow, catching the light from the open doorway.

"Oh, she's so lovely," Rachel whispered. "What is he thinking? How could he leave us? Leave her?"

I shook my head. My own father owned the only answer with no blame attached. Jake had dipped because he was selfish or scared or too broken to do better. Then I realized that Batman had an answer that left him blameless, too: He had no idea his kid existed.

I felt the last of my anger with my niece leaking away. She'd created a connection, an intangible chain. It linked me to Batman as surely as the tether inside me linked me to Digby. Of course she'd gone looking for Digby's dad, powerless as she was to do a single damn thing about her own. The kid was terrified, and when she'd messaged the Batman, it had had zero to do with me. She'd meddled on behalf of Digby, contacting his father because she wished with all her heart that some loving meddler would brute-force contact hers. I'd missed my cue. I'd lost my temper and left her to find her comfort in the testosterone-fueled mercy of teenage boys.

Looking at Lav, thinking of the ticking heart of Digby at my center, I knew what I had to do. For both of them.

Rachel turned away and kicked her flats off, then climbed right into the bed in her sweatpants with her bra still on. I think she was asleep before I got out of the room. I closed the door quietly behind me.

I went downstairs to the sewing room. This room was the last stop for furniture that would soon be retired into the attic. Two slightly sagging wing chairs and a big plush sofa with a stained cushion shared the space with Birchie's old Singer table. The back wall was built-ins, but instead of books Birchie had filed her fabrics here. Rolls were packed into the long, glass-fronted cabinets, and the shelves were full of quilting squares sorted by color. I had hidden my laptop in the purples.

I pulled it out, though yesterday I'd told myself I'd opened enough lids to last me, thanks. But I'd been wrong, and Lav was right.

I plopped down on the sofa, opening the old laptop and hitting the power button. It took forever to boot up; I'd only brought it to make sure Lavender stayed off my Cintiq.

While I waited, I fished my cell out of my pocket, scrolling through to find and punch Jake's name. He wasn't in my favorites.

Five rings, and then I got his voice mail. Jake kept his thousand-dollar midlife-crisis phone, big as a tablet, clipped onto his pants. He had it in his hand every other minute, voice-to-texting, barking at Siri like she was Miss Teschmacher. No way he'd missed this call by accident.

"You've reached Jake Jacoby's voice mail. Let me know what I can do ya for," it said, all good-ol'-boy and hearty. It was a message aimed at his own best customers—aging jocks who bought big-ass trucks out of the section I called Penile Compensation. I waited for the beep.

"Call me, JJ. Now. Sooner than now." I didn't bother to say who I was. He knew damn well who I was. No one else left on this planet called him JJ. "You owe me this. You know you do."

I hung up. I'd keep trying until that turd picked up. Meanwhile my Wonder Woman loading screen had appeared. I put in my password. I'd snapped it closed without properly shutting down, and my oh-so-helpful machine reopened every file and put me right back where Lavender had left off. There was my browser, still open to my Facebook page.

The minimized chat box in the corner blinked smugly to itself. Lavender had sent a call, and now there was an answer. I could read his name in the header. His first name was Selcouth. That was about as far away from Mark or Marcus as alphabetically possible, and unpronounceable to boot. I had a handle on the first syllable, I thought, but did the second sound like "cooth" or "cowth" or "coth"? For all I knew, the last letters could be silent, ending his name in a pigeon sound. His last name was Martin, so I hadn't entirely beervented the *M*.

I'd decided upstairs that I had to open this chat box, read his answer, travel to his page. It felt like the start of something dangerous. Something that I could not control. I hovered my cursor on the X that would close the window, then shifted it down to the bar that would open the chat box. Back to the X. Calling Jake had been easier.

Well, how does anything begin? I asked myself.

Maybe with something as simple as hello.

A lot could come from that small start, for good or ill: A hello in a bar had led to Digby. Violence said hello to Violet, and then they stopped the world.

But my choice had already been made. I moved my finger down the touchpad and clicked. Open.

10

Rachel came downstairs looking crumpled and puffy-eyed, picking her steps all careful and hesitant, which was bizarre. It was as if my unstoppable, bold stepsister had been *Freaky Friday*–ed by a shy deer.

It was still early to be up on a Saturday, but she had showered and changed into khaki capris and a flowered top, and she was carrying a couple of magazines. I smiled at her, but she wouldn't meet my eyes. She must be feeling wary of me, in this new era where I was allowed to know when she was hurting. I'd be careful with her, and hopefully the window into her life would widen. Become a door.

Birchie and Wattie were having their coffee in the living room. I wasn't drinking mine, but I kept smelling it, hoping to huff in a steam-borne wisp of caffeine. Wattie looked as wrung out as I felt, but Birchie had woken up oddly chirpy for a woman who'd been caught hoarding human bones. Maybe because I had canceled the appointment with the estate-sale folks and all talk of moving her to Norfolk had ceased; the county prosecutor had told us through Frank she would "prefer it" if Birchie didn't leave the state while they conducted an investigation. Birchie and Wattie were getting in a round of pre-breakfast knitting, but only Birchie hummed as she worked, as if the darker reasons for her reprieve had escaped her mind. Perhaps, for the moment, they had.

I was trying to read *Watchmen,* which I loved, but I was too distracted to enjoy it. I was waiting to hear back from Batman.

When I'd opened the blinking message window, I'd seen that Lav hadn't sent a plain greeting. She'd picked a hypercute frog emoji, holding up a protest sign that said HELLO! in curly purple font. Awesome.

It hadn't bothered him too much, though, because his message back was friendly. Maybe even flirty: *Hey you. Sure like seeing your name come up on my screen.*

Oh, yeah? I'd typed back, hoping it didn't read skeptical or suspicious. He hadn't responded immediately, and I couldn't sit by my computer until he did. It made me feel like a spotty, lovelorn girl on prom night, waiting by the door in a ruffled dress for a car that wouldn't come. I also didn't want to Message him from my private account. If he saw my Leia Birch Briggs page, he was sure to notice, in a few months, that the feed was filling up with pictures of a baby boy with my eyes and his nose. I'd sent him my cell-phone number with another message that said, *Then text me sometime.* Now my phone was tucked into my back pocket, and I was just as comfortable as I would have been sitting on a bomb.

I'd filled Birchie and Wattie in on Rachel's situation, and they had said that of course she could stay. We stood as she came down, and even as I did the introductions, Rachel was already apologizing for showing up uninvited on their doorstep.

"I'm having family trouble," she added in a small and trembly voice.

"We know," Wattie said. "We are, too, honey."

Their eyes met, and Rachel nodded. I saw an understanding pass between them, and Wattie stepped forward to give Rachel a spontaneous hug. To my surprise, Rachel melted into it, boneless and grateful, making me wish I'd been bold enough to try. They might have stayed there forever, but the grandfather clock chimed seven-thirty.

"Time to make breakfast. While the biscuits bake, I'm going to start you a pot of marrow broth in the Crock-Pot," Birchie said, all smiling sympathy.

"That is an excellent idea," Wattie said, finally letting Rachel go. "I'll come help, and, you know, I want to get those chicken livers out of the freezer. We can fry them up for supper."

These were their standard "building-up foods" for when "folks were lowly." They trundled back to the kitchen to get started. The second they were gone, Rachel wheeled to face me. All traces of the little deer were gone. She pulled my sketchbook out from in between the *Vogues*, then dropped the magazines onto the side table. She turned the pad to show me my own pencil sketch of Violet. I'd left it on the desk upstairs.

"Are you drawing her again?" She spoke barely above a whisper, but it had an edge.

"Yeah," I said, surprised. Rachel didn't usually notice my work lying around, or framed and hung on my wall, or even me doing it right in front of her. She was consistently oblivious, and when I tried to show her panels, she grew palpably bored or dismissive. "I got a contract for a prequel."

She dropped it onto the coffee table with a wrist flick.

"For God's sake, why don't you draw Spider-Dork

or Wonderful Woman, like you've been doing?" she said.

I boggled at her. Even Rachel knew the name was Wonder Woman and that she was my favorite. When I didn't answer immediately, she turned away, as if I'd stopped existing. She plopped down on a love seat and flipped the top magazine open. She stared down at the pages with such laser eyes I worried they'd start smoking.

"This is a chance to do my own stuff," I said, keeping my voice low, too. "I didn't invent Wonder Woman."

She actually snorted.

"You didn't invent her either," she said, waving a hand at the coffee table. "You just drew me." She flipped a page so angrily the corner tore.

"You think this is you?" I asked. "You think *Violence in Violet* is about you?"

"Didn't say that," Rachel retorted, but I talked over her, my temper sparking back, even though I worked to keep my tone light.

"Shocking as you may find this from your seat at the center of the universe, I have several things in my life that are not actually about you."

"I didn't say your thingy was about me! I mean, it could be about me—who could tell? It's so weird. It could be about anything."

"You read it?" I said, moving from surprised to genuinely shocked. Read it and never told me? Well, apparently she'd hated it, so maybe silence was her idea of kindness.

"I looked through it, and I'm not blind. That's my face, that's my hair, that's my body." She paused to flick an angry hand at the sketch. "She's even in my favorite yellow sundress."

"What yellow sundress?" I asked. Rachel wasn't the boho sundress type.

Her eyes narrowed. "You know. The one I had when I was six."

I threw my hands up. "Everybody has a yellow sundress when they're six."

"You didn't," Rachel told me. "Yours was blue, and mine was prettier. We wore them to the botanical gardens, and Daddy called us Sun and Sky."

I was utterly nonplused, and trying to remember. We'd gone to the Norfolk Botanical Garden all the time when we were kids. Mom and Rachel both loved to see what was blooming. Me, I'd always taken a book and plopped onto a bench to read about Conan or Cthulhu every time they stopped moving to ahhh at something.

"Rach, when did I ever care about clothes?" I asked.

"Never. It wasn't about the dress." Her tone was accusing. "You wanted to be Sun."

"I don't remember any sundresses. I don't remember when Keith called us Sun and Sky," I said. "Violet isn't meant to look like you. She's just any pretty blonde."

"You think *I'm* any pretty blonde," she shot back, vehement. She thrust the magazines off her lap and stood up again. Those words resonated. They sounded both so damning and so true. I did think of her that way, smooth as an egg, generic and symmetrical and beautiful. Which was awful of me, except that—was it wholly my fault? When a lovely and untroubled surface was the only thing she ever, ever showed me? But by the time I had my defense, she was already talking, her voice quiet but thick with pent-up anger. "You made me help destroy the earth! You made me be some kind of a lesbian!"

"Violence and Violet aren't lovers," I said, speaking to the point that mattered least. But I didn't want her reducing *V in V,* the best thing I'd ever done, to me calling her gay as if it were an insult—as if in coming to Birchville we really had driven all the way back to 1987. "They're closer than lovers. They're like two sides of a coin."

In the middle of this weird and angry conversation, intense but very quiet in deference to the sleeping kid upstairs and the grandmas cooking in the kitchen, the artist in me heard me say it. The artist in me understood that these words were going to matter.

"Kinda like sisters?" Rachel said, snide. "If it's not me, then why did you steal my baby name and give it to her?"

"Steal your baby name? What?" I asked. "I don't even have a baby."

Digby kicked, calling me a liar, but he barely even had lung buds yet. I ignored him on the technicality.

"Violet," she said, holding up her left hand, as if the name were written on her palm. "Lavender." She lifted the other hand, then bobbled them, as if she were weighing them against each other and they were coming out dead even.

Now I was too mad to stay quiet. "Violet and Lavender are two entirely different words, and—"

She cut me off. "It's the same color!"

"And anyway! Violet came first. I started drawing that character in high school. Lav wasn't even a dreamy star in the corner of your eye. So if you really think Violet and Lavender are the same name, then you stole it from me."

For a second I thought she might explode, fly at me, and slap or bite, she was so enraged. But then she sucked in air and her chin came up.

"Okay, Leia. You are letting me stay here, and I really need this right now, so if that's how you want to remember it, fine. I guess. We'll forget about the dollhouse baby. The one that I named Lavender when I was in preschool."

I shook my head. I was never much into playing dollhouse, preferring to jump on the sofa to zoom my *Millennium Falcon* toy around up as close to the ceiling as I could get it. Playing house way down on the earthly floor didn't interest me, especially since Rachel never let me stage a Sand People attack on the family who lived there. There had been a family. I did remember that. Mommy and Daddy, then a girl and a boy and a baby.

She had named the dolls, but I didn't remember all of them. The boy had been called Jean Pierre or something very like that, and if Rachel had actually been serious about that, how lucky for Lav that she was born female.

"The girl doll was named Lavender?" I asked.

"No, the baby," Rachel said. "The tiny baby doll. The little girl was Madeline. Ugh, just forget it. This is the least of my life's problems. So fine, draw me again. It doesn't matter, because let's be real. No one I know is going to read it. So whatever. Do whatever. Make a supervillain named the Rachenator, give it six or seven evil heads. I forgive you."

She plopped back down and picked up the top magazine, as if she were finished with the conversation, but it didn't play. Her hands were trembling. I heard the rustle in the pages.

"You forgive me?" I said, incredulous.

"You heard me." She sniffed, turned a page. "Oh, look, aqua is coming back for summer. How lucky for you. You look good in aqua. Not that you'll wear it."

"I didn't steal your baby name," I said again.

"If you say so," Rachel said. She lifted the *Vogue* to eye level, until it was a literal wall between us. But she couldn't leave it. She spoke behind the shield of the emaciated teenager on the cover. "I'm just saying. Dad built that dollhouse right after I was born, long before you ever moved in. Before Dad and I knew you existed. I had it my whole life, and the baby was always named Lavender."

Then I finally clued in. This wasn't about dolls. This was about our parents. Somehow we were preschoolers again, and this was about who owned Keith. Had I chosen the color purple to stake a claim on something that she thought of as hers? It was territorial and weird; purple, in all its shades, belonged to anyone with eyes and color vision. It belonged to both of us. So did Keith, to some extent.

"It wasn't conscious," I said. She said nothing, eyes

steady on her magazine. "What do you want me to say? What will fix this?" I asked. When she still didn't answer, I went right into the meat of the matter. "If we were both on fire, Keith would put you out first. We both know it. It's fine."

Which was not to say that Keith didn't love me. He did. He just loved Rachel more. He was the first man that Rachel and I had both belonged to, but she was his in ways I wasn't.

Rachel looked up, finally, and said, "Well, your mom would put you out first if you were on fire. That's just biology."

"I'm not sure that's true," I said, and I wasn't. "Mom would probably try to put us both out and catch fire, and we'd all three burn up together."

"Oh, so Mom is so much better than my dad?" she snapped.

"That's not what I meant at—" I began, but she talked over me.

"Why are we discussing this? What's wrong with your brain? We are not on fire. We will never be simultaneously set on fire in our parents' living room, so that they have to pick exactly who to put out in what order."

Well, we're both on fire now, and neither one of us will tell them, I thought, and out loud I told her, "I call him Keith, you call her Mom. You do the math."

"And whose choice was that?" she said.

I boggled at her. "Yours!" I said. "You bit me!"

"I'm sure that I did no such thing," she said, and she was serious.

"Rachel!" I said. She shrugged, shaking her head faintly, as if I'd just assured her that she'd once picked up Thor's hammer. "I did try calling him Dad, and you bit me."

We were talking about her now, and she didn't like it. She forced her lips into a wry smile, and her eyes cooled. It was as though she'd flipped off her fury switch. Just like that, her wall was all the way up again. All the way up, and fortified. Maybe there were pots of oil, ready and already boiling, all around the top, but I wouldn't know. Not from where I sat. I was far away, outside them.

"If you say so. We're in your house now, and Lavender and I have no place else to go. You're Sun and I'm Sky here. So have it your way," she said.

It took me off my guard. Were we fighting because Rachel was out of her home territory? Worse, her home territory had a For Sale sign on the lawn, and her husband was MIA. She wasn't ready to tell Mom and Keith how bad things were at her place—maybe because she wasn't ready to believe it yet. Or she wasn't braced for the pity and the worry, and with that I could empathize. She'd come to me because I already knew. I was the only one who already knew.

"I hope you know you're welcome here," I said, but it came out stilted and way too formal.

"Thanks," she said, so short it was a mere snip of a word.

Before I could say anything else, Birchie materialized with a home-knit afghan and a cup of rose-hip tea. She went right to Rachel and wrapped the afghan around her. Rachel set her magazine aside to snuggle in. She even took the tea, smiling up at Birchie. She was usually impatient with coddling, but now she looked inclined to sink down into it and bask. So she would take sympathy, as long as it was not from me. Fine.

I snatched my sketchbook and stalked upstairs to my room, and it took a lot to keep me from slamming the door with such a righteous bang it would wake up Lavender. Hell, wake up the rest of the town, even. I wanted to bang it so hard that Martina Mack would sit bolt upright, clutching the covers, thinking Satan had come for her at last.

But it wasn't my room anymore. Not mine alone. Rachel might be mad, but she was not mad enough to leave. Her suitcases lay open on the floor by mine, loaded with silky tank tops and lacy underthings and pairs of summer shoes.

In the bottom of my own suitcase, I had a paper copy of *Violence in Violet*. I'd brought it for reference as I wrote the prequel. Now I dug it out.

I perched on the edge of the bed and flipped through it, hunting images of Violet that caught her at different angles.

Looking at the early chapters, I had to admit there was a resemblance. Violet was blond and tall and slim, with big eyes and a ski-slope nose, so yeah, she looked like Rachel. A little. She also looked like every other anchor on Fox News.

As the story went on, the resemblance faded anyway. She looked less and less like Rachel because she looked less and less human after the warehouse scene.

Her murdered boyfriend was the son of a diplomat. His death sparks an international incident, and Violet weaves herself into the center of ever-intensifying scenes of mortal peril. She's figured out that Violence will save her. She's seen that Violence's solutions are vicious and permanent, but she doesn't care. Her heart is broken. Maybe she's trying to cause so much carnage that Violence will fail and they will both die, but Violence doesn't fail. Violence wins with ever-higher stakes, with greater collateral damage, even as Violet's robins trade themselves for ravens and her butterflies grow ragged and soot-winged. Her pretty body moves from slim to gaunt, the sundress hanging off her skeletal frame.

In the final chapter, Violet squats in a bomb shelter, staring at a television. Her face is practically a skull—jutting cheekbones, lips pulled back in a grimace over prominent teeth. Violence is there. She must be, because Violet has a blackbird on one shoulder, vermin gamboling around her bare feet. The little mice are now rats with long, fleshy tails. The avid, watching rabbits have grown fangs, and there is no light left in them to hold Violence close.

In other bunkers, all over the world, fingers are mashing at red buttons. Bombs are arcing back and forth over the ocean.

Good-bye, Violence thinks. It's the last word in the book. She leaves Violet in the shelter, and she goes out into it. She's delighted to be out in it. She grins her wolfish grin, standing in the spot where the first bomb will drop. Her boots are firmly planted, arms spread wide, spine bending, head thrown back in a rictus of joy as she welcomes the bomb. It's a very phallic missile, actually, and a part of me wanted to go find Rachel, point this out. *Lesbians, my ass. Do you not get art?*

Then Violence is a purple shadow in the center of a blaze, like the wick of a candle flame. The view recedes, backing up in stages. Huge, sooty mushrooms spring up all over North America. The earth is a blue ball, hanging in space, and all the continents sprout with this same, world-ending fungus. The mushrooms dissipate into a dark fog that hangs in shreds and drifts, shrouding the planet, and all of Violet's ruined animals are hidden in its curls and purple shadows. And that's the end. There is no next.

I closed the book, thinking, *Well, sometimes there isn't.*

Did I steal Rachel's face? Her baby name? Maybe. I didn't remember it that way, but she didn't remember biting me. Maybe a dark and daddy-hungry corner of my heart drew Violet to look like her on purpose, to sting her, and it had.

The thing with JJ hadn't helped us. He had loved the idea of her, the hope of her, more than the actual, human me, who had taken him in at his lowest moment. Did I blame her somehow? Because she'd captured JJ with her superpower when we were all still children? She hadn't even tried. She hadn't even wanted him back then, and when she did choose him, she'd ended up wrecked herself.

Still, this is how our story always ended. She took her sorrows to the laundry closet, I waited outside.

When I was ruined, she barged in and helped, because it made her feel so good to be the hero and pull me out of whatever mud I'd mired in.

Sun and Sky, we had started with a crack in us. If we had been born sisters, if my dad hadn't died, if her mom hadn't pulled a fade, if JJ wasn't such a jackass. If, if, if. This much I knew: Our sisterhood had come pre-broken. Letting her stay here, her brief moment of feeling vulnerable, couldn't fix us.

When things began so badly, with a war or a loss or a rift or five shots of tequila, they stumbled along a fractured road that slanted, steeply, down. They could only degenerate, get worse and worse, until you were standing in ruins. When you got to an apocalypse, there was no next.

As if in answer, the bomb in my back pocket trembled and chimed, contrary.

I yanked it out of my pocket, heart rate jacking. I had a text from an unknown number, but I knew who it was.

Been a while. Coming back to ATL? I'd like to see you again.

11

That night Rachel climbed into bed on the side I liked to sleep on, her face shining with moisturizer, and announced she'd already taken an Ambien. She fluffed her pillow and pulled a sleep mask over her eyes, arranging her limbs like it was the most natural thing in the world. She conked out almost instantly. I teetered on the edge on the wrong side, feeling out of sorts and wide-eyed as a bush baby.

Every time I got comfortable, she'd flail a foot into my shin or jab me with a pointy elbow. When we were kids, I'd been the restless one, bothering her with my sleep muttering and humming. Child Rachel had slept the same way she'd done everything—beautifully, with a surface so placid she might as well have been in a glass box with a chunk of apple in her throat, lips preset for an inevitable kissing. Not tonight. It was like sleeping with a bag of upset cats. When she flung out a hand and smacked me in the face, I got up and stomped downstairs to the sofa in Birchie's sewing room. I took my suitcase with me, but even with the racket I made wheeling it away, Rachel didn't wake up.

I envied her that. If it hadn't been for Digby, I'd have dug down into her suitcase and snarfled up an Ambien myself.

She apologized at the breakfast table the next morning.

"I'm sleeping so poorly these days," she said while Wattie slid pancakes and an extra slice of bacon onto her plate. "I'll sleep on the sofa tonight."

Wattie answered her before I could, saying, "Nonsense!"

Birchie chimed in right behind her. "No, no, my dear, that won't do. You're company!"

After breakfast Birchie and Wattie unpacked what looked to me like Rachel's whole wardrobe and hung it in the closet in the room I thought of—rightfully—as mine. Another night passed, and another. Rachel stayed cool to me, and she let them both take care of her. She didn't do much of anything. It was as if she were on a rest cure circa 1800. She dozed and sat and stared at books and magazines. Her phone was always right beside her, and I realized she was waiting. Waiting for Jake to call with his decision. To tell her if he was going to be a man or Lowly Worm.

Then I felt sorry for her again, because I knew from experience that when JJ was done, he was done. He was going to Lowly Worm it off into the sunset.

Day five of Jake Watch, I went and sat beside her on one of the love seats.

"Can I do anything to help?" I asked, even though I knew better.

She looked at me, blinking as if her vision had gone fuzzy, and then her eyes found their focus, lasering in on me.

"Do you want to bring me tweezers?" she asked. "You've gained a little weight. I could reshape your eyebrows for your fuller face."

I shook my head no, smiling close-lipped to keep in the nineteen angry things that I had traffic-jammed in my throat, all trying to get out at once. After that I left her be, because she wasn't going to let me help her. Unless I wanted to count "fleeing my own room" as some kind of assistance.

It turned out to be a good thing. Ever since the bones were found, the whole house had felt out of balance. It was as if that sea chest had held a thousand pounds of weight and the old foundation had sighed and tilted us all a half inch to the left as soon as they'd been taken from the attic. The sewing room was at the very back of the house, past the office, down a long hall. It shared a wall with the kitchen, but there was no pass-through. Since Birchie wasn't sewing much these days, I had it to myself. When I was there, door closed, my newly too-tight bra off, Pandora playing the Smiths for me, I had the most privacy possible in a house this full of relatives from both sides of my family. I even left my phone plugged in here, not wanting the tattletale buzz of multiple messages landing to announce that I was trading secret texts with men. Four of 'em.

The first was only our old friend Frank Darian, keeping me apprised as the justice system ground around in our family business. Our county prosecutor, Regina Tackrey, was a pit bull of a woman. And this was an election year. Frank deposed Dr. Pettery, though, and given Birchie's illness and the bones' unknown provenance or age, he'd blocked any police interrogation. For now. Tackrey had to show that a crime had been committed before anything else could happen to my grandmother. To that end, Tackrey had sent the bones to a forensic anthropologist in Montgomery.

I felt like Birchie was in something's mouth, an ice-eyed reptilian something. It was rolling her around, still whole, as if she were a lozenge. But at any minute that cold-blooded animal's mouth could bite down and shatter her. All I could do was wait and see what it decided to do to her—to all of us.

I was also texting updates and reassurances to Wattie's sons. They'd heard what had happened through Redemption's phone tree. Only Wattie's iron-voiced decisiveness had kept both men from leaping willy-nilly onto planes and coming home.

"I don't want them down here in this mess," she'd said. "Especially Stephen. He was born chock-full of bite, and he's got plenty of bark to go along with it. Trust me."

I hadn't trusted her before, and look where it had brought us. I backed her up, assuring both men that Wattie had not been hurt when my rental car met the mailbox and that the bones were mostly a Birch problem.

Last and not at all least, I was texting back and forth with Batman.

Been a while. Coming back to ATL? I'd like to see you again, he'd sent.

A glance at Facebook, a text, and I already knew his name, where he lived, and that he wanted to see me. Still, it was probably too soon to say, *So I was wondering for no reason if diabetes or mental illness runs much in your family, and if you like kids, and if you're an unmitigated jackass.* I had to be more casual, more circumspect than that, but I was eighteen weeks along now. Digby was the size of a bell pepper, twisting and flexing, more real every day. Lavender had opened a window into the life of his father. I wanted to look through it.

I'd thought all day about what I should text back, but it wasn't until I had settled in the sewing room for the night that I sent my answer.

Yeah, it has been a while. You could have messaged me, though, mister.

The word "mister" softened it. Maybe even made it flirting. I hit SEND, even though this wasn't about flirting. This wasn't about me at all. It was about my kid. I needed to get a sense of who Batman was. My preg book said I could blame the fourth-month hormones for how lush my body felt, my deep-down itchy longing to be touched and soothed and rumpled, and maybe for this, too: I *wanted* to flirt.

He came back almost instantly, with flattery: *Naw, too stalkery . . . you're the famous artist.*

It was really good flattery, reminding me how much he liked my work. I was comic-book famous, which was even less famous than that old double-rainbow guy on YouTube, but I still liked him saying it. My hands had hovered over the keys, full of a thousand questions that I ought to ask, but I saw the ellipses; he was already texting again.

If I'd texted first? Shit, girl, you'd have gone to check your closet. Seen if I was in there making out with your shoes.

So he *was* funny, even when I was sober. I smiled, but damn those fourth-month hormones, smiling wasn't all I'd done. I also had a flash of memory: his full mouth moving against my instep, my ankle, the back of my knee, working its inexorable way upward to where his busy hand was already at work. Not helpful.

I had to nip the flirting in the bud. If there'd been no Digby? I would have leaned in. Maybe even hard. There was obviously a physical attraction here, and meeting at FanCon implied we shared some interests. But I was pregnant, which meant I was actually the stalker, crouching in his metaphorical closet with my secret and a long list of invasive questions. Flirting made what I was doing feel even worse, and every text I sent that left out Digby was so inherently dishonest it felt callous.

It wasn't a decision I made lightly, though. I wasn't

playing, and I didn't want to play him. This was serious business, and I did have a decision to make—one that would echo in the rest of both our lives. This man had fathered Digby, but I needed to know he was at least decent, at least kind, before I gave him the option to become a dad. Absence was a better start for a kid than ugliness. If Batman was some sort of baby-hating basement dweller with a violent temper, Digby needed me to know that.

We texted on and off over the next couple of days. I asked him question after question. Maybe my level of interest in his life, his family, his job read as flirting, but I couldn't help that.

Batman didn't come across like any obvious kind of reprobate. He was a CRNA, a type of specialized nurse who worked with anesthesia. His parents lived in Columbus, Georgia, and he had three older sisters spread across the South, all married and raising families.

He was only thirty-four. It weirded me out to think I'd graduated high school the year before he was a freshman. He was also single, and that hit me with a wave of tardy relief. At least I didn't need to add adultery to my lost night's list of crimes and misdemeanors.

He seemed overly interested in me right back, so much so that if I hadn't known better, I might have suspected him of being secret pregnant, too. He asked about my family, my church, my friends, my life. I told him bits about my Tuesday gamers, being in Birchville, the Lewy bodies, Lavender and Rachel. I didn't mention bones.

The contact snowballed. By the end of Rachel's first week in Birchville, he was texting me in between his surgeries, and I was sneaking off to answer every other minute, as phone-addicted as my teenage niece. Friday night found me tucked into a nest of blankets on the sewing-room sofa, texting with him until almost midnight. That was when he suggested meeting up for some online gaming the next evening. He played Diablo, Counter-Strike, even some old-school StarCraft with his friends from college.

I loved StarCraft, but I texted back, *My gaming comp is back home in VA.* I didn't like gaming with the Cintiq's touch pen, and the old laptop ran so slow. Also, Saturday-night StarCraft sounded too much like the über-nerd version of a date. The instant I hit SEND, I had second thoughts, though. He had a TeamSpeak server, which meant we could voice-talk over the computer while playing. That was tempting. An actual conversation, with tone and nuance, would let me know him faster. Decide faster. The longer I didn't mention the pregnancy, the worse it would be when—or if—I did.

Maybe it was too good an opportunity to turn down. I added, *My old laptop can manage online Scrabble, though. If that's not too weird?*

No such thing, he sent back. *I'm down for some Words with Friends.*

Saturday night Wattie took Birchie off at seven to begin her bedtime ritual. Rachel was sitting on Birchie's love seat with dirty hair, sad-eating carrot sticks the way a normal human would have had potato chips and watching one of those old Merchant Ivory films she and Mom both loved.

Lavender had already ghosted up to the tower room, no doubt to her own Saturday-night virtual hookup via Snapchat or whatever the kids were using now. Since I knew that Snapchat existed, my guess was thirteen-year-olds now used something else.

She was still on the outs with me. She was waiting, like Rachel Jr., for me to tell her she'd been right to contact the Batman. Or maybe I was projecting and she wasn't even avoiding me. After all, she was young, and the world outside this off-kilter house was soaked in golden summer. Hugh and Jeffrey Darian rang the doorbell every other minute to call her out into it.

I went back to my own hidey-hole in the sewing room, where I'd turned Birchie's old Singer table into a makeshift computer desk. I plugged my earbuds in and opened up Facebook and the voice-chat program. While Words with Friends was loading, I heard the robotic voice of TeamSpeak say, "A user has entered your channel."

"Hello, user," I said.

"Hello, you," he said. It was the Batman. I recognized the voice, an echo of memory from way down low in my brain. "Are you up for some one v. one? Scrabble style?"

I remembered his voice as deep, but not this deep. Maybe this was his bedtime voice, a bit scratchy, full of sleepy gravel. It made an invitation to play a board game sound a little dirty. I'd also forgotten how soft-spoken he was. In the bar I'd had to lean in to hear him, which had put us close, then closer, until I'd taken him up to my room to get as close as possible. Twice. Now I was already leaning toward the screen like a dork, as if this could help me hear him better. I sat back and turned his volume up.

"I haven't played this since I was a kid," I told him.

"Me neither," he said, but I immediately got an invite, so he clearly knew the program.

"I smell a ringer," I said, accepting. "How'd you know how to set the game up?"

"I may have . . . um, logged on early to learn how. Smooth, huh?"

"Very smooth," I said. "Especially the part where you just told me."

He laughed but didn't answer. I stared at my letters in a silence that felt more awkward the longer it went on. I'd drawn bad tiles: B F F D R Y N. No vowels, unless I wanted to count that wishy-washy Y. Luckily, he had to play the opening word. Maybe he was quiet because he had bad tiles, too. Still he'd been easier to "talk" to when we hadn't actually been talking.

PHONE appeared in the center of the board, a word long enough to get him to the double-word square. As soon as it was played, he said, "So when are you going to come back through Atlanta?"

Pretty bold. Maybe the awkwardness was all on my side?

Well, I knew things he didn't know.

"Why do you care?" I said, and it came out coy. Maybe even saucy. God, I hoped not saucy. Saucy was like flirting plus.

"You were the best first date I'd had in years," he answered, so straightforward that it paused my breath.

"Oh, that was a date?" I said at last. I could hear I'd overcorrected on the saucy factor. Now I sounded prim and fusty.

"Maybe not at the start. It sure . . . ended like one."

So soft. I turned his volume up again, trying to stop the feeling that he was whispering into my ear.

"My first dates don't end like that," I said, even more prim.

"Well, come back to Atlanta. I'd like to see how you end second ones." *So* damn flirty.

"God, you talk like such a player," I told him.

"Not at all! G-g-g—" He was so surprised he got stuck on the *G*. He paused, then said, "Mm, see? Taking to pretty women makes me nervous."

"Nice save, feminist," I told him, and he laughed, unquelled by my starch.

"I like it when you talk to me like you're a . . . schoolmarm." That made me grin. I'd forgotten this, too, the odd cadence of his conversation. He took pauses in midsentence, as if waiting for the exact right word to come, and most of the time it was not the word I'd been expecting.

I looked at my tiles, and every word that I could make seemed dirty. I didn't want to lay down BODY, much less BOFF. BROOD was out of the freaking question. "Brood," as a word, was even more pregnant than I was. I finally played BENDY, and the second I hit the PLAY button, I realized "bendy" sounded sexy, too.

"You didn't strike me as the nervous type at Fan-Con," I said, to cover my embarrassment.

"Well, you know. I'd had a couple beers, and I never th— I didn't come up to you to make a move. I only wanted a picture for my Facebook feed."

I said, "You understand that's exactly what a player would say?"

He chuckled, pausing to play the word YOUNG off my Y, then said, "Is it? Well, full—revelation. I've had three serious girlfriends. And one was in high school, so I don't think she counts. I'm not mmm . . ." He hummed to a stop for a second. Then he said, "You're really easy to talk to." It was sweet, and maybe even true. I swallowed, awkward again, and busied myself laying tiles. He seemed to feel it, because he instantly lightened the mood. "Did you just bingo? Now who's the ringer?"

I laughed, because I had, playing OFFERING down to his G, and it was on a double-word square to boot. "Suck on that!"

"Oh, girl, you're gonna smoke me!" he said, but cheerful about it. I liked it that he didn't have that boring, e-peen gamer thing about losing to a woman.

By the second game, though, our board looked like it was being played by third-graders with small vocabs and no regard for strategy. We took huge pauses between turns, then set down easy things like BATCH and MEAT and RANK and CAT. Placing tiles was only a way to keep our hands busy while we talked and talked and talked.

I liked how he spoke about his family. They sounded like a close-knit bunch. He was especially tight with his father, whom he described as an "old-school nerd," and his middle sister, Vonda, who had beaten breast cancer last year. They gathered every Christmas, and all spent their summer vacations together at a rented beach house in Savannah. It was after 1:00 A.M. before my pregnant body started signaling that it was going to sleep, very soon, whether I wanted to or not.

"Yeah. I'm tired, too," he told me. A pause, and then he said, quiet, "I gotta work Monday. I can't be up late before a day full of surgery. I'm off Thursday. You want to mmm . . . return Wednesday night and . . . word-Zerg me again?"

This was more than flirting. I recognized it in the pauses and the sudden husky shyness in his voice. He was inviting me into something.

I hesitated, guilt nibbling at my sleepy edges. I was under no illusions that I knew him. Not well. Not at all. All I knew was that I liked his spit-polished, second-date self, enough to say that if I weren't pregnant, I would have been way up for a third. I wasn't ready to invite him into Digby's life based on a fun evening. Still, the more time I spent with him, the nicer he seemed and the worse I felt.

"I think you'll probably need your ass kicked again by then," I said, trying to keep it light, and let him go.

That night I dreamed the bones. They rested, patient, in a sharp-edged metal box in a sterile lab, bathed in light as hard and yellow as an egg yolk. They knew that their time was coming. A pair of gloved hands turned and sorted them, rearranging them into the shape of the person they had once been. The hands recreated the intricate fan of the phalanges, placed the long shins, the pelvis, a cage of ribs containing nothing.

Last of all they placed the skull. I saw the telltale fissure, cracked and gaping, set high on its domed back. The hands began to pick up the bones, cracking them in two. They were long hands, I realized, with preternaturally long fingers. Jagged nails split open the glove tips, poking out, shiny with deep purple lacquer. The hands lifted the rib bones from the tray, out of my sight. I could still hear, though. The sound of Violence, chewing and snapping, guzzling at the marrow, woke me up.

My subconscious mind was clearly not as fervent in its faith that the bones were ancient history, a sad story too old to matter.

It was already after nine. I got up, creaky and sour-mouthed, and went to check on Birchie. Every step out of my private nest in the sewing room brought me farther into the part of the house that felt so very off.

I found her sitting at her formal dining-room table, eating her egg and watching her town wake up through the big bay window, as if this were any given Sunday. On the wall behind her, her grandfather beamed with lofty benevolence from his portrait to her right, while her father's portrait on her left was much the same. Maybe a little sterner, a little prouder. I hurried around the table to drop a protective kiss onto her fluffy white bun. She smelled like her rose-scented powder and mint, as always. It was the smell of home, of love and goodness.

"Morning, Birchie," I said. Lavender was right beside her, not looking at all kissable. She gave me the stink-eye from my own chair. "Hey, Lav. You sleep okay?"

"Mmm-hmm," she said. She was dressed up awfully pretty, in lip gloss and her peacock-blue swing dress.

"Morning, sugar," Birchie said, reaching up to pat my cheek.

Birchie's face was powdered, and her hair was primped. She didn't look like a person who was seriously ill. Much less like a person who'd kept human bones tucked away in the back of her attic. It heartened me to see her so put together. She looked more fully herself than I had seen her since I arrived and found her planting orange candies in the pansy bed. In fact, she looked company-ready, as if she were about to engage in one of her usual lady-type activities: a baby shower, a book club, a lecture about horticulture. . . .

I looked from her nice dress to Lavender's with dawning horror.

"Are we going to church?"

"Is it Sunday," Birchie said, not at all in the form of a question.

"Frank said we should lie low and not answer any questions." I didn't even want them asked. Birchie and her Lewy bodies might say anything.

Excepting for Lavender, we'd spent the week indoors or working in the back garden. We could pretend that we weren't hiding—the kitchen had been so loaded up with curious-neighbor casseroles and salads that we hadn't needed to so much as hit the Piggly Wiggly—but I knew we were avoiding both the pity pats of worried friends and the accusing stares of the less friendly. And the questions. Questions I was trying hard not to ask silently inside myself. I didn't want them coming at me from other mouths this morning, ringing up toward God under His holy rafters.

"Oh, come on, Aunt Leia!" Lavender chimed in. Everyone looked at her, and she put on her pious face. "I don't like missing church."

"That's a good baby," Birchie said, giving her arm an approving pat. I rolled my eyes, under no illusions that Lavender had recognized an abiding need for corporate worship in herself. Church was where the boys were. Birchie went on, "Remember the Sabbath and keep it holy. The Ten Commandments don't change, no matter how poorly your own week is going."

I had to clamp my lips together to keep from asking, *What about that sixth one? Did you break that sixth one, Birchie?* Half the people at church were probably asking the same question of the other half right now. My hands were getting sweaty.

Wattie came in with her own egg and a basket heaped full of biscuits that she set down on the table. Lavender was already reaching. Wattie sat and helped herself to her own homemade blackberry jam. She was in a church dress, too, field daisies and spring green leaves.

"Do you think we should go to church?" I appealed to Wattie.

"Doesn't matter what I think," Wattie said, which wasn't the same as saying that she thought it was a good idea.

"We didn't go to Redemption last week," I said.

"That was my church," Wattie said, setting me straight.

"And you didn't think Birchie should go!" I argued.

Wattie fixed me with an exasperated look. "Child, I did not think I should go."

I was instantly ashamed. I was thinking only of what the people at the white Baptist church would be saying about my grandmother. Wattie, the widow of Redemption's longtime, most beloved pastor, was that church's Birchie. And she had stolen a car and wrecked it while attempting to abscond with human bones found in the attic of the very house she lived in. Her oldest, dearest friend's house. Of course her church community was reeling.

Birchville still lived mostly segregated, especially in the churches. There were parallel versions of Baptists and Methodists and a small, all-white Presby church balanced by an equally tiny AME congregation. The streets and neighborhoods were divided up, too. I lived in Birchie's version of the town when I was visiting, just like Wattie's children lived in hers. I knew this intellectually, but it was easy to forget. These worlds seldom overlapped. The greatest overlap was here, right inside this house, where the matriarchs of both Birchvilles lived together. I was growing another kind of overlap inside me. If Digby were already born, we would have to be back-and-forth members at two churches, as Birchie and Wattie were. Or we'd have to choose a church where one of us belonged less than the other.

"I'm sorry, Wattie, that was thoughtless," I said. "But I think that going over there is downright crazy."

Wattie shrugged. "Well, it's not what I might do, but this is Birchie's church. Birchie's decision."

"Morning, Leia," Rachel said from behind me, startling me. In her pencil skirt and striped blouse, she looked as church-ready as the rest of them. I was the only one who'd somehow missed the rally call. Her hair was limp and oily, though, and her eyes had a Valium glaze. This wasn't the full Rachel. This was the depression-drowsing version that had been on the sofa all week, now stuffed into kitten heels and propped upright, with just enough energy left to be kind of a bitch to me.

"You're going, too?"

"It's the least I can do," she said, so tremble-voiced brave that I felt a sour trickle of vinegar cut into my blood, thinning it.

"We don't want to walk in late," Wattie said, sweeping her eyes pointedly from my hair, tufting up in cowlicks, down to my bare feet.

I made myself step away from Rachel, saying, "I'll be ready."

Birchie and Wattie briefly shone their approval beams on me. I snatched a couple of biscuits out of the basket as I turned to go.

Rachel said, "You know those are a mass of simple carbs."

I wheeled back in a surge of Rachel rage so clear and blue and bright that I was about to make my breakfast protein-rich by means of biting her whole head off. But she wasn't even looking at me. She sat slumped with her own biscuit untouched in front of her. Her phone was beside her on the table, waiting for a deciding text from JJ that was never going to come.

Across the table Lavender was staring at her mother with fear and a heartbreaking kind of pleading in her eyes. In that look I could almost hear the lost and piping voice of three-year-old Lavender, calling from her dark bedroom, *Mumma, halp! Dere a munstras in my closet.*

Lav's phone buzzed, and instantly the scared child with MIA Ken and Walking-Dead Barbie for parents was gone. Instead there was a disaffected teen, sneak-checking texts from boys under the breakfast table. A teen whose father still hadn't called me back, though I'd left him three more messages, each meaner and more insistent than the last.

It was one thing to decide that I was going to help

Lav, but another to figure out how to actually do it. Rachel-style commando assistance—armed, invasive, and permission-free—was an art form, but it was not my medium. Watching Lav sneak-text, I had a new idea.

"Hey, kid," I said. "No phones at the breakfast table." I held my hand out.

She looked up, startled and busted.

"You know better," Rachel said mildly.

Lavender rolled her eyes and passed the phone to me across the table.

"Come and get it after breakfast," I said.

"Let's make it after lunch," Rachel was saying as I hurried away.

I got the phone back to my room, fast. It would lock itself up in a minute or two, and I didn't know Lav's passcode. Jake hadn't taken my calls, but he might well take one from this number. I closed my door and sat down on the sofa.

It took me a sec to find him, because I went looking in the J's out of habit. In Lav's world Jake's number was stored up in the D's. I touched that word, "Daddy," and saw that my hands were trembling. It wasn't a word that had ever been lucky for me.

He answered, though. And fast, picking up on the second ring.

"Lav?" he said, his voice breathy and grainy.

"Guess again," I said.

"Jesus Christ!"

"Strike two," I said, downright bitchy.

It was mean, but for the first time since Jake had cut me out of his life like I was a tumor, I had the option to be mean to him. When he'd reappeared at my family's drop-in Christmas party, thrusting wine at me as he sauntered by to charm my stepsister, I'd been knocked for such a loop. I'd avoided him that evening, then fled back to art school in Savannah. Rachel was courting distance from Norfolk at U Richmond, but I'd been sure that it would come to nothing. He wasn't good enough for Rachel, and my stepsister had a rigorous belief that she deserved the best. I hoped she'd see past the new money and the newer nose. When they got engaged, I'd taken refuge in good manners, hyperpolite and horrified. Once he'd fathered my niece, I was committed to that politeness. But now? I had cosmic permission to tear him a new one, and I had a lot of mean saved up.

"Why do you have my daughter's phone? Is she with you?" Jake asked.

"You don't know? Jesus Christ back at you, JJ," I said, incredulous. "Why haven't you called her?"

A pause.

"Rachel told me not to." Maybe even he heard how pathetic that sounded, because he was talking again before I could answer, defensive. "Anyway, I did go by the house. No one was home. Is Lavender hurt?"

"Of course she is, you douche. All her limbs are still attached, if that's what you mean, but her dad's gone missing," I said. "Every day you spend hiding, that hurt gets deeper and less repairable."

He made a huffing noise. "It's complicated."

I huffed back. "Let me simplify it for you: Call your kid. If you need permission, I am giving you permission. If you need some testicles, I can't help with that, because it sounds like you let Rachel pack them up and bring them with her down to Birchville. Beg, borrow, or steal, but get a set. Get one, and call your kid. Today. This afternoon. She'll have her phone back after lunch."

"They're both with you in Alabama?" Jake asked. "Are they okay?"

"No. No, they are not. When your most important person ditches you, it feels like he pulled the world out from under your feet and took it with him. It feels like a long, fast fall, and there is no soft landing," I said, and I wasn't speaking only for Lav now. I was talking on my own behalf as well, finally defending the kid I'd been back when we were Lay and JJ and everything we did, we did together. Back when he'd screwed me and screwed me over. "It can ruin a kid. Ask me how I know."

"Are you making this about you?" he asked, trying for incredulous. Trying for disdain, but I could hear a hitch in his breathing.

"Me? No. And it's not about Lavender or Rachel either. This is about you. This is big-picture stuff," I told him. "How many times can you do this, JJ? Do you think you have nine lives in you, like a cat? Keep on and you'll have to change nursing homes when you're ninety because you screwed over your roommate. Every time you mess up, you stick the people who love you the most with the consequences. Try apologizing. Try making it right. I know firsthand exactly how shitty it feels when you cut and run because you can't face whatever awful thing you did. I paid for what you did. Every guy I've dated since has paid for what you did, and I was only your best friend. This is your wife. This is your own child. If you do this to your child, Oregon is not going to be far enough to let you get away from yourself. Japan won't be far enough. Mars won't be. You will have to go all the way to hell to get far enough, and if you don't call your kid now, if you abandon her without a word like she is nothing, then you deserve to stay there."

He was definitely crying now, but he didn't speak. I didn't either. I had nothing left to say.

I closed the connection, my hands downright shaking. I'd said words to JJ that I'd had rotting in my mouth for twenty years. I felt oddly fresh, almost minty, clean in the wake of saying all those words. I'd wanted to ask him to promise me that he would contact Lavender, but I hadn't. His promises didn't mean jack, and his tears didn't either. He might be feeling sorry for JJ, weeping for poor Jake, and not for Lavender at all. He would call or he wouldn't. I couldn't control that. But God, it had felt so good to speak the truth at last, biting into him and chewing like a rattlesnake until my venom sacs were spent and empty.

I wanted to savor it, but a glance at the clock told me I had about six minutes before Birchie and Wattie would be walking out the door. I ran a brush across my tufty bed head and pulled on my voluminous Digby-hiding skirt again. At this point I was pretty much living in this skirt, my sweatpants, and pajamas. I rested my hands on my belly and took three deep breaths to slow my heartbeat. With so much happening, my emotions were a pinwheel, paper light and spun by any wind. Once inside the walls of First Baptist, I could not lose my temper or speak my mind.

I sent a little prayer up toward heaven as I hurried down the hall. Birchie was not herself, and she was walking into the lion's den of a riled-up small-town Baptist church. I would not let her go without me. Not when she was the one who had riled it.

12

We headed across the road in a tight battle formation. Me and Lavender first, each of us eager
to lead the way for our own reasons. Then Wattie and
Birchie in their hats and floral dresses and low-heeled
shoes, the elderly-southern-lady version of the Armor
of the Lord. Rachel, solemn and silent, brought up our
rear.

Our bad luck, Martina Mack was standing outside
by the door into the sanctuary in her own floral dress,
passing out the bulletin. Behind her was the familiar
redbrick building with its tall white steeple reaching
up into the bright morning sky. When she saw us,
her bug-eyed face flashed surprise and then a fervent,
ugly joy. She wiped both expressions away so quickly I
wasn't sure anyone else saw. We kept right on coming,

and Martina thrust her stack of bulletins at her hench-crone, Gayle Beckworth, who was passing them out on the other side of the doorway. Martina came forward across the wide front porch to meet us at the top of the stairs.

The Grangers and the Lesters were heading inside, but they paused when they saw Martina step to meet us. I could see the Fincher family, walking to church from all the way across the square. Jerry Fincher was the youngest deacon, and his wife had her fingers second-knuckle-deep in every church pie. When they saw us, Polly Fincher picked up her toddler and thrust him into her husband's arms. Then she sped up so much her baby's stroller jounced up onto the curb.

Lavender, oblivious to matriarch nuance, trit-trotted up fast, then squirted around Martina and headed in-side, looking for her friends. I stayed in front, the last line of defense between Birchie and Martina. The three of us climbed slowly, in deference to Wattie's knees. As I reached the top, Martina Mack's scrawny neck lengthened, and she straightened her spine, look-ing over my shoulder at Birchie.

"I'm so happy you came," Martina Mack said, and she wasn't lying. She smiled a smile so chilling I almost saw Violence in it, a hunger running deep enough to qualify as cannibalistic.

"Happy to be here," I said, even though she wasn't talking to me.

She spoke to Birchie as if Birchie were alone. More than alone. As if Birchie were a lamb staked out on a hillside.

"Did you know I think my grandson's going to take a little trip to . . . Charleston?" She said it like Dr. Evil, but the question itself was so innocuous I blinked, surprised. I'm sure I looked confused. Charleston? What fresh hell was this?

"How nice. It's lovely beach weather," Birchie said, pleasantly enough. Wattie's wide-set eyes narrowed.

Martina pitched her voice loud to say, "Cody won't have time to hit the beach, I wouldn't think. He'll be visiting all of those historic graveyards."

My jaw tensed up at the mention of graveyards. This was something to do with the bones, then? But the Birches' time in Charleston was ancient history. Martina Mack was ancient history in human terms, well into her eighties, but she was not Civil War old. If the bones dated back to Charleston, that ought to be good news for us.

Nothing in Martina's sharky smile, so broad that the sun gleamed overbright off the uniform row of her dentures, said she had good news for us. Sally Gentry and the whole Boyd family came spilling back out of the church to see what was happening. Behind us I heard more people climbing the stairs. Martina was playing to a growing audience. A baby started crying, and I glanced back. It was Polly Fincher's. He hadn't liked the jouncing, so she'd had to stop her sprint toward this weird drama in order to soothe him. The Gentrys and the Cobbs were on their way up, too. No Frank Darian anywhere.

"Stomping all over cemeteries sounds like a misery in this heat. But we each have our own odd pleasures," Birchie said. She was so herself this morning.

"Speaking of the heat, my grandmother shouldn't be standing out here in it," I said.

I stepped forward, but it only brought me closer to Martina Mack. She held her ground, smelling of thin, sour sweat and boiled egg under baby powder. We were now uncomfortably close, but she wasn't moving. Birchie and Wattie had stepped forward when I did, crowding me into the middle of a furious-old-lady sandwich. I sidestepped, and now Birchie and Wattie were facing her directly.

There was a breathless feel of waiting in the folks crowding around us. Whatever damning gossip Martina Mack had learned or invented about the bones, she had already shared it. I could tell, because the gazes of the townspeople had changed since last week, when they brought us all those cakes and casseroles, curious and concerned. Now some looked speculative, some wore an odd, hurt brand of confused, and a few were downright bristling with hostility. I pulled my phone out and shot a quick text to Frank Darian: *What does Martina Mack know that we don't?*

Martina said, "Cody's sure to find your father's grave. Isn't he? He could do a gravestone rubbing for you. I always did think it was odd, burying your father over in Charleston. When you got on that train, we all thought you meant to bring his body home. You've never visited Charleston again, not once, not in all the years I've known you, so it might be nice for you to have a rubbing of his stone." Martina Mack's voice was rich with fake musing.

Small hairs on the back of my neck stirred as she spoke. Was she saying the bones belonged to Birchie's father? She couldn't know that, but if it was purely invented, it was quite a leap. Had Cody told her something?

Lisbeth and Jack Barley had come outside now, too, bypassing Gayle Beckworth, who watched with avid eyes, clutching her double stack of bulletins. More families were arriving, climbing the stairs, craning in to listen, even though Martina wasn't really offering fresh information.

All of Birchville knew that Ellis Birch had died of a heart attack in Charleston, knew how Birchie went away to save the Birch family fortune and buried him there. When she came home, she immediately married a man who Ellis had never thought was good enough. The younger members had heard the story. The older ones had witnessed it. But oh, how Martina's insinuating tone changed the story! In the context of the old, dry bones, these old, dry facts grew flesh and blood. And teeth.

Martina was still talking. "He'll definitely want to pay his respects. See that *legendary* gravestone for himself. Where exactly in Charleston did you say it was that your father was buried?"

I could feel the eyes on us, waiting for Birchie's answer. Most of the congregation seemed hungry more than hostile, waiting for Birchie to deny, explain, defend. The longer she stood silent, the more doubting and anxious and unfriendly that communal gaze became.

Behind Wattie, Rachel was doing her best poker face, or maybe she was actually not paying attention. If only Rachel would snap out of her lethargy for fifteen seconds. She was so excellent at Church-Lady Bitch Fights. She didn't know Birchville history, the long-standing feuds and friendships so tightly woven that they made up the very fabric of small-town life, but she was socially adept enough to come in swinging anyway.

She caught my drowning look and threw back a help-less little shrug. I wouldn't have thought that Rachel's shoulders knew how to do that.

"Good grief—Mrs. Mack, is it? Your Cody is a mor-bid fellow," Rachel said. Her height let her peer over Birchie's shoulder. "Gravestone rubbings? That sounds like the world's worst Pinterest board."

It was weak, but at least Rachel still had a pulse.

"Are you going to give us a bulletin?" I snapped at Gayle Beckworth. "Birchie needs to go sit down."

I'd broken into a thin, slick sweat myself, and it wasn't only from being held captive in the early-summer sun. If Birchie had come here to take the town's tem-perature, then she was sure getting her answer. It was hot, and getting hotter. She'd let Martina's accusation stand unchallenged, and now it was growing Southern Baptist–hellfire hot.

"But why didn't you bring his body home?" Mar-tina asked so very loudly. "You Birches are like our very own First Family here," and she couldn't help let-ting a little Mack bitterness be present in those words. I wanted to step in harder, but I was scared. I had no idea how reliable her information was.

If the bones belonged to Ellis Birch, then had Birchie . . . ? My mind balked, unwilling to go down that road. But I needed to say something. I was genuinely scared of what the Lewy bodies might have Birchie do if Martina kept pushing. I risked a glance at my grandmother and saw that her nostrils had flared delicately. Stress made Birchie worse, and oh, but this was stressful. Around us I could hear people whispering in a wind of breathy words.

Martina stepped in closer still, cleared her throat, and said, "Your daddy is the only Birch not in your family crypt right here in Birchville."

Wattie had Birchie's arm, and I could see her hand tightening, both a reminder of her presence and a warning. Birchie gave Wattie's hand a reassuring pat and smiled her sweetest.

"I am a Birch," my grandmother said, loud as Martina but in a brave, clear tone. "I am a Birch, and I am not inside that crypt."

She didn't say, *Not yet.*

She didn't have to say it to remind everyone that she was sick. More than sick. Dying. And here was known jackass Martina Mack making her stand out on the stairs with the summer sun already beating down upon her head.

"Let her in!" said Mrs. Partridge, stern, but no one else spoke.

"Come on," Wattie said, soft in Birchie's ear.

Wattie moved them forward in tandem. Martina

backstepped in a little skip that defied her age, and Wattie had to stop again. It was either stop or push a small, old, vicious lady backward onto her ass.

"Don't you dare herd me," said Martina Mack to Wattie in a tone she never would have dared to use on Birchie. Her cold amphibian eyes scraped over Wattie, the way a stick scraped at gum stuck to a shoe. "Don't you herd me on the steps of my own church!"

"This is her church as well," Birchie said. "Every other week."

But it wasn't. I could feel it wasn't. Especially not today. I could feel the ripple of movement and negation that ran through the crowd.

"Oh, Miss Wattie, your poor knees! Come inside and sit down. Miss Birchie, you need to get out of this sun!" Polly Fincher said, shoving her way through to us, breathless. She had abandoned both her kids with her husband and come charging up the stairs from the other side. She shot a withering glance at Martina Mack and added, "Aren't you supposed to be handing out the bulletins?"

Cody Mack appeared in the doorway beside Gayle. He was stuffed into a shiny, turd-brown suit instead of his uniform. He stared at us from just inside the narthex, and then he came joggling forward, pushing his way through people, saying, "Gran! Gran!"

He took Martina's arm and pulled her away, practically shooing her on into the sanctuary ahead of us. She went, eyes downcast. He was overflustered, and I realized I ought to be grateful that Martina Mack was such a vicious old crow of a lady.

The cops had found some evidence or gotten some information from the forensic anthropologist that let them draw a line between the bones and Ellis Birch. We weren't supposed to know this, but Cody hadn't been able to keep his mouth shut, and now Martina had tipped their hand.

Gayle held out a bulletin toward us, two of her fingers pinching the corner, as if she were passing rancid meat to a pack of foul animals.

Birchie fixed her with a gimlet eye and said, "Thank you, dear."

We passed into the narthex. Today the red walls seemed so garish, bordello bright, and the long teakwood tables by the entries had a green cast to them, almost venomous, and I couldn't stop asking myself, was it true?

Birchie had insisted that I already knew who was in that trunk.

I told you the first night you were here, she had said. *I told you at dinner.*

I hadn't had a clue what she was talking about, not

then. But now? Martina Mack's insinuations were causing connections. My first night, over the Cornish game hens and the ripe tomato salad, I had asked if Birchie wanted me to take down Ellis's portrait.

You think it would be that easy to take my father out of this house? Birchie had asked me. *You could burn that portrait, but he would still be present.*

Sweet God, had she meant it? Literally? If that was Ellis Birch inside the trunk, then she'd been very right; getting him out had taken all three of the male Darians, a stolen car, and the police. I was shaking my head in an inadvertent no.

Polly Fincher was practically dragging us through the narthex toward the sanctuary now. People we'd known for years milled and morphed in a herd, some trying to get away from us, some trying to get closer to look at us. It was like slogging through upset human mud.

I got my phone out and sent Frank a quick text: *Where are you? The cops think the bones are Ellis Birch. It's very bad.*

"We were all so sorry to hear that you are ill," Polly said to Birchie, loud, glaring around.

As we entered the sanctuary, Pastor Rick came gangling and tutting up the aisle, his long white hands flapping about like flustered birds.

"Oh, well, here we all are, then! Hello! Hello,

Miss Birchie. Polly is right, we are all so sad to hear of your troubles. Your illness troubles, I mean. All your troubles. Oh, look! A visitor. Who is your pretty friend?" he asked, turning to me. "Has to be your sister, yes? Clearly little Lavender's mother?" As if town gossip had not told him a week ago that Rachel was here, at most fifteen seconds after her car pulled in to the drive. He turned to Birchie. "May I walk you to your pew?"

She was now surrounded by friendly faces, Wattie on one side, Polly on the other. I was with Rachel, staunchly holding down the rear. Pastor Rick stepped right, as if he planned to replace Wattie.

"She's in good hands, thank you, Pastor," Wattie said in a quelling tone.

We all froze in tableau, Pastor Rick still angled toward Birchie, hands out for her arm, as if he expected Wattie to step aside for him. That was never going to happen. Wattie cast her eyes to heaven, as if asking Jesus to take a sec to see this nonsense. Birchie stared the pastor down, perfectly willing to wait for the trumpet blast and the first of the Apocalypse's seven horses to come thundering over the hills before she'd ever displace Wattie for this pool noodle of a preacher.

Six endless, awkward seconds ticked by, and then Pastor Rick started walking backward, gesturing them forward with exaggerated hula-girl arm swoops. "This way, ladies! This way!"

I snuck a quick peek at my phone. Frank had sent me a text back: *I'm on it. Meet me in the balcony?*

"Go with them," I whispered to Rachel. She nodded, and I turned back. There were stairs up to the balcony on both sides of the narthex. I hurried back down the aisle to the doors, turned left, and there was Cody Mack. I almost banged into him. I didn't say excuse me. Neither did he.

I glared up at him, wishing I were taller, and said, "You keep your grandmother away from Birchie, you hear me?" I wasn't playing to an audience. I kept my voice low but spoke as meanly as I could.

"Don't mind Gran," he said, but he didn't sound apologetic.

"You're only supposed to talk to us through Frank. Birchie isn't herself, and what your grandmother did? That was low, and the courts could easily see it as you trying to back-door an interrogation."

I made it into a threat. I didn't think Cody had sent Martina—I thought Martina's big fat mouth had actually done us a favor. But I wanted to make damn sure that Cody kept her viciousness at bay from here on out.

He said, "Birchie owes us answers, but I guess it must be right nice for her to be so rich."

"Doesn't suck," I said with snarky cheer.

I didn't get defensive, because it was true. Someone else's poor and unprotected granny, sick or not, would have had to answer for herself to the police by now. My grandmother was a Birch in Birchville. She was the Reigning Birch. Watching his dart roll off me made him shift like he was itchy, and he couldn't leave it. He leaned in, so close I could smell soured coffee and old bacon on his breath.

"Rich or no, the law takes patterside right serious."

It took me a full second to realize that Cody Mack meant patricide, and then I had to stifle a trill of purely hysterical laughter.

It was a big leap from *Is this Ellis Birch?* to *Murder!* Except I couldn't help but remember the deep fissure marring the crown of the old skull. Couldn't escape Hugh Darian's logic: Unmurdered bodies don't get stuffed in trunks. Martina had had a lot to work with when she'd set out to turn our town against us.

I shook my head. Still, they couldn't know that the bones belonged to Ellis Birch. Not this fast. They had to be guessing, and they could be wrong.

But in my head I could hear Birchie saying, *You think it would be that easy to take my father out of this house? You could burn that portrait, but he would still be present.*

Cody smiled an ugly smile at my gigged silence, his upper lip peeling back from his teeth like a smug donkey's. "Maybe you should bring her down to the station. Get ahead of this. Let her tell the tru—" he began, but right then the old organ started the first chords of "Blessed Assurance."

It startled both of us. The ten-o'clock church bells had yet to chime. Pastor Rick must have kick-started the service. Cody turned tail and all but sprinted toward the sanctuary.

I let him go, relieved, and headed just as fast into the left-side stairwell. No one but the youth group ever sat up in the loft, and when I was a kid, we had lined up along the right side. I got up to the balcony, and sure enough, the teenagers were sitting across from me. It was a smaller group these days. Birchville skewed a little more elderly every year, but there were still a couple-dozen teens, sitting with Lavender tucked into the thick of them. Frank wasn't there yet.

I'm on the left side, I texted Frank, and walked to the front pew.

I looked down, seeking Birchie from this unfamiliar angle. My eye found Wattie first, a lone fleck of deep brown in a pinky-pale sea. Rachel was on Birchie's other side. I used my bird's-eye view to try to get a better read on how the congregation was reacting—to

Birchie and her illness, to the bones, and to Martina Mack's thinly veiled accusations.

The congregation had rearranged itself, throwing the church into an odd imbalance. Only on wedding days did families leave their traditional pews to align themselves by their affiliation to the bride or groom. Now every jackass present had rowed up over on the groom's side, behind the Macks. A few staunch families stayed with us on the left, and most of the old families who usually sat in the center had moved to join them: the Alstons, the Gentrys, Frank Darian's sister and her kids. The bulk of the congregation had moved to the middle, crowding up, undecided, shifting uncomfortably in their new, wrong pews.

I had thought that Birchie's illness would buy her more slack, but she'd kept the Lewy bodies secret, and she had ruined two marriages and cost the church an underpastor. Plus, I would have bet cash money that Martina Mack had been dripping poison about the bones into every ear she could find. Birchie, on the other hand, had hidden up on her hill, inside her big white house. Our silence looked like an admission. The town's unhappiness with our family had risen every minute that Birchie stayed inside and offered up no explanation.

Blessed assurance, Jesus is mine! Oh, what a fore-

taste of glory divine! the choir sang, swaying in their long blue robes.

I saw why Cody Mack had turned tail and run away from me. He had the opening prayer and so was seated up on the stage in one of the three chairs backed against the choir loft, right beside the pastor. The associate pastor's chair was empty, of course, and Jeannie Anne was not present either.

Heir of salvation, purchase of God, born of His Spirit, washed in His blood, the choir sang, and half of them faltered on that last word. I wished to heaven that Pastor Rick had had the foresight to choose hymns with no mention of body parts. If they sang "Days of Elijah" next, we'd have a riot when they hit the line about the dry bones.

Pastor Rick was nearly through a sermon that I hadn't heard a word of when Frank Darian finally appeared, slipping into the pew beside me.

"Sorry. I've been on the phone," he said into my ear. "I have a friend in the prosecutor's office who owes me, so I called him. It's not good."

"Tell me," I said, eyes forward on Pastor Rick. Birchie was right. He was a very sweaty preacher.

"Regina Tackrey got the preliminary report from the forensic anthropologist. He says the bones are more than fifty years old. But not much more." My heart sank. Ellis had died about sixty years back. That was bad enough, but Frank wasn't finished. "It's a male, Caucasian, left-handed. The left leg was once broken in three places—"

"Which all points to Ellis Birch," I said.

"Points pretty firmly, especially the leg," Frank confirmed. "They have a theory, now they have to prove it."

"Shit," I said, right there in church. "How do they do that?"

"Tackrey's going to ask for a DNA test. Birchie and the bones."

Pastor Rick had finished, and now the congregation stood up for the closing hymn. Only about half of them were singing, so that the harmonies were odd and off, the voices coming unevenly from all the wrong places in the room:

My hope is built on nothing less
Than Jesus' love and righteousness;
I dare not trust the sweetest frame,
But wholly lean on Jesus' name. . . .

"Here's the worst part," Frank whispered. "The damage to the skull. If this is Ellis Birch . . . well, the anthropologist says he got his head bashed in with something like a ball-peen hammer. From behind."

On Christ the solid rock I stand;
All other ground is sinking sand. . . .

I shook my head against this ugly information. I could not imagine Birchie with a hammer and some bad intentions. Or even with a hammer. A wooden spoon, a tiny garden spade, a pan of toffee cookies, sure. A hammer? I'd never seen Birchie so much as bang a nail to hang a picture. She had old-fashioned ideas about what men and women ought to do around the house. She called Frank for things like that.

"Can they do that? Make her take a DNA test?"

Frank dipped his head in a small affirmative. "I think so. The preliminary report gives Tackrey probable cause, Leia. I'll fight it, but yeah. I think she'll get her motion."

All other ground is sinking sand. . . .

I looked down at Birchie. She stood close to Wattie, their heads bent over a shared hymnal. They knew all these words, of course. Even if they hadn't, the lyrics were projected onto the big screens hanging on either side of the baptismal pool. Still, there they stood, sloping shoulder against sloping shoulder, round hip against round hip, looking at the book as if the screens did not exist. At the sight of Birchie's soft white bun tilting in toward Wattie's silvery halo of curls, a feeling came over me in a wave, so fierce I barely recognized it.

It was love, though. Love, or some other, nameless feeling that was sister to it. I was racked with it. It thundered through me, shook my frame. In that moment I didn't care whose bones were in the trunk, what hand had held what hammer years ago. It didn't matter.

This, I thought. *This is how supervillains start.*

Because in that moment I was looking down on the thing I loved and being told that it was standing squarely in the wrong. Had Birchie and a ball-peen hammer set this ugly story into motion? I did not care. And if this town turned? If this town came after my grandmother? I would eat it. I would eat it up alive.

13

I put Birchie to bed that night. I had an almost primal need to care for her body, the dear and failing case that held my grandmother.

It had been a long and stressful day. In spite of her nap, her supper conversation was mostly non sequiturs, but Wattie said we couldn't let her go to bed early. The break in the routine would hurt her more than being so damn tired would.

Wattie and I walked her back to her room exactly as the clock chimed seven.

She stopped dead at her door and put an urgent hand onto my arm. "They're going to eat the zinnias!"

"It's okay," I told her. "We'll plant more zinnias."

"They'll just make more bad rabbits!" she said, her fingers digging into me.

"Do you want to hear crickets or the ocean?" Wattie asked.

Birchie cocked her head, listening to something I could not hear. Her fingers relaxed. "Crickets."

"She always chooses crickets," Wattie confided as we went on in. "Making a room sound like it's filled plumb up with bugs would not put me to sleep, I tell you that much. But she likes those crickets."

Birchie's room was a riot of early-summer colors. Her love of the Victorian had fuller rein here than anywhere else in the house, from the sage-green wallpaper with its rampant, flowered vine, to the rich prints on the chairs, to the tufted velvet bench at the foot of the bed. I walked her to her panel bed with its tall, carved headboard. Scrolled dressers in matching cherrywood on either side served as bedside tables. Birchie still called the one by the window "Floyd's dresser," though she'd been widowed now for more than half a century.

While Wattie went to the vanity to set up the noise machine, I helped Birchie lower herself to the edge of the bed. Then I knelt before her, sliding her shoes off her feet. She hadn't put on stockings. Twenty years ago, or ten, if I had suggested she go without her stockings, even here in the middle of June, even wearing this dress that came down to midcalf, she would have asked me if we'd gone to sleep in Alabama and woken up in Babylon.

Her bare feet looked younger than the rest of her. She and Wattie went to Pinky Fingers on the square every Friday and got their feet and hands done. Her heels were buffed smooth, and this week she'd chosen a light coral polish.

Wattie moved to the window, drawing the heavy damask drapes against the lingering summer sun. Now almost all the light came from the soft-light bulb on Birchie's bedside lamp. She sank down into the chair beside the window with a sigh that told me exactly how tired she was, and from there she talked me through Birchie's bedtime routine.

First I rubbed Birchie's feet and calves and hands with her rose petal–scented lotion. I took her bun down, putting her hairpins in the glass bowl on the dresser, and I brushed her long hair. It gleamed moon-colored in the lamplight. The pink of her scalp shone through the thin strands as I braided it for sleeping, letting it hang in a slender tail over one shoulder.

When that was done, Birchie stood and put her hands up like a toddler so I could lift her dress over her head. She wore an old-fashioned full slip, with lace at the top and bottom. I peeled that off her, too. It was so strange to see my grandmother in her large, plain bra and the kind of panties named for her. I was wearing granny panties myself these days, baggy, all cotton, and baby blue in honor of Digby. Birchie's were seashell pink. I unhooked her bra and helped her out of it.

Birchie looked like a dumpling in her dresses, small and smooth and rounded. Naked, she was made of folds and creases. Her breasts sat low on her chest, deflated, streaked with stretch marks. Her soft lady belly hung down inside her drawers. Her thighs looked like a baby's thighs, creased and folded, but sadder somehow. The scallops of her legs were not bursting with that good, new milk fat. They were mostly skin, creped and hanging.

I felt such a well of tenderness for this dear old body. Every piece of it proclaimed how tired it was, but it was lovely, too. Her history was written in it, in the stretch marks left by my father, in the surgery scar on her abdomen and the puckered burn scar on the inside of her left arm, in the simple toll of ninety years of fighting gravity. Inside me Digby spun, and my Birchie stood near naked before me, yawning like a child.

She held her arms up again, and I lifted her long, rose-sprigged nightie over her head. Then I took her to use the bathroom, to remove and clean her bridges, and to take her nighttime medication. It was already sorted into a little cup by the sink, and two more pills had joined the ones I knew. There was a yellow-and-orange capsule, garish as a candy corn, and a little blue pill that looked like a bead.

"She didn't have a baby aspirin," I told Wattie as we made our slow way back to the bed.

"She takes that in the morning," Wattie said, peeling the bedding down.

She'd moved the shams to the velvet bench already. I looked at her with new respect, and with apology.

"You do this every night?" I asked. She'd spent the last hour sitting in the window chair, but she still looked flat exhausted. She nodded. "Jesus, Wattie. You should have let me . . ." I trailed off. Hire someone? I'd tried that. Birchie had put a stop to it. Help? I hadn't known she needed this much help.

Wattie said, "If it was me going first, she'd do the same. Don't you doubt that."

I didn't. Wattie was a small, smooth dumpling in her own loose dress, but the artist in me could see under it. I knew there would be history written deep on her body as well. History I would never know. Birchie knew it, though. They had taken care of each other all their lives, through their girlhoods and marriages and babies and illnesses and losses and secrets.

"I need my airplane socks," Birchie said, lisping a little with her teeth out.

I looked to Wattie. "In her bedside drawer."

I opened it and found fleecy socks in a multitude of cheerful colors. None of them had airplanes on them, and Birchie called flying "so much nonsense." Neither she nor Wattie had ever once gotten on a plane, not in their whole, long lives.

"You brought her a pair like this from the airport once," Wattie said. I vaguely remembered that. "She loved them. Frank helped us order more off of the Internet."

I knelt and put the socks on, and then it was time to tuck her between her cool, clean, lemon-colored sheets. I didn't, though. I stayed kneeling, looking up at her.

Frank had told me not to ask. Maybe it was better not to know, but I was going to know soon anyway. Science was going to tell me. I'd rather hear it from this mouth I loved. Whatever truth she told me would change nothing.

"Birchie," I said. "Birchie, is it Ellis? Is it your father in that trunk?"

She looked at me, her eyes bird bright and so, so blue. One soft hand came out to pat my cheek. "Yes, honey," she said, almost like she was sorry for me.

"Leia," Wattie said, a warning bell that I ignored.

"Did you put him in there, Birchie?" I asked her.

"I surely did."

From this angle she looked like an apple-head doll, her lips sinking into her face because her bridges were out. Then she smiled at me, and it was a baby's smile, gummy and wide, sprinkled with teeth.

"Did you . . . ?" This I could not ask, but she answered anyway.

She raised her hand, her arm bent at the elbow. Her hand fisted around an imaginary handle. She brought her hand down, once, in a definitive swing.

"Lord, Lord," she said. "I'll never forget that sound. That bone noise. It was like stepping on ground seashells."

That jabbed the breath right out of me. It was so specific. It sounded true.

"But it had to be self-defense," I said with surety. In Birchville her father's name was linked to words like "hard" and "proud." *He knew his worth, and he made sure everybody else knew it, too,* Myra Rhodes would chime in when Ellis Birch was mentioned in her presence. He'd been "Mr. Birch" to every human in the town, except his daughter. To her he'd been "Daddy." Even so, he must have caused her to do it. But when I tried to say it, it came out like a question. "You didn't have a choice?"

Birchie's gaze on me didn't waver. "I had a choice. I made it," she said, but that could mean anything. That could mean she'd had a choice to live or die, or a choice to save someone in danger. I wanted it to be a choice that put her squarely in the right, but she kept on talking. "He was sitting in his chair, reading the paper. I came up behind him."

She made that gesture again, and in an awful way it reminded me of Rachel. Virginia didn't have a baseball team, so Rachel was a Braves fan. The Tomahawk Chop, she and Jake called it, when they put on their red shirts and had their sportsball friends come over.

"That's Lewy bodies talking. That's not true," I told Birchie, but I did not believe me.

Her nostrils flared, and I saw a sharpness come into her eyes. I was irritating Birchie, the real Birchie, the one who was alive in morning hours and afternoon moments and nighttime sparks like this one.

"Enough. It's too late to get all riled now," Wattie said. She held up Birchie's most recent copy of *Persuasion,* read almost to pieces. "Out you go. Let me tuck her in and do our reading."

I stood in the hall for I don't know how long, crying into my hands and listening through the door to electric crickets and the deep, sweet voice of Wattie reading aloud. I wept because my great-grandfather's bones had been upstairs in a trunk for my whole life, and because my Birchie had put them there. Now she was so frail and folded, brain-sick and as innocent as a baby. I pictured her small hand with its short, coral-colored nails and pale blue veins. I could not imagine those lined, powder-dry fingers wrapped around a hammer.

She didn't even own a hammer. But that chopping motion had been so definitive. She had once swung a hammer at a person. At her own father, and when I'd told Lavender that we Birches had bad luck with fathers, oh, what an understatement that had been.

Ellis Birch had been proud, but also the town's bene-factor. Had he secretly been awful? Even if he had, I knew a lot of awful people. If being awful were reason enough, there would be ball-peen hammers sticking out of the brainpan of every other person walking. The way I'd felt about Cody Mack today, I might have put his in myself. It was one thing to let Violence eat up paper people, but in real life? Dear old ladies didn't kill their daddies and tuck the bodies away up in their attics.

Except my dear old lady had.

I stood hitching and snotting into my scarf until I was flat wept out. Then I stood waiting, hollow and dry inside, because all the truth and all the weeping in the world would not change my decision. That roaring wash of love I'd felt, standing in the balcony at church, it was still in me. It was more powerful than truth or tears.

I'd always thought of myself as lawful good, but I

wasn't going to do the right thing here. I wasn't even certain what the right thing was, but I wasn't going to do it. Instead I would use every weapon in my arsenal to protect my Birchie. Pity, public opinion, her standing in the town, her money. I would use it all.

If Birchie had been younger, and wholly in her right mind, it might have been a harder decision. But this thing she'd done, years and years ago, it was too late to ask her to pay for it now. The law might not set a statute of limitations on murder, but Justice had missed its window. I set my white hat on a high hall shelf, trading it for a gray one and a long dark cloak. This time Justice had to eat the bill.

Damp-faced but decided, I waited for Wattie, listening through the door as she read about Anne Elliot, with her lost Captain Wentworth and her lost bloom.

Wattie came out at last. She was half asleep on her feet, but she took one look at me and said, "Come on, Sorrow. You need hot tea."

I should have let her go to bed, but I couldn't.

"We both could use hot tea, I think," I said, following her toward the kitchen.

She snorted. "Forget that, honey. After today? I need bourbon."

That surprised me. Birchie was a Baptist, but she was a rich, white Baptist, which meant she drank sherry at will and champagne at Christmas and kept a bottle of Blanton's as medicine for shock and head colds. Wattie, a minister's wife, rarely touched the stuff.

The downstairs was deserted. Rachel and Lavender must already have gone up to their rooms. I got out mugs and honey and the box of Sleepytime tea bags, and Wattie put the kettle on. We didn't talk again until we were settled side by side in the kitchen nook, holding our steaming cups. Wattie had put a generous slug of the Blanton's into hers. We both took a sip, and she winced at the taste, reaching for the honey bear. She didn't seem inclined to speak even then.

I said, "I want to know why."

She looked surprised. "I can't tell you that."

"Can't or won't?" I asked.

She shrugged, stirring honey into her toddy, and then she set her spoon down and spread her hands, showing me her pale, creased palms, as if to prove that they were empty of answers.

"You have to have an idea. A guess. Something."

"I could make a thousand guesses, but only Birchie and Jesus know for sure and certain what was in her head, what was in her heart, when she went creeping up on her daddy with that hammer."

I shuddered at the image, but I soldiered on. "Did Floyd know why, do you think?"

Wattie turned her lips down. "Lord no. That sweet man! He never even knew that chest was in the attic. Not any more than you did."

"How can you be sure?" I asked.

Wattie looked at me over the rim of her mug like she was sizing me up. She took another slug of doctored tea and answered.

"That first summer they were married? There was a smell in the house. Very faint, you understand, because we had packed that trunk real nice. Lined it with plastic, put in lime. But still, sometimes, through the vents, a little smell would come. That July, Floyd went under the house four times, trying to find whatever possum or skunk had died down there," Wattie said. She took a large, solemn swallow of her tea. "He didn't know."

My brain had caught on one word: "we."

I asked, "So were you there when she . . . when it happened? Did you see?"

That was not the real question. I was asking how many little old ladies in this house had committed premeditated murder, and she knew it.

"No, baby. It was done when I got here. A bit of time had passed, too. He was cool as icebox pie. I'll never forget the feel of his skin when we went to shift him. Like waxed leather. He was on the rug on top of his crumpled newspaper. His port glass was on the side table, so it had happened after dinner. She only called me because she couldn't shift him on her own, and he was starting to stiffen up."

Wattie sounded so matter-of-fact, so calm and regular, but my eyes felt dry from not blinking. My mouth was dry as well, but I didn't drink my tea. My throat felt like it had forgotten how to swallow. I had to tell my lungs to breathe, because they had forgotten, too, all my body's regular business pausing in the wake of these flat words.

They were new for me, but Wattie'd had them in her for sixty years. Maybe she'd long ago come to terms with her part in it. But maybe not, because she picked up her mug and gulped it all down. From the heat of my own mug, I knew that it was still scalding hot. She powered through, even as a fine mist of sweat broke out on her forehead. She set the empty mug aside.

"Drink yours, too. You need the sugar. You're white as a haint."

"You happened to come over?" I asked, and then sipped obediently.

She shook her head. "No, no. She called me on the telephone. It was past ten, which was late to be using a party line. That time of night, a phone call meant someone was dead or something was on fire, so she knew I wouldn't be the only one to pick up on my ring. Her voice was strained, and she said something like, 'Wattie, can you come over? I need you to help me get Daddy packed.'"

I was so punchy that I snorted and choked a little on my tea.

Wattie didn't seem to get her own gruesome pun. She patted my back until I stopped coughing, and then she kept right on talking.

"She told me her daddy had some bad business troubles. Ruinous, she said. As soon as his trunk was packed, he was heading for Charleston. It was smart, you know, because it gave the town something to be talking about. The Birch fortune in jeopardy. It made sense that the next few days Birchie would be so pale and jumpy. 'Already an old maid,' people said. 'What's she going to do now, if her daddy really has lost it all?' Birch money kept this town alive in a lot of ways. And yet people can't help but ugly-like a riches-to-rags story, seems to me."

She poured another slug of bourbon directly into the dregs in the mug. Added honey. Stirred.

"When she said he had died of a heart attack in Charleston, people believed her. She was Emily Birch. Of course they believed her. It helped that he had always been a portly, red-faced fellow. Big-bellied, you know? And so proud! Kept everything bottled. Dropping dead of a heart attack sounded like exactly what he'd do. It helped that the man didn't have a single close friend in this whole world. He kept himself and Birchie separate, lording like King Poop up on his high, brown mountain." That surprised me. I'd heard Ellis Birch described as a proud man, but usually in reverent terms and tones. Wattie paused long enough to drink the thick, sweet liquid, making a face in spite of all the honey. "Off Birchie went to Charleston. Everyone thought, you know, that she would bring her daddy back, put him in the Birch family crypt, right across the street. But she didn't return. Not for weeks. She sent word that his business problems were keeping her in the city and that she'd buried him there. It didn't make perfect sense, but it made enough. There's plenty of Birches buried in Charleston.

"When she did finally come home, no one knew if she was rich or poor. It was exciting for them, like watching a moving picture. My mother went to collect her at the train station, and I went, too. Birchie had us take her right to Floyd Briggs's store. He was in there, behind his counter. Lots of people were there. More people were there that day than would fit in that store, if you listened to the stories folks told after.

"Birchie—she was still called Miss Emily then—she

walked right up to Floyd, and between us, he wasn't all that much to look at. You've seen his portrait. Gingery fellow, pale as the moon. But he had some chin, you know. Some gumption. He'd been the hardest of her suitors to run off. He had a way with words, and he used to slip her poetry in church, until her daddy caught wind and nipped it. He had a sweet, kind heart.

"She walked right in and she said, 'You wanted to marry me once.' And he said, 'I remember.' And she said, 'Daddy said you were only after our money. Was that true?' Nobody in that store was breathing. Truth be told, there were only six or seven folks, but I was one of them, so I know, and I tell you—no one breathed. He said, 'No, ma'am. That was not true.'

"Now, I knew that the Birch fortune was fine. Never had been in any danger. But Floyd surely didn't know, no more than anybody else in Birchville.

"He was a moonfaced greengrocer, and she was already stout, an old maid with lines around her eyes. But when he dropped to one knee and took her hand, right there, and he asked her in front of God and everybody? Well. They were Bogey and Bacall.

"That was all anybody talked about. It made her daddy's death second-page news. Then the town come to find out she had saved the family fortune after all. Some folks said her daddy had actually done something that saved it, right before he passed. You know, back then fellows didn't like to think about a lady doing money things. Well! That took up two Sundays' worth of jawing. Then someone had a baby, and someone's wife ran off with a vacuum salesman, and the United States put a satellite up right into space. Elvis joined the army. There were always new things to talk about. So that was that."

I tried to imagine what it must have felt like, knowing. Watching nothing happen. Birchie marrying immediately, not willing to waste a day, because any day could be the day that she was caught. But instead time passed and the hot summer did its work. There was the faint smell of a possum dead under the house, and then the smell of fall leaves, and then nothing.

Years rolled by. She'd had a baby. Buried her husband and then her son. Let decades' worth of furniture and books and boxes do the work of burying her father. By the time I was a little girl, neither of them so much as flinched when I asked if I could go and play with all the old things stuffed up in the attic.

I said, "You never asked her why?"

"I helped her when she asked me, baby, and that was all. I loved her. I still love her," Wattie said. Her full mouth twisted down in a way that telegraphed an understatement. "I never did care for him much."

Something like a laugh got out of me. A disbelieving and exhausted noise. If it hadn't been for Digby, I'd have poured the rest of the Blanton's into my mug. Maybe directly into my mouth. As it was, I sat clutching my cooling tea like it was a lifeline.

She pushed her own sticky mug away, like she was finished. Finished drinking, finished talking. She put her hands on the table, preparing to push back and go to bed. I grabbed her arm, pausing her.

"Why would you help her hide a body and not even ask why? Why would you?" In the bedroom she had told me that if their roles were reversed, if Wattie had Lewy bodies and Birchie were still hale, Birchie would care for her just the same. How did she know? What kind of love was this, a love that didn't sell itself out, no matter what? "What did she do for you?"

Wattie patted my hand, but then she stood up anyway. When I did not let go, she put her own hand on my head.

"Sweet girl. I've flat adored you since you were nothin' but a bump inside your mother, but that is not any of your business. Your grandmother and I? We have been on this earth a long, long while. We came up in a different time than you. Some nights these southern trees around here bore some strange fruit. You understand me? Now, I don't talk about that mess. Not with pretty little white girls whose foot never touched the earth until years after Dr. King got buried in it. I will only say this: Every minute of my life, your grandmother has been my good and loyal friend."

Her hand stayed on my head, like she was blessing me, and her large brown eyes were solemn and serious. I wanted to ask her a thousand questions, but she'd made it plain that I was not allowed. It was like I heard the echo of a distant door closing, so far away that the sound had had to travel years and years to come to me.

She was right. I would never know what her life had been like eighty years ago, or seventy, or fifty. Or even now. My arms went around myself involuntarily, holding a brown boy I flat adored, though he was only a bump inside me.

"Get some sleep, Wattie. You're exhausted," I said.

She chuckled. "Baby, I'm more than that. I'm nigh on drunk. For the third time in almost ninety years, Jesus forgive me. You go to bed, too, and don't fret, hear me? Things feel hard now, but it will pass. Everything passes, and something new comes along to fill the space." As she spoke, her tone shifted. She wasn't talking about me anymore. "You can't go around holding the worst thing you ever did in your hand, staring at it. You gotta cook supper, put gas in the car. You gotta plant more zinnias."

She turned away and went on up to bed.

I sat in a slump at the table for a moment. It felt like 3:00 A.M., but my watch said it wasn't even time yet for the nightly news. The whole house was quiet and still. We had all shifted to little-old-lady hours. Early supper, early bed, up with the sunrise to spend time with Birchie at her best. She needed the house quiet after eight.

I got up and went back to my sofa in the sewing room, feeling shipwrecked as I changed into my pajamas and brushed my teeth. I lay down, but I couldn't sleep. I don't know how long I lay there before the chime of a text landing in my phone roused me.

The noise reminded me that about a thousand years ago, back when I was telling myself that the bones were some kind of Civil War archaeology, I had called Jake and let him have it with both barrels. He was a known jackass, certainly, but on the other hand he hadn't murdered anyone. Not anyone I knew about.

I roused myself and reached for the phone.

It wasn't Jake, though. It was Batman. *Still up?*

I was in no shape for stalking the father of my secret baby.

I'm dealing with a family thing, I texted, which was true, but the stark words read harsh. I added, *Looking forward to Wednesday* as a softener. He sent me back a thumbs-up emoji.

I didn't put the phone away, though.

Lavender had living-father problems, and I had sworn to fix them. That was a lifetime ago, but it still mattered. I was hoping against hope that Jake had done something that resembled the right thing. At the very least, he could have sent his daughter a cute frog emoji waving a sign that said HELLO. He could have texted, *I do love you,* or maybe, *Sorry you won shit-all in Dad Lotto.*

I shook my head. Parenthood shouldn't work this way. Fathers shouldn't get to decide if they wanted to father or not, thirteen years in. Fathers who weren't dead should do their damn job. *Assuming they even know they have a kid,* I thought, but I shoved that away for later. This was about Lavender right now.

It actually felt lovely to think about Lavender's problems, to meddle hard in the forbidden lands of Rachel's troubles instead of thinking about terms like "no statute of limitations" and "premeditated." Now, thanks to Blanton's, I could add Wattie and "accessory after the fact" to my concerns.

There was no way to reconcile my long-loved Birchie with a person who could do what Violence did. See a bad man? Take him out. Remove him while he sat sipping his port and reading his newspaper. All I could do was twirl my new black mustache and protect her anyway. Jake, with his money problems and his cowardice, was altogether easier, because I was squarely in the right. I could try to fix that and not think about—

Wait. Was this what it felt like to be Rachel?

Maybe so. I was pregnant with a secret mixed-race baby, carrying on an investigative flirtation with my in-the-dark baby daddy, and I honestly had the least fucked-up life of any adult in the house. At this thought I started giggling. Once I started, I couldn't stop. This was what it felt like to be Rachel. This right here, perched in the catbird seat of least fucked up. It was not a thing I'd ever understood before. God, but it was a good seat. No wonder she didn't ever want to share it.

When I finally got myself in hand, I texted Jake another message:

Call your daughter. I will go full Bloodaxe on you if you don't. Do not doubt me, Jake. I'm capable of anything at this point.

It sounded true, because it was. Blood in my history, murder in my genes, Violence in my heart. Wattie had shared the how, but no one on earth except for Birchie knew the why.

I wondered how long we both had before the Lewy bodies took that answer, too.

14

I hadn't realized I'd been sleeping, but I had, and very hard. There was drool on the pillow. A sound had woken me. Something like a click.

The sewing room shared a wall with the kitchen. Was it morning and someone was making breakfast? It was so dark. I peered at the clock, disoriented. It was 2:04.

Then I heard footsteps pittering down the wooden stairs that led down to the backyard garden.

I sat up. Holy shit, the click had been the door. The back door shutting.

All at once I was fully awake. In my mind's eye, I could see Birchie trying to navigate those long, steep stairs with her tottery balance, imaginary rabbits winding in and out between her ankles. Less than a second later, I was kicking at the tangled quilts, trying to get up and over to the window.

Had the Lewy bodies sent her on some midnight errand? Wattie had told me that she slept restless. On very bad nights, when she was under stress, she would get up and try to go berry picking or to the state fair or, once, to her long-dead husband's funeral. Wattie was a light sleeper, and her room was right next door, so she'd always caught Birchie and gentled her back to bed. But Wattie was resting tonight in the warm and loving arms of Blanton's bourbon.

I ran to the window and peered out into the night. If it was my grandmother, I was about to show Birchville some nerdy-ass pajamas for about the thousandth time this visit, hopefully before she fell and snapped her neck.

It wasn't Birchie, though. It was Lavender.

I could see her blond hair gleaming in the bright summer moonlight. She was already down the stairs and hurrying through the back garden, wearing a lemon-colored summer dress that shone bright as her hair.

Worst ninja ever, I thought.

She had a green bottle in one hand that I hoped was Sprite, and she was carrying something puffy in a plastic grocery bag. I squinted. Was that a pillow? A big white blanket, folded into a square? Either way, not things you want to see a thirteen-year-old toting off into a dark night full of boys.

She'd failed ninja, but her femme-fatale skills were way too precocious. Sneaking out into the night to meet a boy felt like the realm of junior year, not eighth grade. Add in the fact that she was carrying bedding and a bottle? She was heading toward things I hadn't been ready to handle responsibly at thirty-freaking-eight. Digby and I could tell her exactly how this story ended.

Lavender was already disappearing around the corner of the house, but I was barefoot, robeless, and wearing enormous pink plaid pajama bottoms with a floppy black T-shirt that said KEEP CALM AND VANQUISH EVIL. I thought about levering the window open and hollering for her to get her twinkly little butt straight back inside, but I didn't want to wake up the rest of the house. Birchie's routine was sacred, and Rachel would She-Hulk out in mother horror. Lav wouldn't hear me anyway. She probably had her earbuds in, listening to Selena Gomez sing a lot about hotness and kisses and touching and very, very little about chlamydia.

I changed my pajama pants for black leggings and trusted my huge T-shirt to hide Digby and my braless state, then ran quick and quiet as I could through the house to the back door. I didn't have time to muck about finding socks and lacing my Chucks. Wattie kept a pair of electric-blue Crocs by the back door, her "garden shoes," she called them. I stuffed my feet into them and headed out after Lavender. Except for the shoes and the pale pink lettering, I was ninja-ing it up pretty good.

By the time I got down the stairs and through the back garden, Lavender was out of sight. I headed around the house to the well-lit road around the square, unworried. I knew exactly where she was heading. I trotted down the street to the Darian house at a good clip, aiming for the far side yard.

She wasn't there. Jeffrey's bedroom window was primly closed and dark, but Hugh's gaped wide open, letting out all the air conditioning. A neon-yellow fire ladder, the telescoping kind that the parents of second-story kids kept in the closet, hung all the way to the grass. Hugh had put it to unsanctioned use, shimmying down it and out into the night.

I pressed my palms to my eyes for a second, cussing myself for all kinds of stupid. Back when I was a teenager and first became acquainted with insomnia, I'd snuck out plenty to meet up with JJ. We'd take flashlights and sit up in the play fort at a nearby park, reading comics. Back then I'd pinged rocks off his window to get him to come out, because we hadn't had cell phones. Now the pings were digital, and Lavender hadn't needed to go to the Darian house to get Hugh. They'd arranged by text where to meet up. They were already heading there.

I didn't think she was in danger. Hugh was a good kid. It was only that he was a breath away from driving and ready for more than she was on the romance front. She wasn't mature enough to decide how far was far enough. Thirteen should not be out deciding this, un-supervised, with a high-school boy. It was her parents' job to make sure she wasn't, but Lav had slipped out through the gap between them.

I turned in a slow half circle, scanning the sleeping square.

Where would carless kids go on a summer night when they had a bag full of bedding and bodies full of hormones? When I was a girl, young couples met up in the historic graveyard behind the church. I started walking quickly toward it. There was a grassy dip be-tween the Alston and Rhodes crypts, sheltered and private. Something about the proximity of God made French kissing there extra forbidden. Or maybe the silent rows of old gravestones and crumbling angels watching made second base feel more delicious.

One summer, out on a restless midnight ramble, I'd stumbled onto Jeannie Anne and whatever boy she was dating then in another grassy hollow behind my own family's crypt. The one that held every local Birch who'd passed already.

A little voice at the bottom of my brain piped up to say, *Every Birch but Ellis*.

Now, there was a mental road I didn't want to go down. The bones of my great-grandfather haunted the underdepths of my mind, even as I remembered seeing Jeannie Anne on her back in dewy grass, lip-locked with a boy who had one jeans-clad leg pressed between hers. His arm had been jammed way up under her T-shirt, so he could grope at her boob. His hand had looked like a living thing, squeezing and pulsing under her shirt's thin fabric.

I'd apologized and backed away. They hadn't even heard me.

I was sixteen then. Seeing them had made my cheeks flush pink, and not just with embarrassment. I was an unkissed über-dork, awkward and shy with every boy who wasn't JJ.

That will be me one day, I'd thought, imagining myself trading tombstone kisses with a boy, each one a spitball in the eye of death. I hadn't imagined kissing JJ. Never JJ. I hadn't thought of him that way. He'd been so much more to me than a crush. I suppose that's why he'd had such power to crush me.

Now I was out in the dark side of night, race-walking

toward the cemetery gate to chase his daughter through the tombstones because he was at it again—behaving horribly and then poofing. He had not called Lavender back. If he had, he would have texted me and said so, to get me off his back, if nothing else. He'd abandoned her as if life were just as low-stakes as the movies and this summer's blockbuster were *JJ Is a Shit Part Two: Non-Return of JJ.*

At least I'd called him out on it this time. People didn't take this crap seriously enough, acting like sex was something New York advertisers had invented to sell Coke and soap. Sex was offered up like aspirin to the mildly wounded. *You just need to go get laid,* pretty folks on television and in movies told each other after breakups, or work upsets, or if anybody acted mildly grumpy. As if sex were as simple a sin as eating a second scoop of Ben & Jerry's.

In truth it was a force. It was a piece of nature, like the ocean. Living in Norfolk, I spent a good chunk of my summers at the beach with my niece, where we both treated the Atlantic like a private paddle pool. Playing in it, it was easy to forget that it was a mighty thing. It was fun, right up until somebody got sucked out and drowned by riptides or shark-eaten. Sex was the same, such pleasure I forgot its power. I acted like it was something I could own, which was laughable.

Sex had picked me up and set me back down different, twice now.

I reached the cemetery's closest gate. The cemetery itself was directly behind the church, with wrought-iron gates on either side. I glanced back at Birchie's house, right across the street. It was quiet and dark, the porch light out, and no upstairs windows shining. Neither of us had woken Birchie by sneaking out. Good.

I went inside. The moon was high and full, white-washing the crumbling tombstones and the crypts. The stones were engraved with all the old names. The first Gentrys and Grangers and Macks all had honor places here, but there'd been no room for fresh graves for a good century now. Only the five families with crypts could rest here when their time came. I paused by the gate, straining to hear rustling or whispered, breathy voices. Nothing.

I wished I'd thought to bring my own cell phone. I could have called Lavender, told her she was busted. If nothing else, I could have texted her over and over and followed the wind-chime sound of her phone. Now all I heard was an owl calling, mysterious and inquisitive.

I checked the hollow between the first two crypts, but it was empty. I crossed to the other side, fast as I could, to check between the Darian and Fincher crypts, though a rock-strewn path between them made it a bad choice. Lastly, I hurried to the Birch family crypt, the largest building, at the very back and center of the graveyard. It was faced with granite, our name across the top in tall, stern letters. The iron door was locked, and stone angels guarded it on either side. I went behind it and found nothing but the other gate. It opened onto the park, behind the gazebo. I peered out between the rails, and the park was empty, too. The town's shops and restaurants were all closed at this time of night.

Hugh and Lav weren't here. They were getting farther away from me with every passing minute. Had the make-out spot changed?

I spun slowly, listening, racking my brain for an idea of where to go next. Out of the corner of my eye, I caught a flash of movement, all the way across the cemetery, just outside the larger wrought-iron gate. By the time I turned to look, it was gone, leaving me with the impression that a person, or the shadow of a person, had crossed past it in a swirl.

I wasn't scared, not here in my hometown. I didn't think of ghosts either, though I was surrounded by the dead. No, strangely, the word that came into my head was "Batman."

But that was crazy. Birchville was hardly Gotham, and Batman was a fiction. As for my Batman, what possible business did he have here? Our relationship, as far as he knew, consisted of a drunken hookup at a con, some texts, and a datelike night of Words with Friends. If he were here, then he actually had descended way down deep into creepy stalker territory. He didn't seem like the type.

I couldn't shake the feeling, though. The shape I'd seen pass by the gate was tall and dark and definitely male. With ears. Little pointy ears, sticking up from the top of his head.

It had to have been the moonlight playing shadow tricks on my eyes. It must have been Hugh, or a dog, or nothing. I started back toward the other gate to see.

Just then, from the opposite direction, I heard a breathy little shriek, high-pitched and full of laughter. I barely caught it, but it was Lavender. She sounded far away, off the square entirely, the sound carrying on the clear summer air.

Whatever dog or imaginary Batman I had seen would have to wait. I let myself out and ran through the park, going toward Pine Street as fast as I could, near silent in Wattie's rubbery shoes. Pine ended in a T intersection at Oak Street, and I paused there, out of breath, listening for kid sounds. I thought I heard something to my left. Surely they were not heading toward the highway?

These were residential streets, and there was no

traffic at this hour. The houses off the square were smaller and boxier. This neighborhood was mostly tidy brick ranch homes that had been added to Birchville in the forties.

I heard nothing, so I said a quick prayer and sped left, running over to Cypress Street. At the next corner, I stopped, hands on knees, head down, trying to get my breath back and listening. Still nothing. Either they were being quiet or I'd picked wrong and was moving away from them. Where could kids go to get a little horizontal in this neighborhood?

There was no place for that sort of nonsense here. If they went down to Loblolly, they'd be one block off the highway, by a gas station. Had they come out for Snickers bars and Slurpees? I shook my head. Hugh would know that that place closed at midnight.

Everything else, for blocks, was only houses. Who lived here?

That was the right question. In a flash I knew exactly where the kids were heading. I knew what was in the bag, too, and I'd been worried about all the wrong things.

I took off again at a fast trot. The kids would be on Crepe Myrtle, but I didn't want to go all the way around the block. I looked for a backyard with no fence and no doghouse and then cut across.

I pushed through a stand of azaleas, and then I was in Martina Mack's backyard. It wasn't fully fenced, but she had a dog run off the back door, and there was a stake with a chain here, too.

I heard Lavender say something, then Hugh's shushing noise, then stifled giggles. I hoped they wouldn't wake Martina's dogs up. She had three or four of them, medium-size browns and brindles with square heads and small eyes. Together they could bark the dead awake.

As I rounded the corner of the house, I saw them. No Jeffrey. I had half hoped he'd gone through Hugh's room to use the same ladder, but it was only the two of them. I paused, surveying the yard. I'd been a scant few minutes behind them the whole way, but they'd made a lot of progress.

Hugh looked to me like a professional. As I watched, he released a roll of Charmin, holding the end. It sailed up in a perfect arc, streaming a long white tail as it unfurled, soaring straight over a branch of the tall loblolly pine in the center of Martina Mack's front yard. That whole tree was already well swathed, a crisscross pattern running through the branches, bright white and blazing in the moonlight. The fat gardenia bush beside the mailbox had been swaddled, its white blooms mostly covered so that it looked like a single outsize toilet-paper rose.

The grocery bag lay open on the balding grass, and they'd already deployed at least half the rolls in the giant pack of TP.

"Perfect!" Lavender whisper-talked, admiring Hugh's toss.

Lav was clearly new to rolling. She threw hers too hard, and the toilet paper broke, the roll thudding and bouncing away across the grass. She bounded after it, lithe as a fawn, her limbs going so suddenly graceful in her leap that it made my heart swell.

They were giddy with pleasure at their own boldness, rolling the house in response to Martina Mack's horrific baiting of Birchie at the church. As revenge plots went, it was both too mild—given the chance to hurl Martina Mack into the Sarlacc to be digested for a thousand years, I would have been sorely tempted—but also too much. It was wrong to roll the yards of little old ladies, even vicious ones. Especially Martina, who was house-proud. Her tidy nana house had country heart cutouts on the shutters, and she kept her flower beds as beautiful as Birchie's.

I had to nip this in the bud, but damn, they were having so much fun. Watching them gambol and romp in their astounding innocence, it made me happy, too. I needed a little innocence tonight.

I stepped up onto the low brick porch, sheltered from the moonlight in the shadows of the roof and wall, arms crossed to cover my shirt's light pink letters. In my all-black outfit, I was invisible inside the darkness, so I gave them another minute. I would make them come back in the morning and apologize and clean it up. But right now I let them have the glory of watching the high arcs of paper unfurl, the stifled laughter, the simple pleasure.

Movement caught the corner of my eye. Beside me the screen door swung stealthily open. The dogs were silent, which could only mean that someone had told them to be silent.

Martina Mack stepped out in a voluminous flowered nightie, knee length, with a matching summer house-coat hanging open over it. Her skinny calves stuck out like leathery twigs beneath the hem, disappearing into huge puffy slippers. Her hair hung around her shoul-ders in iron-gray witch scraggles. She moved slow and crafty, and the kids, intent on wreaking their small havoc, did not see her any more than they saw me.

Her front lip pulled up like an angry donkey's, and I saw that she'd taken the time to put her teeth in. She must have been up and seen them from the very start.

I was about to speak to her, assure her that we would reverse this process, when I saw what she had cradled in her arms.

I was so shocked to see that double-barreled shotgun that my voice caught in my throat. She raised it, too, flesh hanging down in wrinkled dewlaps from her bare arms. She brought it up to bear in a smooth arc. Not at the sky. Not at the ground. Martina Mack raised the silver barrel, and in her mottled hands the shotgun's arc of wide aim was pointed right at the children.

15

It wasn't the heat. It was the humidity—so dense I felt that I'd been suspended in a liquid. Birchville had become Atlantis, and I was launching myself through air gone thick and salted toward that gun. I was so slow. I floated like Digby, every move blunted, rendered harmless as a flutter. The barrel swung up through the gelled air, and it moved slow as well, in a long, endless arc. The steel gleamed cold in the moonlight. The gun was almost all I could see, my vision pinholed to its shine.

I felt my hands on it, and the metal felt so cold it burned me, like it was iron and I was half fairy. It bucked once in my grasp like an animal, and the roaring boom, when it came, was louder than planets crashing. In the ear-ringing, awful wake of it, in the stink of smoke and chemicals, I couldn't tell if I'd been in time.

I had to actually look, look with my watering eyes, to see that the barrel was pointing up, as if Martina Mack and I had conspired to pepper that fat, smug moon with buckshot, right in his pale face.

Then the air was only boiling summer air again. I shivered in it, drenched in my own panicked sweat. The kids were already sprinting away in two directions. Hugh's T-shirt glowed as white as the tail of a deer in full retreat. They had abandoned the grocery bag, spilling its remaining rolls of Charmin onto the grass. Did Lav know I was here? Or had she just seen a dark shadow moving to block Martina Mack's scraggly head? Catwoman versus Swamp Hag.

The gun's unearthly boom was still ringing in my ears, but now, from very far away, I heard dogs going crazy. Martina did not have three or four. I'd been wrong. She had at least a thousand, all hellhounds judging by the rising noise. They were deep in the throes of whole-body barking, near hysterical with joy or fury, who could tell? The raucous chorus got louder as my ears cleared, and I could see the dogs pushing and jostling in my peripheral vision. The screen door had clicked closed behind Martina, or I might have been swarmed by them.

Martina Mack snarled, her pearly dentures gleaming uniform and square, and yanked at her gun with her veiny claws. She was a thousand years old, though, and I was so swamped with adrenaline that I had superstrength. I yanked back, the force of my pull ripping it right from her hands. She cried out, an outraged squawk under the dog noise.

"Are you insane?" I yelled into her face, and my voice sounded far away because of the noise of that shotgun in my ears and the ceaseless clamor of the hysterical dogs. "Are you fucking crazy?"

This woman who had just shot at children blanched at the profanity, then launched one of her own. "Those li'l shits was trespassers! I had every right!"

"To shoot? To shoot at kids? Was your own life in danger from the Charmin double rolls, Martina?"

I had a white-knuckle grip on her stupid, stupid gun, and I was screaming over all the noise, screaming so hard the words hurt my throat. I took a step back, trying to calm down.

She turned to the screen door and shrieked, "You dogs! Shut it!" The barking stopped. Stopped flat. "Sit your butts!" and they promptly sat. I could see them watching us through the screen. There were only three after all, which seemed impossible, given the huge racket they'd been making.

We glared at each other, Martina Mack and I, so upset that our chests heaved in tandem.

"Give me back my gun," she said.

"Why?" I snapped. "I don't see any babies to shoot. You want to go find Bambi?"

She held her hands out, adamant. "Give it."

I cracked the shotgun open and removed the remaining shell. It was strangely light in my hand. I held the gun out to her, unloaded.

Martina snatched it, saying, "What kind of a grown woman brings a gang of teenagers out into the night to torment a old woman!"

I was so gobsmacked by this that my jaw unhinged. "You think I brought them here to roll your house?"

"Looks like," she said.

"I didn't bring those kids! I heard Lavender sneaking out, so of course I came looking for her so I could shoot her with a gun. Oh, no, wait. Actually, I didn't, because *that's insane*. I came out to find her and take them home." It wasn't completely true, though, was it? I had paused and watched, charmed, for a long, complicit minute. I added a true thing that made me feel better. "Once I saw what they were up to, I had every intention of making them come apologize to you in the morning. I still do. They will be along right after breakfast to clean this up—assuming you can agree not to bury land mines all over your yard to blow their feet off."

She cradled the gun to her chest, her face sour with disbelief. She really thought I'd formed a team of teenage vigilantes to roll her yard.

"Martina?" called a quavery voice from off the left. It was her equally elderly neighbor, Mrs. Teasedale. She was a Methodist, but I knew her to speak to. "Are you okay? Should I call the police?" She said "police" with a long o, the emphasis landing on the first syllable.

"We're fine, Fanny! Go on back inside!" Martina hollered at her.

"What's all that white stuff in your yard?" Fanny Teasedale called.

"We're fine!" Martina said, a vicious shriek this time, and Mrs. Teasedale retreated.

Probably to call the PO-lice, if another neighbor hadn't beaten her to it. Whichever officer was on duty was probably heading in this direction. *Please, Jesus in heaven, let it not be Cody.* "You better clean it up right now your damn self, or I will have you arrested."

I leaned in toward her, uncomfortably close. "Do it. I can't wait to tell the judge how you got up out of bed and took the time to put your teeth in. How you hushed your dogs first, so the barking wouldn't scare the kids off. How big and high the moon was and how both of those dumb-ass kids were wearing summer colors. You saw them, you saw exactly who it was, and you knew what they were doing. You weren't feeling in danger, not a bit, and you weren't aiming at the sky to scare them off either. I saw you. You meant them harm. So please, get your grandson to arrest me, and best of luck with that. I'll use my phone call on the chief, tell him what you did, and you and I can sit out the morning in the cell together. Dibs on the cot."

She cocked her hip at me like Lavender in a snit might, an insolent, easing-back gesture.

"My gun is only loaded up with ice-cream salt," she said, sulky. "I keep it to run off cats and possums."

Ice-cream salt? No wonder the shell felt so light. Even so, I could not calm down. My brain chemicals had hit Digby now, and he was awake inside me, going off like teeny Pop Rocks. I took a deep breath, trying to get my heart rate down.

"Oh, well, if you were only going to shred their skins open and salt-burn them. Maybe put a kid's eye out," I said, dripping sarcasm and venom in equal parts.

"Yes, I meant to burn their vandalizing hides a little. So what? Teach them a good lesson, but that's all. We Macks? We don't kill people." That one hit, and she saw it in my face. Her front lip lifted again, baring those fake white teeth in a sneer. That face she made—it was so familiar that I blinked hard, twice, and stepped back. She followed me, pressing her advantage. "Guess that little jail cell is going to get right crowded, once your granny joins us."

"No one is going to send Birchie to prison," I said, but I had a faint tremor in my voice, and we both heard it. "She's ninety years old. She has a terminal disease."

Martina shrugged, insolent, and reared that donkey lip up again. God, I knew that look! Why was she so smug? Her threat to call the cops had rolled right off me, but she was acting as smug as the moon.

"Maybe so, maybe so. She's rich enough to buy her way past fifty murders, I reckon. But Cody says anyone who helped her cover up? Why, they might as well of done the deed themselves. That's the law."

I felt my cheeks flush, and I said, "Wattie didn't have anything to do with it," before I could stop myself. I should have pretended I had no idea who she was referencing. It sounded defensive and, worse, untrue.

"Course she did. Everybody knows," Martina Mack said, so certain of herself that it sounded offhand. "Train a nigger right, they can be as loyal as them dogs in there." She jerked her thumb at the screen door, her eyes avid on my face, watching to see how her words would land. They hit my heated skin like a slap. I clenched my fist around the unspent shell, feeling the salt shift and crackle in the plastic casing. My other hand went to Digby, as if these ugly words could burn the buds of his ears, twist his little stomach.

Cody really needed to stop confiding in his granny. She could not keep her ugly mouth shut. So they were going to come at Birchie using Wattie, and I should not have needed Martina Mack to unload her ugly words into the summer air to have known this. I should've guessed at Sunday services, in the speaking silence after Birchie claimed that First Baptist was Wattie's church, too. When I watched the pastor trying to take Miss Wattie's place at Birchie's side. When Cody blocked me in the narthex with this same ugly-donkey braying mouth, and that was why Martina's smug face looked so damn familiar.

I'd seen that look on Cody's face before, years ago, when I was a seventh-grader at First Baptist's Summer Youth Lock-In. Thirty-some-odd kids, ranging from sixth grade to seniors, eating microwave s'mores and singing "Blue Skies and Rainbows," playing hide-and-seek all over the building and then gathering for a midnight prayer circle. By 2:00 A.M. most of the kids were sleeping, girls in the youth room, boys in the prayer chapel. I was still awake and roaming, looking for a quiet spot to curl up with *The Dark Knight Returns*.

I ran across Cody Mack, chaperoneless in the kitchen

with three of the other high-school boys. He was doing what looked to me like a magic trick. He had a shallow soup bowl full of water set out on the linoleum counter that ran in between the kitchen proper and the fellowship hall.

"So this here is the swimming hole," he said, not quite a whisper, and something in his tone told me there was naughtiness afoot.

It felt much like last year's lock-in, when he'd snuck in a single Fuzzy Navel wine cooler. Every kid still awake at 3:00 A.M. had shared it. A precocious insomniac, I was the only sixth-grader left standing. As the lowest on the food chain, I got the bottle last, when there was barely a quarter inch of room-temp orange liquid remaining. For years I'd thought that alcohol tasted mostly like human spit. But it had felt brave and naughty-good to be included, so instead of crossing through, I came over to the counter to watch.

Cody'd fetched a set of salt and pepper shakers from the stove, and he upended the salt over the bowl.

"See here? Lookit, here's all the white kids, swimming in the Coosa River. Pretty happy, right?" At once I felt the muscles in my belly going tight. I knew what he'd say a full shocked second before he lifted up the pepper shaker, dumped some in, and said, "But then all the little nigger kids show up."

I'd heard that word before, of course. I'd heard it at school. I'd heard a loud man say it at the Dillard's in Montgomery this very week. But not inside the walls of Birchie's own church. It made me hot-faced to hear it, always, but inside these walls? It felt much worse. Earlier that day Wattie had come over and spent her afternoon teaching me how to make fudge for this lock-in. We'd made three batches, and she'd cut them into fat squares. Hearing one of the same mouths that had eaten her good fudge saying this word, it made my stomach drop like I'd just tipped over on a roller coaster.

"Don't say that," said a high, unhappy voice, and it was mine.

Cody Mack ignored me. Well, almost. "So here's the white kids swimming with all these little *niggers* now, *nigging* up their nice white swimming hole." He did not address me directly, but the repetitions were aimed at me.

One of the boys, James Beecham, said, "I don't . . . I . . ." But his voice was quavery and soft, and Cody Mack grabbed a bottle of Dawn dish detergent and talked over him.

"Uh-oh, look! Here comes the KKK!" He blopped some Dawn into the water, and instantly the floating bits of pepper shifted in a chemical reaction, moving faster than displacement called for, zooming to the edge of the bowl. The salt sat mostly placid at the bottom.

Cody Mack and the other boys snorted and laughed, except James Beecham, who looked as green as I felt. I hated to make eye contact with him, because I knew, we both knew, that we should have done more, said more, stopped him. But James was a skinny worm of a kid with bad skin. I was a Birch, but I was only here in the summer. These were high-school sophomores who played JV baseball and who didn't care what girls said, especially not flat-chested, dorky, middle-school ones. We neither of us spoke again. Our shared silence made it hard to meet his gaze.

I met Cody's instead and saw a look on his face that was being echoed, twenty-five years later, on his granny's. That donkey lip, rising in entitlement. Cody acted like he owned First Baptist, a building that my family had raised to celebrate a faith that called for love and mercy. That word and all the history behind it gave him power, though. His sneering mouth, smeared with Wattie's fudge, had been glad to say that word in front of me, especially, just as Martina liked saying it to me now.

In this frozen moment, Birchville split in two around me. No, more than that. It wasn't Birchville only. I saw there was a second South.

My whole life I'd only seen one. I loved my South, though I could see how it was broken, plagued still with the legacies of slavery and war and segregation. History and a thousand unseen walls divided up the territory, so that we had a black Baptist church and a white one, and the narrow aisle between the color-coded lunch tables at the high school was invisibly a chasm filled with dragons. Still, I always thought my homeland was a single place. I was wrong.

The South was like that optical-illusion drawing of the duck that is at the same time a rabbit. I'd always see the duck first, his round eye cheery and his bill seeming to smile. But if I shifted my gaze, the duck's bill morphed into flattened, worried ears. The cheery eye, reversed, held fear, and I could see only a solemn rabbit. The Souths were like that drawing. Both existed themselves, but they were so merged that I could shift from one and find myself inside the other without moving.

The South I'd been born into was all sweet tea and decency and Jesus, and it was a real, true place. I had grown up inside it, because my family lived there. Wattie's family owned real estate there, too. The Second South was always present, though, and in it decency was a thin, green cover over the rancid soil of our dark history. They were both always present, both truly present in every square inch, in every space, in both Baptist churches, at both tables. Martina Mack had moved me from my South into hers, and yet we stood on the same ground.

The Macks were born and raised inside the Second South, and they lived there all their lives, as if there were no other. Their gaze never shifted. They never saw the duck, or if they started to, they closed their eyes or lied about it. And me? I did not want to see that ruined, bad rabbit.

I dropped the shotgun shell because I needed both hands pressed protectively against my belly now. In the middle of this endless, moon-drenched night, I had stepped into the Second South and seen that my South was a luxury I did not know I had. I could pass through this second one on and off all day and rarely feel the difference.

For the first time, I understood that I was pregnant with a boy who would always know. Right now, se-creted inside me, my son was protected by the lining of my own white hide. I could drift along, seeing only the South's best version of itself if I so chose. But once my son was out, brown-skinned and himself? He wouldn't have that choice.

I had known I would not want to raise this boy in Birchville, but I had not understood why. Not in this deep-down angry way that made my chin come up and kindled a righteous mother fury in my belly.

The Second South was coming after Wattie, too. Wattie who was welcomed at First Baptist by some folks, loved and valued. But there were pews, a lot of them, whose bases were planted in the second one. They tolerated Wattie as an appendage attached to Birchie. The people in those pews could never quite remember that Wattie wasn't—had never been—Birchie's employee. If they could shift us, draw all eyes to the place where Wattie was nothing but that word, they could take her down. Wattie could be lost.

Only I knew exactly how deep Wattie's complicity had been sixty years ago, but everybody knew that she helped Birchie move the trunk. She had stolen my rental car and wrecked it trying to protect Birchie. Birchie was the one most in the wrong, but Wattie was vulnerable in ways Birchie had never been, that I would never be, and it was this injustice that shook me.

"Come after her, then, you racist trash," I said now, and tilted my chin up to match Martina's insolent angle. I thought of Wattie's vehement insistence that her sons and their families not come back to Birchville now, juxtaposed with Martina Mack, het up enough to aim a salt-loaded shotgun at well-to-do white children. What would she aim at quick-tempered Stephen if he came to his mother's defense? What would Cody do, with a badge to back his gun? Wattie had seen where this was headed long before I had, and she'd decided to keep her family out of the line of fire. She was placing her frail, soft body between her sixty-something, grown-ass sons and trouble. Motherhood, it seemed, was a lifelong gig, and I felt my heart swell to bursting pride at her valor. She'd meant to face the Second South alone, but now I'd been unblinded. "She'll take you down. We all will. And don't you dare think we'll fight alongside Wattie because we own some piece of her. She isn't ours. She's us."

I stalked away past the loblolly pine tree, hung with a hundred white crisscross banners that shone pale in the moonlight. I was savagely glad to leave the house marked and marred behind me in this way, if only until morning. The Mack family had left crosses of their own in yards, years back. I turned by the tree, stepping into its shadow with my outsize black shirt swirling around me.

She called after me, "You better make them kids come clean this up! You hear me! You better!"

And I would, too. I'd come down and watch them do it and ask Birchie and Wattie to come as well. The town needed to see us making the kids do what was right. I needed every human from my South to stand behind us. Maybe they would. After all, Wattie was beloved at Redemption, and at First Baptist only twenty or so people had moved to sit behind Martina Mack.

On the other hand, the seats behind my family had not exactly filled to bursting. I'd been heartened to see that some of the younger members of the church, led by Jim and Polly Fincher, had moved into the Partridges' regular pew, right behind ours. The dear old Partridges themselves had simply moved back a row and stayed. We had at least five more families than Martina Mack. Still, most of the congregation had packed itself uncomfortably into the center seats, uncertain. Undecided.

I felt my shoulders squaring. I wasn't twelve years old anymore. I was a Birch in Birchville. My brown-skinned son would be a Birch in Birchville, too, yet he would be nothing but that ugly word to trash like Cody Mack. He could not live in the town as I knew it. He would not live in the South or even America as I knew it. I hadn't truly understood how deep and old and dangerous this was, until tonight.

We couldn't hide up in our house and wait for them to choose. This was a war. An old, old war that had started before I was born and would likely not be finished in my lifetime, but I had to fight it. I was going to have to learn to fight it.

16

I stomped toward home so deep in thought that I
almost jumped out of my skin when Lavender materialized out of Martina's darkened side yard.

"You took her down hard! You are such a badass,"
she told me, grabbing my hand. She'd circled back and
heard the fight then. Good.

"Don't say 'ass,'" I chided, which wasn't very Cool
Aunt of me, but I was firmly on the mother side of the
pond right now. I was mothered up, mothered out,
enmothered in such fierce, protective rage on Digby's
behalf. My son was growing bigger and thumpier every
day. He would be born, and I was seeing with fresh
eyes the world he would be born into. "And also, do
not ever, you hear me, sneak out in the middle of the
night to meet a boy. You should be home already, not

hanging out in the wee hours of the night listening to me shriek like a harpy at a little old lady. You are going to be so grounded."

She shrugged, unconcerned, swinging our hands between us. "Totes worth it."

I shook my head. Well, maybe to thirteen it was. Hugh was very, very cute. I took a cleansing breath, feeling a bit better with my niece's hand in mine. I secretly loved that she had called me a badass, loved that she was on my side. More than that, she was on Digby's side. I hoped hard that her whole generation would be like her.

"Do people still say totes?" I asked.

"Oh, sure. But just, like, ironically," she told me. "Do me and Hugh really have to go back and fix her yard up?"

"Absolutely," I said, and speaking of ironic, I was engaging in some next-level irony right now, wasn't I?

I'd decided to protect Birchie, even though she'd done the worst thing that a human being could do. She'd taken a life. I was firmly on Wattie's side, too, and Wattie had helped her hide the body. But would I let my equally beloved niece get away with some petty vandalism against roaring jackasses? Apparently not.

Lavender blew a raspberry. "She deserved it, though."

"Oh, totes," I said, very California, and she laughed. "I'll help you clean up."

We were at the end of Pine Street now, where it bumped into the square. We turned and headed down the pavement on the side with the old houses. The streetlights were on the other side, by the square itself, but I thought for this conversation we could use a little shadow.

As we passed the Darian house, I paused to check the side yard, to be sure the other budding felon had made it home safely. The ladder was gone, and Hugh's window was closed. I took these as good signs.

Lavender, looking up at the dark window, said, "He wanted to wait with me. I told him I'd be safe with you, and you might kill him."

"I might still, but not for rolling Martina's house. That boy is too old for you," I said. I was calmer, and I thought Digby had calmed, too. He spun in a slow pinwheel at my center.

"It's not like that," she said. "We're just friends."

"It's actually a lot like that, or you would have invited Jeffrey along on your midnight ramble," I said. I shot her some side-eye, but she said nothing. It was a very telling silence. "Be his friend in the living room with your mom right upstairs and me in the kitchen. Be friends at Cupcake Heaven with Jeffrey there, too.

Don't be friends alone at two A.M. You aren't ready for that kind of nighttime friend."

"Okay," she said, too flip and immediate for me to believe for one red second that she meant it. But when she spoke again, she was serious. "It's just that Hugh gets it, you know? I swear we aren't all flirty or talking gushy crap. We talk about, like, our lives. Real stuff. My dad and his mom. Jeffrey gets too upset. He doesn't want to talk about it, but me and Hugh, we do want to."

This was supposed to reassure me, but it didn't. She was too young to know yet that their conversations about the things that mattered most were far more dangerous. They were the conversational equivalent of tequila, a faster path to intimacy than flirting ever could be. She pulled on my hand, tugging us toward Birchie's darkened house. The porch light was off, and only the living-room window had a faint glow to it. Wattie always left one of the side-table lamps burning, to deter all the burglars Birchville didn't have. I pulled Lav to the side, thinking we should go around to the back door. It was unlocked, and I thought we had a better chance of sneaking in that way. I didn't want to risk waking up our exhausted old ladies. Much less Rachel. I'd had enough ballistics for one night.

We turned, but something caught the corner of my eye. Something in the deep shadows of Birchie's porch.

I stopped dead, staring up the hill. I could barely make out the figure of a man. He was sitting in the porch swing. The light was off, and the moon was setting, but he was silhouetted against that faint golden glow from Wattie's lamp.

I recognized him as the shadow I'd seen earlier, flashing past the gate when I was in the graveyard. It hadn't been my imagination or a dog after all. It had been this guy. I could see those points on the top of his head that looked a bit like tiny ears.

There was a crazy moment, hardly longer than a heartbeat, when I knew, I simply knew that it was Batman. Somehow he'd learned that there was a Digby and the news had mattered to him in every way that was right. He'd come racing across the state line, Georgia to Alabama, hurrying to see about his son.

Lavender had stopped with me. She said, "What?" too loud, in a nervous voice. "Why did we stop? You look spooked."

The figure on the porch started and stood up when she spoke. The guy was tall like Batman, but maybe too tall, and definitely too broad across the shoulders. Too bulky. I felt an odd sink of mingled relief and disappointment as he came to the stairs and started down them, toward us. Lavender heard him, and when she saw him, she went dead still, too.

"Daddy?" she said.

Once she said it, I recognized him. He'd gained a little weight in the two weeks he'd been MIA. The points on the top of his head were his messy curls. I hadn't seen him without his hair blown out into that sportsy flop across his forehead, not for years.

But it was Jake all the same, and the moment he heard Lav's voice, he sped up. He hurried down the stairs, and Lav tore her hand out of mine and ran, so fast she was like a teeny Flash in the waning moonlight. He reached the bottom step and started running, too. They met in the middle of the yard. She swarmed up him, and at the same time he was lifting her, and she wrapped her arms tight around his neck. Her feet dangled in the air, and one of her sandals had dropped off onto the ground. She didn't seem to notice. I could hear that she was saying something, too choked by crying for me to make out the words. That was okay. They weren't for me.

Watching them from the road, I felt a small pang for Hugh, because that was done. She might not know it yet, but I did. Jake swayed gently, as if he held a fussy baby instead of a half-grown girl.

He said, "Hush, sweetie, hush. I'm here now," and she was still talking and crying all incoherent with her face buried in his neck.

I looked around for Jake's truck and spotted it across the road. He must have just arrived when I'd seen his shadow cross the cemetery gate.

I climbed up the steep slope of the yard, angling toward them. Up close he looked worse. He had big bags under his eyes, and his skin had an unhealthy sheen, as if he'd been living on Swanson's and bourbon without Rachel there to infuse him with wild-caught salmon and organic beets.

"It's okay," he said to Lav, but his eyes were on me.

"If you guys want to talk out here on the porch swing, I'll leave the back door unlocked," I said quietly.

I tried very hard to sound gracious, and welcoming, and unsour, because this was a good thing. He'd done better than call. He had come, and I could see that it was what she needed.

"Thank you," he said, all meaningful, like he was thanking me for more than the unlocked door.

"No need," I said, and it did come out sour. Too bad. I tilted my head pointedly at Lav and said to him, "I didn't do anything for you."

"I'm sorry," he said. He was still rocking his daughter, holding her tight, but his eyes were locked on mine, his so wide with sincerity I could practically see white all around the iris. "I panicked and I ran. It was

wrong, and I'm so damn sorry. I shouldn't have disappeared like that."

His face was puffy from the weight gain and, I
guessed, some heavy drinking. It softened his chiseled
jaw. Add the hair sticking up in little poinks and he
looked almost more like my old friend JJ than like Jake.
It made me wonder if his plan to flee to Portland had
ever been about creating a third life. Perhaps his recent
setbacks had instead cracked him open, exposed the
raw boy he'd packed away under caring about football,
and playing golf, and booming, manly laughter. Maybe
he'd just been running. Cowardly more than ice cold.

Lavender said a muffled "It's okay" into his neck,
but he hadn't been talking to his daughter.

Not entirely anyway.

Beneath the Jake who was saying he was sorry to his
child, I could see JJ, fat and dorky and hopelessly in
love with Rachel, talking to seventeen-year-old me. It
was twenty years too late and doing double duty as an
apology to Lavender, and it hardly covered everything.
He was still the same jackass who'd breezed into my
parents' Christmas party, almost knocking me sideways, shame-running past me with bravado to get to
Rachel. On the other hand, he was finally acknowledg-
ing that I had been hurt. That he had hurt me. He was

attempting to put paid to an old, old debt here, with shitty coin, but still trying. Perhaps it was the only coin he had.

"You're doing the right thing now," I told him, and it hardly sounded grudging at all. "That counts."

JJ took my words as forgiveness. I saw naked gratitude writ plain on his face, and to my surprise I realized I had actually meant them as forgiveness. He swayed quietly for another moment with his girl in his arms. Forgiving him was like balm on an old hurt place, and it felt sweeter than his apology. Sweeter even than the moment I'd said all the things I'd held in my mouth for twenty angry years. Forgiving him felt like relief.

He set Lav down. She was snuffling, and she kept her arms looped around his waist, her wet face pressed into his side.

"Let yourselves in when you're ready, but be quiet. My grandmother isn't well, and she's sleeping," I said, and left them to it.

I went around the house to the back stairs. *Damn JJ,* I thought, but with less rancor than I would have thought it four minutes prior.

Still, if he'd gotten here a scant half hour earlier, he might have caught his own daughter on the way out, and I wouldn't have to help kids pull dew-soaked shreds of TP off Martina Mack's gardenia bush tomorrow. He hadn't gotten into his car and headed for Birchville immediately, though. Not like Rachel. He'd stewed for a few hours, waffling, trying to decide. As if coming for his grieving, worried kid were a decision and not the only open course.

Forgiveness or not, I thought Apologizing Ken was still a jackass. Sure, there were worse fathers in the world. Jake didn't beat his family or smoke crank, but that was setting the bar pretty low. Jake's run at fatherhood seemed to me a bit like eating chalk. It wasn't toxic. It wouldn't kill anybody, but that didn't make it delicious.

Still, I thought of Lavender's face when she'd recognized him. The way she'd run to him, and even the way he'd caught her up, like he was welcoming a missing piece back to his body, as if his own wayward hand had finger-walked home and barnacled itself onto his wrist again. Maybe, when it came to fathers, kind-of-a-jackass beat an absence.

I wouldn't know for sure. I'd only known the absence.

I went inside, flipping both switches by the door to turn on the back-porch floodlight and the brass chandelier over the breakfast-nook table for them.

Jake would need a nap, but I had no idea where on earth we could put him. The Princess Room? Lavender could tuck in with her mother. Although it might be moot. When Rachel woke up and found him here, we might all be cleaning dew-soaked shreds of Jake off our own gardenia bushes.

I retreated to my nest in the sewing room, even though I was so jazzed up that there was no way I was going to fall asleep. I'd walked home half expecting to find Cody Mack here, waiting for me in his cop car. Maybe he hadn't been on duty, or maybe he was smart enough to know that firing a gun at children trumped toilet paper on a pine tree. Of course, the night wasn't over. He could still ring the doorbell and arrest me for vandalism.

My sketchbook sat on the Singer table, open to the picture that had upset Rachel. I sat down and looked at my version of the ruined town square. On the right, Violet cuddled the apocalyptic Batkitten. She was in the world as Violence had left it, a place that had no next, and I had a sudden impulse to put some hope in it. To put a kid in it. What I wanted to do now was draw in Digby.

I picked up the pencil, and I plopped my boy right down in the middle of Violence's world. I didn't draw him as a fetus or even a new baby. Babies all looked the same to me, like cute potatoes. I drew Digby as he might look in five years or so, when the swaybacked potbelly shape of toddlerhood elongated into straight, thin lines. By age five Digby would have his own distinctive face.

I gave him my high cheekbones, my straight, serious brow line, and my deep-set eyes. I let him have the Batman's lush lashes—you're welcome, kid—and his straight, wide nose. I added a dark stubble of close-shorn little-boy hair. I was working in pencil now, but when I drew him in color, he'd have warm brown skin that seemed lit from inside, like good bourbon. I could see it.

Digby took shape on the scant surviving grass, wearing miniature work boots and khaki shorts, his bare legs thin as strings, each with a knotty knee in the middle. He had a confident stance, with a touch of swagger in it. His hands were tucked into his pockets, and the set of his shoulders was easy, maybe even brave. He was in a scary place, but he was smiling anyway, because the pencil was in my hand and I willed it to be so. I looked at this bright, confident boy, standing on the largest patch of grass that I could make for him in Violet's ruined park.

Digby in the Second South, I thought.

Through the wall I could hear faint voices and the

clink of pans in the kitchen. While I was working, Lavender and her father had come in. They were talking quietly, making eggs or cocoa.

I went back to my drawing. Digby's jawline wasn't right. It was too round. I wanted it to be shaped more like the Batman's. Softer, younger, but still similar.

I turned to my laptop and navigated to Batman's profile page. His privacy settings were so lax, I could have gone through his whole photo album. That felt stalkery, so I opened up his profile pics instead. I'd likely find close-ups of his face there, and I only needed a couple of good angles to get Digby's jawline right.

I began flipping through. Here he was, my baby's father, captured in moments that had happened in his real, full, life. Batman smiling, then Batman serious. Inside on a sofa, then outside by a lake, then in a ski hat with some snowy hills behind him.

He didn't change his profile picture often, because one more click brought me to a shot of his family's Christmas tree from three years back. He'd told me about it while we were playing Words with Friends. That year, he and his dad had conspired with all the older grandkids to scandalize his deeply religious mom. They'd turned her tree into a scene straight out of *Star Wars*.

They'd picked out the darkest dark green Douglas

fir they could find, then dotted it with twinkling white lights for stars and large colored balls for planets. All over the tree, they'd hung TIE fighter ornaments flying in formation against X-wings. Carefully arranged sprays of tinsel acted as laser blasts, and they'd twisted red and orange and yellow tissue paper into flames, strategically gluing them onto damaged ships. His dad had even found a Millennium Falcon tree topper, displacing the angel.

I sat staring at my screen for several endless minutes. I couldn't take my eyes away. It was not because of the tree. Well, the tree was hella cool, no doubt about it, and it was right in the middle of the frame. Even so, it was not really a picture of a tree.

It was a family. A whole family. His parents and him and all the kids who'd helped, clustered around this enormous *Star Wars* tree.

I was having trouble swallowing. Batman's mother was tall and elegant, a very dark-skinned woman with a crown of graying braids, glaring at the tree with comical mock horror. His father, skinny and bespectacled, had an enormous Adam's apple and high-waisted grampa pants. He was the biggest dork that I'd ever seen in a picture, except for maybe my own dad. In a dorkcathlon there would be no clear winner, but the two of them would both make the Olympic team. He'd given Batman his big eyes and those ridiculous long lashes.

Batman was there, one arm around his dad, the other holding an adorable round-bellied toddler. His dad cradled a very new baby. All the older kids were clustered around, the three biggest kneeling in front and making ta-da jazz hands at the tree. There were seven of them all told, and they came in a rainbow of shades that ranged from tan to Cyprus umber. No matter how he came out, Digby was going to fit onto their spectrum.

I wasn't looking at a tree; I was looking at a treasure chest. A mawmaw and a poppy, as his sister's children called them. Aunts and uncles, not pictured, but no doubt close by, one of them holding the camera that had snapped this shot. Seven cousins—no, eight soon. His youngest sister was due in a few weeks, he'd said. Cousins who ranged from Digby's own age to Lavender's. Cousins who looked like Digby's father. Cousins and aunts and uncles and grandparents who knew what it was like to grow up in America with brown skin. They were spread across Georgia and Alabama and South Carolina, a host of relatives who didn't have to shift their gaze to know when they'd crossed into the Second South. Relatives who always knew.

Digby deserved to have them, these smiling human

beings clustered tight together. Poppy cradled the littlest baby with wise hands that looked like they'd cradled umpty babies before her. Those hands deserved the opportunity to hold Digby, and Digby deserved to be held in them.

Most of all Digby deserved a father. I could vet Batman forever if I wanted. I would eventually see past his shiny second-date persona to his flaws, whatever they might be. Maybe he'd turn out to be a bit of a jackass, but there was a righteous jackass in my Birchie's kitchen right now, and he was fixing necessary cocoa for his kid.

"Jesus Christ," I said, a prayer more than a blasphemy, and my voice had gone all funny—breathy and thick. I had to tell him. I had to tell him now, while I was wonky and punchy and exhausted enough to do it. If I waited, I would find a thousand reasons not to. I would coward my way out of it and pretend that it was logic.

I got my phone and opened our long string of texts, then navigated to his number. I pressed it, my heart pounding so hard I could feel it in my eyeballs, in my throat, in my shaking hands.

Two rings and he picked up. Just as JJ had when I'd called him from his daughter's phone. Maybe that was how many rings it took to call a man to fatherhood.

"Hello?" he said. He'd been asleep. Even if it hadn't been past four in the morning, I would have known it from his graveled voice. I couldn't answer. I hardly knew what to say. He must have looked at his screen and seen that it was me, because he said, "Leia? Hello? If this is a butt dial, I may kill you later." He didn't sound mad, though. He sounded amused, if sleepy.

"Not a butt dial," I said. My own voice was scared and small.

"Hey. Are you fff . . . good?" he said. More awake now. A little hesitant.

"I'm okay. I'm good. I'm just . . ." I paused, my heart pounding. Now I wanted to say that this was a butt dial. I wanted to hang up. But I kept thinking of all his nieces and nephews, pressed in close and grinning by that gonzo *Star Wars* Christmas tree they'd made with him. "Pregnant."

It was the only way to end the sentence, really.

"B-beg pardon?" he said, nonreactive. Polite. Like he hadn't quite heard me.

"I'm pregnant. We are. You and me," I said, except he wasn't. It was just me, actually. "Well, no, that's not how biology goes. I mean that you and me together got me pregnant."

There was a silence, and then he said, "I . . . I . . . I . . ." And then stopped talking.

I was gripping the phone so tight I was surprised my screen didn't shatter. He was breathing on the other end like he'd been running. So was I, I realized. We were both panting like dogs, almost in sync. This was going poorly, although I wasn't sure what would have to happen to qualify this call as going well.

"I wish you'd say something," I said.

"I . . . I . . ." he said, and stopped again. "Can't talk."

"Okay," I said into the phone. "That seems fair."

It did. I hadn't wanted to talk about it for months, and now I'd woken him up and blatted the news into his barely conscious ear. But at the same time, a selfish bit of me wanted his immediate reaction to be different, or at least definitive. If he would only yell that this was my damn problem or say he doubted it was his baby and hang up. It would be awful, but at least everything would be decided. Or in some ideal world, he could ask interested questions, say something supportive or hopeful.

I tried to think of the kindest things my pregnancy test might have said to me, if it had been a person.

"I know you need time. It has to sink in. It worked like that for me anyway. It didn't seem real at first, and so I'm sorry it took me this long to tell you. But it's happening, so you have to think about what you want

to do. Me, I know what I'm doing. I'm having a baby."
I thought I would end there, but I wanted all my cards
on the table. I didn't want him to make some bad decision in a vacuum of what was easiest. I didn't want to be
one of those self-sacrificing talk-show ladies who says
to the guy who knocked her up, "You don't have to be
involved. I can do this on my own," and then the audience cheers and claps, as if it's noble to tell a man he
holds no value beyond a scoop of sperm, to tell a man
his own child will have no use for him. I kept talking.
"I also want you to know that I'm happy about it. Your
kid is so, so wanted over here on this side of the phone.
And I'm lucky. I have a good job, a good family, a lot
of friends with kids. Babies get born with much, much
less, and they still have good lives. . . . I know that. It's
just I love this kid like crazy. I want him to have everything. That's why I'm telling you. I want him to know
his dad. I want him to know your family."

A longer pause, and then Batman did talk. He said
one word, very soft. "Him?"

"Oh, yeah. I'm sorry," I said, wincing, because that
was poorly done. When Rachel was pregnant, she'd
planned a reveal party for the day after the ultrasound.
Mom and Keith and I gathered with her closest friends
to find her house tricked out in stark black-and-white

decorations. Rachel brought out an ice-white cake and set it in front of JJ. When he cut it open, we'd all seen that it was pink and stuffed with strawberries. Now Batman had found out he was having a son in a tongue slip in the same fraught conversation where he learned his one-night stand at FanCon had gotten all complicated. "He's a boy. I'm having a boy."

Then my phone buzzed and trembled directly in my ear, like an insect. I pulled it away, startled. A text had landed. I opened Messages and saw that he had sent it. While we were on the phone.

I literally can't talk right now, the text said.

I stared at the words, and I had a flash of fear that he was not alone. I swallowed. His Facebook profile said that he was single, and he'd sounded happy to hear from me when he picked up, but still. I had this image of some other woman that he'd met last night who liked caped crusaders and tequila, too. She could be sleeping beside him right now, exhausted from a long, long night of making Digby's little sister.

Why not? He owed me nothing. Hell, he barely knew me. So we'd had a fun time on Facebook. So we'd been flirting over texts. He was probably alone right now, but he could have fifty women on strings that were fine and light and never meant for binding. For all I knew, he played Words with Friends every night with different women who'd already had his babies, all up and down the eastern seaboard.

Not that it mattered. What was that to me? Nothing. So why were my stupid eyes stinging, and why did my throat feel so thick and closed?

"Well, call me when you can talk," I said, and ended the connection.

17

We walked over to Martina Mack's house right after breakfast, while Birchie had some stamina. She was a little off this morning, but I needed Birchie and Wattie to be seen. Going to First Baptist had shown me that even Birchie's closest community was divided and most folks were uncertain of how to feel about her. Wattie was to Redemption as Birchie was to First Baptist, and that congregation must be equally astir. Wattie had been leery enough of her reception to skip church entirely last Sunday.

I needed more people, pillars-of-the-community types, firmly on our side. The county prosecutor was asking for a DNA test. If—or when—she proved that the bones belonged to Birchie's father, what Regina Tackrey did with them next would be shaped by public opinion. Was Birchie an ancient monster caught at last or the most beloved Birch to ever live in Birchville, now too old and too ill to explain herself? Would filing charges be long-overdue justice or the persecution of old ladies?

The town's answers would spread through the county. So far we'd holed up and left Martina and her ilk to shape this conversation. A bad idea, especially since the Macks and the Tackreys had old ties. If the last day or two had taught me anything, it was that Cody and Martina were pulling us down a path that ended in pitchforks and torches. And shotguns.

We hadn't been working more than half an hour when Alston Rhodes came walking down Crepe Myrtle Avenue, seemingly oblivious to the great crowd of us in Martina's yard. I'd played with Alston every summer, so I recognized her the second she turned the corner. Her hair had not changed since 1994, when she'd cut it to look like she had just stepped off the set of *Friends*. She had on a full face of makeup, but she was wearing sweatpants and Nikes and dragging her fat pug, Punchkin, on a string. Punchkin was being the worst excuse for a power walk I'd ever seen. He tried to sit down twice as Alston marched him along.

She was out of her neighborhood, too, but we'd passed quite a few First Baptist people on the way here. The phone tree had activated, and Alston was the first wave of townly recon, careful to keep her gaze on the sky and the grass and parked cars and trees and anything else that wasn't us even as she beelined our way, a woman on a mission. I was glad they'd picked Alston, or that she'd volunteered. It boded well. She had planted her butt firmly on Birchie's side of the church last Sunday.

I'd stationed Birchie and Wattie deep in the front yard, under the shade of a puffball tree. They were bait, and Alston couldn't get to them without passing Rachel and me, picking shreds of Charmin from the leaves of the big gardenia near the mailbox. I handed Rachel the trash bag and intercepted Alston at the curb.

"Oh, hello!" Alston said, faux surprised but seeming genuinely pleased to see us out of hiding. The second she stopped walking, Punchkin flopped onto his belly, panting. "Goodness, what happened here?"

"You're raising teenagers," I said, grinning at her. "I think you can guess."

We both paused to watch Lavender pluck another string of toilet paper off the azaleas. Frank Darian had to be in court this morning, but Hugh was here. He'd helped Jake carry his dad's big ladder over.

It was odd to see Jake still in Birchville, red-faced and sweating through his polo shirt. When I'd finally quit sketching to scare up some breakfast, Birchie and Wattie were in the kitchen and Lavender was sitting at the dining-room table, cheerfully horking down a fried egg and biscuits with syrup. She'd told me that her parents were taking a walk. I'd wondered if Jake would return from it. Rachel could send him back to Norfolk alone, or, more likely, years from now some descendant of mine might find his bones hidden in their own trunk in the attic. But Lavender had seemed unconcerned that her dad might disappear again. She'd been practically glowing.

"Finish eating and put your shoes on," I'd told her. "We're all going down to fix Mrs. Mack's place as soon as you're ready."

Jake returned with Rachel as we were leaving, sporting a sheepish expression and pink, exhausted eyes. She was cloaked in cool blond dignity. They were not holding hands the way they used to, but he didn't get into his truck and go, and he turned down the nap that Birchie offered him, choosing instead to come along and help us.

Now Jake held the base of the ladder firmly against the trunk of Martina's big loblolly pine. Hugh Darian was at the top, too high up by half for my taste, trying to yank down the white banners he'd lofted so professionally last night. It wasn't going well.

We'd had a heavy dew, and the dampened toilet paper stuck to everything and disintegrated easily. We were practically having to remove it square by square. As Hugh jerked the streamers, they broke off, and the bits at the top were well beyond the ladder's reach. It would take the fire department or Cirque du Soleil to get them down. It probably said something very damning about my character that I secretly wanted those white crisscrosses fluttering on for a few days, until rain or the wind dissolved them or carried them away. They looked like little flags proclaiming Martina's jackassery.

"Oh, goodness' sake, Hugh Darian! You know better. I hope my Connor wasn't helping?" Alston called up to Hugh, then added aside to me, "Those two are thick as thieves."

"No, ma'am!" Hugh hollered back. "It was just me and Lavender."

Behind her, coming up Crepe Myrtle from the other direction, I saw Grady and Esme Franklin walking at a good clip toward us. They were a comfortably portly couple in their fifties, recent empty-nesters. Grady was a deacon at Wattie's church, the one who most often picked up Birchie and Wattie on their Redemption weeks. Our march around the square had activated the Redemption Baptist phone tree, too.

The Franklins lived close, west of Cypress Street. Their part of the neighborhood had the same postage-stamp yards and gardens, the same brick ranches. Most of the houses were tidy and well cared for, though a few had bald yards and moldering sofas on the front porch, just like here. But black families lived on that side of Cypress Street, and on this side the neighborhood was white.

I took ruthless hold of Alston's arm. "Oh, look, here come Esme and Grady Franklin." I headed fast to intercept them, dragging reluctant Alston and exhausted Punchkin down the curb with me, talking with relentless cheery volume over Alston's protests. "Do you know each other? Come and meet them."

As we traded good-mornings and handshakes, Lavender came over and joined us. She knelt down to pet Punchkin, saying, "We should have brought water bottles. This poor guy needs a drink."

"Don't we all," I said, so damn perky. I was wishing mine could be tequila. "Lav, maybe take Punchkin and run the hose for him? I doubt Ms. Mack would mind. She's got dogs, and it's shaping up to be a scorcher."

Martina probably would mind. Well, too bad. I was doing public-relations work here. It would be awesome if she came out into the street and publicly begrudged a pug dog a drink of water. Lavender took the leash and dragged Punchkin off toward the side of the house.

"Yes, it is," Alston said. "Should Miss Birchie and Miss Wattie be standing out here in it?"

It was the opening I needed.

"I don't think so, but they both insisted. They feel responsible. Lav and Hugh were defending their honor, after all." I tipped my head significantly at the house, and Alston followed my gaze. The drapes in the front window twitched; Martina Mack was watching. To Esme and Grady, I added, "The lady who lives here implied some rather harsh things about my grandmother and Miss Wattie down at First Baptist on Sunday."

As I spoke, Rachel drifted toward us, picking up fragments that led her close enough to hear the conversation.

"Oh, no!" Esme said, but then she caught the implication and asked, amused, "You mean the kids rolled her house for it?"

"It's a young way to react, isn't it?" Alston said to Esme, chuckling.

"Yes, but a little too 'eye for an eye' for Birchie and Wattie. They wanted to show Lav and Hugh that you have to turn the other cheek." It was spin, tailored to this small-town Baptist audience, but there was truth in it. I was reminding them of the kind of women Birchie and Wattie were. The kind that they had always been. "Even if that means standing out in eighty-percent humidity making sure teenagers get every bit of the Charmin out of the bushes."

All three of them exchanged approving glances, nodding to one another in parental solidarity. I stood outside the moment, still only secretly a budding member of that club.

Alston said, "I almost don't blame the kids, after the things Miss Martina implied. . . ."

It was a delicate, sideways query, but a query nonetheless. Alston was approaching the subject of Birchie and the bones. This was why they were all here, wasn't it? Grady looked decidedly uncomfortable, sticking his hands into his pockets, while Esme leaned in.

"It was awful. I knew it would be like that. I didn't want to go to church," I said frankly. I turned to Esme and added, "It's why we weren't at Redemption last Sunday. Wattie and Birchie didn't even walk down to the vegetable stand this week or go shop for yarn. They felt unwelcome."

As I spoke, Rachel dropped all pretense that she was working and joined the group. So far she'd been remarkably staunch about not questioning me. She hadn't asked about the bones, not even obliquely, once she'd seen that Lav wasn't in danger. It was as if she had entered into the conspiracy without needing to know what it was, trading silent unasking for the haven of Birchie's house while Jake was MIA. Well, he was found now, and Alston had turned the conversation to the most essential question.

"I hope Miss Wattie knows it isn't true. We wanted her at church," Esme said, then thought to add, "And you and Miss Birchie, too."

"Thank you," I said. I'd visited Redemption plenty of times, and Birchie worshipped there every other week now, but we were welcomed on day passes, because Wattie loved us. "We knew that certain folks would be saying the worst things they could think of, and what could we do? Look what happened when we did go to First Baptist. Martina knew very well she was asking questions that Birchie's not allowed to answer." In an aside to the Franklins, I added, "Her grandson is a policeman. Cody Mack?"

Franklin nodded. "I know him." His tone was cool and so carefully neutral. He did know Cody, then, down to the bone.

"What do you mean she's not allowed to answer?" Esme asked.

Alston chimed in, "For legal reasons?"

I had come to the meat of it now, and all three of

them had eager eyes. So did Rachel, for that matter. Well, they were human, and this was juicy.

"That's part of it," I said. "But look at her."

We all looked, and maybe it was a good thing that Birchie wasn't at her best this morning. Just now she was making shooing hands toward her feet, and Wattie stood in profile, whispering in Birchie's ear.

"What's she doing?" Esme asked.

I wasn't positive, but I could guess. "She's trying to get the sex rabbits to stop . . . well, doing what rabbits do."

"Sex rabbits!" Grady said.

"Yes. She's hallucinating," I said. "This disease makes people see things—usually animals or people. Also, it messes with memory. The police could ask her about the bones five times, but they might get five different answers. Who knows which answer would be true? If any. We can't let her incriminate herself when we have no way of knowing what's real and what the Lewy bodies are telling her to say."

"Dear Lord, how terrible," Alston said. She put a kind hand on my arm and added in a confidential tone, "I knew things were not right with Miss Birchie at the Fish Fry, when she said the P-word and . . ." She trailed off.

It took me a second to realize what the "P-word"

was. A couple of fouler possibilities ran through my head before I realized that Alston meant "penis." It was a medical term, but when Birchie used it to describe a piece of associate pastor that was being put to an illicit use in the choir room? It was profane enough to earn the abbreviation.

I nodded and said, "She may never be able to tell us the whole story."

More spin, but not dishonest. Most mornings, given a good sleep and a nice breakfast, Birchie seemed herself. But I had no way of knowing how many more good mornings Birchie would be granted. It wasn't even 10:00 A.M. today, and she was already shooing rabbits. If the police questioned Birchie on a bad day, she might well say anything.

"So you don't even know?" Esme asked, surprised, looking back and forth between me and Rachel.

"Nope. Not a clue," Rachel said honestly. I shook my head, somewhat less honestly.

"And Wattie?" Grady asked.

"Nope," I lied staunchly, looking Grady right in the eye.

"You asked her?" Esme wanted to know, all pretense that this was anything but a straight-up recon mission dropped now that I was dishing out the goods directly. It wasn't very southern of me.

"Of course!" I said, more comfortable now. I'd told the lie that mattered, the one I had to tell to protect my grandmother and her oldest, dearest friend. Everything I had left to say was pure gospel. "Between you and me? I would have done exactly what Wattie did. I would have helped Birchie move that trunk if she'd asked. The law be damned. She's sick, and Wattie loves her." Three small-town Baptists, and they were so interested they didn't so much as blink at the mild profanity. "I honestly don't think it matters who's in that trunk or how they got there. Not now. I've accepted that I may never know why either. . . ." My voice broke, and it wasn't spin. I wanted to know the why. I wanted Birchie to tell me. But even if she never did, what I had to say next I believed with my whole being. "I do know Birchie, though. I know her character. So do you, and so does Wattie, and so does this whole town. She's been the same person for almost a century. Something bad happened in the middle, but a box of bones can't wipe away ninety years of Birchie being who she is. Whatever she did, or knew about, or kept secret, I forgive her. It's too late for any other course. She's very old, and she's too sick now to explain or defend herself. So I forgive her anything that needs forgiving, and I'm going to defend her. So is Wattie. We're not going to hide in the house like we're ashamed of her. We are going to help Birchie go on about her business for as long as she can, and we won't let people question her or judge her. Wattie won't have it. I won't have it. It won't do."

Those were Birchie's power words. I said them for her, using her authority and her inflections, and Alston's chin came up in response to them. Esme reached out and squeezed my shoulder.

"Good for you," Esme said, and Grady echoed, "Good for you both."

"Of course we all know your gramma. I have known Miss Birchie my whole, whole life." Alston's eyes were shiny, and the whites pinked as she spoke.

"Good for you what?" Lavender said. She was back with Punchkin.

Alston gave her head a little shake. She smiled at Lavender and took Punchkin's leash. "Never you mind, young lady. You have work to do! And here I am standing here chattering and letting my heart rate drop."

"Oh, yes, us, too," Esme said. "Grady's doctor says he needs to walk at least two miles every day."

They paused only to exchange greetings with Birchie and Wattie, and then Esme and Grady hurried back toward their house, disappearing around the corner. Alston took off at a good clip, too, but poor old Punchkin lagged behind her, suffering. After a few hampered steps, she stopped and looked down at him with fond exasperation. He immediately flopped onto his butt again. In Birchville gossip was called "news," and having some was social currency. I'd just handed Alston and the Franklins big fat wads of it to spend, and gossip waited for no exhausted dog. Alston picked him up and tucked him under her arm like a hairy clutch purse, then bustled away up the street.

We all went back to work. Alston must have gotten on her phone the second she was out of sight, because not ten minutes later Darnette and Larry Pearson came out of their pink brick ranch, set catty-corner across the street from Martina. They were each toting a comfy padded chair from their back patio. They went right to Birchie and Wattie and set them up in the shade, then stood chatting with them.

I hoped no one would ask Birchie questions she ought not to answer. Especially since she was already seeing rabbits. Wattie was right there in case someone tried, and I'd been as clear as I could be with Alston and the Franklins both. I kept picking toilet-paper bits, staying out of the town's way as it churned and wavered. The air felt charged with a hundred simultaneous phone calls zooming through the airways overhead.

The chairs were a good sign, though, especially since the Pearsons had chosen to sit in the center section last Sunday. This might shift them to Birchie's side.

For the next half hour, even the most sedentary Baptists from both churches had sudden urges for mid-morning walks that took them right past the Mack house. Most of these folks had not personally witnessed the lid of the old trunk swinging open. They had only heard about the bones, the skull with its empty eye sockets and its telltale stove-in dome. Hearing was not the same as seeing.

Here in the sunny yard, it was hard for folks to imagine Birchie with a hammer or Wattie stealing a car. I was having trouble imagining these things, and I'd witnessed Wattie's crash into the mailbox. I'd tucked Birchie's bare feet into soft socks and watched her do the Tomahawk Chop, her blue eyes blank and unsorry. It all seemed like a bad dream now, as folks from both churches came to rally around them.

I stopped working and simply watched when the first cars pulled up and parked. They were full of folks who lived too far to walk. They came anyway, not bothering with the pretense of happening by. I counted emissaries from more than thirty families, many of them First Baptist folks who had taken center seats on Sunday. We even got RaeAnn Leefly, who I'd seen in the pews behind Martina. She was stiff and uncomfortable at first, but she unbent as Birchie asked about her shingles and her youngest girl, who was having marriage trouble in Montgomery. Birchie, brain-sick as she was, was so hip-deep in the day-to-day life of Birchville that she remembered. Maybe it was Wattie, whispering, remembering for her, but there was no doubting the care behind the questions.

It was doing Birchie good to be out among friends again. Her little blue eyes were bright, and I kept hearing her ladylike trill of a laugh as we finished up. I could still see occasional movement in the curtains. Martina Mack could not be enjoying this now. The pleasure of watching us sweat and pick in her yard must be souring in her mouth. Good.

"They can work a crowd, though, can't they?" Rachel whispered to me, and I nodded.

But it was more than that. My grandmother and Wattie had been a joint force in the lives of all these people. A force for good. They had brought handmade blankets to welcome new babies and warm pans of ham-and-potato casserole to countless funerals. Birchie owned the land their stores were on, and in lean years she'd helped them keep their businesses, in some cases their homes. Wattie's husband had been the pastor at Redemption for decades, and Wattie had pastored right beside him, teaching Sunday school, counseling brides, sitting with the grieving.

The yard was filled, people spilling out into the road, and I realized I had never seen so many members of these two congregations intermingled. It looked like Birchie and Wattie were holding court under the puffball tree, seated side by side with lifted chins and crossed ankles. A steady stream of pilgrims brought them smiles and news and, in Lois Gainey's case, a huge plate of muffins. Birchie and Wattie took all these offerings as their simple due, these little old ladies acting as the hinge between the two communities gathering in the yard. They were the human overlap.

Inside me I was growing a boy who belonged here in this yard. Today, in this unrepeated hour, the Mack lawn looked like his birthright.

A station wagon pulled up, packed to the brim with the enormous Ridley family. The kids spilled out of the back with gallon jugs of ice-cold lemonade and a Tupperware container full of homemade gingersnaps. They started pouring drinks and passing out the cookies.

Little Denise Ridley ran to me, braids bouncing,

carrying a bathroom-size waxy Dixie Cup covered in flowers. She handed the tiny portion of lemonade to me with an equally tiny cookie.

"Thank you, hon," I told her.

I put the cookie in my mouth. I drank the cup, all the while looking at a congregation my son belonged in, knowing that it existed only in this moment. I swallowed, and I felt like I was sharing in a spicy, tart communion, strange and rare. It was a taste of the world as I wanted it to be.

Inside the house the drapes twitched. The world as it actually was, present and watching. This peace, this beauty, was temporary. The world as it was—it was coming for us still.

18

Walking home, Rachel lagged behind in a way that felt purposeful, making significant eyebrows at me. All I could think was, *What now?* This morning had felt like a patch of sweet, clear air I'd stumbled into, untainted by my troubles. I wanted to stay there and go on breathing it. When Rachel plucked at my sleeve to keep me with her, an image popped into my head: a misty-blue-sky picture that kept showing up in my Facebook feed. That meme had a cloudy-white font, and it burbled something about how God never gave a person more than they could handle. I had a sudden, irrational urge to ask Rachel to excuse me for a sec. Just long enough for me to find every friend who had ever shared that thing and smack them right upside their smug heads.

I resigned myself to her pace, though, and Rachel slowed even more. She really had to work to drop back behind Birchie and Wattie. They walked arm in arm, pacing themselves as they toddled slowly home. Jake and Hugh were in front, their lead hampered because they were carrying Frank Darian's long ladder at either end. Lav had gone ahead to walk at the very front with her dad, not even pretending to help carry the ladder, chatting Jake's ear off.

I matched Rachel's snail pace, and when we were so far back that we were definitely out of earshot, she finally spoke.

"Jake told us that you called him." Her gaze was down, and her cheeks went faintly pink. "I wanted to say thank you." It wasn't what I'd expected. I had meddled, Rachel style, in her sacrosanct, closed life. I'd hoped Jake wouldn't tell her and Lav, because I didn't need Rachel's flared nostrils and an icy invitation to step out of their business. "He wants us to go to counseling. So we'll see. We're going home tomorrow to start sorting through the paper part of the mess at least." Not just a thank-you, but actual information about her life. The downside of her life. I'd always been first on her call list when Jake surprised her with a cruise or Lav made the honor roll, but she kept her sadness to herself. Maybe this *was* her good news, though, the best bright side she had available. Even so, the slow pace of our walk felt newly companionable. She snuck a peek at my face and said, "There's already an offer on the house, so that's good. Not surprising. It's waterfront. We have to decide what to do next. You mentioned before that we could stay at your place for a little. . . ."

"Of course," I said. "Just promise me you won't reorganize my closets."

Rachel chuckled and linked her arm with mine. "I'll try not to."

She was a head taller than me, and it pulled us both off balance. Still, I kept her arm as we made our way out of the neighborhood, walking back toward the square. For the first time in our long near sisterhood, we felt strangely even. Rachel wasn't lofting her least-fucked-up trophy and smiling down at me, offering succor. I wasn't holding it either. Neither of us was even making a grab for it.

I was under no illusions that this would last. Rachel would get her life on track, spearheading economic and emotional counseling for her family. She'd go back to work and be amazing; she'd been a hellishly efficient wedding planner in her pre-Lavender years. If anything, she'd honed that skill set after she went full-time wife and mother. I hoped her marriage would survive, for Lavender's sake, but if Rachel divorced Jake, it would be so perfectly done it would make Gwyneth Paltrow's conscious uncoupling look like a bar brawl. I had no doubt that *Rachel: The Comeback* would be an epic, sweeping story, with multiple morals and endless opportunities for her to explain them to me, but I didn't think it would bother me quite as much post-Birchville.

We were coming up on the park on the back side of the square. Jake and Hugh turned left, to go around on the side that would put them closer to the Darian house. Birchie and Wattie turned right, and Lavender dropped back to join them. Rachel and I were still behind, and now I was the one who kept our pace overslow. I wanted, in this rare moment of Rachel being vulnerable, to make some amends of my own.

"Rachel? I'm sorry Violet looks like you," I said. "She's not based on you, but"—and this was hard for me to say—"I wanted her to be pretty. You're what pretty looks like in my head."

That did make her smile, but not the irritating one that seemed to beam down on me from Olympus. She squeezed my arm a little tighter.

"Really? That's sweet. I thought you drew her like that to make fun of me," she said. "She's so stupid. What girl goes skipping down an alley that looks like that?"

"It's a metaphor," I said. "But apparently I do, because she's actually kinda based on me."

We walked on, turning right to follow Birchie, Wattie, and Lav back to the house, and Rachel asked, "Do you think they're lovers?"

"No, I really don't," I said, though it was a popular theory on the *Violence in Violet* forums.

Ship-nerds who wanted them to be in love argued bitterly with the Jekyll-and-Hyde dorks who thought Violet turned into Violence when threatened. There was a third faction who thought Violence wasn't real, just an extension of Violet's will. A smaller set still thought *Violet* wasn't real. That was a huge stretch, but they'd written reams and reams "proving" Violence had invented her to have an excuse for blowing the planet to smithereens.

I got asked about these theories all the time at cons and on my fan page, but I always said people had to make their own decisions. In my head, though? Violence was real, and Violet had to be separate because I really did see myself in Violet. I wanted Violence, who ate people and eventually destroyed Earth, to be separate from me.

But now I'd stood in the balcony of First Baptist, looking down at Birchie and Wattie. I'd felt myself capable of so much ugly. In that moment I'd have pulled the roof down on the right half of the church if I'd had superstrength. I'd gladly have eaten up Martina Mack in two brittle, bony bites. Turned out I had ferocious in me. One day, sixty years back, there'd been ferocious in my grandmother, too.

It was the Violence in me that had blown up every relationship that might have become something real. I'd realized it when I accepted the weak-ass apology Jake had divvied up between me and Lavender and maybe God. When I took my share, I'd felt it as the easing of a hurt so old that I'd grown used to it. So used to it I hadn't noticed its pulse and presence even as I'd destroyed all of my own possible futures, wrecking every family I could have had into a wasteland.

Now I thought the Jekyll-and-Hyde dorks might have been right all along.

I said, mostly to myself, "I always thought of Violence as maternal or big-sistery, not romantic. But I'm thinking now, what if Violet really is Violence? I haven't been able to write an origin story that doesn't include Violet. I can't imagine Violence without her.

The way Violence looks at her, with the songbirds and the rabbits, sweet and innocent, maybe that's how she sees herself, in the beginning. She's protecting herself, and she doesn't even know it."

I found myself excited by the idea, but Rachel was chuckling.

"I wasn't talking about your story thing," she said. "I meant them. Birchie and Wattie. Do you think they're lovers?"

I'd been onto something, but that snapped me right out of it.

"Ugh! No!" I said immediately. Birchie and Wattie walked on ahead of us, rounding the last corner, arm in arm, chatting with Lavender. They were almost exactly the same height, and their sloping shoulders met in a perfect, gentle angle. "They were both married!"

"So?" Rachel said. "It was a different time. Maybe they—"

"Absolutely not," I interrupted. My grandfather had died before I was born, but I'd known Wattie's husband. She'd had a good marriage. He always seemed to have a hand on her hip, her back, her shoulder, and she'd leaned into his touch. I couldn't imagine Wattie having his babies, working beside him down at the church, calling him "Big Bear," the whole time secret-pining for my granny. "Don't be gross!"

"And you say I'm homophobic," Rachel said, primly but with no rancor.

I laughed. "You are. A little bit. Look, it isn't that. They shared a crib, Rachel. They practically had the same mom." Birchie had told me Vina stories the way I'd one day tell Birchie stories to Digby. The piecrust she and Wattie made was Vina's family piecrust. Birchie was at Vina's bedside with Wattie and all of Wattie's older brothers when she died, and she took flowers to her grave four times a year. "Vina gave Birchie every bit of mothering she got. She and Wattie were born barely a year apart. They nursed together."

"But they aren't actually blood-related," Rachel said, head cocked slightly sideways as she considered them.

"You and I aren't blood-related either," I said. "You're saying that if we were lesbians, you'd want to French me?"

"Ew!" Rachel said instantly.

I grinned. "You'd want to lay me down on a beach and make sweet, sweet—"

"Stop! Ew, stop!" Rachel shrieked, laughing now, too. "Oh my God, my brain. I need brain soap. Okay! Fine! Point taken."

It was another very good moment. We both picked

up the pace, gaining ground, maybe to bring this almost perfect conversation to a close before it turned on us. We were coming up on First Baptist now, almost home. Looking ahead at my little old ladies, I wished I'd thought to bring an umbrella. I didn't like to see the sun beating down on them, turning Wattie's short, crimped hair to molten silver and bouncing off Birchie's fluffy bun.

As we caught up, Rachel said, "Incest aside, I think you could have made Violet look like you. You're very pretty, Leia." I warmed to the compliment, but then she added, "Although more people would know it if you would let me shape your brows for you. You *have* put on a little weight. Maybe when you're home, you could come running with me? I'm going to have to give up my gym membership—"

I shook my head and bumped her shoulder with mine. Here was Rachel, unable to help herself, readying to step in and take charge of my weight and anything else that wasn't perfect. Somehow today it didn't chafe me.

Lav saw we'd caught up and dropped back a step, inserting herself between us, grabbing our hands. She set our arms to swinging.

"You ready to go home tomorrow?" Rachel asked.

"Yup," she said, unconcerned. Poor Hugh!

She pulled us forward, almost skipping, resetting our pace with a young vengeance, bringing us abreast of Birchie and Wattie as we crossed the street to the edge of our yard. I groaned but matched my feet to hers, eager to be home. Digby and I needed to lie down.

Beside me Birchie and Wattie turned in tandem up the driveway, but then they pulled up short, staring at the porch.

"What?" I said. "Are you—"

I followed the line of their gaze, and I saw him sitting in the porch swing, reading. I froze, and my mouth stopped talking. It felt like my heart stopped, too, or maybe it was only time, taking a pause.

"Holy crap! It's Batman!" Lav said.

It wasn't actually Batman, though.

It was Selcouth Martin, near stranger, with a sharp in-line haircut, straight across and squared on top, instead of a cowl. No cape or even a utility belt, just dark jeans, a gray T-shirt, and red low-top Chucks. He was deep into a graphic novel, waiting in the sun where Jake had waited in the shadowy night, sitting in the same swing and with the exact same purpose. Selcouth Martin had come to see about his kid.

"Batman?" Rachel asked, confused.

"Yeah!" Lav said excitedly, squeezing my hand so hard it almost hurt. "It's him, isn't it? It's him!"

My mouth wasn't working yet, so it was a good thing she'd answered her own question. He was here, alive and in person, on my doorstep only a few bare and busy hours after my phone call. He'd known I was staying with my grandmother in Birchville, so he must've put the town name in his GPS and pointed himself in my direction. I'd talked about Birchville quite a bit. I remembered telling him that Birchie lived right across from First Baptist on the square. Had he found the house on his own? I hoped to God he hadn't stopped at Brother's Café or Tiger Gas and asked where I was staying. The town would be ablaze with speculation, especially if he'd then sat out waiting on our porch for longer than five minutes.

Birchie and Wattie looked to me, and Birchie's eyes were bird bright.

"Is that him?" Birchie whispered. She clutched tighter at Wattie's arm and released an odd, trilling giggle. It had an edge of hysteria in it that I didn't like. *Maybe we should have driven down to Martina's house,* I thought, but then Birchie added, "Wattie, I think that's the father!"

Wattie squinted, speculative, then said, "That young man is not what I expected," her voice very dry.

"Whose father?" asked Rachel, but I was too floored to answer. She looked at Batman, watched him turn a page. We were all still down at the end of the drive and talking quietly, so he hadn't seen us yet. "Is that— Do you have a boyfriend, Leia?"

"You know?" I asked Birchie and Wattie when my mouth decided to let me get two words out.

"Oh, sugar. Course we know," Wattie said, like I was being silly.

"Know what?" Rachel said. "Is he a secret boyfriend? Did you keep him secret because he's black?" Her voice dropped even lower on the last word. She flashed an apologetic look at Wattie and told her, "Because we are not like that. No one in our family is like that."

"We knew the second we laid eyes on you," Wattie said, ignoring Rachel.

Birchie chimed in, "You look exactly like me when I was four months gone."

"Gone where? What am I missing?" Rachel said, getting frustrated. "Who is Batman?"

She said it loud enough for him to hear us. He looked up. As soon as he saw us, he tucked his book into a gym bag at his feet. He stood, lifting one regular,

ungloved hand up in an awkward wave. His shirt had
a picture of the evolution of man on the front, *Homo
habilis* at the beginning of a line of figures that grew
taller and straighter. At the end of the line, a giant
robot was throttling modern man. It was a joke, but
it wasn't going to play in Birchville. Neither Birchie
nor Wattie thought there was anything amusing about
evolution.

"You're carrying mostly in your hind end," Wattie
said.

Birchie said, "In our family that means a boy."

Rachel looked at each of us in a confused round-
robin. She blinked, shook her head in a tiny no, and
then I saw understanding come into her face. Her gaze
snapped to meet mine.

"Does Mom know?" I shook my head, and her eyes
widened, suddenly horrified. "Oh God! I never should
have said that you were fat! You aren't fat at all!"

Which was so perfectly Rachel that I felt a wild,
hysterical bubble of a laugh rising up inside me and had
to work to quash it down.

"Come along," said Birchie, and she crossed the
lawn to the porch stairs, letting out a long exhale. It was
made of words, a breathy string of syllables, near silent.
"Daddy, Daddy, Daddy," she was saying. I didn't know
if she meant Batman or her own father. The one she'd

ended with a hammer. Either way, she had overdone it this morning.

I followed her. We all did. As we reached the bottom of the porch stairs, Selcouth Martin picked up his bag and came forward to the top of them. He looked different—better—than his profile pics. I'd assumed I'd looked at him through slightly rosy beer-and-tequila goggles back at FanCon, but actually he wasn't photogenic. Now I saw the man I'd taken right upstairs to bed with me. Here was the beautiful mouth and narrow jaw, those wide-set eyes with their ridiculous long lashes. Pictures didn't convey how well his features worked in person. *Worked for me, anyway,* I thought, and I felt heat come into my cheeks.

Lavender let go of our hands and went springing up the stairs, past Birchie and Wattie, and she reached him first.

"Hello, Batman," she said, grinning up at him.

"Hello," said Batman.

"Lavender knows your boyfriend?" Rachel asked in a whisper. Then, louder, "Wait, Lavender knows that you're pregnant?"

Selcouth Martin heard her. His jaw went tense, and I shrugged at him, helplessly. I'd thought that he would call me back in a few days or text me for a meet-up in his TeamSpeak channel. I'd assumed I would have time to think of what should happen next. Instead next was happening right now.

"Come on in out of the heat," Wattie told him, unlocking the door.

I followed them all in, but it didn't feel like escaping the heat. Not a bit. I was walking into it.

19

We filed into the entryway between the parlor and the big formal dining room. Lavender had left her sticky breakfast plate and a fork with egg yolk congealing on the tines sitting out on the table, but Birchie's house was otherwise immaculate, as always. Birchie and Wattie stopped in front of the stairs and the center hallway, turning back toward us. We formed up into a loose half circle facing them, as if we were all children who'd been varying degrees of naughty.

It was me, then Rachel, then Lav, and Selcouth Martin on the far end, holding his gym bag. Lav was sticking close to him, all big eyes and dazzled smile. I'd conjured her father, and now her HELLO! frog emoji had magicked Digby's into being. She was delighted with herself.

I stole a peek down the line at him, and his face was unreadable and stoic. His arrival had been so fast it seemed decisive, as if he already knew his course. That scared me. My mind ticked through scenarios: He was here to demand I sign a paper absolving him of fatherhood. No, he wanted to claim shared custody from the get-go. Could he legally make me mail a brand-new baby twelve hours away from Norfolk every other weekend? I'd called because Digby deserved to have a father, to know his father's family. But now Selcouth Martin was here in Birchville. He was a real, whole person. He had a heartbeat and a brain full of his own ideas. I was terrified of what those ideas might be.

I stopped, frozen in the entry with my family like a deer who feels safer in the center of a herd. But deer couldn't talk. What a luxury! I wished I couldn't either, the second I started to introduce him and realized that I'd never heard him say his name. Not sober. Not that I remembered. What if I said "Sel-*cowth*" and he corrected me—*Actually, it's Sel*-coth—making it instantly plain that I was pregnant by a man whose name I did not know how to say? Which was true, actually, but it wasn't the sort of thing I'd put on a birth announcement. I couldn't very well declare, *Y'all, this is Batman,* like I was Lavender. Introducing him as Mr. Martin seemed way too formal, considering that I was chock-full of his baby.

So I floundered. It was only a second of gigged silence, but Birchie sailed into the gap, so fast that even my socially adept stepsister was left in her mannerly dust.

"I'm Emily Birch Briggs, young man. Leia's grandmother," she announced, stepping forward with her hand out. Her eyes were still overbright, as if a blue-hot fire had been lit behind them. "And you are?"

"Selcouth Martin," he said, shaking her hand. Sel-*cooth*, so at least I knew that now. He added, "Most of mmmm . . . I go by Sel."

"We are all, as you can imagine, very interested to meet you, Mr. Martin," my grandmother said, seemingly in control, but there'd been rabbits afoot already this morning, and then that "Daddy" chanting in the yard. She was pale, and though the house was so cool the air had a crisp edge to it, a fine sheen of sweat was forming on her forehead. "How long have you known about the baby, is my question."

Selcouth—Sel—took a quick peek at his watch and said, "Uh . . . about seven hours?"

"Six hours and fifty-five minutes longer than I have," Rachel said to me, sotto voce and a little snotty.

"Well, he is the father," I whispered back. He would

have had a much bigger lead on her, in an ideal world. One where I knew his agenda and how to pronounce his name. My head was still spinning with sinister reasons for his instapresence, my worst-case scenarios expanding at both ends: He wanted primary custody. He was going to try to bully me into an abortion.

"And yet my teenage daughter knows?" Rachel whispered, and I missed the first part of whatever Wattie was saying.

". . . flights from Norfolk. You were lucky to have gotten right onto a plane," she finished in an approving tone.

I felt the blush as a heat in my cheeks. Atlanta was only a two-hour drive away, but, like Rachel, Wattie was assuming that Sel Martin was my boyfriend and that he had flown down from Virginia.

That, of course, made zero sense to Sel, who said, "I . . . I . . . I . . ."

I saved him by bulling on through the introductions, putting off the inevitable by way of good manners. "This is Mrs. Wattie Price, our dearest family friend." He reached out to shake her hand, nodding, silent and solemn. He seemed shy here in a way he hadn't been at FanCon. Of course, this room was stuffed with my relatives and his unborn kid. "And this is my stepsister, Rachel, and her daughter, Lavender."

He glanced over at me as he turned to shake with Rachel, and I had forgotten how very dark his eyes were. Out of the sunshine, at this distance, they looked solid black, so that I couldn't tell his irises from his pupils. It made his expression hard to read. I had a sudden urge to get closer. Very close, so I could peer in and see what he was thinking.

He turned to Lavender, putting out his hand. She took it in both of hers and beamed up at him, so excited she could hardly stand to be in her own skin.

"I'm the one who found you!" she proclaimed.

He blinked, nonplused, and said, "Was I luh . . . luh . . . llll . . ."

Lost, I thought. That was the word that ended his question, but it was stuck in his mouth. I could practically see it jammed up in there. I had a strong urge to say it for him, but I quashed it. It felt intrusive and oddly presumptuous to speak for him.

He closed his mouth, swallowed, and then a different word came out. "Mislaid?"

"You didn't tell him?" Lav asked me over her shoulder, grinning, and then she said to Batman, "I sent you that frog emoji."

"What?" he said to her, and his gaze flew to meet mine again.

"What?" Rachel echoed, very, very sharp. And

then, to Sel, "I don't see how you got here so fast from Norfolk."

"No, he's from Atlanta," Lavender corrected, as happy-jittery as a puppy.

"Mm, mm, mm," said Wattie, almost to herself. "You two children are in a red-hot mess."

Lav was still explaining. "They met at FanCon, and she lost him, but I found him on Facebook. Well, me and Hugh did."

She said it as if this were all so damn romantic, as if we were in a scene from one of those old Julia Roberts movies that Rachel liked so much, and I should say, *I'm just a pregnant girl, standing in front of a Batman,* and soaring violin music would play, and everyone would clap, delighted, watching us kiss.

Rachel, undelighted, said, "FanCon? You told my daughter, my thirteen-year-old daughter, that you picked up a guy at—" Her voice cut out for a half second as something else occurred to her. "My God, Leia, do you even know him?"

Wattie fixed me with a very, very Baptist look. "Well, speaking biblically, we have good reason to think Leia knows Mr. Martin quite well."

Birchie was the only one who seemed unfazed.

"Good words!" she said, as though a dog named Words were in the room and had brought her slippers.

Then her tone changed abruptly, and she asked me, "Are you going introduce us?" in a querulous voice, overloud. "You should have introduced me first. I am your grandmother."

I started to explain that she had already introduced herself, but Wattie turned to her and talked over me.

"We're so sorry. That was not well done. Mr. Martin. This is Emily Birch Briggs, Leia's grandmother."

To his credit, Sel rolled with this, shaking Birchie's hand again and smiling. He was a nurse, after all, and I'd told him about Birchie's Lewy bodies.

He started to ask Birchie a question. It began with a *W*, and he got stuck on it, hard. It sounded like there was a wind trapped in his mouth. He kept blowing the *W* out, but the rest of the word would not come with it. He stopped and put a hand briefly over his eyes.

Too many pieces of my family and secrets and wrong assumptions were colliding. Birchie was more off now, before lunch, than she was even at bedtime. Rachel wanted to murder me, and Jake could be back any second, maybe even with Hugh and Jeffrey in tow. The last thing this room needed was a jackass and a few more teenagers.

"Good words!" Birchie barked again, and Wattie turned full profile, whispering directly into Birchie's ear.

Batman pivoted to me and spread his hands, like he was making an apology.

"I stutter." It was the first thing he'd said to me directly, and the only thing he'd said so far that had come out clean.

"Okay," I said, puzzled. He hadn't stuttered when we played Words with Friends or at FanCon.

His beautiful, quick smile flashed, and he said, as if he'd read my mind, "Beer helps, and it's wuh-wah . . . it intensifies when I'm under stress. I'm fff-mm . . . stressed now. I'm surprised I've muh-managed to say anything." That all came out with only a few blips, as though his telling me he stuttered had relaxed him enough to make it less true.

Rachel was tucking her hair back behind her ears, embarrassed for him. I knew her so well; she wasn't sure it was politically correct to continue on with righteous fury now that he'd announced a minor disability. Lavender looked flat dismayed. She'd found him for me, brought him here like he was a present, and already he was turning out to be imperfect.

"Okay," I said again, and the main thing I was feeling was relief. It came over me in a wave so intense that a foolish grin spread across my face. It was overwide, but I couldn't help it. He stuttered! That was why he "couldn't talk" when I told him about Digby. He hadn't burst into silent hatred, and he hadn't had female company. He quite literally had not been able to get words out. "This is pretty stressful, for all of us."

He smiled back, and for a second it was like we were the only two people in the room. "I wanted to show up. I wanted you to know, I will show up."

It came out perfect, right to me, and this was what we needed. To be the only two people in a room. I dug a twenty from my pocket and held it out to Lavender. "Lav? Run go catch your dad before he gets here. Tell him to take you for ice cream and take any Darians that are headed this way, too."

"Oh, come on!" Lav protested, but Rachel backed me up.

"That is an excellent idea. Go." It was spoken in Unbrookable Mother, and Lord, but I would have to learn that language. It was so effective. Lav rolled her eyes, but she took the money.

"Rachel, best if you go with Lavender," Wattie said, calm and quiet. It wasn't only to help me, though. Birchie was swaying to some internal rhythm, staring into the dining room. "I think Birchie needs some quiet in the house right now."

"Do you need help?" Rachel said, refocusing.

"I don't think so, hmm, Birchie?" Wattie said. "We

need a cool drink and a bite of something and to have a little lie-down. We will do much better on our own."

"We're never going to be on our own," Birchie said darkly, staring into the dining room. She shook an angry finger at her own seat near the head of the table. "Get out of there."

She wasn't talking to us, though. She was talking to bad rabbits or whatever animal she saw defiling her table by Lavender's dirty breakfast dishes.

Rachel shot me a speaking glance, but she took Lavender's shoulders and steered her out the front door.

"Sorry," Lav whispered again as she went, and I said, "S'okay, kid."

Wattie was back in profile, whispering to Birchie, coaxing her to come and sit down and rest, promising a cool drink of lemonade.

Birchie looked on the verge of angry tears. "It should be champagne. Floyd teetotaled, you know. His whole life. I didn't. Daddy didn't either, but that's not what's going to put us both in hell."

Even with the front door closed, I heard Lav calling to her dad as she clattered like a pony down the porch stairs, which meant that in another thirty seconds we would have had Jake here, on top of everything. So that was a small mercy.

Wattie's whispers were so soft now that they were for Birchie alone, and she eased her along toward the table.

"We are having lemonade. You are not," Birchie told all the nothings that were not in the empty chairs, still angry, but also cold and flat, as if she were reciting facts. *The sun's a yellow star, gravity works, and silly rabbits, lemonade is only for old ladies.*

Wattie made a shooing hand at me behind her back.

"Come on," I whispered to Sel Martin.

I led him silently down the hall, back to the sewing room. I opened the door for him, and he went in. All the way in, walking to the far side to stand in front of the rainbow of quilt squares stacked in the shelves, his gym bag held awkwardly in front of him. I closed the door behind me, and I stayed right there, by the door.

I wished I had a bag to hold. I couldn't figure out what to do with my hands. Everything possible felt fake and posed and full of silent messages. Clasped in front was judgey, behind my back turned me into a naughty child, and crossing my arms felt defensive or, worse, angry. I hung them by my sides, where they felt obvious and unwieldy.

This is what I'd wanted, but now, with the door closed, I was remembering that the last time I'd been alone in a room with him, we'd made Digby. I knew that this near stranger had a hairline scar on his abdomen. *Appendix,* he'd told me as I ran my tongue along it. This was the same man who had kissed the tiny birthmark I kept hidden high up on the inside of my left thigh, now fully clothed and on the opposite end of the room.

"So we should talk," I said, and instantly blushed. World's worst opening for a conversation with a man who'd just told me he stuttered. I corrected, "I mean, I want to apologize. I shouldn't have called you at the butt crack of dawn and sprung Digby on you."

"Dih . . . Dih . . . D . . ." he said, trying to repeat the name, and I had done it again—given him vital information in a casual side spill, like when I'd told him I was having a boy via a pronoun slip.

"I'm sorry. Digby is what I've been calling the baby."

"Oh," he said, and very carefully made no facial expression.

"You don't like it?" I asked, because whether Digby's father would like the name was not something that had crossed my mind. Not until I was facing Digby's father.

"I luh-luh-love it," he lied. He wasn't very good at it.

Strangely, this obvious lie to please me made me

feel a little better. Maybe he was like that cliché about snakes—as scared of me as I was of him. I stayed on my side of the room, trying to read his silence, his dark eyes, his carefully neutral body language, as awkward as my own. Did he have his own worst-case scenarios running in his head?

The first thing he'd said to me was, *I wanted to show up. I wanted you to know I will show up.* That was the thing he'd said that mattered anyway. He'd dropped everything to appear bare hours after I told him I was pregnant.

Meanwhile I had his kid tucked inside my body. That made Digby wholly mine for now. I hadn't contacted Sel for months, and when I finally did, I hadn't mentioned the baby. I could have kept Digby to myself forever, and he knew it.

Maybe that was his worst-case scenario. Was he scared of being locked out of his own kid's life? I wanted his words, for him to tell me, but they were trapped inside his mouth. So I took it as my best, most hopeful guess, and I rolled with it.

"Digby can be what we call him while I'm pregnant, like Rachel called Lavender 'Beanie' before she was born. We can figure his real name later. Something we both love. If you want."

His smile appeared, relieved and beautiful, and I

knew I'd guessed right even before he said, "Gug-guh-gggg . . ." trying to get out some affirmative. *Good,* or maybe *Great.* He snapped his mouth shut, nostrils flaring, frustrated.

I said, "Don't be nervous. We're on the same side here, I think. Aren't we? I think about Digby—Digby-for-now, or whatever we end up naming Digby—and I'm on his side. Are you?" He nodded in sincere, vehement silence. "Okay, then. So we have to find a way to talk. I'd offer you a beer, but there isn't any in the house. We have bourbon, but between your evolution T-shirt and drinking before noon, Wattie might go find the old shotgun and run you off." His gaze had turned speculative. I was flat-out babbling, my own nerves causing the words to run out of me, trying to make up for all his stuck ones. "What if we got our phones? We could sit in the same room and text. It's very modern. Lavender and her friends do it all the time."

He put his hand briefly over his eyes again. When he took it away, his expression was rueful. He held one finger in a wait-a-sec gesture, and now he was the one blushing. Furiously. So furiously that I could see the red wash rising in the undertones of his skin, especially in the tips of his ears.

He turned away and set his gym bag down by my laptop on the Singer table, opened it, and set his book aside. It was a hardback of *Saga*, as battered around the edges as my own beloved copy back in Norfolk. He really did have damn good taste in comics. He pulled out a wad of black cloth and unfurled it, his back still to me, and then he pulled it on over his head.

It was the cowl, the same one I remembered from FanCon, with the bat ears poking up. The long cloak fell behind him to midcalf. He pulled at the neck, simultaneously twitching his shoulders, getting it all to lie correctly in one practiced motion, and then he turned back around to face me.

"Hello," said Batman. And it was him. Sel Martin was gone. This was the hot Batman with the lush mouth, flashing the cocky smile that had caught me at the hotel bar. His eyes glinted through the slits in the mask.

"Hel-*lo*," I said.

The gym bag was empty. He hadn't brought the rest of the suit, but it didn't matter. The pieces he had worked fine with the gray shirt and the dark jeans, kind of like I'd run into Batman on casual Friday.

"Let's talk about this kid." No stutter. Not even a hint of one.

"Damn," I said, and I realized I was grinning back at him, hugely, dorkishly. I shut it down, embarrassed. I gestured at his cowl, his cape. "That works?"

"Always." He shrugged. "Even when I was a kid,

running around the house in Dark Knight Underoos and a black pillowcase with home-cut eyeholes."

"Do you wear it to your job?" I asked him, fascinated.

I almost wished he did. I personally would love to be rolled back for surgery to find that my twilight sleep would be managed by one of the Super Friends. It might be a little disconcerting for non-nerds, though.

"I don't stutter much at my job," he said, soft like always, but I could hear him fine in the quiet room. "Or with my friends. Not since I was a kid. It only gets bad when I try to talk to pretty women. Or when I find out I accidentally made a baby. Or when I'm alone with one of my favorite artists. I'm three for three today."

"That's a total player line," I said, taking one step closer. The dreadful art monster in me wanted to know who his other favorite artists were and where my stuff came in the ranking, but I shoved that aside for later.

He shrugged, unabashed. "You're pretty. You're pregnant. And you're Leia freakin' Birch. You know how many times I've read *Violence in Violet*? Plus, I've got every series that you've drawn for in sleeves."

"Every series?" I said. "Not my Hellboy one-shot." It was a limited-release thing I'd done with a writer I liked.

"Oh, yeah," he said. "That sequence, when Hell

Boy's running through the tunnels and the fire rolls over him? His face? So good."

I found myself touching my hair, flattered. I'd been grossly proud of the way I'd caught Hell Boy's pleasure and his shame as the flames engulfed him. I made my treacherous girly-flirt hands go back down by my sides.

"Nerd Test," I said, changing the subject. "DC or Marvel?"

"Uh, DC?" he said like this was a no-brainer.

Wonder Woman was DC, and he was wearing half a Batsuit, so it actually was. It was a place to start where I felt sure we would agree.

"Fantastic Four or Doom Patrol?" he asked back, which was bolder. Riskier.

"Doom Patrol," I said. "Especially Grant Morrison's run."

"Yeah, damn. Richard Case," he said in full agreement, and now he came a step toward me. "I didn't come straight here. I went to Macon first, to my parents' house." It was as if our successful round of Nerd Testing had made it okay to talk about scarier things. "It was four A.M., but I had to go talk to my dad."

"You guys are close?" I said, and drifted closer, as if saying the word out loud made my body act it out. I already knew they were tight. It was obvious in the picture of the *Star Wars* Christmas tree.

"He's my best friend," Batman said. "Does that sound dorky?"

"Absolutely." I smiled when I said it. "I like dorks, though. Hell, I am dorks."

"Okay, then. I told him. About the baby. You. FanCon. He gave me some good advice, but it didn't matter. I knew I was coming straight here to see you. I knew when he opened the door. It was so early I'd woken him up. His face was grumpy, but he saw me, and before he thought to be worried, he lit up." He was very serious now, his low voice intense. "I don't want my kid to grow up twelve hours away. I have nieces and nephews, and I love them, but I only see them three or four times a year. Every time they've grown into different people. I don't want to know my own kid like that. In snapshots. I want to be the kind of father that I have."

Now my hands were in front of me, twisting together in a tangled bother. Here was everything that I wanted for Digby, offered freely, as his birthright. I wasn't sure how to grasp it, though. I was too much of a pragmatist.

"I love what you're saying, but how would it work? It's not like you're going to pack up all your crap and move to Norfolk tomorrow." I said it the same way I might say, *It's not like you're going to take up fly-*

ing Douglas Adams style, just throw your body at the ground and hope to miss.

"Of course not," he said, but then he added, "Not tomorrow anyway. I've never been to Norfolk. I might hate it, who knows? But you're growing my kid there. I sure as hell want to take a look at the place." Now I was the one who couldn't speak. Whatever smart-ass answer I might have had jammed up in my mouth and left me silent. "I want you to come and see Atlanta, too. You might fall in love. There's a lot more to my town than FanCon."

I swallowed. Jesus, this was high-stakes stuff. "What if I hate it?"

"Come and see," he said. "What if you don't?"

"What if you hate Norfolk and I hate Atlanta?" I said, and I sounded panicky. "What then?"

He shrugged. "I don't know. We look at Wilmington. We look at Asheville. Why not? You work freelance, and I'm a CNRA, which means I can get a job almost anywhere. If we hate Wilmington and Asheville, we go visit Myrtle Beach and Greensboro. We'll pick a place together, same way we pick his name." As he spoke, we had both moved even closer to each other. We were near the middle of the room, and now I could see the deeps of his eyes inside the mask. His pupils had expanded, so that the iris was a slim, near-jet ring.

He made it sound so doable, and maybe it was. I hoped so, because inside me Digby was awake and spinning, small and certain, absolutely on the way. I wished then, hard, that I were an optimist. Rachel was. Once, irritated with my dark-siding, she'd said, "Is the glass never half full for you?" and I'd snapped back. "Sure it is. Half full of bees."

She'd laughed and said, "Half full of poison. Half full of deadly radiation, but always half empty when it's sugar or sunshine." She had a point. My mind never went jumping to the rosiest conclusions. Look how I ended *V in V.*

"What if we argue, and hate each other so much we can't live in the same town, and screw our kid up, and ruin our lives, and then we die?" I said, mostly joking. But not joking.

He considered my dire scenario for a few seconds, and then he said, "Nerd Test: *Preacher?* Or *Pretty Deadly?*"

That one I had to think about.

"*Pretty Deadly,*" I said. "But only by a hair."

"You see? It's going to be fine," he said, fronting like he was cocksure.

I laughed. I couldn't help it. "Oh, smooth sailing," I said. "Here on out."

"Maybe not," he said, smiling back. "But there's

a town somewhere, between your family and mine, where we can both be happy. Where he can grow up with both of us," Batman said, and then his gaze dropped for a moment, and his soft voice dropped even lower, making me step in again. "I'm here. Let's start. Spend the day with me. Show me around this place."

That shocked me. "Birchville? You'd consider Birchville?"

"Sure," he said. "You got strong ties here. It's close enough to Montgomery for me to work."

"It's maybe not the best place for a mixed-race kid? There's no church where—" I began, then stopped, embarrassed to realize I was about to explain racism to a black man. He'd surely noticed once or twice, with no help from me at all, that our shared homeland had some trouble in this department. "I'm sorry." Now I was the one blushing.

He stepped in, close. "Hey, stop. That's everywhere," he said. "He'll be black no matter where we raise him."

I started to object, because Digby was half mine after all. He would not be black. He'd be— And this time I stopped myself before I got even one word out. Sel Martin was right.

My son was going to be black. Even when he was nursing in my arms, I would be a white woman with a black kid. There was no such thing as mixed-race in the South, or in America for that matter. The whole country had called a mixed-race man our "first black president." Lou Elle Peterson, who ran Redemption's All Sisters Service Club, had light gold eyes, and her skin was no darker than Rachel's got in summer. But she was black. Everyone thought of her as black. I thought of her as black, and when I admitted this, a weird wave of panic washed through me. A thousand Facebook videos I'd cried over became hideously relevant to me in whole new ways. My hands went to my belly, and I shook my head at Sel, all my words stuck inside me now.

"He can never wear a hoodie," I finally said, which was nonsensical, but I was fully freaking out.

"Okay," Sel said, very calm. "We have a lot to talk about. But, you know, there's time."

I looked at him with drowning eyes, but he was so calm that I felt calmer, too. There was barely a foot of space between us now, and it was good to be this close to him. I could read his gaze, and it was kind on me. He wasn't thinking I was stupid; he wasn't blaming me for being blind. He could imagine Digby's life in ways I couldn't, and he knew the world our boy would navigate. He was present, already stepping in, stepping up for a son he'd learned only hours ago even existed.

My heart swelled up inside my chest, and he deserved the cape. He'd earned the cowl, and what baby could be safer than this nascent one, now curled up barely a breath away from Batman.

"Okay," I said, leaning in toward him. "There's time."

"Oh, yeah. We've only got one immediate problem," he said.

"What's that?" I asked, and he bent down and kissed me.

No body contact. Only his mouth, firm and sure, fitting itself to mine, seeking a response. My body gave it, swaying into his. Then his hand cupped my neck, reaching under my hair and tangling in it.

My stomach dropped in that weightless, rollercoaster feeling. I lost my breath, and my arms went around him, under the cloak, my fingers remembering the smooth lines of muscle in his back. His free hand was on my hip now, pulling me into him. My heartbeat left my heart and became a beat that happened all over my body. I felt its pulse behind my eyes, in my shaking hands, low down in my belly.

He broke the contact but stayed close.

I drew a ragged breath, and I said, "Damn."

I could tell myself it was second-trimester hormones. I could tell myself that it was just the cowl. I was old-school nerd—God knew I liked a fellow in a cowl. But it wasn't only these things, just as it hadn't been only the tequila that night at FanCon.

Now that he was this close, I remembered his smell. Under the faint, crisp linen of some kind of aftershave was the scent of a man that was this specific man, and it was correct. When he kissed me, it was right like facts were right, like hard science, chemical and sure. I did not know much about Batman, but this part? This part worked. This part worked way too well.

He pushed the cowl off, letting it hang down behind him with the cloak.

"Oh, good. I was worried it was just my puh-problem," Sel Martin said.

"Nope. That's both of us," I said, and he grinned. "Don't grin like that. This is so scary." His face changed not at all, so I made stern eyebrows at him. "Really. We need to be careful with each other." He did not stop grinning.

"Leia freakin' Birch," he said, a world of admiration in the words, all kinds, and damn it all if my mouth wasn't grinning back at him.

Stupid mouth. We'd actually solved exactly noth-ing. We were still near strangers, and pregnant, and had full lives in separate cities that were far away. We lived in different Americas. His was more dangerous than mine, and our kid was going to live there, too. We'd actually undone one solved thing, because Digby would need a real name in a few short months. But we stood too close, grinning at each other anyway like natural-born fools, like idiots who'd been kissing when we ought to have been having scary talk and making hard decisions.

Brilliant idiots. His hand was still resting on my hip like it belonged there, and I thought maybe the wisest thing I could do would be to pull his face down to my face and kiss him, just a little more.

Which, of course, was the exact same second Birchie started screaming.

20

It was a staccato burst of screams, short and sharp, echoed by a heavy thump and clatter. I ran out the door and back up the hall, spurred on by the sound of breaking glass. Batman ran with me, the deflated cowl flapping at the nape of his neck and his cloak billowing out after us. We passed the stairs, skidding to a stop behind Wattie just as Birchie's longest scream began, an enraged, near-endless "No!"

Frank Darian was near the foot of the dining-room table, on our side, clearly panicking. He had his hands raised in an almost comical defensive posture toward my grandmother, as if propitiating a fluffy-haired mad god.

Birchie stood with her legs braced on the far side of the table. Her face was shiny with sweat, and hectic red circles were burning in her cheeks. She had Lavender's dirty fork in one fist, lifted like a weapon.

Wattie, talking so sweetly it was almost a croon, said, "Now, then, hush," while putting one herding hand out as Batman and I came up, keeping us behind her. She shot us a quick glance over her shoulder. "Don't, now. Birchie needs a little room."

I'd never seen Birchie this way, violent, weaving, puffing. Wattie was so calm, though, that I thought, *She's seen this. She's seen Birchie this way before, and more than once. God help us.* I obeyed her, putting one hand on Sel Martin's arm for a second to hold him with me.

Birchie's chair was tipped over, and the pitcher of lemonade had fallen or been pushed off the table. It was now a large puddle dotted with melting ice and chunks and slivers of glass near us. Birchie's cup was overturned on the tabletop, and her lemonade was still flattening and spreading across the wood. One liquid finger, then another, reached the edge of the table and began drip-dropping onto the floor. It was a soothing sound, a pattering, like summer rain.

That sound had no place in this electric room, where Birchie told us in a screechy, rage-filled voice, "I said no, I said no, I said no, I said!" She turned from one of us to the next, the dirty fork held up by one ear in her bent arm, tines facing us, like it was a butcher knife.

Frank Darian was talking to Birchie, apologizing for something? I couldn't follow because Batman was asking quietly, "What meds is she taking?"

I could not remember the names, but Wattie answered, "Exelon and Sinemet."

"I'm so sorry," Frank said again. "I should have called."

"Nothing for anxiety?" Batman's stutter had not come into the room with us. Maybe it was the feel of the long cloak, still hanging down his back, or maybe he was in nurse mode.

"What are you whispering about?" Birchie said, turning her fork toward us, glaring. "Are you having secrets from me? Are you making more secrets?"

"I was telling Mr. Martin here that you have Valium for when you're mad like this," Wattie said. "In the kitchen cabinet, left of the stove. Maybe Frank can get one for you?" It was a sweet-voiced question, yet every person in the room but Birchie heard it as an order.

"Of course," Frank said, and started forward.

"Go the long way, Frank," Wattie said, and he obeyed her, turning away from the dining room and going through the entry and up the hall as Wattie went on, saying, "Maybe we should all sit down," ignoring the fork and the way Birchie's chest was heaving.

"How on earth can I? He took my chair!" Birchie said. "This won't do! This will not do at all!"

"Your chair fell over. Frank didn't take it. He went to get your pills," Wattie said, sweet and reasonable.

"You're bleeding," Sel Martin said.

"What?" I said, but he was speaking to Wattie.

"Not Frank! Don't be stupid. I meant him," Birchie said, turning to jerk her fork toward no one, toward nothing, toward her own empty spot at the head of the table.

While she was in profile, Sel stepped forward, through the wreckage of the shattered pitcher. He ignored the crunch of glass under his shoes and grabbed Lavender's linen napkin off the table. He went to Wattie and bent to examine her arm, up high near the shoulder.

"Mm, that's pretty deep," he said. He pressed the napkin to her arm, and red splotches came soaking through the white linen.

"Did she do that?" I asked Wattie, but she ignored me. "Did Birchie hurt you?"

"How'd you get back in my house, you salty bastard?" Birchie talked over me, furious. She was staring at the portrait that hung to the left of the table's head.

Her father, Ellis Birch, stared back with his proud painted eyes. "We took you out. How did you sneak back in my house? We crashed you in the car!" She was outraged, as if the bones had escaped the evidence locker, refleshed themselves, and come straight home to reclaim the head of the Birch table. It had been her spot for sixty years now.

It made me want her rabbits back. Birchie's rabbits had gone bad, but at least she knew they weren't really there. She didn't curse or yell at them. That was saved for Ellis Birch, her father, the man she'd ended with a hammer. The worst part was, this shrieking version of my Birchie, lofting her fork, had no remorse. She looked ready to end him all over again.

"Keep pressing on it, and keep it lifted. We need to get it clean," Sel told Wattie, folding her hand over the napkin. "When's the last time you had a tetanus shot?"

Birchie heard him and glanced his way, fork still lifted high. When she saw Sel, she began to giggle. It was a high-pitched, girlish sound, almost garish coming from her small, elderly mouth.

She shook her fork at the portrait and asked, still tittering, "Do you know he's black? Look how black he is!" She leaned in, smacking her lips.

"I did notice that," Wattie said, unfazed, as if Birchie were talking to her. She was working hard to get Birchie to notice or talk back to someone, anyone, who was actually present.

I felt my cheeks flush and said to Sel, "She's sick."

"S'okay. I knew I was black." He flashed me a quick smile before turning to Frank, who'd returned with the pills. I hadn't noticed him come up behind us until he was handing me an amber bottle. Sel said to Frank, "Can you get their first-aid kit?"

"Look how black he is, I said, you salty bastard!" Birchie was still talking to the portrait.

Frank, his whole face gone pink with embarrassment and stress, said, "Sure, yes, it's in the pantry," and went back up the hallway.

Birchie stared the portrait down. "We're having ourselves a little, tiny black baby. Come next year there'll be a tiny black Birch sitting at your table, eating up Vina's recipe for sweet potatoes. Eating right off your spoons. Little toasty marshmallows. Off your spoons. How will you like that?" That girlish, awful laugh got out of her again. "How will you like sitting at this table then?"

She was blowing, puffing her air out, then pulling in a tiny panted sip on the inhale. The hectic splotches in her cheeks had spread to stains that ran from her chin to the outside of her brow line.

"How do we make those sweet potatoes?" Wattie asked, holding the napkin tight to her arm. "I forget. Do they take brown sugar or molasses?"

Birchie swayed, her head cocked. She was listening, but not to Wattie. The lifted fork trembled in her hand. Drool had collected in the corners of her mouth.

Birchie said, "He doesn't like it, Wattie," staring the portrait down, weirdly joyful.

"I'm sure he doesn't," Wattie said. "But I need you to tell me, how much butter?"

"Fuck those sweet potatoes," Birchie said, her fury reigniting, but at least she was talking to Wattie now. Not a painting. Not the bones. "Why won't you hear me, Wattie? You know him. You know, but you will not ever hear me." Her gaze went right back to the portrait, and I knew we'd lost her again. "She knows you, you fuck, you fuck, you fuck-fuck-fuck."

"Birchie?" I said, but she was gone.

She ran at the painting in a blur, screaming obscenities, faster than I had seen her move in decades. She drove the raised fork into her father's painted face. The curse became a high animal keening, and she stabbed again and then again, as hard as she could, aiming for his right eye. Spittle ran down her chin, spraying his face as the fork caught. She jerked it out, tearing the eye away entirely. She took aim at the second one, stabbing true, then dragging it down the eye, scouring it.

I didn't know her. I didn't know this version of her, and my hands were on my own cheeks, and my cheeks were wet.

Sel was on her side of the table so fast I hadn't clocked him going. He came up behind her, ignoring her banshee wail and the wild tomahawk chopping of her stabbing hand. He took Birchie in his arms in a single smooth movement, catching her wrist before she could stab the painting again. His long arms locked around her, pinning hers. She screamed and reared, her feet lifting off the floor as she kicked the air in front of her, her fluffy bun unraveling as her head thrashed back and forth.

"Oh, no, oh, no!" I said, helpless, watching my grandmother flailing and screaming in his arms.

"It's all right, it's all right," Sel Martin said, as calm as Wattie, dragging Birchie back a few steps so she couldn't kick the wall and hurt her feet. Both her shoes had come off, and I hoped the broken glass was all on my side of the table.

"Don't hurt her," I said, but he wasn't hurting her.

His arms around her were firm and sure, holding her as she thrashed like a caught fish.

Birchie's screaming thinned, devolving into a word. A name.

"Wattie! Wattie!" Birchie called, her voice shaking. Her body stilled, in pieces. Feet first, and as soon as she stopped kicking, Wattie was there, in front of her, dropping the bloody napkin to the floor so she could peel Birchie's fingers open and take the fork. "Wattie!"

"Hush, baby, hush," Wattie said, dropping the fork, too. It clattered onto the hardwood, and she put her hands on Birchie's cheeks to still her thrashing head. Her arm continued to bleed, but she ignored it. She put her face near Birchie's face and looked into her eyes. "I'm here. I'm here. Hush. Hush."

"Call an ambulance," Sel said to me, calm and sure.

Wattie said, "Don't you dare," in that same voice Rachel had used to send off Lavender. Unbrookable Mother, and it worked on all of us. Except the medical professional.

"I think we should," Sel told us. "At least call her doctor."

"I'm so sorry. I did not mean to upset her!" Frank said. He was back with Birchie's first-aid kit from the pantry clutched in his hands. He set it down on the table, then put Birchie's chair upright, and I was instantly so grateful. It was one less wrong thing in this room full of wrong things.

"It's all right," Wattie said. She kept her eyes fixed on Birchie's eyes. "I'm here. You see me? I'm here. It's just us here. We'll have our medicine? Yes?" She held Birchie's face firm in her hands, with Birchie's long white hair loose from its bun and hanging down in strings over her face and Wattie's hands. Birchie started crying.

"I'm so tired," she said. "I'm so tired."

My hands were shaking, so it was hard to get the bottle open. I got the cap off and managed to spill a blue cotton-candy-colored pill into my palm. One cup of lemonade was still miraculously upright, sitting half empty in front of Wattie's usual chair. I set the amber bottle down, wiped my eyes, and got the cup.

I came around the table and said, "Birchie? I have your pill. Okay?"

After a long moment, Birchie said, "Well, all right."

Sel was still holding her, but he released her wrist. I handed her the pill, and she put it in her mouth, then drank some of Wattie's lemonade, swallowing it. Sel's grip had loosened, and her feet were on the floor. She stood swaying slightly in his arms, her blue-button eyes gone blank and her mouth crumpling in on itself. She looked like she was a thousand years old, her white hair streaming all down her shoulders in a tangle of thin ribbons. I set the glass back on the table, and when I looked up, Birchie was blinking at me, confused but smiling.

"Leia! Honey, when did you get here?" Her eyebrows knit in mild concern. "I don't think I got the turkey. Wattie, did we get the turkey?"

"I got it, not to worry. A nice fat Thomas he is, too," Wattie said, and then to Sel, "You can let her go now."

He didn't let her go so much as hand her to me. I turned, winding one arm around her waist, supporting her. I kept her near the wall as we walked, keeping myself between her bare feet and the broken pitcher. I glanced at the portrait of Ellis Birch as we passed by, and it wasn't fixable. One eye had been ripped away down to bare canvas. The other looked as if a tiny Wolverine had slashed it.

I asked Sel quietly, over my shoulder, "Can you see to Wattie's arm? Frank brought the kit."

"Yeah. Let's—" Sel began.

"Shhh, Mr. Martin," Wattie interrupted, not loud but very firm. Wattie could speak Unbrookable Mother even at low volume. It was a nice trick. "Wait just a minute. If she hears you, sees you, it might set her off again."

I was whispering to Birchie, walking her away, "Do

you want your nap? Do you want to come lie down with me? We'll go upstairs and turn the ceiling fan on, and you can have a nice rest in the cool."

"That sounds lovely, sugar," Birchie said.

We made our slow and careful way up the stairs, to Birchie's room, and I closed the door. I moved the shams and peeled the covers down. My adrenaline had faded, and every single piece of me felt like sea glass, sanded away and worn. Even Digby, making little turns deep inside me, felt smooth-edged and slow.

Birchie sat yawning on the edge of the bed, and I brushed her tumbled hair out gently and then braided it for her. She was as placid as a sleepy child. By the time I had her tucked in, the lamps off, and the ceiling fan going in a lazy whirl, her eyelids were heavy from exhaustion and the Valium.

I kicked my own shoes off and lay down beside her on top of the covers. I was exhausted. I'd been up all night, chasing Lavender, calling Batman, fretting, but there was no way I would fall asleep. I was too anxious. Wattie was hurt—worse, Birchie had hurt her. Frank's news must be very bad, to set her off like that. Had Tackrey gotten the court order? I needed to get back downstairs and find out. Not to mention I'd abandoned Batman. Wattie would want to take his measure, plus Rachel could come back any second. I couldn't leave him unsupervised and unprotected with those two women. Even so, I wanted the Valium to take full effect before I left my grandmother. I waited quietly, gently rubbing her back until her breathing eased and became regular.

I thought, *I'd better wait another minute, be sure she's* . . . and that was the last thing I remembered thinking.

21

When I woke up, the room was nearly dark. Evening sunshine glowed faint orange at the edges of the damask drapes. Birchie was gone from the bed. I got up and went to the top of the stairs. I wanted to go straight down to find out exactly how bad Frank's news had been, but I heard Batman's voice in the hum of conversation in the parlor.

That made me pause and then go back up the hall, into the guest bathroom. I didn't want to talk to Batman while my teeth had this post-nap hairy feeling. I'd moved my toothbrush and other toiletries to the downstairs bathroom, though. I thought about stealth-using Rachel's, but if she ever found out, it would put her directly into therapy. I used one of her flossers and gargled a shot of her Listerine instead. My eyes looked tired and puffy, but it felt too obvious and girly to stand here primping, borrowing her tinted moisturizer and brown mascara and lip gloss like a belle whose beau had come a-courting. I compromised by stealing a dab of her million-dollar eye cream and running her brush through my tangled hair.

Downstairs, empty cake plates dotted the side tables; I'd slept all the way through supper. Birchie and Wattie sat side by side on one of the love seats. Wattie had a fresh white bandage on her arm. Lavender sat close to Batman on the other seat, proud again, almost proprietary, which made me suspect that the afternoon had gone well. She was repleased with herself for finding him, stutter and all.

Jake and Rachel, clearly not love-seat material, had taken the chairs facing the fireplace. There was a good two feet of cool air between them. Still, they were both in the same room with their daughter. Until I'd stepped in all entitled and unasked, they'd had a buffer zone of four full states. It felt like I'd won a prize for jackassery and given it to Lavender. When I looked at Jake, I felt oddly proud and almost proprietary right back. It was a bizarre thing to feel about Jake Jacoby, of all people.

I hoped Lav hadn't learned a taste for Rachel-style commando meddling. I was pretty sure I would return to my regular my-own-business-minding self when I got home, but Lav might have more trouble; meddling was in her genes, and our first real runs at it had so far worked out well. The parlor currently held two missing fathers, which was a record number in this house. Granted, one was a mystery and the other was kind of a tool, but still.

Birchie, in the love seat facing the stairs, saw me first. She looked pink-cheeked and smiley. Either the Valium was still working or Wattie had doubled down and given her another. I descended two more steps and saw that she was barefoot. Downstairs. Before today, I had never seen Birchie's naked feet in any room except her bedroom. It was as disconcerting as if Rachel had pranced in wearing a teddy. I wanted to run back upstairs and get the airplane socks. Or maybe I only wanted an excuse to run back upstairs.

"Oh, good, you're up!" Birchie said, and every set of human eyes in the room turned toward me. I immediately felt as garish and attention-calling as a traffic cone. If Birchie had ever allowed mice inside her walls, they all would have been looking at me, too. "We didn't want to wake you. You need your rest. But I was getting worried you'd sleep right through to morning."

As she spoke, Lav turned around entirely to grin at me, getting on her knees, her arms crossed on the back of the love seat. Sel lifted his hand in a rueful wave, as if not sure of his reception. I was mostly impressed, and I let him see it in my face. Jake was a nonfactor, but I knew the women in this room, including the teenage one. The interrogation must have been relentless, but Sel had stuck it out. At the same time, his gym bag was sitting at his feet, repacked, so he was good to bolt. Smart. I wished I could bolt, too. Everyone was peering back and forth between us. My every twitch and breath felt cataloged and measured and interpreted.

"We didn't want you to miss Sel," Wattie chimed in, and now I knew it had gone well. When I'd taken Birchie up the stairs, Batman had still been Mr. Martin. "He needs to leave quite soon. He can't miss work again tomorrow."

"He waited for you, though, didn't you, Sel?" Birchie said. "And now he's going to have to drive home mostly in the dark."

Batman rose, saying, "At least I'll muh-miss rrrr—"

"Rush hour," Rachel finished for him, and I knew, I knew he hated it. Not that he reacted, much. But I saw how his blink took an extra beat, a move I often used to gather patience. I'd done it plenty in my tenure as Rachel's stepsister.

Jake put in, "I hear it's a beast in Atlanta," very man-to-man.

"Mm," Sel said, an affirmative-ish hum of sound.

I hoped a single afternoon of Rachel wasn't enough to put him thoroughly off Norfolk. At the same time, it occurred to me that thirty-five years of living with or nearby Rachel might be just about enough.

"I'll walk you out," I said.

"Me, too," Lav said, leaping to her feet.

I froze. I owed her too much to shut her down. Rachel, thank God, stepped in and did it for me, saying, "No, ma'am. You need to take all these cake plates to the kitchen." I had to admit for the millionth time that Rachel had her uses. She made me crazy half the time, but I had no doubt that she loved my ass.

Jake added, "Might as well load the washer while you're in there."

Lav groaned and protested, but just a little. Part of her, I think, was basking in the tandem commands of double parenting.

Sel rose to say good-bye to her, then to Birchie and Wattie. I took the opportunity to tell Rachel, "Hey. I'm sorry I let Lav get her nose in my very adult business. It really was an accident."

"I'm not mad anymore. Lavender told me what happened. She can be a little . . . unstoppable," Rachel said, and she and Jake stood up to say good-bye, Rachel adding a very pointed, "Hope we see you. Soon."

Once the front door had shut behind us, Sel and I breathed a sigh of relief in perfect unison.

"You lived!" I said, as we headed down the stairs. "That must have been quite a grilling. How did you manage?"

"I stuh—" He stopped and shook his head. His hand slipped inside the half-open gym bag, fisting in the cloak. He breathed in. Out. Looked at me. "Stuttered. A lot. So they couldn't get muh-much out of me."

"Very crafty," I said. We took each step down very, very slowly, as if by agreement. "Thanks for staying. It eased their minds, to get to know you some. I can tell. And any stress or worry we can get off Birchie right now really helps."

"It wasn't a lot of work," he said, and quirked an eyebrow. "Your suh-sister ended all my sentences for me."

That made me laugh. "I bet. She finishes mine, too."

"Hmm. Way I see it, you owe me one hella awkward luh-luh . . . meal with my puh-parents now," he said, changing the subject. He didn't say any more about Rachel, and that was a first, or close to it. Most men noticed that Rachel was gorgeous—and felt compelled to mention it to me—long before they noticed how controlling she could be. If they ever did.

"At the very least," I said. I wanted to meet his parents, actually.

We'd reached the bottom of the stairs. He turned right, following the walk to the driveway, and I turned with him. We kept a careful six inches of air between us. I think both of us felt my family watching from the house. He was a city guy, so I might have been the only one who also felt watched from the windows of every house on our side of the square. All the phones in Birchville were in use right now, I would put money on it.

"You're so close right now to Muh-muh-mm . . . Atlanta and Muh—"

He was trying to say Macon. I knew it, but I waited. I wasn't going to Rachel him. His nostrils flared, and he was blushing again, deeply. I put a hand on his arm, in spite of all the eyes, stopping us at the very edge of our yard and looking up at him.

"Don't worry about it," I said. "Your stutter doesn't bother me. If you really need to say something and it won't come out? I kinda like you in that cowl." I felt my own cheeks heat, because that was such an understatement. I really liked Sel Martin in that cowl. Add the long, swirling cloak and I'd start to wonder why people had ever invented underwear. Keeping them on could feel downright gratuitous.

"Sure," he said. "Right here in Suh-Smallville's town square."

"Why not?" I said. "They're used to Big Nerd Doings whenever I'm in town. I ran around here every summer in a Wonder Woman unitard and completely unbulletproof plastic bracelets."

His ridiculous thick eyelashes dropped over his eyes. "Buh-but you were probably fuh-ffff-five."

"Try fifteen," I said. "I told you. Big. Nerd. Doings. I only stopped because I finally grew boobs. Birchie said it was a scandal, and she and Wattie wouldn't make me a new one."

He chuckled, at the same time sizing me up to see if I was serious. I was dead serious, and the set of his shoulders eased by a degree.

"Macon," he said, clear as day, and then made ta-da hands at me. "I wuh-won't always be this nerved up around you. I hope."

We started walking again, slower than a creep, dawdling across the street to the line of parked cars around the square. This was how it was when the guy was new, and smelled right, and everything he said seemed so very interesting. It had been a while, but I remembered this. We were like kids playing no-you-hang-up-first, but with a whole town watching. He must have felt watched, too, city boy or not, because he hadn't kissed me. And he wanted to kiss me. I could feel it.

"You make me nervous, too," I told him. "But it's a good nervous. You know?"

He flashed me the cocky smile I liked. He did know. "You have a lot going on here, but in a tuh-t-t . . . small place like this you must have slow days. Take one, soon. Come see my city. Muh-meet my folks."

"I will. As soon as I can. I have to get Birchie back into her routine and stable before I take a day trip."

Sel nodded his agreement. She was so far from stable she'd stabbed her dearest Wattie with a fork. Of course, this was assuming that Regina Tackrey would see reason and Birchie and Wattie wouldn't be jerked out of their routine and into prison.

"It's complicated. Birchie's in kind of a mess right now. More than the illness. It's long, and awful, and very hard to nutshell, but there's stuff happening here that I need to be around for."

"Yeah," he said. "The buh-b-bones."

I literally did a double take. "How did you . . . ?" But I had no need to finish the question. "Lavender," we both said. He stuck briefly on the *L,* so he lagged a syllable behind me.

"Useful kid," he said, and I waited, braced, but that was all.

I was relieved he wasn't going to ask me avid, ugly questions. Not right this minute anyway. Also, I'd been a little worried he was going to man-pout or guilt me ever since Lavender had spilled that she was actually the one who'd contacted him. On the one hand, I was glad to be absolved of sending cutesy-tootsy HELLO! frog emojis. But now he knew that back at FanCon I'd woken up and thrown out the note with his phone number. I'd actually flushed it, right along with the one used condom where there damn well should have been two. He had to know that if there'd been two, there would be no baby and he never would have heard from me again. A guy like Jake Jacoby, say, would have felt that as an ego kick and needed smoothing and soothing. Batman let it go with two kind words—*Useful kid*—and I was getting the sense that Sel Martin was an easygoing kind of guy.

"The bones. Yeah," I said. His not asking made it easier to say, "It seemed like a lot to explain over Words with Friends."

"It's nuh-not a second-date conversation," he agreed, and stopped by a dark gray Outback. "This is me."

"I didn't think the Batmobile would be a Subaru," I said, and he smiled. It occurred to me that if he was up to speed, he might know more than I did currently. He might know why Frank came by and sent Birchie into orbit.

"Did Tackrey get the court order for a DNA test?" I asked.

"Oh, yeah, you missed that. She did," he said.

"Shit," I said. "Just shit." But I wasn't surprised. I'd been expecting it.

Rachel was right. I was not an optimist. I hadn't believed, not down deep, that my impromptu public-relations picnic in the Mack yard could halt the grinding of legal wheels already in motion.

"So . . . it'll be positive?" Sel Martin asked, human and curious.

"I think so," I admitted. "But at this point it's ridiculous. I wish I'd thought to film Birchie this afternoon. This is not a woman who can be held responsible for something she saw or knew about or even . . . even did. It was sixty years ago, and now she can't defend herself." The Lewy bodies had returned her to her own initial innocence. They were stealing her memories and her intellect and her ability to choose, until I could almost see her rabbits gathering around her. At the same time, I doubted a film of Birchie remurdering her father with a fork would be all that helpful. That wild attack had been the opposite of sorry.

"Agreed," he said. "At some puh-point, her doctor's testimony, maybe, will make them stop."

So he was an optimist. Even if Birchie was uncon-victable, if Tackrey dragged this on, the stress would kill her or exacerbate her illness to the point that she moved to Rabbit Land entirely. Also, there was Wattie to think about. She was of perfectly sound mind, and she didn't have Birchie's family name and influence. If Tackrey pushed it, Wattie could very well end up spending her last good years in prison. I wondered, not for the first time, if I should let her sons know how real the danger was. She wouldn't thank me or forgive me, though, and Wattie was in her right mind. I had to let it be her call.

"Anyway. This isn't a second-date conversation ei-ther," I said. "I'm just so frustrated. At a certain point, when everything gets this wrecked, there can't be a next, you know? It's done. Game over. The end. There is no next."

His gaze on me was frank and curious. He leaned on the car.

"I'm not saying anyone should prosecute your grandma. But speaking philosophically? There's al-ways a next."

"Speaking philosophically, not if you die," I said, so over-the-top dour that he laughed. I was happy to change the subject to something less tangible than human remains and the prosecutions of my dear old ladies.

"Even if you die," he countered, interested. Maybe he'd forgotten to be nervous, because right now he wasn't stuttering at all. "You don't see it, but next happens anyway and always. With or without you."

"No, I know, but—" I began, but then I stopped, because that phrase, "next happens anyway and always," those words, in that order, clicked with some buried something in my own brain. "Do you really believe that?"

"Yeah. At least until the world ends," he said, but maybe he was righter than he knew. Maybe there was a next even then, I thought, and then my brain did that irritating artist thing, where I stopped being in the road, or even in my body. All at once I was in Violet's world, and Violence's. A ruined place, with no next. When I came out again, I had a question.

"Nerd Test," I said. "This is for the big money. Are you ready?"

He nodded, mock solemn, and I asked him Rachel's question. "Violence and Violet, are they lovers?"

"Nah," he said, sure and immediate. Like it was obvious. "Violet *is* Violence. She just doesn't know it." I'd been leaning that way, but when I heard him say it out loud, the artist in me knew that it was true. "In the warehouse scene? Violet has her hands over her eyes, and most of her little birds and animals hide, too, but the rabbits give it away. They watch Violence eat that drug lord, and you hid those little shadow rabbits in Violence's hair. I missed it on my first read. You're pretty slick. But once I saw them, it's obvious. They're reflections."

He was right. I'd hidden all kinds of things in that book, Easter eggs and references and visual jokes, often in Violence's hair and in the shadows around her. In that panel the watching rabbits were reflected, one to one. They were pieces of Violet, and they saw themselves when they looked at Violence. I'd drawn them that way, so I must have always known, way down in my subconscious, that they were one and the same, and both alive in me.

I had to call Dark Horse and get out of this contract. Change it. I couldn't write the origin story they wanted, because there was no going backward. I'd left Violet and Violence in a world that was a wasteland of their—her—own making, but now I knew that a few things had survived. I'd drawn them already. Cats, in some form, and those spindle-limbed, toothy, slouchy Lewy bodies. Those personified Lewy bodies could be what remained of the human race, mutated into monsters. There might be little pockets of real human survivors, too, frail and vulnerable. There might be a few with other, interesting mutations. Supermutants. They would all be trying to survive with very limited resources. . . .

Images were unfolding in my head, the start of a story. I could see it. I could see the world, and V and V had to find a way to live in it. To live with it, with what they had done. There was a next, even after an apocalypse.

I don't know how long I stood there, lost in my own mind, but when I came back into my body, he was waiting for me.

"You're right. They're the same," I told him. "Flashing lights and bells and prizes. What would you like?"

"Yuh-you. Vuh-vvv-visiting Atlanta," he said, shy again but saying it anyway. "Soon."

"I will," I said. "I promise."

"I better guh-get on the road," he said, but neither of us moved.

"Yeah, you should," I said, and still we stood there.

"Mm-hm," he said.

You hang up first. No, you.

"Go on," I told him. I wanted to kiss him, but Lord, the eyes on us. Instead I told him, "There's a next here, too," and he smiled. I wasn't an optimist, but even I knew this was true.

He got into his car, and I watched him drive off into the sunset. Literally. He headed west up Main Street, a dark silhouette against the spectacular sinking orange ball. But only literally, because I would go to Atlanta. Sooner rather than later. Sel Martin and I had together made a big mess and a baby, and there was a next coming for all three of us. The difference was, I wasn't scared of this one. I'd always walked away from possibility, but I didn't think that I would again, if it came down to it. Something had been put to rest when I confronted Jake, wringing that shoddy, shared apology out of him. Some new bravery had started, when the Fetus Formerly Known as Digby had quickened at my core. Together these things felt like a sea change. There would be a next, and in a place where half my relatives and a third of a small town weren't peering out windows at us.

I turned back to Birchie's house, and immediately the drapes twitched and folded, people backstepping in a hurry. The weakest piece of me wished I'd gotten into the Batmobile and ridden off into the sunset with Sel.

Instead I started walking back to the house. There was a next inside, too, and I had to be there for it. Next was Regina Tackrey, armed with swabs and science, coming to scrape some truth out of my Birchie's frail body.

22

This early in the morning, the attic was a dry and dusty kind of pre-hot. I could feel almost-sweat prickle my skin as I clambered around the piles of junk. Frank Darian and his boys had dug quite a hole in the back room to unearth Birchie's trunk. They had stacked decaying furniture and boxes and chests in and among the more familiar front-room landscape. Rachel and I had been searching for that pair of ship paintings Birchie liked for nearly half an hour.

I had to find them, because Cody Mack, of all damn people, was coming to the house at 9:00 A.M. to collect the sample of Birchie's DNA. Birchie's sacrosanct routine had been dipped into hell and hauled back kicking over the last few days; we needed to keep her quiet and in places where she felt comfortable and calm. Dragging her off to an unfamiliar lab where a stranger would poke around in her mouth seemed like the short road to another fork stabbing. Tackrey had agreed to collect the sample at our house but insisted on sending Cody. It was a savvy choice; Birchie had donated everything from trauma kits to body armor to the Birchville police force, and Cody was the only officer in town whose Birch bias ran against us instead of for us.

I didn't want Cody to see that picture of Ellis Birch with his eyes scratched out, like broad hints in the world's worst game of Clue: *Miss Birchie in the dining room with a dirty breakfast fork. Miss Birchie in the parlor with a hammer.*

Last night I'd pulled the portraits down and stored them in the attic's back room, wrapping Ethan but not bothering with ruined Ellis. I'd stacked them on a dresser, Ellis on top, faceup, blind eyes pointed at the vent fan.

Unfortunately, taking down the portraits had left tattle-tale rectangles of brighter wallpaper in the dining room. As Birchie would say, it would not do.

Searching the attic was slow work, both because we had to be careful not to cause a junk landslide and because I felt so antsy. I didn't really think there were more long-dead relations packed away up here, but at the same time I got a spine shiver every time I peeled a trunk lid open.

Rachel and I were on our own. Jake had rolled out at 7:00 A.M. sharp, wanting to get an early start on the ten-hour drive to Norfolk. Lav went with him. I thought she was scared her dad might poof again if she let him out of her sight.

Rachel pulled a rolled-up area rug off a row of very large, promising boxes. She was doing all the heavy lifting—a pregnancy perk—and she worked much faster than I did, eager to get on the road. Every minute put her farther behind her family, and Lavender wasn't the only one who didn't trust Jake left unsupervised.

As I knelt to open the first box, she said, "So I had an idea last night."

"Uh-oh," I said. These were dangerous words.

"No, it was a good idea. I think I should tell Dad and Mom about the baby," she said, dragging the heavy rolled-up carpet back out of the way. "When I get home."

I looked up from the first box's jumble of old clothes and weird kitchen gadgets from the 1970s. "My baby? Why on earth!"

"Because you know what's going to happen," Rachel said, blowing a strand of hair off her face. "Mom will freak out, worrying about what people will think, and Dad will bluster around trying to solve everything instead of letting her talk." She propped the rug up against a wardrobe we'd already searched, then came and knelt by me to open the next box. "They'll fight, and then she'll cry, and then he'll stomp off and do fifty hours of penitent yard work. In the end it will be fine. This is their grandbaby, after all. Why should you stress through the fussy bits? You have enough going on."

I did, actually. I'd had trouble sleeping last night, thinking about the DNA test. All I could do was stand by Birchie's side. I felt helpless, like I was twiddling my thumbs and watching a huge rock coming at her, fast, to roll over her and ruin her. Then I'd twiddle more and watch the splash damage ruin Wattie.

I couldn't take one more thing, so I shook my head at Rachel in an emphatic no, saying, "They'll freak out. They'll leap right into their car and come straight here." Why not? Everybody else had.

"No they won't," Rachel said. "I'll say I'm only breaking your confidence because you're worried about how they'll react. I'll make them swear not to mention it until you tell them. See how that works?"

It took me a second to process her idea, but once I did, I saw that it was genius. Evil genius, but still. It gave Mom and Keith time to plan their reaction, and it took a big chunk of worry off me. It was manipulative, and a very Rachel-specific kind of awful, and God, so very tempting. I hesitated, arms buried in heaps of Easter-colored polyester, and she pressed on.

"By the time you get home, they'll be past panic and deep into supportive."

"It does sound like the easy way out," I admitted, but there was no way I could sign off on it. It was Rachel's style, not mine.

"Good. Because I already did it," Rachel said. "I called Dad last night."

I plunked onto my butt, surprised that I was surprised, because of course she had. That was also Rachel's style. "Damn it, Rachel—" I started, but she interrupted me, pointing.

"Is that the ships?" From our low position, we could see a couple of tarp-wrapped rectangles leaning on the wall behind a coffee table.

"I think so," I said, because there was nothing else to say. Mom and Keith knew. Done was done, Rachel was Rachel, and truthfully, it was a relief. Maybe I should give Margot Phan a call and enlist her to spill the news to our Tuesday gamers and my church friends in the same way. They could all chew it over together without me. I'd come home to a not-in-the-least-surprising surprise shower, and my Diaper Genie/ onesie problem would have solved itself. "I know you meant well, Rachel, but please talk to me first next time, okay?"

Those exact words had come out of my mouth so often that I ought to have a pull string that would trigger them by now.

Fruitless, too, because even as we carried the paintings down, Rachel was saying, "Since I'm staying at your house, I should start getting your nursery set up. I'm at least going to paint. You can't be around the fumes."

I saw my imagined Superman-blue walls disappearing in a wash of Modern Dove Gray or Mint Wisp Green.

"Thanks. That's nice of you. But Sel may want to help pick out the color and the theme."

I said it purely as a defense, then realized that it might be true. He'd cared about the name, but did men care about baby bedding? He was a Dark Knight guy, so he probably thought Supe was a prig. Maybe the nursery's theme should be John Henry Irons? His alter ego, Steel, wore Superman's colors and shared his ideals, and he looked more like Digby might.

"Oh, of course!" Rachel said, backing off. She looked

almost sheepish, and that was such a new look on her face that it had no set, faint lines. She peeked at me from under her lashes and said, "You guys pick, and I'll paint, if that works? I wouldn't want to get in the way of . . . whatever's happening there. With you two."

It wasn't quite a question, but I answered anyway.

"Something is. I'm keeping it separate. Like, in my head I'm kinda dating Batman, and that could go any number of ways. Sel Martin, though? He's in our lives forever. I have to stay on good terms with him, no matter what happens with his alter ego. Does that make sense?" I asked.

"Actually, it does," she said, which surprised me. Very few sentences that had "Batman" or "alter ego" in them made any kind of sense to Rachel. She stopped at the bottom of the stairs, and her voice was very stiff, very prim as she added, "I'm having similar feelings about my husband."

I stopped, too, shocked. Rachel was confiding in me. A little. Eight words, given in the wake of her latest maneuver with my baby news. But still, it was a whole sentence that was vulnerable and reciprocal.

I'd felt guilty for stepping in and calling Jake, but ever since then she'd been more open with me than she'd been in our whole lives. For Rachel, to meddle was to love. Maybe, by interfering, I had finally told her I loved her back in her own language. On impulse I leaned my ship picture against the wall and hugged her, painting and all.

"Oh, goodness!" she said, hugging me back as best she could with her arms full.

"Thanks, Rachel," I told her, and this time I said it with no qualifiers.

"Thank you, Leia," she said, such foreign words that it was practically like hearing Rachel speaking Klingon. She added, in her old familiar bossy tone, "Come home soon."

Her lips to God's ears, I thought as we went to the dining room and hung the pictures on the same old nails that had once held up Ethan and Ellis. I wanted to go home. Or at least I wanted this part—bones and sorrows dug up sixty years too late—to be over. Even the regular human heartbreak of my grandmother's aging, her failing mind and memory, would be better than digging in these ancient, moldy secrets. Reading assisted-living brochures and fighting with Birchie and Wattie was shitty, unless the other choice was watching Regina Tackrey send them both to prison.

"Yours is higher," Rachel said as she stepped back to eyeball the pictures.

Even I could see that she was right. The schooner had a slightly longer wire, but the patches of shiny wallpaper were hidden.

"It's good enough," I said.

"It's going to drive you crazy," Rachel said, meaning that it would drive her crazy. She was leaving, though, and the schooner listing a half inch lower than the clipper ship was not going to keep me up at night. I shrugged it off, but she said, "Let me fix it."

Not everything was fixable, even by my stepsister.

"How will you do that? You think Birchie keeps a hammer in the house?" I asked her, and that ended the discussion, fast. Birchie kept no tools at all. Maybe she had banished them superstitiously, like Sleeping Beauty's mother on a spindle-burning run sixty years after her kid had gone down for the Big Nap.

Birchie and Wattie came in bearing a pot of oatmeal with berries and a platter of biscuits and bacon. Strictly spoon and finger foods, I realized, and sure enough there were no forks on the set table. No knives either, not of any kind. Wattie had even prebuttered the biscuits and put out the honey pot instead of jam.

"You might as well eat," I told Rachel. "It will save you a stop."

Birchie was pretty good at first glance. She was

dressed in a long floral skirt and a lightweight summer twinset. Maybe her eyes were a little overbright, but her fluffy bun was tidy and her powdered cheeks were pink with liquid rouge. She knew who Rachel was with no cuing. Considering the hell of yesterday and the stress of the morning's agenda, she was better than I expected. We kept up a steady stream of kindly conversation around her, talking routes and road times over the meal. Birchie put in a comment here and there. Most of them made sense. Only one was directed at the rabbits. By the time we were ready to see Rachel off, I was moderately reassured that Birchie wouldn't attack Cody Mack with the honey twirler.

In the entryway Rachel thanked Birchie and Wattie for the hospitality, kissing each of them on the cheek. She saved me for last, holding me tight and whispering, "See you soon, preg," in my ear. Soon? She *was* an optimist. I was worried that Digby might get himself born in Birchville after all.

"Should we walk Rachel out?" Wattie asked Birchie, cuing her, but Birchie didn't answer. She was staring back at the dining room, toward her own seat.

"Birchie?" I said, and a laugh got out of her.

It was cousin to yesterday's high-pitched, tittering noise, the one that had been a harbinger. It raised every little hair on the nape of my neck.

"Birchie?" Wattie said, trying to call her back. She took my grandmother by the shoulders and gently turned her to face us. "Birchie?"

Birchie stopped laughing, and her eyes focused.

"My father is a boat," she told us, and her voice was filled with wonder.

23

Cody Mack arrived sporting mirrored cop sunglasses and a smirk. He was carrying a briefcase, of all things. It was brown faux leather, very glossy, with bright brass corners, downright odd for the occasion. The hinges were dusty. It looked like a prop you'd give a kid playing a big shot in the high-school musical, so the audience would understand he was important.

Frank Darian arrived with him, carrying his own actual briefcase. Frank looked tired, and this would be one of his last acts as our lawyer; he'd advised that it was time for us to hire a criminal attorney. *A really good one,* he'd said, handing us a list of names, and those words scared me more than anything. It had nothing to do with his own ongoing troubles with his divorce either. He'd made that clear. When the DNA results were back, when it was proved definitively that Birchie had been hiding her own father's body in her attic, he thought Tackrey would pursue the matter. Vigorously, unless public opinion shifted. She was running opposed in the primary for the first time in years.

They came into the parlor, and Birchie and Wattie did not get up from their side-by-side spots on their love seat. I took my cue from them and stayed planted in the chair closest to Birchie, steaming in a welter of separate hatreds. I hated that my family was in the wrong. I hated that Cody Mack, racist jackass, was here repping law and order. I had pent-up urges to make all this stop pinging through my body with no place to go. Most of all I hated feeling helpless.

Frank took up a vigilant stance in front of the fireplace, feet spread, hands behind his back, and we all exchanged polite, cool greetings. Or everyone but Birchie did. She said nothing, though her face indicated that a smell had come into the room.

Cody swayed his hips forward and back before plunking the showy briefcase down on the side table that sat catty-corner between Birchie and me. He took his time, popping the tabs and swinging the lid up. The briefcase was even dustier inside. He must've dragged it down from his own granny's corpse-free attic as some kind of compensation thing, because it was dead empty except for three swab kits, each in its own small box. He could have carried them in a plastic Piggly Wiggly bag, or with his hands.

"So this here is going to be easy, and it don't hurt," Cody told Birchie, who had yet to overtly acknowledge him. As he spoke, he reached for one swab kit and unpacked it, laying the pieces out on the bottom of the open briefcase: a padded envelope, a clear evidence bag with a zip top, a swabbing stick sealed in paper, a pair of bright blue latex gloves, and a little pile of forms and stickers. "If you cooperate, I can be out of your house in five flat minutes. Less," he continued, snapping on the gloves. Now that he was addressing her, her gaze had dropped. She looked down at her hands, folded tidy in her lap, almost demure. Wattie, beside her, took a near-identical posture, both leaning in so that their sloping shoulders touched.

"Please walk us through the process," Frank said, for Birchie's benefit.

Cody picked up the swabbing stick and unwrapped it. "I'm going to put this here stick in her mouth," he said, and then, to Birchie directly, "It goes in kinda off to the side, so don't worry about gagging or nothing. Then I'll scrape at your cheek on the inside. This takes a little time, because I got to collect cells on it. I have tried this on my own self, so I know it isn't uncomfortable at all. And that's it. Your part is done. Okay?"

He was on his best behavior, and I thought Tackrey must have put the fear of God into him. Tackrey herself couldn't be present, or she risked becoming a witness in her own case.

Birchie finally looked up from her hands. She gave him her most polite, bad-company smile, the dangerous one. The one with frost and steel behind it.

"I think . . . not," Birchie said to him.

Cody turned his face toward Frank, then to me. No help either place. Wattie was still in demure mode, though it fit her face about as well as sheepish had fit Rachel's.

I tried to keep my breathing slow and steady, for the baby's sake. The way these first four months had gone, my child was going to come out either tough as nails or thoroughly neurotic. I needed to take up yoga or Zen meditation, stat. That pulsing, purple urge to act went through me again, pushed hard by my heart and carried in my blood. It zinged through my limbs, and it had no place to go except back to my center, where my relentless heart sent it rushing back through me again.

Cody tried once more. "Now, Miss Birchie, you don't get to think not. You don't get to think at all, because we got a court order. I can show it to you if you want. I already showed it to ol' Frank here. You don't have a choice on this."

Frank finally stepped in. "Let's get this done, okay, Miss Birchie?"

"Thank you, no," Birchie said, politely, and closed her mouth.

Really closed it. She had always had a rosebud, too small for her face, and age had further thinned her lips. Now she pursed it into a teeny, puckered star. Her eyes sparked frosty fire at Cody Mack, who was frustrated enough to pull off his mirrored cop sunglasses and glare around at all four of us in turn. He ended on Frank.

"You need to get your client to comply," Cody said, swaying those hips again. Forward, back, like the standing-still version of a swagger. He turned to me and Wattie. "Or you do. Only reason y'all're here is to get this woman to cooperate."

"Miss Birchie, this is not optional," Frank told her. "This is the law."

Birchie was listening, but not to him. Her eyes flicked to a spot behind Cody, toward the dining room, and her head tilted. Birchie was listening to rabbits. Or something worse.

"Can we do this another day?" I asked, trying to

sound sweet. I didn't want it done at all, but later was better. Never was best. "She's very off."

"Naw, we cannot," Cody said to me. "We are bending ass-backward for you Birches already, having me do this here. Now, if you want it to get ugly, we can get ugly. If she refuses, I got the right to yoink some hairs. That'll be more invasive-like, because I need the root."

Cody said "root" so it rhymed with, "mutt," and for a second I didn't understand what he was saying. Then I did, and I said, incredulous, "Are you actually threatening to pull hairs out of Birchie's head?"

"Yes, ma'am," Cody said. "And if she fights me on it, I might have to use a little force, restraining her."

I had a vision of how well that was going to go. She'd fight. I had no doubts. No one who had seen her yesterday could doubt it, and she was frail and so small. She'd fight, and she'd get hurt.

Wattie started whispering in Birchie's ear. I could catch words here and there. She was trying to get Birchie on board. Peacefully. Forklessly.

Birchie patted at her knee and said, "Now, you know that won't do, Wattie. It will not do at all," and I despaired.

I just wanted to stop this, but thinking of the damage Cody's rough hands on her could do, I said, "Birchie, please. Let's get this over with."

"It's nasty." Birchie peeped at me through her pin-hole.

She screwed her mouth shut even tighter, and this was getting ridiculous. It was like I was watching three human adults trying to get one sweet-toothed baby to eat spinach. Any moment Cody Mack would be swishing the stick toward her, saying, *Here comes the airplane, zoom, zoom!* But this sweet-tooth baby had Violence inside her, and her bones were as brittle as starfish. My eyes went around the room, cataloging all the things Birchie could use as a weapon. The fireplace poker, the heavy scented candle in its mason jar, her own coral-tipped nails. She could hurt him, if she got the element of surprise. Cody, with his barrel chest and meaty arms, would then crush her old bones into powder trying to protect himself.

"It isn't nasty!" Cody said with a pissy-sounding edge. He leaned in toward her with the stick, waving it in her face. "I took it right out of a sterile wrapper. You all saw me do it. Now, last chance, open your dang mouth."

Birchie was losing her temper back. I could see it in the firm set of her chin.

I stood up, and it felt good to stand, even though I was acting against everything I wanted. "Give me the stick, Cody."

"No, ma'am. I got to collect it. Chain of evidence."

"Well, you have two more kits there. Let me show her what you're doing," I was trying for sweet and rational, but my words got away from me. "Maybe we can finish this up without bloodshed, and before the rest of us turn ninety, too. I'm sure you have a long list of old, sick ladies to torment today."

He shrugged and made a little sarcastic bow, then passed the stick to me.

I leaned toward Birchie. "I'm just going to show you," I told her. "Can you please open your mouth?"

If anything, she managed to squinch it shut even tighter.

"Great job!" Cody Mack said, enjoying my failure. That jackass.

"Show her on me," Wattie said, and opened her mouth, leaning forward.

It was a good idea. I moved down a step, Birchie's overbright eyes tracking my every move from underneath her sparse, suspicious brows.

Cody said, "Put it in the side. Then scrape it up and down on the inside, like brushing her teeth. Except on her cheek."

"I heard you explain it not three minutes ago," I told him. I did what he said, inserting the stick and scrubbing it up and down with some pressure. "How long?"

"Forty-five seconds, and I got a timer going on my watch," he said. I kept scraping, and Wattie made affirmative-sounding noises, side-eyeing Birchie encouragingly with her mouth stretched wide into the most plastic smile I'd ever seen. I realized she was boiling with it, too, this deep purple desire to make it all stop. Yet here we both were, helpless to stop helping. After what felt like twenty years, Cody said, "That'd about do it."

"There, now, that was nothing," Wattie said as I took the stick out and showed it to Birchie. It was bloodless and not in the least upsetting. It was only a wet looking stick.

"You see there? That's all. Wattie did it." Threats of labs and hair pullings had rolled off her, but I remembered how Wattie would use recipes and the regular beats of her real life to call her home. Now I used them against her, saying, "Wattie wants y'all to plant the pumpkins today, and if we don't, you are going to have store-bought pumpkins on your porch come October. Is that what you want?"

That got her mouth open, but only to berate me. "Leia Birch Briggs, I would sooner have no pumpkins at all! Did you know last year half those ones in the Pig were not even from America?"

"Well, do the stick, and let's go plant. June won't last forever," I said, though no matter how this all came out, Birchie would not be here to pick those pumpkins come October.

Birchie eyed the stick, mistrustful, but Wattie gave me a little nod, almost imperceptible, encouraging me.

"It isn't ladylike," Birchie said. At least she was talking to me now, the pinhole gone. "Look, it has her spittle on it. Her human spittle, and there you stand holding it in the parlor."

"It gets put right away," I said. I muscled Cody aside and picked up the little bag with the plastic zippered top. I held it where she could see, then I put the stick in and zippered it shut. "You see? It gets sealed, even. Let's do this. No fun in the garden until this is done!"

It was my first try at Unbrookable Mother. I tried to sound like Rachel telling Lavender to clear the breakfast dishes. I tried to sound like Birchie herself had sounded on all my childhood summers, telling me I had to put away my coloring supplies before I could go out and play on the square. It felt wrong to be using it on one of the very women who had taught it to me, but I found I did own this voice after all. To my mingled rage and sorrow, it worked. It unmothered her, turning her into the child.

"Goodness, no need to make such a fuss," Birchie said, sulky, and she opened up her mouth like a baby bird.

I got out of Cody's way, super fast, before she forgot that she'd consented. He stepped in, smart enough to keep his own mouth shut for a minute. I lurked behind him making hyper-encouraging eyebrows as Cody tore open a new box and made a big show of putting on clean gloves. Wattie leaned in, whispering a soothing list of all the seeds they needed to get into the ground now—sweet potatoes and lady peas and melons—while Cody took the sample. It was such a long minute that Wattie was reciting their winter planting schedule before he finished. But then the stick was out and he was popping it into the bag, and thanks to us nobody was stabbed or broken. Thanks to us the state had everything they needed to ruin us.

Frank pantomimed a fast *Whew,* and I smiled back, but wry. This was not a victory I could celebrate.

"Now, was that so hard?" Cody said, holding up the plastic bag for her to see.

She put a hand to her chest, distaste registering in her turned-down lips and lowering eyebrows.

"Really?" I said quietly behind him. "Because when she slaps that out of your hand, I am going to laugh my ass off. And good luck getting another sample. Can't wait to hear you call Ms. Tackrey and explain—"

But he was already setting the bag in the bottom of his briefcase, saying, "Okay, okay, okay," over me until I stopped talking. "I was only showing her," which was crap. He'd been trying to bait her. He was the same bully he'd been in childhood. Instead of growing out of his worst traits, he'd only gotten big enough to do real damage with them.

Birchie dropped her eyes, hands folded, back in demure mode.

"Now what?" I asked as Cody fished in his shirt pocket for a pen to fill out the label on the sticker.

"Now I box it up and drop it off straight to the lab," he said, checking the dusty briefcase and then feeling in his back pockets for a pen that wasn't there.

I think, if I had a plan at all, it happened then. Not even a plan. More like a noticing, a logical click of understanding much too fast to think in words: there was a little bag full of cells sitting in the dusty bottom of his briefcase. Cells I'd helped gather, though they could put Birchie into prison. There was another little bag full of cells, anonymous, identical, in my hand. Cells that wouldn't help the cops or Regina Tackrey at all.

"I have one," Frank said, holding out his own pen.

Cody turned toward the fireplace to take it, blocking Frank's view of the briefcase. He was turned away for a second, maybe two. Not enough time, if I had thought about it. But I didn't think. My body had been ready, waiting, filled with pent-up purple action this whole time. My body moved, setting my little bag down, picking his up. Boom and done.

Wattie saw me. Just her. Her eyes went wide, horrified, and she opened her mouth. She snapped it shut again. Cody was already turning back. He was writing on the sticker. I watched him affixing it to the wrong bag, as horrified as Wattie was. My bad hands buzzed and trembled, so that I had to work to not drop the bag holding the real sample.

This is a felony, I thought. *I am holding a felony, and I did it. This is how fast a person's hand can move, almost without permission. An impulse, a breath, and then it's done, and then you did a felony, forever.*

I didn't want to think about Birchie with a hammer, about what she did in her own worst moment, but I already was. I clutched the bag so hard my knuckles were white.

Wattie was purely panicked. I could see it in her wide, wide eyes. She opened her mouth again and then closed it. We were telegraphing urgent eye messages back and forth in total silence.

She was telling me that I was stupid, and God, but she was right. My hands had done a felony, and it could not be undone. Cody had already put the wrong sample in the box and labeled it.

If it had been our chief, Willard Dalton, I could have said, *Oh, wait, I did something bad and stupid.* He could have switched them back or taken a whole new sample. Hell, if it had been Willard Dalton, observant and smart, my bad hands would never, never, never have had the opportunity. But this was Cody Mack. If we spoke up now, I'd be leaving the house in handcuffs.

Hush! Hush! I don't want to have my baby in a prison, I thought-beamed at Wattie, and she closed her mouth up for the third time.

Frank, oblivious, began a round of cool, polite good-byes as Cody clicked his stupid briefcase shut. I croaked out some kind of good-bye, too, and so did Wattie. I hoped I didn't look as red and sweaty as I felt. I could hardly hear myself over the blood roaring in my ears.

"How long until we get results?" Frank asked.

"Well, this kinda thing, it can take months," Cody said, and I felt his words both as relief and as a heavy sword on a thin string, hanging over my head. Months? Months of not knowing if I'd be caught. Months of this baby growing here in Birchville with my grand-

mother unable to leave the state, stuck in this dangerous, fork- and stair-filled house. I couldn't put her in
a temporary place until I could move her close to me.
Not when I had no idea where I'd be living and every
tiny change was so hard on her. But this also meant
months of putting off a prosecution. Which was worse?
Then Cody flashed a big, shit-eating grin and added,
"But Tackrey'll fast-track this one. So say a week? Ten
days?"

I had my answer. Fast was worse.

Frank was walking Cody out now, leaving with him,
mouthing polite things. Birchie and Wattie stayed glued
to the love seat, both dead silent for different reasons.

I closed the front door behind the men. Turned and
leaned against it because my legs were weak and shaking now, made of rubber bands and putty.

"Let's go plant pumpkins," Birchie said, cheery, as
if all the unpleasantness were done now.

I didn't answer. Wattie and I both cocked our heads,
listening to the voices and the clomp of big man feet
down the stairs until we couldn't hear them anymore.
Then Wattie stood so fast it was like she'd borrowed
better knees. She was across the parlor and over to me
in a flash, grabbing my arm in a grip so tight it hurt.

"Girl, what have you done?"

"I don't know, I'm sorry, I don't know!" I said, clutching the tops of her arms.

"What happened?" Birchie asked from the sofa, still sitting, unalarmed.

"You are going to be sharing a cell right down the hall from us. Your fingerprints must be all over that plastic bag," Wattie said, in a state, trying hard not to flat-out yell into my face.

"Why would they fingerprint that bag? They won't know. Maybe it's a good thing. If they can't identify the body, how can they proceed? With no working theory?" I was trying to convince myself as much as her. "The case will never be solved, and one day people will talk about the bones the same way they talk about the Pig Man in the Holler, or the giant alligator gar down in Lake Martin—the mysterious remains found in the Birch house."

Wattie rolled her eyes to heaven, calmer now, but not by much. "Are you stupid? You gave them my genes, child! My genes! Lord help you. Lord help your baby—do you think that I am black here like a paint upon my skin? Do you think he will be, too?"

I didn't understand her for a moment. "You mean they can tell from that swab that you're black?" That didn't seem right. In fact, it seemed a little racist, for genes to know that. For genes to tell that. I wanted us all to be the same, under.

"Of course they can! Lord help your baby," Wattie repeated, throwing her hands up. Then she fisted them in her short curls, walking away from me, back into the parlor. I trailed after. "We have to call Willard Dalton. Now. Get him to swap them back."

I shook my head. "We can't. Tackrey doesn't trust him. Cody is going to take that box straight to her or to the lab. It's not going to stay in Birchville."

"What did you do?" said Birchie, and she was alarmed now. Wattie's distress had penetrated whatever fog had gathered around her, and she was sitting up as tall as she could.

"She swapped the tests out. Yours and mine," Wattie said, pacing, frantic, hands still fisted in her hair. "She gave them my cells."

Birchie put a hand to her heart, her eyebrows rising.

I was still talking to Wattie. "It doesn't matter. They won't look to see if the genes are from a black person or a white person. Not on a paternity test." I spoke with all the authority of a person who had once been trapped in a dentist's waiting room with no book and a trashy daytime talk show on the TV. They'd been doing a thing the smarmy host called "father reveals," where the guy who thought he was the daddy never was and they told him so on TV. "They only look at those markers. Specific ones. I think. I'm pretty sure." I wanted to go ask Google, but I didn't want that particular search in my browser history. I needed to go to a library. A big one with a lot of anonymous computers. Far away.

"You switched them? My cells and Wattie's?" Birchie asked me. She stood up, hand still pressed to her heart.

I nodded, surprised she understood that much.

"I'm so sorry," Birchie said. To Wattie. Not to me.

Wattie's nostrils flared, hands pulling at her hair, and she said, "Don't."

"I'm so sorry, so sorry," Birchie told her. She came across the room, already reaching for her.

"We don't know," Wattie said, stiff and unmoving in her arms. "You do not know."

They were having a conversation that I was not having.

Birchie said, "I do know, and you do, too," and Wattie crumpled. She burst into sound, hands still pulling her hair. It was an awful noise, long and rising, a shuddering howl. Her hands finally unfisted from her hair, moving to cover her face. The sound broke, becoming sobs so deep and racking that they shivered her foundation. She shook so violently that without

Birchie's arms around her I thought her body might come apart. Her hands pressed so hard against her face it must be hurting her.

"What's happening?" I said, but to them I wasn't even in the room. I was as unpresent as one of Birchie's rabbits, practically imaginary. Birchie rocked her back and forth while Wattie wept.

"You do know," Birchie said. "I am so sorry."

Wattie shook in her arms, saying something I could not understand.

"What's happening?" I said again.

Birchie met my eyes over Wattie's shoulder, and now her words seemed made for both of us.

"That test is going to come back positive. Doesn't matter that you swapped them. The answer will come back the same," she said.

"No," I said, a red bolt of negation.

That could not be so. But my artist's eyes were looking for it now, without permission. Once it was said, my eyes could not help seeing it.

Not in their faces. Birchie had small eyes, close set. Wattie's were large and round and spaced wide. They had different noses, different mouths, and they were made of such different color palettes.

The truth was written in their bodies. As they held each other, Wattie racked with weeping, Birchie's arms around a sorrow that was larger than the room, I could see it in the shapes of them. The downslope of their meeting shoulders, the rounding of their hips and bellies, the curve of their equivalent short calves. They had broad foreheads and small pointed chins, so that their disparate features were set in matching hearts. Their bodies told my future, and my body spoke their past; they had looked at me, and each had known that I was pregnant. They'd known because they both recognized their shape in me.

"Jesus," I said. "Jesus, Jesus."

I could not unsee, so I stood witness. I didn't know how else to be in the presence of such ugly pain.

Wattie finally looked up, eyes streaming.

"Hear me," she said, clear as day. "My daddy was Earl John Weathers, and that's all."

"I know. I know he was," Birchie said, and tears were spilling down her cheeks as well. "And Vina Weathers was the only mother that I ever knew. Whether she bore me or not."

She was saying Vina's love had made them sisters, but my artist's eyes saw that they were sisters twice over. Sisters in their hearts and in their histories, two halves clasped together in a tangle of good love and bad history.

I'd thought that every human secret must eventually

get too old to matter, but the echoes of this one filled the room. They wept in each other's arms, and I was crying, too. They became a single thing in my blurred vision, smashed together, leaning on each other. They turned their heart-shaped faces toward me, their very different features painted on the same-shaped canvas, and now that I had seen it, I would always see. This was the past rising up alive to eat us. History breathing. Alive in their bodies, mirrored in mine.

24

Emily Birch was firmly on the shelf when she was twenty-nine, but it was a shelf of her own making. She was the rising Birch in Birchville, and the boys who came a-courting in her girlhood were overdiffident, cringing like dogs before her father. She knew it without being told: They would not do.

It was plain in the amused, pitying way Ellis Birch invited them in when they showed up in fresh collars with combed-back hair. They sweated through their half hours in the parlor, and no vase of cool water could stop their field daisies and Queen Anne's lace from wilting in his presence.

Clayton Mack took a different route. He joined Emily when she walked out alone, cocksure and overly familiar, coming up behind her to tug on her braid. He made her laugh. He did not come by the house, properly, to genuflect, and he soon found himself invited to pursue opportunities elsewhere. In Georgia, say, or Mississippi. As Alabama sealed itself shut behind him, the already sour blood between the families curdled thoroughly.

Emily was too beloved and too busy to be lonely, especially since her father practiced what he preached; she was the only person in Birchville he found worthy of his love. He was an early, wealthy widower, so maidens and spinsters and widows alike took solid runs at him. He was immune to casseroles and sympathetic ears and mothery dabbings at his baby, marching unscathed through a hundred honey traps with the same amused condescension that he gave Emily's suitors.

This very public attitude meant Ellis Birch was revered far more than he was liked. His father had been "Ethan" to quite a few families, but Ellis was "Mr. Birch," always, to everyone. To Emily, however, he was "Daddy," and she basked in every bit of his scant sunshine. It was rare, and all for her.

Lord, he loves his girl, though, folks in Birchville said, like a refrain, like a forgiving chorus, when his pride had chilled the room. Their small, cold god had been big enough to carry Birchville through the Great Depression and beyond. He never treated Emily as decorative either. From birth on, she was told her life had higher purpose, sleeping on his knee through deacon and town-council meetings before she could talk. By twenty she was running all the ladycentric clubs her mother would have managed, had she lived: Library Friends, Garden Club, the Mary-Marthas.

Floyd Briggs didn't start out as a suitor. He was only friendly and funny and kind when she went to his shop to supplement her garden with his fresh produce, and she noticed he'd sit out on the park benches in fine weather, reading poetry and novels by Austen, E. M. Forster, any Brontë. All her favorites. Soon they were trading books back and forth at church. He began slipping his own poems, handwritten and unsigned, into the pages. They were quite good, and one day Emily found herself at his shop buying spring onions when she knew very well the ones in her own garden were ready.

She also knew, before he asked, that Floyd Briggs would not pass muster with her daddy. Ellis had dismissed boys with finer pedigrees, better prospects, older names. Ellis was the One True Birch and Emily his rising, only heir. But when the question came, she was tempted enough to talk it over with her father. He did not rail or forbid—these things might have tipped his strong-willed child into Floyd's arms.

He was cool and thoughtful, questioning Floyd's motives. After all, Emily would be quite wealthy. He didn't try to guilt her with the knowledge that if she married, he would be alone in his big house up on the hill. She knew that already. He himself had not re-married, and the unspoken message was that she was enough. In the end it felt too much like betrayal to tell him he was not enough back. She kept her name and let Floyd go.

That was when her girlish figure started getting away from her. It was only Emily and her father, eat-ing the good suppers Vina left behind for them each evening. One day Emily would be the Last Birch in Birchville, and at that thought she'd have another fried tomato, another slice of pie.

At twenty-nine, had her name been anything but Birch, she would have been pitied. Another old maid sitting in the small row of the passed-over, running to fat. Instead she married the town. She cleaved to Birchville, carrying it forward as Birches always had, and the town honored every vow she made to it. She moved past ladylike committee work, becoming the fund-raiser and planner who rebuilt the town's library. Jesus had clearly stated in some unfindable verse some-where that women could not be church leadership, but the deaconate elected her to be their secretary. Then they rewrote the bylaws to give the "secretary" the right to speak in meetings and to vote.

She loved the town, and she loved her father. She loved Vina and Wattie, and she loved the Reverend "Big Bear" Price when Wattie married him. She loved Wattie's babies when they came. Everything she loved loved her right back. It was a good life. Her father told her by example that it was good, and filling, and enough. She believed him.

She believes him until the day she comes home from Garden Club early with the beginnings of a sick headache. She goes back to her father's office to tell him she will nap until supper. The door is open, and she sees. To see, in this case, is to unbelieve.

She understands what is happening. Of course she does. Birchville is a small town, a country town, full of dogs and horses and barn cats. The Partridges keep goats, and Birchie herself has chickens and a strutting banty rooster. She has seen animals stacked this way, their eyebrowless faces blank, muzzles incapable of grimaces or smiles. Animal faces stay passive, strangely disinterested even when they are making other animals.

This is what Vina's face looks like now. Vina, bent over her father's desk, is all animal. Only animal, because Vina is not inside this body. The mouth is slack.

The eyes point without seeing. Vina's cheek is squashed against the wood, and her face slides back and forth on it, squelching her features into shapes that are only shapes and not expressions. She is rocked on her cheek by the thrusting of the body behind her.

It is perversion at its most primal, because Vina is the only mother she has ever known. This man, her father, still has his human face on, concentrating. His face seems separate from his body as it attends to the animal business of its pumping. She has seen this face when he's balancing his ledgers, calculating, straining toward conclusion.

She backs away, but a noise comes soft out of her throat. Vina, gone from the room, the house, the planet, does not react at all, but her father sees her. His face is all shock now, but his body, engaged, keeps pumping, once, twice. She flees before his shocked human face can make his body stop.

She runs up the hall and into the kitchen, where a pot of lady peas are slow-bubbling, glistening with bacon fat. Vina made this. It is meant to feed them once the horror in her father's study is completed and Vina can go home. She runs to the dining room. Ethan's portrait is on the floor, leaned against the wall. His nail has fallen, and her father is supposed to be rehanging the portrait, now, while she is at Garden Club. He is not. He is attending to other matters.

Her father is still back in his office, but his portrait's eyes follow her as she walks in distraught circles, twice around the table. She goes to the parlor, and the painted eyes follow her there, sterner than his real gaze on her has ever, ever been. Then she hears his footsteps, leaving his office. He is in the hall. She runs fast up the stairs, slamming the door to her room with a loud, announcing bang. He does not follow.

She paces through her room, into the turret. She sits at the window seat, and her body cannot sit. She paces back and forth, and she can hardly stand to be inside her body. In every other moment, Vina has a human face. A face that looks on her with love. What Emily saw was worse than seeing Bill Palmer's she-goat, blank-faced and resigned. Worse than her own hurtful rooster, who hops on any hen that takes his fancy. A horror happens, secret, in her house.

She goes into the turret and sits again, then immediately rises to throw up in the white ceramic bowl in the shelving. Downstairs, Vina's skirts have rustled back into place. Vina will be stirring the peas, counting eggs for cornbread.

She thinks of Wattie in her own home with Big Bear

and their newest small, fat baby. And now? Now that she has seen, she sees. She sees how it is written in the way her body matches her friend's. How long has this been happening, under her roof? Her good Birch brain, well acquainted with sums and figures, is taking bad account here. Wattie is twenty-nine.

As Emily stands in her room, the sun races across the sky. The cornbread is out of the oven now. She can smell it, but for Emily no time has passed. How is Vina already ringing the brass bell on the porch that means supper is served? How is Vina already headed home to her own husband? How is it that the sun is nearly down?

Someone must stop her father. Someone must tell him that he must not do this thing. She cannot think who. Not the good white men of the town who run their businesses inside her father's buildings, work in his mill, come to him for loans when their children are sick or the weevils eat up half their cash crop. The police all tip their hats when he passes. The deacons approached her father not a week ago to ask for money for a new organ. They watched him write a check for the whole sum.

Not the good black men of Redemption who drink from the colored fountains and call Ellis "sir." If one of them took a white woman to his bed, there would be strange fruit hanging in the trees outside town.

Can she go to the women, then? The wives. What do they know? They likely do this thing facing their husbands, smiling, making their human babies eye to eye, hands clasped, the way that Wattie has with Big Bear. Wattie has told her in secret; it is a lovely thing, what happens in the marriage bed. It is not the same as what she saw.

No man here has any power to stop him, much less any woman, any child of any shade.

Vina herself cannot make this stop. Has not been able to stop it for longer than Wattie has been alive. Vina's husband lost his leg to gangrene. This job saved her husband's life, paid for his surgery and medications, fed her babies, kept a roof over their heads. If Vina tells, who will believe her? If the Birches turn her out, who in Birchville will take her? Vina has no voice.

The only equal whom Ellis Birch acknowledges is hiding in the tower, throwing up. His daughter owns the only voice that he might hear.

She does not remember going down the stairs, but more time has passed without her. Her father has eaten, and his empty dishes tell a story: His appetite is fine.

Her own plate is empty and pristine. The lady peas and collards wait in covered dishes for her. The cornbread is swaddled in a napkin to keep warm.

Her father has rehung Ethan's portrait. The hammer and a small tin of nails sit on the close side of the table. In the morning Vina will find them and carry them back to the tool hutch under the back porch. Emily wonders if Vina will do this chore before or after she is raped again.

Her father sits in his comfy chair in the parlor, having his port. His back is to her, his real eyes turned away. His painted eyes watch her, unreceptive.

"Well, there you are," her daddy says. "Did you fall asleep?"

"No," she says, because she has to talk to him. There is no one else. "I was being sick from what I saw."

"Well, of course," her father says, sympathetic, calm. "It's not a sight or a subject for ladies. Don't think about it. Go on and have your supper."

Her obedient feet walk to the table, but she cannot imagine putting lady peas in her mouth. They smell like sulfur laced with rancid fat. She removes the lid from the collards, and they gleam with slime in her ruined eyes.

"You have to stop," she tells the collards.

These are all the words she has, but he has more.

They come to her from very far away, and the sky is dark, though she cannot remember when the sun went down. Maybe it didn't. Maybe it is still afternoon and the sun has gone black, a testament to how the world has turned to ruin. Yet it is the same. Nothing has changed except her way of seeing, the image shifting, showing her a secret, second father. She sees there is a secret, second town, too, always present, alive inside the lines of the town she sees. The town she loves.

Maybe this darkness came to eat her eyes for seeing. She wishes it would. She wishes it would shroud her ears, too, stop them with soot so she cannot hear her daddy telling her in a wash of calm, cool words that men have needs that Emily will never understand. No lady truly can, and that's all right. That's only proper. He tells her not to worry about Vina. Vina is not like her. Vina, he says, doesn't mind.

He is saying Vina is an animal. He is telling Emily that the mother of her heart is always, every moment, nothing more than that blank thing she saw splayed across his desk. She knows better. Her father evicts Vina from her body when he makes her body a bad place to be. He is killing Vina in those minutes, and he believes he has this right. Emily Birch is now deep inside the Second South. Her family helped make it, and her father has maintained it. He is it, and she is him.

"You have to stop," she says, because no one else in town will tell him. "You have to stop. You have to stop." They are the only words she has.

"All right, sweetheart. Not to worry. Have your supper," her father tells her, and he is closing the conversation. He turns back around. He sips his port. "There's lemon pie for after, in the icebox."

He will not stop, and no one can help. Not one soul. She knows because she is married to the town. She and the town share this powerful father, who has made both of them in his image.

Emily stands by the table, looking at the hammer, and she says it one last time. "You will stop."

"Darlin', we are not going to discuss this," her father says, getting impatient. "Trust me. They aren't like you. They don't mind it."

They. Not Vina's name, or even the dignity of the singular pronoun to make her a person. Emily knows that "they" is niggers, though this is not a word he says. Birches say "colored," because they are not trash, like Macks or Beckworths. They are better. She herself was too good to waste on Carter Mack, who made her laugh. Too good to be thrown away on Floyd Briggs, who asked for her hand in a poem so lovely it made her heart jump in her body.

She chose instead to be a worthy daughter to this

man, and he is a horror. Her heart swells with an awful love for him. He is full of decency and sweet tea and Jesus, and he is a good place to live if you are white and well-to-do and Baptist and if you never let the people who are not these things be human. He will not stop hurting Vina, he will keep believing Birches are better than and too good for.

Her hand takes up the hammer, and she says it one last time—*You will stop*—despairing, because he will not stop and she will not allow it to continue. Her hand rises behind him, and he says, his voice now stern, *It is not fit to discuss this any further. It is done,* and he is the town, and he is the times, and he is right: It's done. The hammer has already come down, and the crush and shudder felt the same as stepping on the white seashells he imported for their driveway.

She always knew she was this strong, because he told her so. She never knew she was a horror, but this means that she is still her father's daughter.

No one can accuse me of being too good for Floyd, now, she thinks, and hears herself laughing. The sound is sick and mirthless.

She sits in his vacated chair with the bloody hammer in her lap and drinks the port and waits for morning. Time, which moved so fast before, has paused. In a thousand years, when the sun rises, Vina will come, and see, and put the nails away. The police will take the hammer. She will be dragged out, a chubby old maid found beside her father's cooling body. She finds herself wondering what story will grow out of it. Nothing pretty, and is this her family legacy? They will drag her off to squander her next thirty years the way her father has squandered her first thirty. The town, the world, will go on as he made it. It is not the town she wants to make.

She thinks, *No.* Then she thinks, *Not if I can help it.*

She has done the worst thing a person can do, but in that dark hour she decides that she will pay her penance on her terms. She is Emily Birch, after all.

She sets to work, making her own story. She marries Floyd and replaces what she's seen with a better truth of what a man is to a woman. Time passes. A smell comes into the house and leaves the house. The USA puts a satellite right up into space, and Elvis joins the army; Wattie is right. A person cannot hold the worst thing they ever did in their palm, staring at it. Emily Birch Briggs packs her sin away, piles days and months and years on top of it, and serves the town in payment.

This is the story that my grandmother told Regina Tackrey in her offices near Lake Martin. It was morning, Birchie's best time, and we sat in a sterile conference room with Frank and Wattie and Willard Dalton on our side of the table. The other side was packed with Regina and four staff people I didn't know. Tackrey's yellow hair was lacquered into a pouf, and she wore a floral-print dress with a green jacket over it. They were pieces of a costume, sops to southern ladyhood that were at odds with her sharp eyes and squared-up shoulders. Behind her another man ran a camera on a tripod. I could see Birchie beside me and also on a large screen at the head of the table. In her pink belted suit with pantyhose and a small pink hat perched on her bun, she looked as gentle and sweet as a thousand-year-old Easter egg.

Wattie sat beside her, and she wept and rocked quietly, listening, holding Birchie's hand. Birchie was calm and sad, and her story was as true as time and the Lewy bodies let her make it. On her other side, I felt tangled in the shreds of all their shared and secret stories. The Lewy bodies gathered in the shadows, eating Birchie's stories up in every future. Six months, a year, they would have eaten this truth, too, and watching Wattie weep, I almost wished they had.

Only three days had passed, but Birchie'd had nine good meals and three good sleeps, and she wouldn't wait any longer. She wanted to give her confession before the DNA test came back. She would not listen to Frank, or me, or Wattie. She would not hire a new lawyer. She insisted that we bring her here, to tell the whole truth and nothing but the truth, right up to the hammer. Then she started bending it, and I thought that this was why she had insisted. Birchie wanted to confess while she was still canny enough to lie well.

I saw a stiffness enter Wattie's spine as Birchie's story took a turn; she gave all the parts Wattie had done to Floyd. Floyd, who had loved her, and who was past minding, and who could not be prosecuted. She said Wattie never knew what was in the trunk until she saw it opened; she helped Birchie move it only because Birchie begged. Wattie said nothing, though her lips were tight with disapproval.

"Why are you telling me this now?" Tackrey wanted to know. "Why now, and not when we first found the bones?"

Birchie's blue eyes went bright, but no tears fell, and her voice did not shake as she said, "I didn't want Wattie to know. I never wanted her to know that my father was her father, too." This was gospel. She held her sister's hand, and I could see how the skin of Wattie's fingers had gone gray and ashy in the last hard days. Her eyes were red from nights spent weeping. She looked like a woman whose world had been turned. It had, though I suspected that Wattie had always known some of it. She knew why Birchie picked that hammer up, but she'd never done the long math. She hadn't wanted to be Birchie's sister, not this way.

"But she knows now?" Tackrey asked. "How?"

"The Lewy bodies told her," Birchie said, regretful. "I say things I don't mean to say. I do things I don't mean to do. Awful things. Just ask Frank here." I saw two men on Tackrey's side of the table exchange a knowing glance. They knew about the Fish Fry, and that meant they had Birchville ties. Now that I was looking, I could see that the left one was some kind of Partridge, with his ginger hair and bubble hips. So Birchie's tale would beat us home. Birchie was still talking, though. "Sometimes I see my father. He comes to make me sorry when the Lewy bodies let him. I see rabbits, you know, too. You have six of them lined up right behind you."

"So you told Mrs. Price?" Tackrey said.

"Not exactly," Birchie said, and smiled beatifically. "I switched our DNA out. Hers for mine."

All at once, my face felt burny and my lips felt as thin as Wattie's looked. My eyes went down, too, and I felt my mouth opening. How many shared sins could Birchie be allowed to eat alone in one confession? Birchie reached over and took my hand in her free one, squeezing it hard. So hard the bones hurt, and my mouth snapped shut. "Wattie gave a sample first, to show me how to do it."

Tackrey, startled, said, "How on earth . . . ?"

Birchie made a tutting noise. "My granddaughter set Wattie's stick down near me, and I swapped it right out when Cody wasn't looking. He's a terrible policeman, I will have you know. You really should have sent me Willard here," Birchie lectured. She turned to Willard. "You never would have let me get away with that, now, would you?"

Chief Dalton, looking as horrified as I felt, but for his own reasons, choked out two words: "Lord no!"

"But why?" Tackrey asked, appalled. "It makes no sense!"

"Lewy bodies often don't," Birchie told her, shaking her head.

"Why would you?" Tackrey asked, talking over her. She was filled up with a righteous fury, but behind that her politician's wheels were turning. She'd insisted on Cody. He'd been her man, and he had screwed this up. Well, that much was true—he had. "Why swap the DNA if you didn't want Mrs. Price to know?"

"The rabbits told me it was a good idea. Though now, of course, I see the problem," Birchie said. She touched her hat and let her voice go petulant. "I also don't know why they should all be on your side of the table. Lined up against me. They are my rabbits, after all."

I almost spoke, but just then Digby tapped and stretched, keeping his own small council. I put my hands over him, and I decided to keep mine. I didn't see how letting him be born in prison would help anyone. Birchie, demure in her pink hat, was more in control than she had been in weeks; I didn't think there was a single rabbit in the room as she confessed to the worst things every human in the room had ever done.

That was where Frank stopped it. "I think my client has almost reached her limit," he said. "She isn't a well woman."

Tackrey was savvy enough to reach over and turn the camera off before she said, "No kidding."

We left the building and walked to our cars.

It wasn't until Frank was getting into his that he told me in low tones, "That may well be the end of it."

If he meant legal proceedings, I thought he was right. It would be an ugly scandal if the swap got out and the blame could land on Tackrey. Birchie's story absolved Wattie, and no one was left alive to dispute her version. Legally, I thought we might be in the clear. But if Frank thought it was over, well, that was naïve. There had been a Partridge in the room, and Tackrey, whose family had always been in tight with the Macks, would have a bellyful to say to that family now.

The air was electric with telephone lines lighting up in crisscross patterns all over the county. The three of us got into my replaced rental car, and we followed Birchie's story home.

25

It begins with Digby. Digby in the Second South.

Months before my son was born, I'd hoped Digby into being with a pencil. When I'd set him by Violet in the ruined town square, I'd released the name into my art. He belonged there, an avatar of the real boy I couldn't wait to meet. He started the story in ways that even Violet couldn't.

Digby doesn't realize he's in danger in the opening panel. He leaps through the scant grass on the edge of the park, running along the back side of the square. A few of the shops are visible to his left, and behind him the roof of the brick church rises up into the blackened sky. The steeple is broken, pointing its jagged finger at a shrouded sun.

He is in his shorts and work boots, using a slingshot

to hunt a postapocalyptic rabbit monster. It looks like the tattered rabbits that remained around Violet at the end of the old graphic novel, but its katana ears owe a little bit to Kelley Jones's Batman in *Red Rain*. Digby is so skinny, so hungry, that his skin is stretched tight over his skull. You can see his swagger, though; his immortal baby braveness is present in the lines of his body as he hunts. There is only one word on that first page, written inside a small white square to show that it is a thought, not dialogue.

Hello.

The view expands. Violet, sheltered by the cemetery's stone wall, watches him through the wrought-iron gate. She's wearing camo togs, the pants belted by a frazzled length of rope. Her hair is looped and knotted down her back in six long braids, held off her face by the tattered rag of what used to be her yellow sundress. In this second panel—and in every panel where Digby is seen through Violet's eyes—his footsteps leave a trail of leafy vines and birds and mice and yearning baby squirrels and unmutated rabbits. His grimy red shirt glows for her.

Violet thinks, *A person. A real person, like a living sunbeam in this dark and filthy place.*

The view pans out farther: Digby hunting, Violet watching, and slouching shadow shapes that coalesce in the ruined shop windows and listing doorways. My lumpy, stick-armed Lewy bodies have evolved into a pack of postapocalyptic cannibals that Digby calls the Exes. Ex-people, he means. They hunt Digby as he hunts the rabbit.

Violet sees them first.

Like any light in darkness, you attract, she thinks. The Exes are not aware of Violet's presence. If she warns him, she will give away her own position.

"Hey, kid!" she calls to him anyway. She is no longer that pretty bit of nothing in a sunshine dress. She's tougher. She has sinned, and she is sorry. "Kid. Behind you."

Digby's bravado turns to fear, and he looks back and forth between her and the monstrous Exes. And then he runs. Toward them. As if they are the lesser of two evils, and perhaps they are.

"Oh, poo," Violet says, but she does not hesitate.

He is running directly into monsters, so Violet leaps after him, snatches him up. She drags him back toward the cemetery, hampered by his struggling. She slams the wrought-iron gate shut behind them, but more Exes are coming in the front gate and streaming out of the church's back door. Violet and Digby, flanked, are brought to bay with their backs against a crypt. She lets go of Digby. He sidles a few inches away, but there is no place to go. They stand side by side, pressing them-selves into the cool stone. Digby has his slingshot out and cocked, ready to go down fighting.

"She'll come," Violet tells him.

"Nobody comes," Digby says, the little pessimist. "Nobody ever comes."

The Exes sidle closer with their eye bulges shining blind-white, reaching with their ragged-jagged fin-gers. They sniff at Digby with their high-set, slitted nostrils. They huff the taste of Violet from the air and smile. Their teeth, dripping hungry spittle, are square and blunt and huge.

"She'll come," Violet repeats, and Digby takes his eyes off the Exes long enough to shoot her a cynical look.

Then a close-up of his face, his eyes gone wide, sur-prised. Closer still, and now the whites are visible all around the irises. Violet's change is seen first this way, in the reflective lens of his innocent gaze.

"Hello, kid," Violence says, and then she does what Violence does.

I'm proud of the fight scene. It's some of my best work, the kinetic bodies color-soaked against dark, static backgrounds. Violence is rampant, and Digby backs her, pinging rocks at Exes with his sling. Seeing this, she grins a red-black grin. As she chases off the few surviving Exes, her booted feet smash apart the two dusty skeletons who are lying in each other's arms in a hollow between two smaller crypts.

She turns again to Digby, and he's standing with his own feet planted wide, slingshot aimed at her face.

"Oh, kid, what heart," Violence tells him.

She lets him back away. She lets him run. It is Violet who follows him, watching over him at a distance until she earns his trust enough to get close. It's not easy. She is blond and blue-eyed, and in this brave new world with its limited resources, the few survivors who are still human have banded into small tribes. Digby's whole group fell victim to genocide while he was fishing. He came back to find himself thoroughly orphaned, but he could not find his sister's body in the carnage left behind. He's looking for her, and Violence-in-Violet goes along; tough as he is, he's too small to survive alone. Digby will come to love the double woman he calls Vi. He knows that she is beauty and the beast all in one package, just like most of us.

Dark Horse went crazy for that opener. They loved my antiheroine seeking redemption in a blighted version of America. It was chock-full of monsters and lost children, race wars and superbeings, and I had plans for some individual humans with mutations, too. Super-villains that could challenge Vi and Digby for years to come. They traded the prequel for a series, and I signed on for a longer, more extensive contract.

If it did well, then down the line some other team would run it. They might write Vi's origin story, and I might be part of that or not. For now it was enough to begin, letting her go on to what was next in the shadowland version of Birchville.

I had to set it there; Birchville was the place where I had come to clearly see the monsters plaguing my homeland's real landscape. They all had their avatars in Vi and Digby's world. The artist in me wanted to explore the Second South in large terms, but I wasn't above putting in a Mack Monster at some point. I'd rename her, of course, but she'd for sure have those iron-gray witch scraggles and a lip-lifted donkey's mouth. I might put in Tackrey—though our dealings with her had mercifully closed after Birchie made her grand and almost honest confession.

That day, when we got home from Regina Tackrey's office, we saw that the Franklins were already standing on our porch. Wattie's son Sam opened the door for them. Sam and his wife and their middle daughter had all arrived two days earlier. Wattie had finally come clean with both her sons.

Sam stepped out and waited with the Franklins on the porch when they saw my car pull up. Esme was holding a casserole dish that I knew contained her famous corn pudding. I couldn't imagine how she'd had time to make it. When we reached the top of the stairs, she thrust it into my arms so that she could hug Wattie, and her dish bit me with cold.

She'd pulled it from her freezer, premade as testimony to the human condition. Trouble and hunger always came, and most of Birchville kept an emergency casserole at the ready. Esme had grabbed hers and run to us, not waiting to thaw or bake it. Even cold, this was funeral food, rich in butter and comfort, and Esme and Grady were wearing black. They had come to mourn.

While Esme and Wattie were still clasped, a blue Honda pulled up and parked on our curb. Grayle Peck, another Redemption deacon, got out, and I saw that Wattie's cousin, 'Genia Price, was in the passenger seat. He'd checked 'Genia out of her nursing home and brought her over so Wattie would have more family here; Stephen couldn't fly down until next week.

Birchie opened the front door, letting Esme and Grady inside to preheat the oven. Sam led the way, but the three of us waited on the porch. As 'Genia began her slow creep up the walk on Grayle's arm, another car was pulling up, and then another. Two more turned onto the square. All the cars were packed full of folks I recognized from Wattie's church. They wore dark clothes and carried food. Redemption was coming, and in force.

Birchie and Wattie formed an impromptu receiving line at the top of the long staircase, greeting Wattie's gathering church. I stepped back out of the way and watched them.

Arm in arm, Birchie and Wattie were a living hinge. They were the place where the South met itself, and I thought that it was good, even though their very sisterhood had called forth a mourning party. It was ugly, but it was where we were. This was where history had brought us, and inside me the baby I would not name Digby spun like a small promise of better things. He belonged to me and to both of them. He was the future that Birchie and Wattie had risked everything to preserve.

I walked to the far end of the porch, out of earshot. I sat down on the swing, got out my phone, and called Polly Fincher.

"Oh, honey," she said instead of hello. She must have seen my name on the caller ID.

"You heard?" I asked, though I knew the answer. In fact, I didn't wait for it. "Then come. Please come."

A hesitation, and then Polly said, "We weren't sure Birchie would want . . . We weren't sure."

"We need you," I said. "And we need Alston, too,

and the Partridges, and Frank Darian. Anyone else that you can think of. Birchie needs her church."

"All right. Let me start the phone tree, then I'm on the way," she said, staunch, and I closed the connection.

Not everyone who heard the call would come. Some of the First Baptist members who did hurry toward us would turn back when they saw the house already full of Redemption. In the same way, when First Baptist began arriving, some of the Redemption folks would cool, and some would leave. But not all.

In the intersection of who would come and who would stay was a church that did not exist. Not yet. But I had glimpsed this congregation eating ginger-snaps and drinking lemonade in Martina Mack's yard. I would re-form it now, on purpose.

Together we would comfort Wattie. We would offer Birchie absolution. I could feel it as a nascent presence that might move and grow inside Birchville the way my son moved and grew in me. Something possible. A promise. An intersection where my son belonged.

The first wave of Redemption folks had all been offered greetings and entry, but I caught Birchie and Wattie before they could follow their guests inside.

"I'm staying," I told them, and I meant it. For as long as Birchie needed me, for sure. Perhaps after, for Wattie, because why should she have to move? Sel had been open to it, and if he could be happy here, I might even stay longer. After all, I was a Birch, and so was my son. This was our town. It would become what we made it. "I'm staying here with you, in Birchville."

"I know, child," Wattie said, like no other path was possible. Which it never had been. Not once she and her sister had decided.

"That's a good baby," Birchie said, pulling my face down to kiss me.

"We're putting in a ramp on this porch, though. Those stairs are a death trap," I told them, stern, and Birchie tutted.

"And ruin the lines of this house?" Birchie said. "Now, that won't do."

"It will do, very well, and you're moving down-stairs," I said.

I'd go back up to my own room, turn the tower room into a nursery with silver-blue walls and true red bed-ding.

Down the street I could see Polly Fincher's blond ponytail shining in the sun as she hurried toward us, carrying her own frozen emergency casserole. Frank Darian was coming out of his front door with a bag of store-bought chips, Hugh and Jeffrey in tow.

It was starting. I got out of the way and let it.

Birchie lived long enough to meet him: James Birch Briggs-Martin. He was born the day after Thanksgiving, in Alabama. He landed yelling, slick, and bloody, seven pounds, one ounce, and crazy beautiful. Sel caught him and put him on my chest.

Birchie's best last hours were spent rocking my son with me beside her. Sometimes she knew him.

"James, James," she said to him then, rocking and reminding, though more and more she thought that he was one of Wattie's long-grown babies or her own lost son. Near the end she did not recognize him at all. She would still reach for him, though, readying to take her leave even as she welcomed him, staring down into his earnest face.

"Hello, hello," she said, when I put him, a small stranger, into her arms. Her eyes brightened, and she smiled. My boy called her to immediate love in that way that babies have; it is their birthright. It is their superpower. She touched his open, tiny palm, his cheek, the burring of black fuzz on his head. "Hello."

Acknowledgments

D ear Person-Holding-This-Book, thank *you*, first and most and always, for reading. Without readers, there are no books. You are valuable and precious, and I am one of you. Thank you for buying my books in particular, and for passing them on, and for telling others about them. Thank you, Righteous Handsellers, especially those of you who have pressed my books into the hands of the right readers and said, "You are going to love this." You make my work possible.

Thank you, Emily Krump, editor, champion, and quite possibly the patron saint of patience. Thank you, Jacques de Spoelberch, for your guidance and your endless supply of spine. This one is for you. Endless gratitude to everyone at Morrow who has had this book's back: Liate Stehlik, Lynn Grady, Jennifer Hart,

Carolyn Marino, Tavia Kowalchuk, Kelly Rudolph, Kate Schafer, Libby Collins, Mary Beth Thomas, Carla Parker, Rachel Levenberg, Tobly McSmith, Ploy Siripant, Mary Ann Petyak, Madeline Jaffe, Shelby Peak, and Maureen Sugden (aka she who stops me from putting the word "little" into every other sentence).

Sara Gruen, Karen Abbott, and Lydia Netzer, you are more than notes and feedback and the right kind of pressure. You are *my* Almost Sisters. My beloved local writing partners kept this book grounded and me (relatively) honest: Anna Schachner, Reid Jensen, Ginger Eager, and The Reverend Doctor Jake Myers. Thank you, Caryn Karmatz Rudy and Jill James. Thanks, Alison Law—without you there are only technical errors and foul language.

Thanks to the glorious and gifted nerds who helped me get the art part right. All errors are mine: Bobby Jackson, Ross Boone and his alter ego Raw Spoon, and Katie Cook. Speaking of art—I love Cig Harvey, and this cover is exquisite.

Thanks to the folks who helped me get the medical and murder parts right. All errors are mine: D. P. Lyle, MD (author of *Forensics for Dummies* and the Dub Walker series), Dr. Steven Rippentrop, and novelist-slash-litigator Frank Turner Hollon.

My recent years of teaching have changed my heart,

my stories, and my relationship with writing itself. I am grateful to my students at Lee Arrendale State Prison. Thank you, Reforming Arts, both for creating a space where these women can find and explore their voices and for letting me be present in it.

I love you, Scott, Sam, Maisy Jane, Bob, Betty, Bobby, Julie, Daniel, Erin Virginia, Jane, and Allison. I love you, people of Slanted Sidewalk, small group, STK, and The New Revised Standard Version of Fringe. I love you, as well, First Baptist Church of Decatur. Thank you for trying to be a place where we broken humans of all flavors can be welcome and beloved. It's an uphill walk, isn't it? But damn, I love the view. Shalom, y'all.

About the Author

JOSHILYN JACKSON is the *New York Times* best-selling author of seven novels, including *gods in Alabama* and *A Grown-Up Kind of Pretty*. Her books have been translated into a dozen languages. A former actor, Jackson is also an award-winning audiobook narrator. She lives in Decatur, Georgia, with her husband and their two children.

HARPER LUXE

THE NEW LUXURY IN READING

We hope you enjoyed reading
our new, comfortable print size and found it
an experience you would like to repeat.

Well — you're in luck!

HarperLuxe offers the finest in fiction and
nonfiction books in this same larger print size and
paperback format. Light and easy to read, HarperLuxe
paperbacks are for book lovers who want to see
what they are reading without the strain.

For a full listing of titles and
new releases to come, please visit our website:

www.HarperLuxe.com